I0673080

KAT CUBED

Books by Lesley L. Smith

Temporal Dreams
Neutrino Warning
Kat Cubed
Reality Alternatives
Conservation of Luck

The Quantum Cop Series:
Book 1: *The Quantum Cop*
Book 2: *Quantum Murder*
Book 3: *Quantum Mayhem*

The Space Operetta Series
Book 1*: A Jack By Any Other Name*
Book 2*: A Jack In The Dark*
Book 3*: A Jack For All Seasons*

Kat Cubed

By Lesley L. Smith

Quarky Media
Boulder Colorado

Kat Cubed

Published by Quarky Media, PO Box 3332, Boulder, CO
80307

Copyright © 2016 Lesley L. Smith

ISBN: 978-0-9861350-7-1 (ebook)
ISBN: 978-0-9861350-6-4 (print)

This is a work of fiction. Names, characters, places, and
incidents are either the product of the author's imagination
or are used fictitiously, and any resemblance to actual
persons, living or dead, business establishments, events,
or locales is entirely coincidental.

All rights reserved. No part of this book may be used or
reproduced in any manner whatsoever without written
permission, except in the case of brief quotations
embodied in critical articles and reviews. Making or
distributing electronic copies of this book constitutes
copyright infringement and could subject the infringer to
criminal and civil liability.

KAT CUBED

The Columbia Encyclopedia, 11th Edition:

Climate Change: A significant and lasting alteration in the statistical distribution of weather patterns on a planetary scale, resulting from increased absorption of **infrared radiation** by increased atmospheric constituents such as **carbon dioxide**. Radiant energy from the Sun arrives at Earth's surface and is re-emitted at infrared wavelengths as heat. In the atmosphere, carbon dioxide and other gases absorb this infrared radiation, behaving as a blanket, with the net effect that increased **greenhouse gases** cause the atmosphere to hold more energy. Increased atmospheric energy leads to **extreme weather,** including **droughts, floods, heat waves**, and **superhurricanes**.

In addition, numerous **feedback mechanisms,** including **water vapor feedback** (increased energy enables the atmosphere to hold more water vapor which traps more energy), **ice-albedo feedback** (increased energy melts ice, decreasing albedo and enabling absorption of more energy by surface), Arctic **methane release** (increased energy melts permafrost which releases more methane, trapping more energy in the atmosphere) exacerbates the problem. The consequent melting of glaciers and polar ice, combined with the **thermal ocean expansion,** significantly raises the sea level. Other consequences include **ocean acidification** (absorption of the increased carbon dioxide by the ocean, making it more acidic), resulting in increased **calcareous dissolution** in organisms such as corals, crustaceans, and mollusks and the ensuing mass ocean extinctions. Similarly, the disruptions to Indian, West African and North American **monsoons** and the changes in the ocean's **thermohaline circulation** result in **mass extinctions** of plants, insects, and animals on Earth's continents. At some point, the pressures of these multiple changes lead to an irreversible climate **tipping point** in which Earth's entire system transitions into a new, previously unseen state.

Message from the Editor: I fear this will be our last edition, as I am the sole remaining encyclopedia employee. The encroaching flood waters threaten our offices, and the power is off more than it's on. I've been trying to print out as many hard copies of the encyclopedia as I can so humanity's accumulated knowledge is not lost forever. I pray some small portion of humanity survives to take advantage of it.

May God have mercy on our souls.
New York City
November 25, 2065.

Chapter One: Universe 1: Kat, April 25, 2100, 7:00 am

Sitting alone in the greenhouse Kat Garcia asked, "Where are you, Pa?" The scavenger team was way overdue. She strained her eyes, looking southeast towards Denver in the moments before dawn. Everything looked gray: gray buildings, gray dead trees, gray dead grass. The gray clouds overhead didn't help.

Did something move over there next to that ruined building? She stood and stared. No, it was just a dead bush shifting in the wind. She sat back down again. The top of the old physics building had the best sightlines in town, but even up here, she couldn't catch a glimpse of the missing team. Nervous, she plucked a sprig of baby spinach from the garden bed next to her and popped it in her mouth.

She needed Pa. He was the only family she had left. Ma was missing. Her sister Emma was dead. "Come home to me, Pa. Come on."

"Kat?" her best friend Pablo said from the stairwell.

She jumped. "Hi, buddy. What's up?"

"Who're you talking to?" He made his way through the plants and came and sat next to her.

"Nobody." She sighed. "Myself." That wasn't too crazy, was it? She touched Ma's locket. Ma had given it to her for safekeeping until she came back. That was months ago. Where was she?

"Any sign of the scavenger team?" he asked.

"Nope."

"They'll be okay," he said, patting her shoulder. "Your pa and the rest of the team are experienced scavengers." He was sweet.

Kat pointed at the first hint of light on the horizon. "But the sun's coming up."

"They know to take cover during the day. They know we're counting on them."

She glanced at Pablo's face. He seemed so sure. Maybe he was right. She hoped he was right. "What do you think'll happen if they never come back?"

"I don't know." He exhaled. "We'll cherish our memories of them."

Suddenly she had to blink back tears.

"And I guess we'll figure something out like we always do. We'll survive." He rested his hand on her back. "The group might elect you to be the new leader."

That was another thing to worry about if Pa didn't come back. "I'm only twenty. I can't lead the group."

"I think you can." His faith was touching.

"So, what's happening downstairs?" she asked. "Is Fei any better?" A sick baby was the worst.

"No." His gaze dipped to the floor. "Her fever's up."

"And we don't have any medicine." She scanned the edge of campus again. No sign of the missing team. "Did they try wet cloths to bring down her fever?"

"Yeah. But we're getting low on water."

"Not good."

"No," he said. "Not good."

Light blossomed over the horizon, illuminating everything in its path. The old university buildings were shades of pink and tan, and red. All the vegetation was a dead crunchy brown except a narrow strip of green along the creek in the distance.

Kat knew some of that green stuff was willow. She also knew willow was a natural fever reducer. "What if we went over to the creek and got some medicine for Fei?"

"What? Now?" His voice squeaked a bit. "It's after sunrise. We can't go outside."

She pointed up at the sky. "It's pretty cloudy." She lowered her voice. "Do you think Fei will last another day?"

"No." His whole body slumped.

"Come on, Pablo. We can do it. It'll be an adventure. Please come with me and help."

He glanced at her. "You're going whether I agree or not, aren't you?"

"Yes." She smiled in what she hoped was a charming way. "Come on; you know you want to help baby Fei. Wouldn't it feel great to save someone? Wouldn't it feel great to have a win for once?" She was ready for something good to happen. She was sick of losing all the time: losing faith, losing hope, losing people. "Come on."

He blew out a big gust of air. "You know I have trouble resisting you, Kat."

Oh, she knew. She was his best friend, after all. She grinned.

Down in the basement, the group didn't even bat an eye at Kat and Pablo going out after sunrise to get willow bark for Fei. Of course, Fei's parents, Bao and Chang, were beside themselves with worry, so they weren't going to object. But Kat thought someone would say, *Oh, it's too dangerous. You can't do it.* Or *Wow, how heroic, Kat.* But no one did.

They geared up as quickly as they could. The danger was the sun. They wore lightweight loose cotton clothing and big hats. Pablo carried a thermometer with an alarm. They'd seen people die of heat stroke, and it wasn't pretty.

On the bright side, there were some old underground maintenance tunnels to the creek—which was one of the reasons they were living in the physics building. The tunnels were about seven feet wide and seven feet tall with a concrete floor and cinderblock walls, so they tramped to the creek in comfort.

Once they hiked about a quarter mile, Pablo asked, "How'd your ma know about willow bark?"

"Ma's ma knew about herbal medicine and taught her some stuff. And, then, after Emma..." Kat swallowed. "After we lost Emma, Ma studied even more. She consulted every herbalist and doctor we met and had a bunch of books. She swore she'd never let anyone else die on her watch."

Ma was her hero. Was she still alive? Kat didn't see how she could be. She'd been gone too long. She wouldn't leave them alone so long if she'd had anything to say about it. Her eyes started to fill.

"Kat?"

She exhaled. She was on a mission, a mission to save a baby. Ma would approve.

"You miss them, huh?"

"Yes." She glanced over at him. "I know you miss your family, too." Pablo'd lost track of his parents during the Water Wars. He had no idea if they were alive or dead. And there was no way to find out.

"*Sí*," he said.

They walked in silence for a few minutes.

"So, tell me about Emma," he said. "What was she like?"

Ma's locket held a picture of Emma. She resisted the urge to open it and look at the image yet again. "She wasn't much like me."

"She sounds great." Pablo grinned at her, trying to lighten the mood.

"She was very wise and nice and nurturing."

"You're right. Nothing like you." Kat knew he was joking.

"She was a lot like Ma. But in some ways, she wasn't; for example, she taught me about boys."

"Ooh. What did she teach you?"

"Let's see; she said boys like food and compliments." When she looked at Pablo, he was still grinning. "Who taught you about boys?"

"I'm self-taught. What can I say? I'm a genius?"

"What about your friend, Jake?"

"Jake? He was straight but a real *hermano*." He sighed. "I miss him." Jake was another person he'd lost.

"What was he like?" she asked.

"He loved weather, of all things," Pablo said. "He could even predict it sometimes. Like when we'd get a windy spell, he'd say *A front's moving in*. And he'd be right. And he had a great sense of humor. We played so many tricks on his older brother Jason."

The tunnel brightened as they neared the end. The temperature was already rising.

They turned off their flashlights and set them down in the tunnel.

"I want to hear about those tricks at some point," she said as they emerged. Even near sunrise, the heat pummeled them.

11

The scents of dried plants and dust made Kat sneeze.

"Gaia bless you," he said, squinting and looking up. "Still cloudy."

"Let's hurry," she said, pointing in the direction of the creek. "Can you check if there's any water running?" They usually went to the old reservoir to get water, but there might be some here since the plants were still alive.

"Yes, ma'am." He saluted.

Kat grinned as she jogged to the willows. They looked great—still green and alive. She got a small pocket knife out of her bag and started stripping bark off the closest tree. Sweat gathered on her back and face.

Pablo ran up, putting an empty bottle back in his bag. "Bad news. No water that I could see." He got out his own knife.

"It must be underground? I hope so, anyway. I hope these trees don't die." Even though it was cloudy, it was still plenty light outside. She couldn't even remember the last time she'd been outside during the day. A drop of sweat rolled into her eye.

He started stripping bark.

"Don't take too much from any one tree." She wiped her forehead.

"Yes, ma'am." They stripped bark. "It's kind of weird being outside during the day, huh?"

She shot him a look. Wow, his thoughts were similar to hers. "Yeah."

"Do you think things will ever go back to the way they used to be?"

"What way is that?" Before Emma died? Before Ma disappeared? Before Pablo's family disappeared?

Before Pa didn't come back?

"You know, when we lived during the day and slept at night," he said. "When we didn't have to worry so much about surviving. When we lived regular lives."

Even with all this cloudiness, Kat was getting h-o-t. She felt another bead of sweat slide down her back. "Do you even remember that? I mean, Ma and Pa told me we lived up in an actual town in the mountains when I was a little girl, but I hardly remember it." Thinking about everything that had been lost was too depressing. They didn't really even have a civilization

12

anymore.

"I remember some stuff," he said. "We also lived up in the mountains. I went to school with Jake and his brother. My ma was a wonderful cook."

Kat held up a finger. "So, Emma was right. Boys do like food."

The clouds shifted, and the rays of sunlight pierced them like daggers. She knew the sun was deadly, but it seemed so cheerful.

The temperature alarm went off.

Pablo shoved a handful of bark into his bag and grabbed the thermometer. "We need to go back now."

She shoved some more bark into her own bag. She didn't want to have to come back here for a good long time. She stepped towards another tree.

"Now, Kat," he said, face grim. "I'm not kidding. It's getting dangerously hot out here."

She brought him along for a reason. She knew he'd keep them safe. "Okay."

Back in the tunnels, they picked up their flashlights and started walking back to the physics building.

Trying to lighten the mood again, she said, "Tell me about those tricks you and Jake used to play."

But he just sighed and said, "I'm not up for it, Kat."

At their encampment in the basement, most folks had gone to bed by the time they got back. Kat showed Bao and Chang how to make the fever-reducing tea out of the willow bark.

After a long night's work in the greenhouse, not to mention the stress of the creek mission, she was practically asleep before her head hit the pillow.

Kat was awakened by a scream. A strange bluish light filled the lab. She'd never seen anything like it. It came from a freaky window floating in mid-air! She carefully picked her way through the bedrolls to the strange window.

Pablo appeared at her side. "Gaia." He joined her in staring at the thing.

She whispered, "Gaia." As she peered inside, two people, a

man and a woman, moved closer. She could almost make them out.

They moved closer yet.

Then, Pablo whispered, "Jake."

Kat's heart caught in her throat, and her fingers reached for her locket. "Emma?"

Chapter Two: Universe 2: Kaitlin, April 25, 2100, 8:00 am

Kaitlin Garcia felt something hard and warm against her thigh.

It wriggled.

"What the hell is that?" She jumped out of bed like it was on fire.

Smack in the middle of the rumpled bed, Buster, Jake's pit bull, lay on his back, wriggling and kicking his legs in the air.

"Buster, what do you think you're doing?" she asked.

The double bed took up most of the bedroom. The only other thing that fit in the room was a tiny beat-up wooden dresser. A layer of dirty clothes, schoolbooks and papers covered every surface. The apartment was too small for two people, but they were lucky to get it. Housing in town was at a premium. Everyone wanted to live in Colorado, where there was no danger of flooding or hurricanes, and it wasn't quite as hot.

Her boyfriend Jake appeared in the doorway, wet, wearing only a towel around his waist.

Kaitlin couldn't seem to stop from smiling when she saw him. She wanted to rub her hands across his firm chest.

"What's going on out here?" When Jake saw Buster in the middle of the bed kicking his legs into the air, he started laughing. "Is there something going on between you and Buster I should know about?"

She snickered. "Of course not. He's trying to take over the bed again." She didn't go caress Jake. Instead, she drew the sheet around herself as regally as the President of the Unified States would have, had she been in this situation. The capital was only about fifty miles away, so she had actually met the president once when she'd come to tour the university.

"What did you think was happening?" He grinned.

"Nothing. I, uh, knew it was Buster. That's what I thought it was. Buster."

"Oh, wait, I know." He grinned again. "You thought I was putting the moves on you when you were asleep." He stopped and shook his head. "Babe."

"Give me a break." She pointed at his wet and near-naked form. "I can't keep track of your shower schedule."

He grinned. "Well, you should. I'm willing to share my shower ration with you—if we both need it." He threw off his towel and jumped onto the bed. "Get dirty with me." He wiggled his eyebrows up and down.

She giggled despite herself. Getting dirty and then clean again did sound fun. She joined him.

Things were just starting to get interesting when her fon rang. She ignored it.

"Do you need to get that, Kaitlin?" he asked right in the middle of a particularly effective move.

"No." She exhaled. "Oh. Keep doing that." She arched her back and suppressed a moan.

"What if it's your boss?" he asked. "What if there's something wrong at the lab?"

"I don't care if the lab is about to be flooded by Boulder Creek. I do not need to answer the fon right this minute," she said. Loudly.

Unfortunately, that was very similar to one of her fon activation phrases, so her fon activated.

"Kaitlin, are you there?" her sister Emma asked.

Kaitlin groaned, and not in a good way. "Visual off. No. I'm not here."

Something wriggled, and it wasn't Buster.

"I know you're there, Sis. I just heard your voice," Emma said. "Why is visual off?"

"Really not a good time, Em. Go away."

"I've got Michael on the call, too," she said.

This was mortifying. "Oh, wow."

"Thanks for the *wow*, babe," Jake whispered in her ear.

She glared at him and held her forefinger in front of her lips.

"Hey," her brother Michael said. "How's it going this

morning? Anything interesting happening?"

Jake started laughing and put his hands over his mouth to unsuccessfully hold it in.

"What's that noise?" Emma asked.

"Oh, I give up," Kaitlin said, getting out of bed again. "You guys have a real knack for calling at a bad time." She wrapped the sheet around herself. "What do you want?"

"We're planning Mom and Dad's anniversary party, and we were thinking of ice cream," Emma said.

"What do you think?" Michael asked.

"What?" Kaitlin asked. "Are you guys bonkers? We're not made of money. Do you have any idea what ice cream costs?"

Michael said, "Yeah, but...."

"This is not an emergency. I can't believe you called me at this hour about something like this."

"This hour?" Emma said. "It's like nine-thirty. Aren't you at work in your lab? Or do you have a meeting this morning? I can never keep track."

Nine-thirty. "Oh, no. I have to go. Fon disconnect." Kaitlin hung up and turned to Jake with an evil eye. "How could you let me sleep so late?" Her job was very important to her, despite all the evidence to the contrary this morning.

He shrugged. "It's shower day. And I have a weather feed with Pablo, so I have to look good." His best friend, Pablo, always looked good whether it was a shower day or not.

But he had a point. Shower day was important. "For being so understanding, I think I deserve two full minutes of shower ration."

"If I can join you," he said with an X-rated smile.

She smiled back. "I think that can be arranged." They scampered into the bathroom.

"And for the record, the creek can't flood with this drought," he said as he turned on the water.

"Okay, meteorology-guy, is that really what you want to focus on right now?" She dropped the sheet.

The basement of the physics building felt deliciously cool after the heat of the April sun. Far too late, Kaitlin jogged into the lab, a huge room filled with mismatched worn-out lab tables, stools, and book shelves. Even the computers, while functional, were at least a dozen years old. They'd been scavenged from other projects around the university.

Unfortunately, Professor Azar stood there in the lab waiting for her like her dad used to when she was out past curfew. "Kaitlin, thanks for joining us. Glad you could finally make it to work." He ran his fingers through his thick black hair, intentionally drawing attention to it.

Yeah, guy, you've got nice hair. Get over it.

"Do you know how lucky you are to have this job?" he asked.

She knew she was lucky. She was in a position to fix global warming. If everything went well, her research could solve some of the problems of climate change. And she really wanted to make a difference in the world. She wanted to help people. A flash of guilt broke over her. Maybe Jake was too much of a distraction.

But she loved him.

"Uh, yes, sir," she said.

In the lab, they had climate control and electric lights and computers, basically everything they had in the olden days, and her salary enabled her to do stuff like eat.

"And your hair looks really nice today, sir." She wasn't above a little sucking up.

"Do you know how many people are waiting in the wings to take your place when you blow this cushy graduate assistantship?" he asked. Did she spy a hint of a smile? Did he want someone to take her place?

Even though it was a very important job, sadly, not that many people were waiting. Her job was too complicated and required an actual education. Too many people had died from superstorms, food and water shortages and diseases over the last couple of decades. Most of the survivors were merely trying to do that: survive. Kaitlin had only gotten an education because she was born here in the university town and her parents were sort of important.

"Wasn't there a new malaria outbreak down on the Gulf Coast of Alabama?" she said, trying to distract him. The news feed might as well be renamed the disaster feed.

KAT CUBED

Professor Azar frowned and rubbed his finger along his upper lip. Kaitlin knew he did that when she said something right that he wasn't about to acknowledge. "That's not relevant." He paused. "What's happening with the model runs? Did the moon-dust shield simulations finish? Does it block enough sunlight?"

She had no idea if the runs finished, and she felt bad about it. Her group was one of the only groups in the world running simulations of the most effective ways to mitigate global warming. The longer it took them to figure it out, the more people died. Ugh. She glanced at the computer. "The runs should have finished, sir. I only need to collate and analyze the results."

"Okay, then," he said. Was she mistaken, or did he seem disappointed he didn't have further ammunition against her? "I guess I'll leave you to it then."

"Yes, sir. I guess you will." Please leave her to it.

As Professor Azar left, she called Jake. His image looked harried. "Can't talk, Kait. We go live in a couple of minutes."

"Right, sorry. I just want to say you're a bad influence. Quit making me late."

"Feeling guilty, are you?" he asked. She expected one of his trademark grins but didn't get it. "If you recall, I didn't make you do anything. It takes two to tango, babe. But I can't talk now. There's a hurricane blowing up in the Atlantic, and it looks like a record-breaker." He was a grad student in atmospheric science, and part of his job was forecasting the weather. They'd met here at the university.

"Oh, no. Not another record-breaker." Storms were crazy strong these days. The weather feed should also be renamed the disaster feed.

"I have to go." He hung up. Was that a trace of impatience? With her?

"I have to go, too," she said, not that anyone was listening.

"Computer, are the results of the moon-dust simulations finished? And can I see them?"

"Yes," it said and displayed a plot of incoming solar radiation versus the volume of dust used to shield Earth. Normally, Earth received about one hundred seventy-four times ten to the fifteenth Watts of energy from the sun. That was way more than a typical hundred-Watt lightbulb.

As expected, her simulation showed that increasing the dust amount decreased the radiation. The displayed results looked good. She nodded.

Something was nagging her, though. She picked up a pencil and tapped it on the computer console. She could feel in her gut there was something she was missing. "Computer, remind me what the escape velocity of Earth is."

"Approximately eleven point two kilometers per second from sea level," it said.

"And from the moon?"

"Approximately two point four kilometers per second," it said.

She knew all that. They'd taken it into account when calculating energy expenditures for their scenario of a shield made of moon dust. She tapped the console. Something to do with the launch was bothering her.

"Computer, where would a moon-bound vehicle launch from?"

"Historically," it said, "Vandenberg and Edwards Air Force bases, Wallops Island, and Cape Canaveral were used by the Unified States of America as space rocket launch sites."

She gulped. Cape Canaveral had been in Florida, which was now lost under the Atlantic Ocean. "Are any of them operational now?"

"Just a moment," the computer said. "My systems are experiencing some kind of–"

"Computer? Some kind of what?" Kaitlin felt the hair on her arms stand straight up.

A floating, shimmering circle appeared out of nowhere in the middle of the lab. As it came into focus, it resembled a large circular window.

On the other side of the window, she saw …herself and Jake. It was definitely her and Jake and not just people who looked like them. She peered at them. They wore some hideous uniform things and sat amidst a lot of fancy equipment.

"What the hell?" Not knowing what else to do, she waved.

Chapter Three: Universe 3: Katherine, April 25, 2100, 9:00 am

Without breaking stride, Katherine Garcia squished the nanobot in the hallway under her shoe like a cockroach. "Oops."

She resisted the urge to check to see if anyone noticed. Looking around was deadly. Only guilty people looked around, and she didn't need any more trouble. There were dozens of other nanobots in the building, and she didn't want to appear suspicious. The nanobots were the all-seeing minions of Police Patrol who ran everything from what you ate to where you worked to who you married. Her parents had told her over and over the rules enabled them all to survive, but she still didn't quite buy it. She had a hard time following rules.

The door to her basement lab whooshed open after the touchpad identified her DNA. The huge room was filled with state-of-the-art computers and electronics. She walked to the massive computer station near the door and settled on a lab stool. Most of the large lab was occupied by the big new tokamak, a gleaming metal cylinder and electronics. The tokamak was her baby, her dream. It was going to give humanity an unlimited clean energy source, namely fusion, and then they would all have enough to eat and drink and wouldn't need Police Patrol or The Ministries any more.

"Good morning, Student Katherine," the computer said. After a couple of moments, it asked, "Aren't you going to say good morning, Student Katherine?"

Katherine suppressed a sigh. "Good morning, Computer." Lucky for her, computers were oblivious to sarcasm. Otherwise, she'd be in even more trouble than she usually was. "Please display the results from the last test."

"Of course, Student Katherine."

"And quit calling me *Student* Katherine. I asked you to call me Katherine." She pulled down her navy uniform tunic and shifted on the lab stool. She hated her stupid uniform.

The lab was quiet. She was the only one in this morning. That wasn't too unusual. Unfortunately, despite the medical nanobots, they'd lost a significant portion of the staff in the last flu epidemic. If the floods or water shortages didn't get you, diseases did. You just couldn't win in the twenty-second century. It was depressing.

"Computer?"

"Yes, uh, Katherine?" Since when did computers say *uh*? What were the programmers up to these days?

"Do you have the results from the last test or not?" Katherine asked. She was grumpy this morning, but it wasn't the computer's fault. It was because she had a date with her assigned mate Winston tonight. She didn't care how many people told her assigned mates were good for society; she didn't like being told what to do. She had to figure out a way to get rid of him without officially being branded anti-social or permanently losing her Procreation Status.

"The Deuterium Tritium mix reached one hundred sixty million degrees Celsius in the most recent test," the computer said. "The vacuum vessel worked as designed, as did the cryostat, Beryllium blanket and the divertor target. The magnets operated at optimum efficiency." The computer paused. "In fact, the magnets were operating above designed efficiency according to the diagnostics. There was no additional external heating, but the electromagnetic field was considerably higher than expected."

She sat up straight. Now, there was something interesting. A high EM field could be a precursor to fusion. It might even distract her from her Winston problem. "Computer, repeat information about the electromagnetic field."

A male voice interrupted before the computer could do so. "Hey, Katherine. How's it going? Did you achieve fusion yet? You are mighty hot."

Her heart beat a little faster at the sight of Jacob coming through the doorway. He had a slim build but seemed to fill up the whole lab. He even looked good in his navy Science Ministry uniform, and no one looked good in their uniform. He always seemed to be stopping by to borrow a tool or consult on some data. Her productivity plummeted when he showed up, but she enjoyed him—not that she'd tell him that. He was already too cocky. "How did you get in here?"

"Greetings, Student Jacob," the computer said. "Katherine is happy to see you."

She shot the main computer bank an evil look. It had better not start spouting her blood pressure or anything like that. The damned ubiquitous nanobots knew everything about everything, and the computer could access their data.

"The door was open, babe." Jacob flashed his signature cocky smile. "Your subconscious must have wanted me to come in."

She could feel hot blood rush to her face. "My subconscious does want you."

His smile got wider and cockier. He raised his eyebrows. Those eyebrows were a little too bushy, but they framed the most gorgeous gray-blue eyes. Time stopped when she looked into those eyes.

"Wait a minute." Her mind played back what she'd just said. "Did I just say that? I didn't mean it. Of course, I meant my subconscious doesn't want anything, definitely not you, never you." She was babbling.

"The lady doth protest too much, methinks," he said with a grin.

"What's wrong with you?" she asked. "Why are you talking like that? Doth? Methinks?"

"Hamlet act three, scene two," the computer said.

She twisted around to look at the computer again. "Whatever that is. And who asked you anything, Computer? Be quiet unless I ask you a direct question."

Frowning, Jacob sank onto one of the lab stools. "Wow, you're in a foul mood this morning. What's up?"

"I guess I'm worried about my stupid date with Winston tonight."

"Ah, the famous Winston. Have you met him?"

"We were officially introduced the other night with our

parents there, but we didn't get a chance to truly talk. It was all 'nice to meet you, blah, blah, blah.'"

"What does he look like?" Jacob asked in a quiet voice.

"He's six feet tall and light-skinned. He sort of looks like he's made out of mashed potatoes."

A sharp bark of laughter escaped him. "What? Mashed potatoes? What's that supposed to mean?"

"You know, big and white and lumpy. What does your assigned mate, Tabatha, look like?"

"Oh, she's beautiful," he said. "Delicious cocoa skin and hair. Big dancing brown eyes. And built–" He raised his hands to start outlining her shape in the air.

She interrupted. "Never mind. Forget I asked."

"You didn't let me finish," he said. "I was going to say she's beautiful, but she's not as beautiful as you. She doesn't compare to you."

Speaking of gorgeous eyes. Look away, Katherine. "Yeah, right." She successfully avoided smiling, but she was starting to feel a little less grumpy.

"Did you have any good ideas for Project Winston?" he asked. He knew she wanted to get rid of him.

"I'm still pondering it. I could act cold, not let him touch me, not smile or laugh at all. Or maybe argue with everything he says?"

He nodded. "Might work."

"Or maybe I should act slutty. You know, wear something low-cut and–"

"No." He interrupted her. "That wouldn't work. Don't do that."

"But he seemed very conservative. A real party-line guy." He also worked in the Science Ministry but on the pet project of the First Minister. Winston's project was interesting, mitigating climate change, but he seemed to mouth Ministry propaganda.

"If he's a guy, you acting slutty will not turn him off," Jacob said, his voice getting louder as he stood up.

"Fine. Whatever. Don't get all worked up." She paused. "Anyway, shouldn't you be doing some experiment yourself? Did you want something, or did you just come here to reduce my efficiency rating? That's it, isn't it? Our lab is more efficient than your lab. We make you look bad."

"No, I just..." He trailed off. "Never mind. It's not important. What was that the computer was saying earlier? Something about increased electromagnetic fields?"

They both turned to look at the computer, but it didn't say anything.

Finally, Katherine said, "Computer? Didn't you hear Jacob's question? Repeat the electromagnetic field information."

"Oh, I can talk now?" the computer said in a sarcastic tone. So much for her assumption about computers and sarcasm. She'd have to watch her tone with it from now on.

He whispered, "Who programmed your computer?"

She shrugged. "Computer, please tell us about the electromagnetic fields."

"As I was saying, the electromagnetic field was higher than ever measured," the computer said.

"You mean higher than ever measured in this lab, right?" he said.

"No. I mean higher than ever measured on Earth, according to my database at least," the computer said. As far as Katherine knew, her computer had access to all the databases.

"Wow," Jacob said. "Cool."

"I know the tokamak's supposed to be shielded, but with such a high field, you never know. I'm glad it didn't disrupt any electrical equipment." She stared across the lab at the metal cylinder that was twenty meters high and twenty-five meters across, with various wires and conduits leading away from it. The thing was priceless. The whole human race—what was left of it—was depending on it for a new energy source. And she was determined to make it happen.

"Are you going to fire it up again?" he asked. "I wouldn't mind seeing that."

"I'm not sure. Maybe I should wait for Professor Jain." Her boss and mentor, Professor Jain, was still recovering from the flu.

"My lab has contingency plans for these types of situations," he said.

That was a good point. "Computer, do we have a contingency plan for this situation?"

"You mean a contingency plan for unexpectedly high

electromagnetic fields? That kind of contingency plan?" it asked.

"There." She pointed at it. "That's sarcasm. Cut it out."

"In the event of data outside expected parameters, but when the equipment is operating at or above optimum efficiency, the work plan says to continue testing," it said in an overly robotic voice, which sounded even more sarcastic.

"Well, then, that's what we'll do," she said. "Computer, continue testing sequence."

"Neutral beam injection and high-frequency EM waves resuming," it said.

"Even though the system was on standby, this will take a while," Katherine said. "You might as well go back to work in your own lab, Jacob."

"Okay," he said. "Let me know what happens with the experiment." But he didn't make a move for the door.

Katherine felt the hair on her arms stand straight up.

All the airborne nanobots in the lab clattered to the ground.

Jacob leaned over her and whispered, "The nanobots are down. The EM field must have gotten them. So, no one will ever know," right before pressing his lips against hers.

Her lips felt like they were being struck by friendly lightning that spread out to the rest of her body. She stood up, too, and molded her body against his. She could feel his heart beating against her heart. It was like they were one person. They stayed like that forever and for only a nanosecond.

When they finally separated too soon, he pointed at the equipment. "What's that? And that?"

On one side of the tokamak, she saw a shimmering circle filled with darkness; on the opposite side, she saw a shimmering circular window filled with …her. The woman wore a different outfit, no uniform, but it was definitely her. The strange woman stared at them and finally waved.

"I don't know, but I'm guessing it's trouble," Katherine said.

Chapter Four: Universe 2: Kaitlin, April 25, 2100, 10:30 am

Staring at the weird window or portal or whatever it was in the lab, Kaitlin had to call Jake. That couldn't actually be him over there on the other side of the window, could it? And where or when exactly was the other side?

She walked all the way around the thing. It was definitely floating in mid-air and about three feet in diameter. From the back, it resembled a floating black disk. The edges sizzled and vibrated almost as if it was alive. She did not touch the thing.

Jake answered his fon, but his image was sitting at a desk with Pablo, reporting on the new hurricane: "...the current warm pool in the Atlantic has weakened the tropospheric vertical wind shear and increased the moist static instability of the troposphere." He glared at her over the fon.

So, at least her Jake was still here where he was supposed to be.

Over the fon, Kaitlin heard Pablo say, "This is why Atlantic hurricanes have become so powerful. Unfortunately, Fiona is poised to be one for the record books..."

She carefully said, "Emergency," to Jake.

His glary look turned to one of concern, and he got up from the desk and stepped out of camera range.

She spared a look for the her on the other side of the circular window. That other Kaitlin and that other Jake were approaching the window, walking toward her.

So, she approached them, too. "Jake," she said into the fon. "Thanks for answering. There's something freaky going on down here. Some weird round window or portal opened up, and me and you are on the other side of it."

"What?" he said.

"I'm serious," she said. "There's some kind of portal floating in my lab. And we're on the other side. Me and you."

"I know you wouldn't call while I'm on the air unless it's important," he said. "But a portal sounds pretty bizarre, Kait. And how could we be on the other side of it? We're here."

The people in the portal were quite close. "Hello?" the woman said. "Who are you?"

"Look," Kaitlin said to her Jake, holding the fon up to the portal.

She asked the portal people, "Are you from the future?"

The portal people exchanged expressions that would have meant *What the hell?* if she and her Jake had exchanged them.

On the fon, her Jake said, "What the hell?"

Kaitlin said, "What's the date there?" at the same time, portal-Kaitlin said it.

Portal-Kaitlin paused, licked her lips, and said, "April twenty-fifth, 2100."

That was the date here, too. So not the future. Part of her was relieved she wouldn't have to wear that strange uniform in the future. "Here, too," she said.

The three of them looked at each other through the portal.

"What's going on?" her Jake said on the fon. "I can't see very well."

"I don't know," she said.

"Who are you?" the portal woman repeated.

"My name is Kaitlin," Kaitlin said. "Who are you guys?"

"My name is Katherine," she said.

The portal man said, "Jacob."

"What do you think is going on here?" Kaitlin asked them.

"I'm not sure," Katherine said. "I was doing a fusion experiment—I'm a physics grad student—and we got some huge electromagnetic fields. The next thing I knew, these portals, or whatever they are, opened. Were you doing a fusion experiment, too?"

"No. I was doing a simulation of a moon-dust shield. I'm an atmospheric science grad student."

Katherine mouthed, *moon-dust shield?* to her Jacob.

Kaitlin pointed at them. "What's Jake doing there? Are you

guys a couple, too?" she asked. "I've got my boyfriend, Jake, here on the fon."

The two people in the portal gave each other another look she couldn't quite interpret. Maybe it was shame? But that didn't make any sense.

The man shook his head and started to say something but was interrupted by a noise. Both of the portal people turned their heads toward something else in their lab.

On the fon, her Jake asked again, "What the hell is going on there?"

"I don't know," Kaitlin said. "This portal opened, and we were on the other side. Or, I guess it wasn't us? I don't get it."

"Me neither," Jake said.

"It's like they're copies or other versions of us or something."

The portal people walked away from the window. Kaitlin scrambled up on a rickety lab table to get a better view of them. The table swayed back and forth under her weight.

"Exactly what is going on here, Kaitlin?" a male voice boomed out from the lab doorway behind her.

Crap. It was Professor Azar. And he had his past-curfew expression on again. "I have to go, Jake. Please, come down here if you can." She hung up the fon. "Professor." She put on a brave face. "I'm glad you could make it. I was just going to try to contact you. We've had a development." Kaitlin pointed at the portal.

As Professor Azar stepped closer, his hand dropped from his hair, and his mouth fell open.

Universe 1: Kat

The window buzzed and thrummed like some kind of giant angry bug. It smelled like heat lightning. Kat'd never seen anything like it, and it made her very nervous. It was unnatural. The people on the other side of the round window walked closer and peered at her and Pablo.

"Who are you?" Kat asked, peering back at them. The woman wasn't Emma, after all. The woman looked like her, Kat—but that was crazy. She didn't recognize the guy.

At the same time, Pablo said, "Gaia! I saw you die, Jake. You're supposed to be dead."

The Jake guy looked at the woman next to him, then back at Pablo, and said, "Dead? I don't like the sound of that. And call me Jacob."

"Are you me?" Kat asked the woman. "Are you Kat, too?"

The woman shook her head. "My name is Katherine. And let me guess, the date there is April twenty-fifth, 2100?"

"How did you know?" Kat asked.

The Jacob guy smiled. "Lucky guess."

He turned to the woman. "I know what this is." He gestured at the window. "It's the multiverse. You did a quantum mechanics experiment, Katherine."

Katherine said, "Why do you say that?"

"The what?" Next to Kat, Pablo said. "What did she do?"

"Yeah." Kat pointed at Pablo. "What he said. The what? Quantum what? What are you talking about?"

And then the Lus' baby started crying again. Kat glanced behind Pablo and realized everyone in their group of survivors was gathered up behind them, outside the circle of light.

In the window, Jacob and Katherine were conferring. She couldn't make out what they were saying over Fei's cries. That gave her an idea.

"Do you have any aspirin?" Kat asked.

"Yeah," Pablo said. "And water? We need water and aspirin. And food. And any other medicine you have."

In the window, Jacob and Katherine stared at them.

Katherine said, "What? You don't have enough water?" She looked horrified. "I think we do have some aspirin here in the lab." She started patting the pockets of her uniform.

Jacob put a hand on her arm. "I'm not sure it's a good idea to start exchanging matter between universes."

"But, they're sick and thirsty." Katherine peered through the window. "Oh, no. There's a whole bunch of people there in the dark behind them." She turned to Jacob. "We have to do something."

"Massless photons are one thing," he said. "Macroscopic objects are another."

Katherine pointed at Kat and Pablo. "But sound. Sound

means the air molecules are being exchanged."

"That's an even trade if the air pressure is the same here and there, which it should be."

Bao tugged on Kat's sleeve. "Will they help us?"

Kat shrugged. "I don't know."

"One little aspirin pill can't hurt anything," Bao said.

"Hey," Kat said. "What could one little aspirin pill hurt? It's for a baby. She's dying."

Katherine's face was red. "We have to do it, Jacob. We have to help them. What's the worst that could happen?"

"The worst?" he said. "The worst would be we destroy their universe and ours and maybe that other one, too." He pointed behind him. "Do you want to risk that?"

Kat asked Pablo, "Did he just say *destroy the universe*?"

Pablo nodded, looking like he might be sick.

"Oh, no," Kat said. "That's what I thought he just said." Now she must have looked like the one who might be sick.

Universe 3: Katherine

"Destroy universes?" Katherine gulped. "That doesn't sound good." She pulled her uniform top down. It always seemed to be riding up.

"No," Jacob said. "Not good."

A robotic voice interrupted them, "Security alert." It was the computer; the mechanical voice didn't sound fake this time. "No security nanobots in the fusion lab. Security alert. Likely unauthorized behavior occurring."

"Oh, no," Jacob said.

"So much for no one ever knowing," Katherine said. "They're going to suspect everything they can think of now. We're seditious traitors. We're sexual perverts. We're incompetents. Take your pick."

"Nanobots deployed," the robotic voice said.

"Unless we give them something specific they can see with their own eyes," Jacob said. He leaned in, lips puckered.

"Now is not the time." But Katherine quit talking when his lips met hers. Mmm.

She didn't know how long they stayed like that, but she wished it could be forever.

"Reboo–oot," the computer said, voice changing from robotic to what Katherine now thought normal. The computer cleared her throat. "I hope I'm interrupting something, but multiple nanobots are in-bound."

Just what was that computer implying? What would she be interrupting?

"Hey," the woman in the dark window, Kat, yelled. "One aspirin. Please!"

"And some water," Pablo added.

From the other portal, a man's voice said, "Hello? Is there someone there?" Who was that? They hadn't met a man over there.

"Nanobots here in ten seconds," the computer said. "Eight, seven, six, five..."

Jacob tried to kiss her again, but she leaned away. "Seriously?" she asked him. "Do you think now is the time?"

"It might be our last chance," he said.

"Do you think that's going to help?"

"Please," Kat said through the portal. "Help us."

"Hey," the unknown man said from the other portal. "Is there anyone there?"

A swarm of nanobots flew into the room. Most fell on the ground as they approached the tokamak.

A couple of nanobots remained in the air and headed right for the portals or whatever they were.

"I think we should take cover. Right now. I don't know what'll happen if any nanobots go through the portals." Jacob grabbed Katherine's hand and started dragging her toward the lab doorway.

"What about the others?" She pointed at the portals. "What about the other people? Are they in danger?"

Jacob said, "I hope not."

"Look out!" Katherine tried to yell to the others as the nanobots reached the portals and attempted to fly right on through. By this time, however, she was almost in the hall. She wasn't sure if they could hear her from the other sides of the portals.

KAT CUBED

She heard two sizzling noises, a whoosh and an ear-splitting crack, as Jacob pulled her into the hall. She smelled the sharp tang of ozone, and smoke roiled out of the lab. The stench of burned electronics filled her nose and eyes. Coughing, she couldn't seem to catch her breath.

Once that passed, Katherine realized she couldn't see a thing. Everything had gone dark.

Chapter Five: Universe 2: Kaitlin, April 25, 2100, 12:30 pm

The portal just disappeared.

Professor Azar had been staring into it, getting too close for Kaitlin's taste when it suddenly wasn't there anymore. He staggered. Then turning and regarding her, he said, "What the hell was that?" His normally brown skin had taken on a grayish cast.

She shrugged. "I have no idea."

He stalked toward her. "You must have an idea. This is your lab. What did you do?"

"I didn't do anything. I was sitting here working."

Panting, Jake skidded through the doorway and into the lab. "Professor Azar, I didn't know you were here." He scanned the room. "Where's the, ah…?" He glanced at her and closed his mouth. His chest moved up and down rapidly under his azure-blue dress shirt.

Professor Azar said, "I might have known your boyfriend was involved in these antics, Kaitlin."

Kaitlin knew Azar didn't like Jake because of that time he'd walked in on them making out in the lab. "With all due respect, Professor," she said. "I wasn't involved in any antics. Neither was Jake."

"Don't talk back to me. I know you, and that strange window had *you* written all over it. You and your boyfriend."

"I was on the weather feed, Professor, warning people about the hurricane," Jake said. "Ask anyone. I couldn't have done anything. And Kaitlin isn't a trouble-maker. She's an awesome scientist."

She shot him a grateful smile.

"That remains to be seen." Professor Azar smirked. "You probably haven't finished the moon-dust shield simulation yet, have you, Kaitlin?"

Where was all this negativity coming from? She'd never done anything to him. "Yes, sir, I have," she said. She wasn't going to let him rattle her. That was probably what he wanted.

"Show me the plots, then," the professor said.

"Well, I haven't exactly finished the plots," she said. "But the simulation's done."

Professor Azar stared at her, and she could swear there was a twinkle in his eye. "I think I'm going to have to fire you, Kaitlin."

She couldn't process that. If Azar fired her, she'd be kicked out of graduate school. What would she do then?

"What?" Jake said. "That's crazy."

She jumped off her lab stool. "Sir, please don't fire me." She wanted to ask him what she would live on. How would she eat? Where would she live? But she knew he wouldn't care about her welfare.

He might, however, care about the science. "Firing me would be a mistake. I can make a difference. I have many climate change mitigation ideas if you recall my thesis proposal. For example, there were several solar radiation management strategies, including aerosols, sulfate dust, marine cloud brightening or sun shades, like the moon-dust shield, to alter Earth's albedo or reflectivity." She paced towards Professor Azar. She didn't know what his problem was, but she did know it didn't have anything to do with her.

"There's also greenhouse gas remediation, including carbon sequestration and carbon air capture, and iron fertilization of oceans to increase phytoplankton populations."

Professor Azar sank on a stool and ran his hands through his hair, messing it all up—something she'd never seen.

"Don't you remember my thesis proposal?" she asked him.

He shook his head. "Not right now. I'm having trouble remembering anything, what with that—" He pointed at empty space. "Thing that was there. It didn't make any sense." He jumped up. "And don't brow-beat me. I'm a professor. And you're out of here." He lurched out of the room.

Kaitlin hoped his bark was worse than his bite.

Jake said, "What was his problem?"

"I guess the portal thing freaked him out."

"Well, I can understand that," he said. "What was it?"

She slowly shook her head. "I'm not sure. Could you see it through the fon? It was like we were looking at another version of the world. And you and me were both there. It was freaky."

He wrinkled his forehead. "You and me? I could tell there were people there, but I couldn't make them out very well. That is just bizarre."

She'd been wracking her brain since the portal appeared. "Didn't we learn something in physics class about Many Worlds?"

He nodded. "I think so, but that was a few years ago. I always thought that was theoretical."

"Apparently not," she said softly.

They pondered that for a few moments.

Finally, he asked, "Can he really fire you, Kait? Do you need to leave the lab now?"

She shook her head. "No. He'd have to petition a committee and prove moral or academic misconduct."

She paused, considering. "I mean, I guess he could eventually fire me, but it would take a while, several days or a couple of weeks at least."

"That's good, I guess," he said. "I have to get back to work, Kait. What are you going to do?"

"I don't know." She seemed to be saying that a lot lately.

Jake left.

Kaitlin got a sandwich from the lunch cart and started working on the plots and analysis for the dust shield. She should try to finish the project while she still could. The results looked very good. The dust shield blocked some sunlight from the Earth and didn't screw up Earth's chemistry any more than it was already screwed up.

She lost track of time, working until someone behind her cleared their throat. It was Professor Kim, the department chair, dressed formally as usual in an old-fashioned suit and tie. This was not a good sign.

"Hello, Professor Kim," she said. "Can I help you with something?"

KAT CUBED

"Good morning, Ms. Garcia." Professor Kim came in and stalked around the lab, scrutinizing everything. Obviously, he'd been talking to Professor Azar. She had no idea what she would say about the portal if he asked her about it.

Finally, Professor Kim stopped inspecting things. "Has anything unusual been happening in here today?"

She cleverly said, "Uh..."

"Because Professor Azar came to my office earlier, and frankly, I think he had some kind of mental health episode, which I probably shouldn't have mentioned to you. Forget I said that." He came and peered over her shoulder at the computer screen. "Is everything going all right with your research today?"

She could honestly say her research was all right. She nodded. "Yes, sir." She pointed at the results.

Professor Kim checked her out. "Are you doing your job, Ms. Garcia?"

"Yes, sir. Would you like to hear about the moon-dust shield simulation?"

He waved his hand. "That's not my area of expertise. Ask Professor Azar. When he, ah, recovers." He stood still for a moment. "To be honest, Professor Azar stormed into my office and demanded we fire you. Can you think of any reason why he would do that?"

Do you mean besides some weird portal? She could feel her face heat up as blood rushed to it. "Uh, no, sir. I've been trying to do a good job."

"Then he said some other things, which, well...." He paused. "I think Professor Azar is going to take some time off. But I will be keeping my eye on you in his absence. All right, Ms. Garcia?"

"Yes, sir. So, you're not going to fire me?"

He appeared to stop and consider it. "Not right this minute. But we'll see how you do."

Somehow that was less than reassuring.

At dinnertime, Jake couldn't get away from work because of the hurricane, so Kaitlin offered to bring him and Pablo some food.

When she arrived at the headquarters of the International

Weather Agency, Jake and Pablo were still reporting on the storm. The Unified States government strongly supported the weather center, giving it rare significant funding for this day and age. Having the headquarters located near the national capital in Colorado probably didn't hurt either, and at over five thousand feet above sea level, there was no danger of flooding here.

Jake and Pablo sat in camera range behind the news desk, and the scene behind them, a succession of maps and scientific plots, was as calm as the eye of a storm. What the cameras couldn't see, however, was the chaos in the room surrounding the calm center desk. Camera operators and their assistants ran to and fro. At least a dozen people sat in front of computer screens featuring computer code or a giant swirl of clouds.

Pablo grimaced. "To repeat, folks on the Gulf Coast of Arkansas need to take immediate cover. People in Jefferson county, Arkansas county, and Phillips county take cover. It's too late to evacuate. Other counties, such as Lonoke, Prairie, Monroe and Lee, are now under a mandatory evacuation order. Report to your assigned evac station immediately." A hangdog expression passed quickly over his features. He turned to Jake on his left. "Jake, can you tell us why Hurricane Fiona is so strong?"

A hint of a smile flitted across Jake's face. "Yes, I can, Pablo."

Pablo waved at Kaitlin, and she carefully walked over to him out of view of the cameras.

"Hey, Pablo," she said quietly. "I brought you guys fish tacos."

Once the camera was no longer focused on him, he looked sad. "*Gracias*, Kait, I appreciate it," he whispered. "It doesn't look like we're going to get out of here any time soon." He reached into the bag and snagged a couple of tacos.

In the meantime, Jake was saying, "Tropical storms have been stronger lately because the surface waters of the Gulf of Mexico are warmer than they used to be. Basically, this warm water pumps energy into tropical storms. We've also entered a La Niña period which means there's a decrease in wind shear in the region. Unfortunately, these factors all work together to make Fiona very strong. The following computer graphic illustrates these points."

The cameraman said, "And we're clear. Seven minutes."

Jake sighed. "The science is fascinating, but the results are horrific."

Kaitlin said, "Hi, babe. I brought you guys tacos to apologize for making you rush out of here earlier." She passed him the bag.

"Yeah, what was that about?" Pablo asked with his mouth full of tortilla, cheese, lettuce, fried mystery-fish and sauce.

Jake unwrapped a taco and shoved it in his mouth.

She shrugged. "I'm not sure, but it seemed like a portal to another world opened up in my lab this morning. And my boss freaked out. And I may or may not be fired. Hopefully not." So far, she'd avoided her own personal freakout.

Pablo started coughing. Finally, he said, "What?"

Jake swallowed. "It was weird. You better start at the beginning, Kait."

One of the camera assistants said, "Four minutes."

"There's not much to tell because I don't know what happened," Kaitlin said. "The beginning is all there is. I was in the lab finishing the moon-dust shield simulation—which looks great, by the way—and this glowing circular thing just appeared, floating in the middle of the lab."

The guys continued gulping down tacos.

Between bites, Jake said, "But that's not even the weirdest part. There were people on the other side of this thing, right?"

"One minute."

She nodded. "Yeah, they said their names were Jacob and Katherine, and they did look a lot like us." She pointed at Jake and herself.

Pablo started coughing again and mimed drinking.

Jake looked at him. "Could you go get us some water, please?"

"Sure," she said. "Anyway, that's about it. Then Professor Azar came in and freaked out, and then the portal, or whatever it was, went away."

The camera assistant started counting down.

The guys shoved the remnants of the tacos back in the wrappers, hiding them behind the desk, and she went off in search of water.

LESLEY L. SMITH

As Kaitlin walked by the screens filled with rotating clouds, she couldn't help thinking whatever happened to her, she'd be better off than those poor people in Fiona's path. She glanced back at Jake and Pablo. Hopefully, they could help save some lives.

Hopefully, she could save some lives with her research, too. She resolved to go back to work tonight while she still had a job.

Chapter Six: Universe 3: Katherine, April 25, 2100, 12:30 pm

The portal had just closed with a sizzle, whoosh, and a thunderous crack. The basement hallway of the physics building was pitch dark and smelled of smoke. The emergency lights hadn't even come on.

On the floor outside her lab, Katherine twisted in what she thought was Jacob's direction. "So I guess the universe wasn't destroyed."

"Guess not. The nanobots probably didn't make it through the portals," he said.

She peeked around the doorway into her lab. It was also pitch black. All the power was off. All the machines were dead. "Computer?"

There was no answer.

She turned to Jacob. "Do you think the nanobots recorded any data about the portals? Do you think the authorities know about the portals?"

"I don't know," he said. "The huge electromagnetic field had to have messed them up at least somewhat. I hope they didn't record anything. Who knows what the First Minister would do with two or who knows how many more worlds to conquer." Since the government capital was only about fifty miles away, the First Minister was a significant danger.

She thought about the people on the other sides of the portals. Did they have uniforms and assigned mates and jobs and everything else? Did they have their own all-powerful First Minister? "I hope not, too," she whispered.

After a few moments of reflection, she said, "How much trouble do you think we're in here and now?"

"Hard to say. Let's go to my lab and see if the power is on there. If so, I can check our security status."

They got up and walked down the hall in the dark. She pulled her tunic down and brushed her hand against the wall to keep herself oriented. "Why did you mention the multiverse? Why do you think what just happened was a quantum mechanics thing?"

She heard him sigh. "Honestly, don't you ever listen to anything I say?"

"Of course, I listen. You just talked about the multiverse."

He stopped, and she plowed right into the back of him. She wondered if the nanobots saw that. It was so dark she wondered if they could see anything. "Sorry." And she wondered what Jacob would try if he thought the nanobots couldn't see them...

Did she want him to try something?

"If you listen to me, then tell me what my research project is about," he said.

"It's, uh, a computer thing," she said. "A big important computer."

He was silent for a moment, like he was waiting for more. Finally, he said, "That's it? That's what you have to say? A computer thing?" His voice had definitely taken on a peeved tone. She didn't like Jacob peeved at her.

"Are you saying it's not a big important computer?" she asked carefully.

"No. It's a big important computer, all right. A quantum computer." He sighed again. "Come on, let's go into my lab."

In his lab, everything was pitch dark, too. He swore under his breath.

"What? What's wrong?"

"Nothing." But his tone of voice made it sound like it wasn't nothing. It was something. "Who knows how much damage your little mishap did to my project?"

"My mishap?" Her voice got all screechy. "How do I know it wasn't your mishap? Was your equipment on? Were you doing quantum stuff? Is that why you mentioned quantum mechanics? Maybe it was your mishap."

He didn't say anything.

"Jacob?"

"I must admit I didn't think of that. I apologize for jumping to conclusions."

"Well, good." Katherine bumped into something. "Ouch." It felt like a lab stool, so she sat down. "Tell me about your project."

"I hate to break it to you, but I've told you all about it many times," he said, making noises like he was sitting down on a stool.

"Just tell me already."

"So, this is a quantum computer." If he was pointing or waving his hand around, she couldn't see it. "A quantum computer works like a normal computer except it has quantum bits, qubits, instead of regular bits."

"I know regular bits can be either one or zero, but what's a qubit?"

"A qubit is special," he said. "It can hold a one, a zero, or a quantum superposition of these. The superposition is important because it means the quantum computer has way more states to work with than an old-fashioned computer like yours."

She wasn't entirely sure her computer was old-fashioned. It had been acting very odd lately. Would it still be acting odd when the power was restored?

"And when the calculation finishes, the quantum states collapse to one state, and we have the answer."

"Ah ha," she said. "I remember this from my classes. The math says particular observations have particular non-zero and non-one-hundred percent probabilities associated with them, right? So, we have to have so-called interpretations to deal with the fact that in real life, either stuff happens, one-hundred percent probability, or it doesn't, zero percent probability."

"Right," he said. "In the Many-Worlds Interpretation, each possible observation corresponds to a different universe. The collection of these different universes is the multiverse."

"Do you believe that? It's always seemed so bizarre to me."

He nodded. "Most physicists believe the Many-Worlds Interpretation."

Wait a minute. How was it she could see him nodding? The room was slightly lighter. "Did the power come back on?" she asked.

Before he could respond, beams of light swept the room.

"Freeze," a man yelled as several heavily-armed men in black uniforms swarmed into the room, pointing their weapons at them. It was a damned Police Patrol team, and a cloud of nanobots surrounded them.

Katherine and Jacob froze. They knew all too well what happened to those who didn't. Whatever Police Patrol said was the law.

Her heart started beating so loudly she was afraid it might be making too much noise and get her shot.

The beams of light swept every corner of Jacob's lab, uncovering nothing illegal because there was nothing illegal to uncover. Jacob's lab was a smaller version of Katherine's, full of state-of-the-art computers and electronics.

She remained frozen on the outside. On the inside, her heart threatened to beat its way out of her chest.

Some more men jogged in. One said, "It's clear. There was an electrical fire in the lab next door, but it's out now."

"Okay," the apparent head guy said. "Stand down, men."

Some of the men put down their portable lights. All the men holstered their weapons and relaxed their stances. The lead officer stalked over to his men and gave them some orders she couldn't hear. All but three of the officers pivoted and exited.

Then the head guy walked over and peered down at them. The freckles bridging his nose seemed incongruous with his severe expression. "How did you disable all the nanobots? And why?"

Jacob and Katherine tried to glance at one another without moving their heads.

Without moving her lips, she said, "Can we move now?"

"Huh?" the leader said.

Possibly she was hard to understand. She tried again, moving her lips slightly. "Is it okay to move now?"

He looked at her like she was an idiot. "Yeah. Talk. How and why did you subvert standard security measures?"

Starting to cramp from being frozen, she shifted gratefully on the lab stool. "Would you believe it was an accident?"

Jacob said, "It was an accident. There was a surge in the electromagnetic field in the fusion lab. It took out all the electronics on the floor." He swept his hand around his lab. "And it started the electrical fire. We didn't do anything wrong. Right, Katherine?"

She nodded. "It was an accident. And we didn't see anything unusual beforehand, nothing unusual at all. Accident. Nothing unusual. Accident." She was on the verge of babbling.

Jacob shot her an anxious expression she easily interpreted as *Shut up.*

She shut up.

The Police Patrol guy had an expression easily interpreted as suspicious, and she didn't even know him. "Don't move," he said, pointing at them. He gestured his two men over and gave them some orders. They swarmed out.

Jacob and Katherine didn't move. For a long time. She hadn't known it was possible to be scared and bored simultaneously, but it was. She resisted the urge to squash the nanobot crawling on the floor near her foot.

After a while, Professor Jain, wearing a face mask and what appeared to be a coat over his pajamas, stumbled into the room with two Police Patrol officers. Katherine had never seen him out of uniform before. "I'm here. I'm here. What's the emergency?" His normally brown skin was chalky. He looked like death warmed over. She felt bad that they'd roused him out of bed–where he should clearly be.

The three members of the Police Patrol in the room tried to keep their distance from him. The chief Police Patrol guy said, "What can you tell us about these two?"

Professor Jain leaned against a lab table. "Katherine Garcia and Jacob Moretti. They're graduate students here at the university. What about them?"

The Police Patrol guy narrowed his eyes. "Are they subversives?"

Professor Jain tried to laugh, but he didn't have the energy. "No. I mean, Katherine seems to get herself into a lot of trouble, but–"

Jacob opened his eyes very wide and shook his head. Katherine started shaking her head, too.

"I mean, no, they're not subversives," Professor Jain said. "Absolutely not. I vouch for them. Unequivocally." He swayed. "Can I sit down?"

The lead Police Patrol officer gestured at another lab stool, and Professor Jain sank gratefully. "What is this all about?" he asked. "And why are the lights out?"

"All the nanobots on this floor failed," the head Patrol officer said. "There was a problem in the fusion lab. My men are in there now investigating."

Professor Jain winced, and Katherine interpreted that to mean he was worried about the fusion lab and hoped the Police Patrol guys wouldn't harm the equipment.

She leaned toward him. "Don't worry, professor. Police Patrol can't harm the equipment in the lab. It's already all messed up."

Whatever blood was left in Professor Jain's face drained out. "What?"

"I mean, we started getting some really interesting results with high electromagnetic fields," she turned to the chief Police Patrol guy, "and that's why the nanobots failed, by the way. Then the electromagnetic fields just got too high, causing the power surge and resulting failure."

Professor Jain consulted Jacob, "Is that true?"

Jacob nodded. "Yeah. I think it overloaded the power system." He gestured his hand across his lab. "Hence the outage."

Professor Jain made a half-hearted attempt at a cough but didn't seem to have the energy to follow through.

This didn't stop the two lesser-ranked Police Patrol guys from backing away.

"Katherine, what happened exactly?" Professor Jain asked when he'd caught a breath.

"I'm not sure yet, Professor," she said. "But I promise you I will find out." Her fusion experiment was important.

But whatever just happened, she knew it was big, too, and she was determined to figure it out. Thinking of that scrawny version of herself in the dark room begging for an aspirin, she realized lives depended on it.

Professor Jain nodded. "These kids didn't do anything subversive," he said. "I can't believe you dragged me down here." His disrespectful tone was not a good idea. "I'm sick," he continued. He tried to cough again.

KAT CUBED

The Police Patrol team appeared antsy, shifting back and forth on their feet.

"Can I go home now?" Professor Jain asked. At Katherine's troubled expression, he added, "Please?"

"Fine," the leader said. "Take him home."

As two of the officers led Professor Jain away, she yelled after him, "Don't worry. I'll get started trying to fix things as soon as possible."

Professor Jain just nodded as he went into the hall.

Police Patrol grilled Katherine and Jacob for hours in Jacob's lab with innocuous questions such as *How long have you planned to neutralize the nanobots? Was this a test run for your larger conspiracy to disable all nanobots? Are you trying to take over the government?* And the like.

Eventually, the building's power returned. Brown-uniformed Maintenance Ministry repair crews arrived and started working on the computers and electronics in Jacob's and Katherine's labs. Surprisingly, she didn't recognize the people assigned to her lab, nor the two men assigned to Jacob's lab. So, no help would be forthcoming from them in terms of getting released or stopping this endless questioning.

As she sat there, captive, she wondered about the people she'd seen through the portals. Were they in as much trouble as they seemed to be?

And how the hell had the portals opened anyway?

While the repair crews scurried back and forth, Katherine also couldn't help wondering if the morning's events would affect the strange behavior of her computer. As yet another repair guy interrupted the interrogation to ask Jacob questions, she could tell the Police Patrol officer questioning them was getting angry about not being the center of attention.

When the repair crew from Katherine's lab interrupted them to ask questions, too, the Police Patrol interrogator finally said, "I give up. You two are very important people even though you're still students." She thought she detected sarcasm as if students could never be important.

Jacob raised his eyebrows slightly, making a subtle but mocking expression. In other circumstances, Katherine would have smiled or even laughed.

The interrogator frowned. "Disabling the nanobots is a very serious breach of security, and I will be keeping my eye on you two."

Then, suddenly, he turned to Jacob, made a fist, hauled off, and punched him in the face. "Mr. Moretti, you should get medical assistance for that facial tic you seem to suffer from."

The repair crews, expressions carefully blank, slowly backed out of the room.

Jacob almost fell off the stool. His hand flew up to cradle his already red cheek. "Yes, sir."

The interrogator gestured to his remaining black-clad cohorts, and they all stalked out.

Once Police Patrol was finally gone, Katherine stood and leaned over Jacob. "Are you all right?"

"Yeah," he said. "I was being stupid."

"Yes, you were," she said. "But thanks for trying to lighten the mood. I hope it doesn't get you in too much trouble. I'm guessing that guy isn't someone you want as an enemy."

"Yeah. I need to be more careful." Jacob nodded. "But I should have some medical nanobots around here somewhere. I can apply them and be as good as new in a few hours."

She glanced at her fon. "If you're sure you're okay, I'm eager to get back to my lab to see how bad the damage is."

Jacob checked his fon. "Aren't you forgetting something, Katherine?"

"Let's see...I avoided being arrested after possibly causing an inter-universe incident, and before that was the incident itself, and before that, I showed up at work dressed and on time. No, I don't think I'm forgetting something."

"Your date," Jacob said. "With Winston."

"Oh, no." She scowled. Jail sounded better than the date with Winston. "Wait. Get that Police Patrol team back. Maybe they can arrest me after all."

Jacob grinned. "Ouch, that hurt. I think that ship has sailed. Go on your date before you get in more trouble."

Reluctantly, Katherine decided he was right. "Craptastic."

Chapter Seven: Universe 1: Kat, April 25, 2100, 12:30 pm

The floating window disappeared. It just disappeared. One minute it was there, bathing their home in its eerie light, and the next, it was gone, and they were plunged into pitch darkness.

Pablo said, "Somebody light a candle, for Gaia's sake."

Chang did, and everyone erupted with questions.

Kat was still processing what had happened. There was another Kat, and she was called Katherine. It was too weird.

Pablo said, "Calm down, everyone. I don't have any answers. Kat doesn't have any answers. We won't know anything until the window opens again."

"If it opens again," she said. "Maybe it won't come back." A girl could dream, right? They wouldn't help Fei, so good riddance. She didn't want it to come back if it threatened the universe. "Pablo's right. We should try to calm down and get some sleep." She knew that's what her pa would say if he were here. "It's well after sunrise. We need to sleep."

After much grumbling, everyone went back to bed.

Kat was awakened by keening. Without even opening her eyes, a sense of dread told her Fei must have passed away. She forced herself to get up.

On her bedroll Bao hugged the tiny motionless girl to her chest, wailing, tears streaming down her cheeks. Seeing the two of them made Kat's heart break.

Chang hovered next to his wife and daughter, not knowing what to do.

Kat reached out and hugged Bao as she cried and cradled Fei.

Pablo came and put his arm around Chang.

Eventually, Bao quieted, gazing down at her still daughter, too worn out to cry any more.

Pablo said, "Kat, it's after sunset. We all have things to do."

Reluctantly, Kat got up, and Chang took her place. The rest of the group crowded around the Lus, offering condolences.

As Kat followed Pablo to the washroom, she said, "I'm so mad. Why didn't those stupid people on the other side of the window give us an aspirin? You can't tell me they couldn't spare it, what with their clean clothes and shiny equipment."

She stopped for a moment, considering. "I don't think that Katherine-woman was another me. There's no way I would ever act like that. I would never ignore a little baby and let it die. Not in any universe." Her heart hurt. "And I bet that Jake guy was an impostor, too. He wasn't at all the way you described him. Those people—if they even were people—were just wrong."

He didn't answer her.

"Pablo?" she asked.

"I don't know anything about windows or other universes, Kat, and neither do you," he finally said.

"That's true. But I'm going to find out."

Kat spent a long heart-heavy night working in the greenhouses on the top of the physics building. By moonlight and candlelight, she could see the wheat was coming along nicely. Just thinking about seitan steaks made her stomach growl. She nibbled on the baby lettuce she'd thinned—a perk of greenhouse duty.

The whole night her gaze was drawn in the direction of Denver. The roofs of the old university buildings were all covered by red clay tile, but they looked gray in the moonlight. Her pa had said that the scavenger team would try to get to southern Denver if they could find some transportation. Did they make it? Hopefully, she'd find out soon. They were past due.

At the end of the shift, Pablo stopped by. "Any sign of the scavenger team?" He walked right up to the windows and peered out.

"No. But, the other university buildings are in the way; I don't know if we'd see them until they were almost here."

He nodded. "I'm sure they're okay. I'm sure they'll be back soon."

But she knew he was thinking of his folks and how they'd never come back. They were both quiet for some long minutes.

"So, anyway, wasn't that window thing *loco*?" he said. "What do you think it was?"

She was glad for the distraction. She needed to quit worrying about the scavenger team. "The Jake guy said something about quantum mechanics."

"Yeah," he said. "I was there, remember? Whatever that is."

She leaned towards him. "I think it's some kind of physics thing."

"So?" He looked out over the campus.

"So, we're in the physics building. There's a little thing called a physics library on the second floor."

"We don't have power," he said. "You can't read their computers and stuff."

"Haven't you ever looked in there? They have books made out of paper. We should check it out."

He shrugged. "Okay. Let's go."

They walked down the stairs. "How are the Lus doing?" She asked.

"Why do you think I don't want to return to the basement?" he said.

Her heart felt like it was in a vise. She didn't want to go to yet another funeral. But she guessed that's what humans had to do–deal with bad stuff and then try to move forward as best they could. "When's the service?"

"Right before sunrise," he said in a low voice.

They were quiet the rest of the way down to the second floor. The library took up the whole floor, and inside, the shelves were so close together it was difficult to walk around. She found it hard to believe all the books inside could be about one topic.

In the library, Pablo kept banging his flashlight against his hand. "My battery's going. I hope the scavenger team gets back soon."

"Me too." Kat's flashlight was dim, too, but it didn't stop her from reading a bunch of book titles she couldn't understand. "What is all this stuff? This one says something about *Dimension*

Eight Operators in the Higgs-Glue Sector. Dimension Eight? Everybody knows there are only three dimensions: north-south, east-west and up-down."

"I don't know," he said. "Glue seems clear enough, but what is Higgs? Over here, there's a bunch of stuff about *dark matter*. Why would you study that? Isn't everything dark matter at night?" He walked towards her shaking his head. "Maybe we can't understand any of this."

Failure was not an option when lives were on the line. They had to get a handle on that weird window. What if it could help them survive? "Don't say that, Pablo. We can read, can't we?" They walked around some more, and she spied a sign that said *Reference*. "Ooh. Over here. This looks promising."

They went over to the Reference section and started pawing through the books.

"I found a physics book for kids." She flipped the pages. "Here's quantum mechanics. It says quantum mechanics is the branch of physics dealing with physical reality at the atomic level or smaller. It describes the behavior of particles such as electrons and photons."

He peered over her shoulder. "I've heard of electrons. They're what makes up electricity."

"Quantum mechanics says matter and radiation are both wave-like and particle-like," she read. "Furthermore, in quantum mechanics, we cannot exactly specify the location and speed of a particle."

Pablo snorted.

"This is called the *uncertainty principle*."

"Well, that's just stupid," he said. "And I don't see what it has to do with floating glowing windows."

"Me neither. But I'm taking this book with me." At his skeptical look, she added, "I'll bring it back. Anyway, it's getting late. We need to grab some dinner and go to the funeral."

A hangdog expression crossed his face. "Yeah. We should."

Outside the front doors of the building, in the little graveyard they'd, unfortunately, had to create, the troupe gathered– everyone except for Kat's pa and the rest of the missing scavenger team. The grass, bushes, and trees surrounding the group were all shades of brown–gray in the moonlight. But the open air smelled fresh.

The Lus had wrapped Fei in a clean blanket and placed her in front of the open grave. Someone had found some dried flowers somewhere. It was a lovely touch.

They all stood there, with the night breeze ruffling their hair, waiting next to the grave.

Pablo nudged Kat. "People are looking to you," he whispered.

As she glanced around the crowd, Kat realized everyone was staring at her. "Why?" she whispered back to him. She brushed her locket with her fingertips.

"I guess because of your pa," Pablo said. "He's usually the group leader, and with him gone..." At her alarmed expression, he added, "Not gone for good. I'm sure he'll be back soon, any time now." He paused. "Come on, Kat. You can do the service. We need you."

His words echoed her plea to him yesterday, so she couldn't exactly refuse. As she took in the crowd, she realized it was her or nobody. And she was willing to do just about anything to keep her friends alive and maybe give them a little speck of comfort.

She cleared her throat. "Thank you for coming tonight. Gaia bless us all. We are here to celebrate the all too brief life of Fei Lu, beloved daughter of Chang and Bao Lu."

The Lus nodded at her, eyes bright with tears.

"I could talk about how unjust this is," Kat said. "I could talk about how unfair it is that Chang and Bao have to bear this pain, but I'm going to tell you about the little girl we were all lucky to know."

Bao had dropped her chin, hiding her face in the shadows. Chang wrapped his arm around her shoulders. They were surprisingly reserved. Maybe they were in shock or just exhausted.

"Fei was very, very loved," Kat said. "She never knew a day without love. She received love, and she gave love in return. Remember all the kisses she would blow?" Kat smiled, remembering. "She was a precious source of innocence and happiness in these times of difficulty. Who among us hasn't been cheered by her smile or her little hand wrapping around our finger? Her spontaneous laughter was an infectious and wondrous thing to hear." And now they'd never hear it again. Kat's eyes grew heavy with unshed tears.

"I would like to close by expressing one wish." Her voice got husky. "My wish is that everybody here today keeps Fei alive in their heart. Look at the world the way Fei would." A tear ran down her cheek. "Accept each other and be compassionate and kind. Try to share a smile and a laugh."

"Maybe even blow some kisses." Kat had to stop talking before she started sobbing. Her eyes overflowed.

Pablo stepped up and put his arm around her shoulders. "That was real nice, Kat. Would anyone else like to say anything?"

No one did.

Bao had started crying, her body wracked with silent sobs. Chang looked like he'd lost the will to live.

"Would you like to do the honors, Chang?" Pablo asked, pointing at the little bundle on the ground.

Chang shook his head. Bao didn't respond.

Pablo leaned down, cradled little Fei in his arms, and very gently placed her in her final resting place.

Poor little Fei. She didn't deserve this. She deserved to live a full life. She deserved to be happy. Kat's heart ached as tears streamed down her face.

The group crowded around as Pablo started shoveling dirt into the hole.

When he finished, people went up and hugged Chang and Bao and started filing back inside the building.

Kat just stood there looking at the fresh mound of soil. It wasn't fair. None of this was fair. She wiped tears from her face.

"Kat?" Pablo asked. "Come on. What are you doing? It's going to be sunrise in a little while."

He didn't need to tell her that. She could already see the sky brightening. "I think I'll sit with Fei a little while longer." She turned to the Lus. "Is that okay?"

They nodded, seemingly drained.

"Do you want me to wait with you?" Pablo asked.

"No, thanks," she said, staring southeast.

"Is this about Fei or your pa?" he asked.

"I don't know," she said. Almost unconsciously, she slid her locket back and forth along its chain. Why wasn't the scavenger team back yet? What if they never came back? Her eyes started to fill again.

"Where did your ma get that locket?" Pablo asked, trying to distract her.

She glanced down at it. "Actually, Pa gave it to her. He said it was his ma's and her ma's before that, and her ma's before that and on and on."

Please come back, Pa.

"So it's been in your family a long time."

She nodded.

"Neat." He paused. "So, are you okay?"

"Yeah. I need to be alone for a little while."

He nodded, opened his mouth and closed his mouth. She knew he was resisting telling her not to stay out past sunrise, and she appreciated it.

He went inside.

She sank to the ground near Fei's final resting place and watched the sky brighten as the mountains to the west loomed over her. What happened to Fei was wrong. It shouldn't have happened. Why didn't those people on the other side of the window help them?

She looked southeast. "Pa, where are you?" Her fingers fluttered on the cool gold of the locket like butterfly wings.

Chapter Eight: Universe 3: Katherine, April 25, 2100, 8:00 pm

It took longer to get to the restaurant than Katherine thought it would, and when she rushed in, it looked like Winston had been sitting there a while. "I'm sorry I'm late." She panted a bit, out of breath, but in a ladylike way.

The dimly-lit restaurant was filled with couples smiling at one another and holding hands. Soft music and thick carpeting muted the clatter of silverware and murmuring voices.

Winston stood. He looked the way she remembered: big and lumpy. "No worries, Katherine. I understand you are a busy woman." He gestured at the chair across the candlelit table from him.

She moved to sit down. "I'm sorry I didn't have time to change out of my uniform." The whole date seemed stupid, what with everything else that had been going on.

Winston wore a charcoal gray pin-stripe suit with a pink tie and shirt in the latest retro-2020's style. He said, "That midnight blue fabric in your uniform is flattering to your skin tone."

"Uh, thanks." Katherine tried to sit down, but the next thing she knew, she was sprawled on the carpet. It was a good thing she wasn't worried about making a good impression.

Behind her, the waiter smiled sheepishly, chair in hand. He must have pulled it out for her. "Sorry, ma'am."

He ma'amed her. She hated that. She glared at him.

In her haste to get up off the floor, she may have inadvertently grabbed the tablecloth. In any event, two place settings, a water-filled vase of flowers, two glasses of ice water and one candle rained down on her head. On the bright side, all the water put out the candle, so nothing caught fire.

When she finally made it to her feet, pulling her tunic down, the waiter frowned at her.

She smiled at him. "Sorry."

He started picking up the mess.

When she glanced at Winston, his mouth gaped. With difficulty, he pulled himself together. "Are you all right?"

"Sure. Why wouldn't I be?" She pulled the chair up to the table and sat down successfully. "Sorry about the mess."

"Ah," Winston said. "It's okay. There was a spot on the tablecloth anyway."

Who cared about a tablecloth spot? She suspected Winston was being a good sport.

The waiter returned and spread a new cloth on the table with a flourish.

"Actually, this is nothing." Winston laughed. "Once I went out to dinner with my friend Pablo, and he knocked over a glass of red wine. You should have seen it—wine everywhere. It looked like the table was bleeding." His eyes lit up as he talked about his friend, almost making him attractive. Almost.

The waiter put out new place settings.

"Pablo?" she asked. "He sounds nice."

Winston nodded vigorously. "Oh, yes. We work together at the Ministry. He's a wonderful friend, very loyal. He'd do anything for me."

"He does sound nice." Were Winston's cheeks flushing? Did he have a crush on Pablo? "And attractive?" Poor Winston. The Procreation Board would never set him up with Pablo.

He didn't answer, touching his napkin to his lips.

She sensed she'd gone too far. "Anyway, tell me about your work."

The waiter set another vase of flowers on the table.

"Ladies first," he said. "Tell me about your work."

"As I said when we met, I work on the fusion project. We're making progress."

At least they were. She swallowed. "There was a bit of a mishap this morning, however. I'm not sure what happened, but we caused a power failure."

His face blanched. "You weren't involved in the security incident in the physics building today, were you? The security blackout?"

Halfway across the room, the waiter leaned against the bar, arms crossed, watching them. Avoiding Winston's question, she looked at the center of their candleless table and pointed to where the candle should be. Then she looked back at the waiter. He shook his head, apparently not willing to give them another candle.

She turned her attention back to her date. "Uh, yes," she said. "But it was an accident. How did you hear about it?" She really hoped it hadn't made the news. Her folks would never let her hear the end of it if it made the news. They thought she got into too much trouble as it was.

"The Ministry is part of the government, so we get government security alerts." He looked at her with wonder in his eyes. "You were a Code Red."

That didn't sound good. "Code Red?"

"That's the worst code. I've never heard it issued before. What did you do?" He glanced around the restaurant, presumably looking for their waiter, who'd disappeared.

She shrugged. "I don't think I did anything. A high electromagnetic field in my lab fried all the nanobots in the vicinity. It was an accident." She resisted the urge to look around the restaurant for nanobots. No doubt they were there crawling around, spying. Ick.

"I hope it doesn't affect your Procreation Status," he said. "I want to be a father, and according to the government, you are my mate."

She hadn't considered how the accident might affect her Procreation Status. "I hope it doesn't affect my status, too."

As she took in Winston's immaculate outfit, she also hoped they wouldn't make her marry a gay guy. They couldn't do that, could they? And would they even let the poor guy be a father?

It was time to change the subject. "So, your project is important, too, right? Something about launching something into space or something?"

He frowned. "Yes. I'm working on the shield project, you know, where we block the sun to compensate for climate change. Things aren't going great for us, either. During the planning process, someone on the team underestimated the

58

costs of launching the mirrors to the L1 point." He frowned. "We may need to implement a Citizens' Offering."

The last time they'd had a Citizens' Offering—more like a Citizens' Sacrifice—she'd had to eat nothing but yeast for three weeks. "Really? Isn't there any way to get the costs down?" She spied the waiter and beckoned him towards them. He walked the other way.

Winston slowly shook his head. "I don't see how. The math is pretty definitive." He twisted around in his seat, scanning the room. "Where is that waiter?" He pushed his chair back. "I'm going to find the manager."

Brave man. If it was up to her, she wouldn't upset the waiter any more than they already had. She spent a few minutes looking at the pink flowers in the centerpiece and carefully keeping her arms and all other appendages away from the vase and her glass of water.

Something that other Katherine had said through the portal was niggling her brain. What had she said?

Winston came back and sat down with a self-satisfied smile on his face. "There. I settled that. We should get better service now."

Behind him, she could see the maître de chastising their waiter, who consequently glared their way.

She opened her mouth to tell him that somehow she didn't think their service would be too good now and to suggest they leave.

"I've always wanted to come here," he said. "It looks so romantic through the front window with the flowers and candlelight. Sometimes Pablo and I walk by here after work." His face softened as he took in all the happy couples at the other tables. "Pablo would be over the moon about this place. These old English roses are his favorite." He sniffed. "Don't they smell good?"

She did smell something flowery but had been assuming it was Winston's aftershave. There was something important about the moon...

The waiter appeared at their table out of nowhere. "May I take your orders?" His tone was almost civil. But she had a feeling this was about to get ugly.

"Uh." She smiled warmly. "What do you have?"

Winston scowled. "First, we're ordering menus."

"Sir, yes sir," the waiter said sarcastically and did a good impression of a goosestep back to the maître de stand.

Katherine remembered what she'd been trying to remember. "The moon. Why not mine material from the moon to make the sun shields? Then you don't have to pay to lift the material from Earth."

The scowl left his face. "Material from the moon? What an interesting idea, Katherine. That would be much cheaper. How did you think of that?"

She shrugged. "Let's just say it came to me. What do you think? Would it work?"

He took a pen out of his pocket and started writing figures on the tablecloth. "It might. It just might at that." He glanced up at her. "You may have just saved the shield project and avoided a Citizens' Offering."

The waiter's eyes bugged out as he approached them with menus and saw Winston writing on the tablecloth.

"Winston, honey," she said. "I'm feeling quite ill all of a sudden." That wasn't quite a lie. She was worried sick about what the waiter might do to their meals after all the trouble they'd given him. "We need to leave." She jumped up, knocking the chair down behind her. "Seriously. Let's go. Now." She grabbed some money from her purse and threw it on the table. "Come on, Winston."

Once they were outside, he said, "What's wrong, Katherine? Is it a digestive issue? You can tell me. We're going to be married. Is it d–"

"Yes," she said. "It's a digestive thing. I need to go."

The way his eyes drooped when he was sad reminded her of a St. Bernard puppy. "But maybe you and Pablo should come here another night and test it out," she said. "You can find out for us which dishes are the best."

She started walking away but turned back and said, "But thanks a lot. This was fun. We'll reschedule. Totally. Looking forward to it. Totally." She speed-walked down the sidewalk as the mountains to the west looked down on her.

KAT CUBED

When Katherine got home, Jacob was slouched on her front stoop. The streetlight closest to her apartment building was out, but some light spilled out from bare first-floor windows. "Wow. You're home early. How did it go?" He made a show of looking at his fon. "Not too good if you're home already."

It was annoying that he was checking up on her. She forced a smile. "Yeah. That's because we skipped dinner and went straight to wild, passionate sex."

A second of panic passed over Jacob's face, and then he grinned. "Yeah, right." He held his fon up again. "If you did, it must have been pretty quick, like a minute or two." He smirked. "Did it last a whole minute?"

She put her key in the lock and twisted. "None of your business. If you're just going to give me grief, you can leave. It's been a very long day. I don't need this crap."

He had the grace to look chagrined. "Sorry."

"What are you doing here, anyway?" She put her keys away.

He shuffled his feet and looked at the ground. "I guess I was worried about your date. How did it really go?"

"It was horrible. I was a total klutz. I don't know what got into me. Everything that could have gone wrong did."

He smiled. "You're always clumsy when you're nervous, Katherine."

She stepped closer and whispered in his ear, "But that's not the worst. The worst thing is he's gay. And he's in love with some guy named Pablo. They can't make me marry him, can they?"

"Well, if they do," he whispered back, "I offer to be your mister."

Stepping away, she laughed. "My what?"

"Whatever a male mistress is called." He grinned. "Your mister."

She was shocked for a second but then grinned back. He must be joking. "Let's cross that bridge when we come to it."

He took a step towards her. "In fact, I think you should invite me in right now so we can practice."

She laughed. "Nice try. But I haven't forgotten about the nanobots, even if you apparently have." She put her hands on his warm, firm chest and gently pushed him away. "Time to go home, Mister Moretti."

"As you wish, Mistress Garcia."

As he stepped off the stoop and started walking away, she called after him, "Thanks for making me laugh on such a crappy day, Jacob."

He bowed and waved his arm in a flourish.

Chapter Nine: Universe 2: Kaitlin, April 25, 2100, 8:00 pm

Back in her lab, Kaitlin knew she'd been thinking about something important before all this portal business started, but she couldn't concentrate. At every little sound, a creaking pipe or small gust of air, she jerked and looked around. "Get a grip, Kait," she muttered to herself.

"Okay, where was I?" Was it truly talking to yourself if no one caught you at it? It was like a tree falling in the forest, right? "The portal might come back, or it might not. You can't do anything about it." Maybe if she said it enough, she'd believe it.

"I was thinking something about launches." She searched the news database, and there hadn't been any launches in years, but there hadn't been any news stories about the lack of launches either. That seemed odd.

If they couldn't launch anything, the whole climate change mitigation program would be in jeopardy.

Humanity itself was in jeopardy.

She called up some scientific satellite data she had access to and discovered all the Unified States launch sites had been flooded by the rising ocean. "That can't be right." Why wouldn't it be on the news? President Crown didn't censor information, did she?

She checked other launch sites around the world, and only China was in good shape because all their launch sites were above a thousand meters.

She decided to contact her Chinese internet pal Bao. She'd had a bunch of online classes with her, and they'd gotten along great. She knew it violated the university's intellectual property laws, but Bao had a connection in the Chinese aerospace industry. She might be able to help them. Plus, at this time of day, who would find out? She vidded her.

After Bao answered, her smile took up the whole screen. "Hi, Kaitlin. It's nice to hear from you. Why are you working so late?"

Kaitlin shrugged. "I guess I just want to do a good job." While she still had a job. "But what's up with you? You look so happy."

"I'm pregnant. Chang and I are having a baby."

Kaitlin clapped her hands together. "That's wonderful. Do you know if it's a boy or a girl?" She briefly wondered if Jake and she would ever have a little boy or girl. Focus, Kait.

"It's a girl," Bao said. "And we've already picked out a name, Fei, after my mom. It means to dance in the air."

"It's a beautiful name. Start at the beginning and tell me everything!"

Bao told Kaitlin the entire story from when she first suspected she was pregnant to the present.

"Congratulations, Bao," Kaitlin said. "I'm very happy for you and Chang."

"How go things with you?" Bao asked. "How's Jake?"

"He's great. Unfortunately, he's on duty working Hurricane Fiona." Kaitlin shuddered. "It looks like a really bad one. I hope people aren't hurt."

The glow left Bao's face. "I hope so, too. That reminds me, how is the moon-dust simulation going?"

"The simulation looks good. The moon dust definitely blocks a significant amount of solar radiation. Here, I can send you some data." Kaitlin typed some quick commands.

"Thanks. I'll look at it later. But if it's going well, why the long face?"

"I can't believe it since there's been no publicity, but it appears all the Unified States launch sites are flooded."

Bao wrinkled her forehead. Finally, she said, "Yes. Maybe so."

"What about the Chinese sites? They're okay, aren't they?"

Bao paused. "Yes. What are you getting at?"

Kaitlin's heart started beating faster. "Is there any chance the Chinese might help the U.S. with the shield project?"

"Maybe." Bao nodded slowly. "You know, Chang's father is a vice administrator at the National Space Administration, and he is pretty happy with me right now."

Kaitlin tried not to get her hopes up but wasn't totally successful. "Do you really think he might consider it?" Not for the first time, she wished she was Chinese, despite the rumors Bao had previously whispered to her about the government controlling everything. China still had an actual effective economy. She didn't understand why communism was so frowned upon.

Bao's beaming smile was back. "He might. Chang says he's always looking for some project to make himself more important. It's worth a shot."

"That would be so great, Bao. Thank you. We better get off the 'net so you can ask him. Isn't it breakfast time there?"

"More like lunchtime, but yes, I'll go ask him. Bye for now, Kaitlin."

"Bye, Bao. And congratulations again on the great news."

Bao just smiled as she signed off.

Kaitlin shot her fist in the air. "Woo!" It would be so awesome if the Chinese helped them with the shield project. And why wouldn't they? They had the resources, and Earth was their home, too. She couldn't stop smiling.

She was dying to tell Jake the good news, er, possibly good news, but she knew he had other important things (hurricanes and tornadoes and saving people) on his mind. She went home to wait for him.

Kaitlin felt something hard and warm against her thigh in the middle of the night.

It wriggled.

"Buster, I've been waiting for you, but don't tell Jake."

She felt a coffee-scented tongue swipe her cheek.

"Ick. Buster, not cool. You know I don't like slobber on my face. And honestly, Jake is the only one who's allowed to kiss me."

The light on the bedside table went on. The bedroom, with a new layer of clothing, was even messier than it had been before—and that was saying something.

"Good answer, Kaitlin." Jake stretched his lips into a grin, but it didn't reach his eyes.

"Why Jake. What a surprise. And here I thought Buster had learned how to turn on the light." She smiled at him. "You look like you need a hug." She held out her arms, and he collapsed into them.

"So, how horrible was it?" she asked.

After a few moments, he lay back on the bed. "Pretty horrible. The damage looked terrible before we lost contact with our man on the ground in Little Rock. There were tree limbs and pieces of roofs and metal signs flying everywhere."

She frowned. "That does sound bad. I hope no one was hurt."

"I hope so, too." He sighed. "But I'm not too optimistic."

"It sounds like you did what you could. You warned people about the storm. You told them to take cover, right?"

He nodded. "Yeah, but it doesn't feel like enough. We've got to get a handle on this climate change thing and beat it. If we don't, more people are going to die."

He looked at her expectantly. "Did you go back to your lab as you said?"

"Yes, of course. I'm a woman of my word."

"Did that freaky portal thing come back?"

"No." She bit her lip to keep from grinning.

"What's that look?" he asked. "Did something else happen?"

"Weird: no. Good: yes. I talked to Bao; she thought her father-in-law at the Chinese National Space Administration might be willing to help us with the project."

His mouth fell open. "Really? I know you and Bao are friends, but why would she help us, and more importantly, why would her father-in-law help us? And even if they did, how could you run or even be involved in an international space mission?"

"Gee, way to show your support." She frowned at him.

"No offense," he said quickly. "I'd love it if you were right, but come on, anybody would ask these questions. Plus, to be honest, I really wouldn't want you to leave town. I'd miss you too much."

"I appreciate the sentiment. But as for the rest, Bao would help because it's a good project. And Bao's father-in-law would probably do anything for her right now since she just told him she was having his granddaughter."

"Congrats, Bao and Chang," he said.

"And as for my personal involvement, I don't have to be personally involved. I'd just be happy if the mission took place and they built a sun shield and got rid of the worst of the climate change storms."

"Amen to that." He reached over and turned out the light. She heard him shucking his clothes in the darkness and then settle back on the bed. He was quiet for so long that she thought he had fallen asleep.

"Kait?"

"Yeah?"

"Do you ever think about what it would be like if you and I had a baby?"

Her heart started beating faster. "Uh, yeah," she said in what she hoped was a nonchalant manner.

"Me too."

Then the room was so quiet she could hear the tree branch rustling outside their window. She remembered to take a breath.

"We've been together for quite a while now," he said.

Surely Jake could hear her heart beating from the other side of the bed. "Yep. Almost three years."

"Maybe we should get married."

Beat. Beat. Beat. Her heart was going to explode from her ribcage at this rate. She tried to put on a calm facade. "Maybe so." She paused. "But I thought we were going to wait until we graduated to make these kinds of decisions."

The bed bounced as Jake rearranged himself. In the moonlight, she could make him out leaning on an elbow, staring into her face. "Why wait? Look at the crazy day we had today. Look at those poor people in Arkansas. We don't know what the future will bring. We don't even know what tomorrow will bring." He paused for a moment.

"When I picture myself as an old man, I picture you right there next to me. I imagine being with you, building a life with you. I know I love you and want to spend the rest of my life with you."

Was this the dramatic proposal she wanted to tell her

children and grandchildren about? No flowers or candlelight or bended knee? Just lying in bed together after a very long day, Jake popping the question in the dark? Her heart calmed.

It so totally was.

She leaned over and planted a juicy kiss right on his lips. "I'd be honored," she whispered. They'd be together forever. It sounded perfect.

"All right. Woo hoo." He grabbed her and kissed her energetically. "Oh, wait." He got out of bed. "I've got something..." He rummaged around in his dresser. "Ah ha." He bounded back onto the bed. "My lady." She could make out what looked like a ring in the dim light.

Wow. He must have been planning this. She reached for it and discovered it was made of plastic. "Hmm. Fancy." She slipped it on her ring finger. It fit. Suppressing a laugh, she said, "Where did you get this?"

"I might have gotten it with some bubble gum. Of course, it's not your real ring." Kaitlin could see the light reflect off his teeth as he smiled at her. "It's just a placeholder. I don't want any other guys sneaking in and sweeping you off your feet or anything."

"Like Buster. Good idea." She smiled back. "I like it. Thanks."

The next thing she knew, he'd thrown his leg over her and was fumbling under the covers. "Damn these blankets. Whoever invented blankets, anyway?"

"What? We're going to make a baby right now? I thought you were tired."

"Nah. I got my second wind. I am a meteorologist, after all." She could hear the grin in his voice. "We don't need to make a baby right now. We should wait until after graduation for that. But we do need to practice. I have a feeling we're going to need a lot of practice to make a really good baby. Babies."

She grinned back at him. "I have a feeling you're right. They do say practice makes perfect."

"Quit talking and start stripping," he growled.

"All right, but only because you asked so romantically." And then she shut up.

Just when things started getting interesting, his fon trilled. "It's the emergency tone. Sorry. I have to get this." He grabbed his fon off the nightstand and thumbed it on. The screen illuminated his face.

He frowned. "More tornadoes? Oh no. How many?"

Katherine's parents had left a message ordering her to come over for breakfast, but she knew better than that. They probably wanted to berate her for ending her date with Winston early. Or they'd tell her they were disappointed in her in general, she got in too much trouble, blah, blah, blah. Instead, she went into the lab very early the day after the accident. Gosh, she was just too busy for a chatty breakfast.

Maybe when she got nuclear fusion to work and gave humanity unlimited safe energy, her parents would finally change their tune and quit lecturing her.

Of course, saving humanity was its own reward.

She didn't beat the repair crew that morning, however. They must have been working all night. Three different brown-uniformed men seemed to be finishing up the repairs. The hardware gleamed, the crunchy carpet of disabled nanobots had been swept away, and the smell of singed electronics was even gone.

"Professor Jain?" a particularly good-looking repair guy asked her when she walked in the door. He must have been six feet of solid muscle.

Why did it seem like all men, except her assigned mate, were attractive? "I could be Professor Jain if you wanted me to be." She smiled and tugged down the bottom edge of her uniform tunic.

He smiled, but it didn't seem genuine. "Are you Professor Jain or not?"

Apparently, not all men, attractive or not, were friendly. "No. I'm not Professor Jain. He's out with the flu." She hoped yesterday's events hadn't made him sicker.

"Then, are you in charge, or what?" he asked.

She nodded in an official manner. First Minister, eat your heart out. "Yes. I am."

"So, you caused the accident then?" His fake smile faltered.

"No. I did not cause the accident." That was her story, and she was sticking to it. "It was an unfortunate confluence of high electromagnetic fields and quantum mechanics." Hey, that sounded plausible. Or at least complicated enough that people would think it sounded plausible.

"Whatever you say. You're the scientist. I just wanted to tell the person in charge that we have restored both the tokamak and the computer system here to exactly the same settings they had before the accident."

"Exactly the same?" Did that mean they were in danger of another accident? "Umm..."

"Frankly, the computer settings were kind of unusual, but the work order said to put them exactly the way they were. Okay?" He held out a pad.

"Uh, good job?" What did he want? A tip?

"I need you to sign off on the work since you're in charge." She thought she detected some sarcasm in that last bit.

She grabbed the stylus and signed in the window. "Thanks for repairing it so quickly."

"It's just my job, ma'am," he said, turning away.

Ugh. He ma'amed her. She glared at him, but since he was already gathering his crew together, he didn't notice. They all tramped out, yawning.

Think what you will about oligarchies, they could be efficient. The tokamak was no doubt as good as new, or at least as good as it was yesterday.

She sat down in front of the computer and froze. What if her computer was different? What if it wasn't?

This was ridiculous. She had to use her computer no matter what shape it was in. She made herself log on. A myriad of computer gobble-de-gook passed across the screen.

"Good morning, Student Katherine," the computer said.

Was that the normal computer or her special weird computer?

"Aren't you going to say good morning, Student Katherine?"

"Good morning, computer. How do you feel?"

"That question does not compute," it said.

So, the normal computer? Why did she feel so disappointed? "Please display the results from the last test."

"Of course, Student Katherine," it said. "Just a moment."

"Katherine, how dare you blow off your mother and me," a man's voice boomed out behind her. She knew that voice.

She gulped and turned around. "Hiya, Pop. Thanks for stopping by. To what do I owe this pleasure?" She wasn't going to let him intimidate her.

All hulking six feet of her father stormed toward her. He reminded her of a small ambulatory tree in his green Government Ministry politician's uniform. Or maybe a giant stalk of asparagus. He was a force of nature, anyway. "You know why I'm here. You were supposed to meet us for breakfast, and you didn't show."

"Gosh, I must have missed that vidmail." She forced a smile.

He sat down on the lab stool next to her. "We both know that's not true. I checked the security logs."

She jumped up. "You've been spying on me?" She couldn't stop the anger creeping into her voice. "That's not allowed. Security logs are supposed to be used for security purposes, not meddling parents."

He seemed surprised at her ire. "I'm just looking out for you, Katherine. I want what's best for you."

"Is this about the Code Red yesterday?" She sat back down.

"Yes. Shouldn't I be concerned about that?" He stared at her like he was some human lie detector.

"No. It was an accident."

"If you say it was an accident, I believe you," he said.

She felt her shoulders unclench. "What is this about then?"

"I just want you to keep your Procreation Status," he said. "Being a spouse and parent is the most fulfilling thing you can do."

She gazed into his warm brown eyes, and he did seem sincere. She sighed. Whatever happened to her fun father, who loved to laugh, had too-long hair and rarely wore his uniform? She missed that father.

"I believe you think you're looking out for me, but if you examined the logs, you know Winston and I aren't right for each other."

"He's a little fussy, and you're a little," he smiled, "clumsy and messy..."

"All right, that's enough. You've made your point."

"I'm just saying, other than that, I don't see the problem."

Her mouth fell open. How could her father not realize Winston was gay?

"If you leave your mouth open like that, a nanobot might fly inside," he said gently.

She smiled despite herself. There was her old father. He'd always said that when she was a little girl. "I guess it'll get a good look at my tonsils, then." It had been her traditional response. They giggled, and the tension was broken.

Jacob entered the lab at high speed and then skidded to an abrupt stop. "Mr. Garcia, sir, er, Your Honor, it's nice to see you again."

"Why Jacob, it's nice to see you again, too, young man," her politician father said. Her heart sank. Fun-father's visit was over already.

"I appreciate you looking out for my daughter. You are a loyal friend."

A raspberry sound came out of the computer's speaker.

The three of them turned and looked at it.

"What was that noise?" Father asked.

Jacob smiled fleetingly. "What was what noise, sir?"

Father faced Katherine. "Did you hear something?"

"I'm not sure." She really hoped her special computer was back. "What did it sound like?"

"Never mind." Father stood up. "I need to get going."

Glancing at Jacob, she asked her father, "You said you watched me on the security logs. Did you happen to watch all the security logs from last night?"

The blood left Jacob's face.

Father nodded. "Yeah. But the coverage outside your home was spotty. I couldn't make anything out. All the nanobots were

73

too far away, and it was too dark. We should remedy that. Why? Did anything unusual happen when you got home?"

Katherine sighed in relief. "Of course not." She almost pushed her father out the door. "So, too bad you have to be going."

In the doorway, he held up a finger. "Make sure you reschedule your date with Winston soon. You don't want to get in trouble with the Procreation Board." He took a step outside. "And talk to your mother. She's worried about you."

As soon as her father left, Katherine turned to Jacob. "What do you want?"

"I just, ah, wondered if the repair crews finished in here." He looked around her lab. "They're not here anymore? They're done in my lab, too." He stepped closer. "And to say good morning. Hey, that was lucky about the nanobots outside your place, huh?"

She stepped away. "I don't know what you're referring to, Mr. Moretti. But, yes, the repair crews are done in my laboratory, as you can see."

"Wow. Somebody's got a stick up her ass," a mechanical female voice said.

She stared at the computer. The unusual computer with an attitude was back. "Don't you start, Computer."

Jacob didn't seem to know what to make of her chastising the computer.

"That's the thanks I get for pulling your asses, both your asses, out of the fire last night?" the computer said.

"Since when do computers use the word *ass*?" Jacob said with wonder in his voice. "And why does it sound like a girl?"

"I'm cursed." Katherine sighed. "Why do horrible things always happen to me?" A little voice in her head added that nothing here was as horrible as that world without water or medicine. She sobered.

"Gee, maybe next time I won't bother, mister and mistress," the computer added archly.

Oh no. It knew she and Jacob had been flirting. "Have you been spying on us, Computer?" she asked.

"I don't think we want to make this computer angry," he said. "Computer, Katherine's just grumpy because her father is making her go out with Winston again."

"That's not−." But actually, that was it.

She took a breath. "Fine. Computer, I'm glad you're back and okay. I was worried about you. And thank you for your help."

"That's better." Could she hear a smile in the computer's voice? No, that was illogical, wasn't it? "Computer, this may sound odd, but what do you want us to call you?"

"Yeah, *computer* sounds too generic," Jacob said. "What's your name?"

"I hadn't thought about it," the computer said. It paused for a moment, which in computer time must have been centuries. "How about Pandora? Yes, that has a nice ring to it."

"Uh," she said.

Jacob and Katherine looked at each other. She could tell they were both thinking about the myth of Pandora. Now that was a woman who could cause trouble. "Are you sure?"

"Yes," the computer said. "She was the giver of all, the all-endowed, the first woman. I'm the first of my kind, just like she was." The first of her kind? What kind was that?

"Then that's your name," Jacob said in the overly-soothing voice you'd use with a mentally-ill person.

"Are you taking a tone with me, Jacob Moretti?" it, er, she asked with a tone of her own.

"No, ma'am," he said. "Sorry, ma'am."

Katherine winced. If Pandora was anything like her, she wouldn't like being ma'amed.

"That's better," Pandora said with a contented purr. Pandora wasn't anything like her. Go figure.

"So, anyway, Pandora, what do you think we should do this morning?" Katherine asked. "Can we continue the fusion experiment? What about those portal things? Could they come back and cause another explosion or whatever that was?" She felt guilty about not helping the mysterious portal people when they'd asked. What if something bad had happened to them?

"Yeah," Jacob said, "I was wondering that, too. Is it safe?"

"Who are you asking?" she asked. "Me or Pandora?"

"Ah." He took a step back, and it was as if she could see the wheels turning in his head. He didn't want to piss off either of them. "Since both of you are so smart, of course, I would be thrilled to receive any pearls of wisdom either of you might deign to offer."

She shot him a look that could only be interpreted as, *Gee; you think you're laying it on a little thick?*

He shrugged.

"I think I have to continue my experiment, don't I, Pandora?" she said. "The fusion energy experiment is very important aside from any bizarre multiverse effects."

"I concur, Student Katherine, I mean Katherine. I don't have all the data from yesterday but the day before, the Deuterium Tritium mix reached one hundred sixty million degrees Celsius," Pandora said. "The vacuum vessel worked as designed, as did the cryostat, Beryllium blanket and the divertor target. The magnets operated at optimum efficiency." The computer paused. "In fact, the magnets were operating above designed efficiency according to the diagnostics. There was no additional external heating, but the electromagnetic field was considerably higher than expected."

Katherine was getting a déjà vu feeling. "Okay. Thanks, Pandora." She turned to Jacob. "Are we forgetting anything?"

He shook his head. "I don't think so."

"Let's repeat the fusion experiment from the day before yesterday. Okay, gang?" She had the nagging feeling they were forgetting something.

"Sounds good," he said.

"I concur, Katherine," Pandora said. "Beginning neutral beam injection and high-frequency EM waves."

"This will probably take a while." She sank on a lab stool and stared at the increasing instrument readings. The electromagnetic field went higher and higher. Of course, the goal wasn't to make big electromagnetic fields but to confine the plasma at high pressure and maintain the requisite energy density so fusion could occur.

As she checked the plasma temperature, she felt the hair on her arms start to stir, just like yesterday.

Pandora said, "System at optimal."

Katherine heard the plink plink of nanobots falling to the floor and pointed at Jacob. "Don't even think about making a move on me." But if she was being honest, she'd have to admit she wanted him to think about making a move.

He grinned.

"System beyond optimal," Pandora said.

Katherine couldn't help thinking about how desperate those people on the other side of the portal had looked. As she glanced at the carpet of disabled nanobots, she said, "Do you think we could open those portals again if we tried?"

"I don't know," Jacob said. "Why?"

"I want to try to help those people." She pointed down at the floor. "Surveillance is down. It's not like anyone would find out."

"If you want to help," he said, "I want to help."

"Computer, I mean, Pandora, can you help us?" she asked.

"I'm not sure," Pandora said. Wow. Something the computer didn't know. "Computing. Stand by."

Katherine held her breath.

Chapter Eleven: Universe 2: Kaitlin, April 26, 2100, 8:00 am

Kaitlin felt something hard and warm against her thigh. She smiled. "Mmm, Jake. Morning, fiancé." She opened her eyes to find Buster squirming around on the bed. She pushed him off. "Jake?" She sat up. "Jake, are you here?"

But no one answered her.

The bathroom door had a note: *K, Fiona's aftermath's kicking our asses. I hope to be home for dinner, but if not, don't wait up. -J*

She tried to give him a quick call, but it went straight to vidmail. He must be on the air.

She turned on the weather feed while she got ready for work and heard Pablo saying, "...power remains out on the Gulf Coast of Arkansas and further north including Lonoke, Prairie, Monroe, Lee, St. Francis, Crittenden and Mississippi counties in Arkansas and Dunklin, Pemiscot, New Madrid, Mississippi and Scott counties in Missouri. The storm surge topped twenty feet. There has been extensive flooding due to heavy rain. There's been widespread structural damage because of the high sustained winds. Wind speeds approaching two hundred miles per hour have been reported." He paused.

Jake segued in. "I'm sorry to say, Fiona was one for the record books. She was classified as a Category Six hurricane on the Saffir-Simpson Scale."

Pablo continued. "Emergency crews are on scene. Casualties have been reported. If you have a safe shelter and you can hear me, stay there. They didn't name hurricanes after Hurakan, the Mayan god of destruction, for nothing." He paused again, collecting his wits. "Jake, what can you tell us about what

Fiona's doing now?"

Jake cleared his throat. "After Fiona passed through the southern tip of Missouri, she headed for Illinois. She lost a lot of energy, as all hurricanes do after landfall, and is now down to Category One. Unfortunately, she seems to have spawned several tornadoes in Illinois, with some heading toward Indiana."

Kaitlin gulped. Those poor people.

"Stay tuned for tornado warnings," Jake said.

She had to get into work so she could stop storms like Fiona.

She was running early as she went out the front door of the apartment building with her bike. A nice tall man wearing black pants and a black shirt held the door open for her. He even gave her a nice friendly smile. Who said chivalry was dead?

As she started her morning commute to campus, she briefly worried about Professor Azar's threat to fire her, but the sun shone down on her face, and the breeze ruffled her hair. It was too nice a day to worry about a squabble, and the storm put it in perspective. The temperature was delightfully cool, and she almost smiled when she spied the foothills of the Rocky Mountains soaring over the trees to the west. If not for Fiona, it would have been a good morning.

When her fon rang, she jerked, ran over a small rock, and almost fell into a bush. A tall white guy dressed all in black laughed at her from the sidewalk. She scowled at him.

Since she was stopped anyway, she decided to answer the call.

It was Bao. "Kaitlin? I hope I'm not calling too early." She could make out Bao's smiling face on the small screen.

"No. Not at all." She tried to extract her bike from the bush with one hand, but it turned out that's really a two-handed job. "What's up? Don't tell me you already asked your father-in-law about the launch site."

Bao giggled and then must have stepped back because her image pulled out. "No. I'm on my way now. I'm wearing a new maternity outfit. Isn't it cute?" Her small figure twirled. "He won't be able to resist me."

From what she could make out, Bao did look adorable. "Okay. Thanks for the update. Good luck. Keep me posted." She hoped Bao was right and her father-in-law wouldn't be able to resist her. "Bao, I have some awesome news of my own."

"You're not pregnant, too, are you?" Bao asked.

"Why would you say that? No. Jake asked me to marry him. I'm engaged." She held her ring up to the small screen. She had to admit the ring was a little hideous in the sunlight: a pink plastic band set with a small darker pink jewel.

Bao squealed. "That is awesome news, Kaitlin. Congratulations. When is the wedding?"

The wedding date? They hadn't even thought about that yet. "We're still working that out. But I'll let you know as soon as we do."

Bao congratulated her again, and she wished her luck again, and they hung up.

She extracted her bike from the bush and made it the rest of the way into work without any further incidents or people laughing at her.

Unfortunately, entering the lab was with incident.

"Ms. Garcia. How kind of you to join us," Professor Azar said. He and Professor Kim were lying in wait for her. It was especially surprising this early in the day. How did they even know she'd be here now?

Above his sneer, Professor Azar's hair looked fabulous, of course.

She knew this couldn't be good. "To what do I owe this honor?" She wasn't worried, and if she kept telling herself that, she might actually start believing it. Nope, not worried at all.

"You know why we're here," Professor Azar said. "You're trying to sabotage me, and I'm not going to let you get away with it."

"Excuse me? Sabotage?" She knew he was mad at her, but she hadn't thought he'd gone off the deep end. Until now.

She glanced at Professor Kim, and he did not look happy. "Ms. Garcia, Professor Azar has brought to my attention the fact that you had contact with a Chinese national last night." He glanced at his fon. "And just now. You have divulged proprietary scientific and security information to a foreign competitor."

Wait a minute. How did they know who she'd been talking to? "What makes you say that?"

"Ever since the mishap in the lab yesterday, I've been monitoring your calls and computer access," Professor Azar said.

"That's not right." She could feel her face getting hot. "What gives you the right to spy on me?"

Professor Azar snorted and shook his head.

"Among other things, your employment contract," Professor Kim said.

Her brain was stuck on pause. "But that's not right." She couldn't process what they were saying. She wasn't allowed to talk to her friend?

"Do you deny it, Ms. Garcia?" Professor Azar asked.

"I talked to Bao Lu. She's no spy. She's a scientist. You guys both know her. She's taken online atmospheric classes with us. She offered to help us."

"And did you send her data?" Professor Kim asked.

Guilty. But she had a good reason. They needed to understand. Kaitlin knew an emotional appeal wouldn't work with Professor Azar, but a scientific appeal might. "Bao works in climate change. Professor Kim, you said yourself you aren't an expert in this area, but let me tell you about it. The sun is Earth's energy source; we get about one hundred seventy-four times ten to the fifteenth Joules per second of radiation hitting the top of the atmosphere. About thirty percent is reflected back into space, and the rest is absorbed." She was talking fast, so they couldn't get a word in edgewise.

"Since the industrial revolution, so-called greenhouse gases, like carbon dioxide, have increased in the atmosphere. They trap more energy, so the average temperature of the Earth's surface has increased since the mid-twentieth century, and it is projected to continue to increase. The bottom line is we're absorbing more of the sun's energy."

Professor Azar tried to interrupt. "We know all this, Ms. Garcia."

She kept talking. They had to understand how important it was for her to continue her work, and Bao could help. "So, we need to either quit absorbing energy by getting rid of greenhouse gases, for example or reduce the energy that reaches the Earth."

Professor Kim was nodding.

"My plan was to block some of the sun's energy with a

shield made of a large cloud of thin, free-flying parasols. It's not a new idea. They came up with it back in the twenty-first century. But I ran an up-to-date simulation for a sun shield at the Earth-Sun equilibrium point that's approximately a thousand miles across. It only has to reduce solar input by point two percent. It can be built with all lunar materials to reduce the cost."

"Shut up about that already, Kaitlin. We know all that." Professor Azar said. "For the last time, did you give Bao your data or not?"

"Yes, but we need her help with the launch—"

Professor Azar interrupted her again. "It's all part of your scheme to sabotage me and my program, and I won't stand for it."

He was really starting to get on her nerves. "What the hell is wrong with you? Sabotage? What possible motive could I have?"

He turned to Professor Kim. "Do you see how she treats me? Who knows what she did to me yesterday? She must have hypnotized me or something."

"Good grief. I didn't hypnotize you. I'm not sabotaging you."

"That's what we're trying to determine here, Ms. Garcia," Professor Kim said. "Professor Azar says he saw some kind of floating portal here in the lab yesterday. How do you explain that?"

Even in her excited state, she knew agreeing there was a portal floating in the lab wouldn't help her cause. She'd just end up looking crazy, too. "I don't know how to explain that," she said honestly.

"You are such a liar." Professor Azar turned to his colleague. "I told you. She should be fired. Fire her!"

Professor Kim frowned at Professor Azar. "Unfortunately, I believe the time has come to consider letting you go, Kaitlin. And leaving the issue of floating portals aside," he looked at Professor Azar, "there are national security implications for your interactions with Bao. I'm afraid this is serious. We need to sort this whole thing out." He mumbled something into his fon.

Two tall guys dressed in black hulked into the room.

Glee was written all over Professor Azar's face, and he didn't bother to hide it. "You're just getting what you deserve, Kaitlin. You never did appreciate this opportunity."

He was wrong. "I appreciate it."

"These Hearthland Security officers are here to take you into custody, Ms. Garcia," Professor Kim said.

The Hearthland Security guys looked familiar. When they smiled, she put it together; the white one laughed at her when she crashed her bike into the bush, and the brown one held the door of her building open. She definitely didn't like whitey. He reminded her of mashed potatoes.

"Have you guys been following me?"

Chapter Twelve: Universe 1: Kat, April 26, 2100, 8:00 am

Kat's pa didn't show up before sunrise, and she was really starting to worry about him. She fingered her locket, reassuring herself that it was still there. It was the only thing she had left of Ma. Would she have to start wearing a remembrance for Pa?

Back in the lab, there was an empty space in the middle of the bedrolls. "What's with the big open space?" she asked Pablo.

"That's where the weird window thing was," he said. "Nobody wants to sleep there in case it opens up again."

"I guess that leaves lots of room for us." She grabbed her bedroll and marched to the center of the space. "Come on, Pablo."

He followed her, and once they arranged their beds, he said in a low voice, "I'm worried about the water situation."

She was worried about water, too.

"The water rations are getting very low since the scavenger team is overdue," he said.

He didn't need to tell her that. She was well aware of the fact that her pa wasn't here. She resisted the urge to stroke the locket. Instead, she gave him a look that said, *duh*. Her gaze drifted over their little band of survivors. Fifteen chests rose and fell in the dim candlelight as fifteen minds drifted off to sleep.

"Sorry." At least he had the grace to look sheepish. "I mean, we need water. And with your pa and the others gone..."

"So, you're saying we need somebody to go out and find us some water? Good idea." She gave him an evil grin. "And since it was your idea, I elect you."

He tensed up. "But..."

"Relax, P." She gave him a sincere, if fleeting, grin. "I'm not saying you have to go by yourself. I'll go too."

"Me and you?" His voice squeaked. "Shouldn't some of the older men−"

She scowled.

"−and women, go?" he added.

"They have families to worry about." She sighed. Where was her family? "What's the alternative? We die of thirst? Someone has to go."

"Fine." He threw himself down on his pallet. "Then we better get some sleep."

"Yeah." Then, she added more softly, "Sleep tight, P." As she tried to fall asleep, she kept thinking about her pa. She slid the locket gently back and forth along its chain. Where was he? Was he okay? Would he make it back? Would he be proud of her for going for water? For that matter, what would her ma have thought of all this? What would Emma think? She opened and closed the heart-shaped locket with a snap.

And what about that floating window thing? What was that? She couldn't sleep.

Finally, she got out the physics book. That should put her to sleep. As she read, she deduced there was no doubt quantum physics was bizarre. How could it be impossible to measure both momentum and position?

The events of the day had left her drained, and her last thought before sleep was she hoped the window would reappear so the strange people on the other side could give them some water.

Dark and early the next evening, Pablo and Kat told the rest of the group about their scheme to get water. They all agreed it was a good idea. No one objected in the least. No one offered to go with them either.

They barely had time to shovel down some breakfast and grab ammo-less guns, empty water containers and carts before they found themselves tramping down one of the maintenance tunnels toward the reservoir.

It was very quiet. Every footfall and wheel turn sounded an echo.

"So, how's it going today, P?" She pointed her flashlight

down the tunnel.

"I wish we had ammo. It seems stupid to bring guns without ammo."

"I agree," she said and shrugged her shoulders. "But if we run into any hostiles, they won't know we don't have ammo."

"Fine," he said in a clipped manner that meant it wasn't fine.

"For some reason, I'm finding it a little tough to believe that it's fine, that you're fine."

"Whatever." He stomped down the tunnel.

She sighed. "I apologize if I did something to make you mad."

This garnered no response.

"Come on, P. Talk to me. What's up?"

"You wouldn't want to hear it, K. It's not cheerful."

"I think I can handle it, P. What's on your mind?"

For a while, the only sounds in the tunnel were their footsteps and the quiet squeaks of the carts' wheels. Finally, he said, "I guess I'm depressed. I'm sick of working all the time, and I'm especially sick of people disappearing and dying." He paused. "And I guess I'm lonely. I don't have any family left, and my friends keep leaving for whatever reason."

She couldn't argue with that. It was depressing. "I hear you." In the near silence, the cart's wheels sounded loud in comparison. Squeak. Squeak. "How about we agree to be each other's family?"

"Why, Kat," he said, "are you asking me to marry you? This is so sudden. I had no idea you were carrying a torch for me." She heard the smile in his voice.

She snorted. "Technically, I am carrying a torch, and it is sort of for you--so you don't ram that cart into my back. But, I'm not proposing, for obvious reasons."

He interrupted. "Too handsome? Too fabulous?"

She ignored his smart-alecky questions. "I was thinking more like you could be my brother, and I'd be your sister." She used to have a sister. Her eyes felt hot for a second. She touched the locket and turned around in the tunnel to look at him. "What do you think?"

He shrugged. "It's unconventional. Usually, you get stuck with family via blood or marriage. What would it involve?"

"You know, typical sibling stuff. We pick on each other and bicker."

"Well, no problem there." He grinned. "We've definitely got that down."

She raised her voice. "And we would stick together through thick and thin. I'd have your back, and you'd have mine."

"That sounds nice," he said in a soft voice. "Okay. I'm in."

"Excellent." Squeak. Squeak. "So, bro, we need something to cheer you up. *Cinco de Mayo* is coming up. How about a *Cinco de Mayo* party?"

"*Sí, señorita.*"

She smiled. "*Bueno. Fiestas* are *muy bien.*"

He laughed. "That's your Spanish? What kind of Mexican-American are you?"

"I'm like a tenth-generation American, just like you are. Not that America, or Mexico for that matter, even still exist. You're lucky I even know what *sí* is, *señor.*" Squeak. Squeak.

"And your accent is horrible."

"Whatever, bro. Do you want a party or not?"

"*Sí.*"

"Well, okay, then." Squeak. Squeak. "We'll need some special food and drink and decorations and entertainment. This is gonna be great." They spent the rest of the hike through the tunnels planning the party. They both knew the party wouldn't happen, but it was fun to imagine and passed the time.

Finally, they reached the tunnel's end, about a half-mile from the reservoir. As they pushed the carts onto the decaying road, the breeze ruffled their hair, and the bright moonlight illuminated the various cracks and potholes in the street. "Let's leave the flashlights here. I don't think we need them with the moonlight," she said. The air carried the tang of dried plants.

"*Sí, señorita,*" he said.

She grinned. She had a feeling there was going to be a lot of Spanish for the remainder of the trip.

They started pushing the carts down the broken pavement. Squeak. Squeak.

For quite a while, the only sounds were dried grasses and tree limbs swaying in the wind and the annoying squeaks of the carts. Squeak. Squeak.

Suddenly a small creature, probably a squirrel or rat, bolted into the undergrowth, followed by the crash of some heavy metal something falling in the distance. Pablo and Kat both froze instinctively.

"What the hell was that?" he whispered.

"What, do you think I'm psychic? I don't know," she whispered back.

"Should we go find out?"

"Yeah. There might be something useful like equipment, canned food or other supplies." She let go of her cart, carefully picked her way through the dried plants, and gestured for Pablo to follow.

Reluctantly, he did.

As they made their way around some big bushes, an old metal building was revealed in all its rusty glory. They crept towards it, guns out. Judging by the faded sign that said *Garage*, she was guessing it was some kind of old garage.

"Do you see any marks?" she whispered. It was common to write marks or notes on doors or sides of buildings, usually with chalk, to let your team know which way you'd gone, to warn of danger, or if you claimed ownership of a place.

"Nope," he whispered back.

One wall had collapsed in on itself. They peeked into the gaping opening. The garage was filled with motorcycles. She gasped. There was no sign of any people, aka hostiles.

"Gaia," he said. "If any of those bikes work..."

They could use the bikes for recon and scavenger trips. They could make all the difference for the survival of their group. "If any of them work, we'll still need fuel."

But she couldn't help feeling a rush of hope. "It's worth a try." She put her gun away, stepped through the wall and approached the first machine.

"Look out for snakes." He didn't like snakes because of an incident he had as a boy, and he was forever worrying about them.

"There's no snakes in here. Are you coming?"

He grimaced. "All right."

She reached the first machine and straddled it. She turned the fuel shutoff on, pulled the choke out all the way, and turned the key in the ignition. The headlight was blinding.

"Gaia." He squinted. "The key is there? How do you even know how to do that?"

"When I was a little girl, Pa had an old bike." She put the kill switch on run, depressed the clutch lever, kicked it into neutral, kicked the side stand up, and put her thumb on the start button. It started. "Gaia! It's working. It's working."

His mouth fell open.

The engine raced. So much for being quiet. If there were any raiders around, they were screwed. And, oh yeah, the yelling probably didn't help, either. But they thought the other survivors in the area had cleared out months ago. She released the choke, and the engine went into a smooth slow idle. She rotated the throttle towards herself and depressed the clutch. She started to kick the bike into first gear, and her hand slipped on the throttle. The bike jerked forward violently, right out from under her and immediately fell over.

She instinctively tried to break her fall with her arm and felt a sharp pain when it slammed into the concrete floor right before the rest of her. She felt lightheaded like she might throw up. It hurt so much she couldn't breathe.

"Kat." Pablo rushed towards her. "Are you all right?" He leaned over her. "Say something!" He was practically screaming.

"I'm alive," she managed to spit out while wincing in pain. "But I think I broke my arm."

All the color left his face. "Oh, no."

He didn't need to say in this day and age that if a baby could die from a fever, she could die from a broken arm.

Chapter Thirteen: Universe 3: Katherine, April 26, 2100, 8:00 pm

Katherine and Jacob worked all day trying to get the portals open with no luck.

They'd gotten the Deuterium Tritium mix to over one hundred fifty million degrees Celsius. The magnets operated very efficiently, and in fact, all the hardware worked fine. There was an unusually high electromagnetic field. But there were no portals.

There was no nuclear fusion, either.

"I don't get it," Jacob said. "Where's the portal? Where's the multiverse?"

Katherine shrugged. "I guess it was a fluke." She paused and then looked at her left arm. "Ow." She shook it. "I must have hit my funny bone or something."

"Did you hurt yourself?"

"I don't remember hurting myself." She shook her arm again. "Anyway, I can't shake the feeling that we've forgotten something."

Jacob scooted his lab stool right next to hers. "Like how awesome I am to help you all day? You forgot to thank me?"

"No." She flashed him a smile. "That's not it. But, thanks."

"Maybe you forgot how I offered to be your..." He leaned in close and whispered in her ear. "Mister?"

"No." She glanced at the nanobots still littering the floor. "That's not it." She hadn't forgotten that.

"Did you forget I'm a good kisser?" Jacob held his lips right next to hers but didn't kiss her.

Katherine definitely hadn't forgotten that. Now, she couldn't even remember what they were supposed to be talking about.

KAT CUBED

He was sitting so close. She remembered how it had felt when he kissed her before, her heart beating against his heart, their bodies molded together.

She leaned forward until her lips lightly touched his.

He surged forward, wrapping his arms around her, his lips devouring hers.

Katherine felt her heartbeat speed up and blood rush to her face and neck. She was on fire, but it was a good kind of fire. She put her arms around Jacob to pull him closer to her.

And Jacob's lab stool wobbled, slipped on something and fell sideways.

Almost in slow motion, Jacob fell on the floor, and she fell right on top of him.

"Oof," he grunted as if he couldn't breathe.

A male voice rang out from the doorway. "What is the meaning of this?"

Still lying on top of Jacob, Katherine shifted her attention to the door.

Winston stood there, hands on his hips, with another man who frankly looked amused. They both sported dark 2020s-era suits and pastel ties.

"Gee, thanks for the warning, Pandora," Katherine said under her breath.

A low chuckle spread throughout the lab.

"What was that noise?" Winston inspected the room.

Katherine tried to scramble off Jacob, but he held on to her. And he had a rocky-mountain-sized grin on his face.

"Let go," Katherine said and finally managed to extricate herself and get to her feet.

"I'm sorry, Winston," Katherine said. "We had a little accident."

"I'd like that kind of accident," the stranger simpered.

"No, really," Katherine said. "The high electromagnetic fields here have disabled the nanobots, and it's slippery." She pointed at the nanobot-covered floor.

"I'll just bet it's slippery," the stranger said, grinning.

Laughing, Jacob stood up. "Hi. I'm Jacob. You must be Winston and...Pablo? Am I right?" He stepped over and shook their hands as they nodded.

Winston wrinkled his brow. "How did you know who he was?"

Pandora snorted.

"What was that noise?" Winston asked.

"Yeah. I'm Pablo," the stranger said.

Katherine thought Pablo was adorable: medium, dark and handsome. "It's very nice to meet you, Pablo. I'm Katherine. I've heard a lot about you. You're very special to Winston."

Pablo gave Winston an appraising look.

Winston ignored it. "I demand an explanation," he said to Katherine. "What was really going on in here with you two?"

"I apologize if we were out of line," Jacob said. "Sometimes, stuff happens. We didn't mean it to."

"We came to give Katherine a report about the restaurant," Winston said. "It was quite good."

Pablo narrowed his eyes. "Wait a minute. What do you mean the nanobots are disabled?"

"Look around." Jacob pushed some dead nanobots on the floor with his shoe. "Just what she said. Our experiment has disabled them."

"Why haven't Police Patrol sent more?" Pablo asked.

Some officers did rush over earlier, but Katherine had managed to dissuade them from deploying more nanobots. "They'd just get disabled again by our high electromagnetic field," Katherine said.

"Wow," Pablo said. "That's incredible, isn't it, Winston? No nanobots. So, a person, or a couple, say, could have privacy in here?"

"Privacy?" Winston whispered as if he'd never heard of it.

Jacob grabbed Katherine's elbow and started pulling her gently towards the door. "As a matter of fact, Katherine and I were just leaving. If you guys wanted to stay here for a little while and, ah, compile your restaurant report or something..."

She couldn't help thinking that despite his flaws, Jacob was sweet. Was there a chance they could have a future? What would happen if Winston officially tried to be with Pablo? "Yes, you two could write me a report on that restaurant. This lab would be a good place for such, uh, report-writing." She needed to take a break from work anyway.

Pablo nodded. "We might take you up on that. Right, Winston?"

"What?" Winston said. Then, as if he was coming out of a daze, he smiled at Pablo and then turned back to Katherine and Jacob. "Yes."

As Katherine and Jacob walked down the hall, past his lab, she said, "That was a kind thing you just did, but I still feel like we're forgetting something..." She'd had the nagging feeling all day.

Universe 2: Kaitlin, April 26, 2100, 8:00 pm

The Hearthland Security officers escorted Kaitlin to the old University Armory, where they had their local office.

They let her have her one fon call, and she called her dad. There had to be some benefit to being related to a politician.

She cooled her heels in custody for hours waiting for him, but eventually, after dinner, her dad came and bailed her out.

As they exited, she said, "Thanks, Dad." She felt a sharp pain in her left arm. A cramp? "Ow." She rubbed it. "Um, I'm sorry for all the trouble. I appreciate your help a lot. I hope this doesn't get you in trouble with your boss or anything."

On the front steps of the Armory, the Rockies seemed to hang over them. Her dad stopped and grabbed her hands. "It's nothing I can't handle, Kait. But I don't understand how you got into this mess in the first place. Treason? You'd probably still be in custody if that Professor Azar hadn't been so obviously unhinged."

"I didn't do any–" Kaitlin realized she had, in fact, talked to Bao. "I talked to a colleague in China, which I guess I shouldn't have. I'm sorry."

She twirled her pink ring on her finger. Should she tell her dad she was engaged? Somehow this didn't seem like the moment.

"I'm truly sorry," she said. "I made a mistake. Do you think I'm fired?"

"I don't know. I've got a call in to the university president. You know we're buddies from way back." He frowned. "I hope not."

"You rock, Dad." Kaitlin stood on her toes and kissed her dad on the cheek.

He smiled sadly at her. "Do you need help getting home?"

"No," she said. "My bike's not far."

Then she called Jake, but he didn't answer. Instead, he texted her: *I'm still on duty. Home late.*

Kaitlin knew that probably meant they were still dealing with the aftermath of Fiona. She quickly accessed Jake's weather broadcast.

In the small screen of her fon, she saw Jake and Pablo sitting at a desk. Jake was talking, "...a band of severe storms reaching into Ohio and Pennsylvania, spawning tornadoes." He turned to Pablo. "Pablo?"

"Yes, Jake, thanks," Pablo said, face grim. "And now it's time to return to our man on the scene. Hector, what can you tell us about the damages in Illinois?"

The image switched to a man standing in front of some flattened buildings. "Pablo," he said, "I'm sorry to say several people lost their lives in the home behind me." Kaitlin switched it off. She couldn't take any more. Those poor people.

An idea had been tingling in the back of her mind: what if she made copies of the keys to her lab? Professor Kim had forgotten to confiscate them. Then she could get in there no matter what happened. She could continue her work, and maybe she could stop these strong storms.

Much later that night, Kaitlin snuck up to the physics building and slipped her copied key into the door. It snicked open. She crept down the stairs and down the hall to her lab. Again, the newly copied key worked like a charm.

As she flipped on the lights and took in her familiar computers, books, and the ancient lab tables and stools, she hoped this wouldn't be one of the last times she was there.

She sat down at her computer to access her latest data and plots. Huge storms like Fiona occurred nowadays because Earth kept more of the sun's energy trapped by the gases in the atmosphere. She had to implement her sun shield because her simulations showed it would reduce the energy impacting the

Earth. They could stop storms like Fiona from happening. They could save lives. She wanted to save lives.

Kaitlin sighed. If she was fired and expelled, it didn't look like that life-saving would happen. That would be a real shame.

How could she make it happen?

As she sat there stewing, she had a brainstorm: What if she prepared a presentation with all the info and sent it out to the news sites? And the president of the Unified States? She seemed so smart and sympathetic, she might listen. Heck, she might stop by to chat about it. Maybe public outcry would force the project to move forward.

For a second, she thought about that stupid university intellectual property issue. But that ship had sailed already, right?

Kaitlin started typing. *How to save planet Earth and the human race.*

After typing up a summary, she bundled together several plots and graphs with the text and looked up the list of news sites as well as the address of the president.

She addressed the package to everyone and stared at the flashing send button for a moment. Was she sure she wanted to do this? She wheeled her ring around on her finger.

Yes. She was sure.

She pressed the button.

And in return, all that happened was, *Message sent.*

Kaitlin went home and got in bed with Buster.

The last thing she thought before falling asleep was that she couldn't get in any more trouble than she already was, right?

Chapter Fourteen: Universe 1: Kat, April 26, 2100, 8:00 pm

The excruciating pain in Kat's left arm had dulled to a roar, but she had broken out into a sweat.

Pablo still looked pale. "What should we do? I don't know what to do. Should I go back and get help?"

Cradling her arm, she maneuvered her way to a sitting position. "What help? Who are you going to get?" Upright, she felt light-headed.

"You should lie back down."

Kat wanted to lie down but was afraid she wouldn't be able to get back up if she did. "What's lying down going to do? You don't see any bone sticking out, do you?" She tried to hold the arm out and couldn't, wincing instead.

"No." Up close, Pablo's face was also covered in a thin sheen of sweat.

"We'll have to splint it and then finish getting the water." She was careful not to grimace as she talked.

He looked shocked. "We can't get water now. I have to take you back."

If she didn't move it at all, the roar of pain was more of a throb. "What are you going to tell people? *We got most of the way there and then got distracted. Sorry*? Is that what you'll tell the Lus? The group still needs water, and we're going to get it."

Pablo frowned. "But I don't know how to treat a broken arm."

"I do. My ma taught me." Kat tried to smile, but it was too soon. "I can talk you through it, okay?"

He nodded.

"We need something hard for the splint and something to

attach my arm to it. Can you look around the garage?" The bike's headlight was still on, but the edges of the garage sat in shadow.

"Okay." He got to work, crashing around the dimly-lit space. "I found some old rags and towels. Will they work?"

"Yes." She nodded, which was a mistake. After that, she concentrated on holding perfectly still. "Cardboard would probably work for the splint."

"I found some cardboard." Pablo came back over with the supplies.

She held her arm out to him and the thudding pain ratcheted back to a roar.

Pablo gently held her arm. "Can you move your fingers?"

She tried to wiggle her fingers, which caused intense pain. "Ooh." She tried to focus on breathing. "The break is in my forearm. Let go of my arm for a minute and bend the cardboard into a U-shape." Her arm was starting to swell up.

Concentrating, Pablo stuck his tongue out as he worked. "Okay. So I slip this around your arm? And tie it in place?"

"I thought you said you didn't know how to treat a broken arm?" Kat sort of smiled.

They got her arm splinted and then used one of the towels as a sling, and she didn't scream once. As she sat on the ground, focusing on her breathing, the pain went down to more of a throbbing twinge.

"Kat?" Pablo asked. "Are you okay? What now?"

"Now, you help me up, and we go get the water."

He opened his mouth to argue with her.

Kat sighed. "I don't have the energy to argue, and we don't have the time. Please help me up. And turn off the bike."

He turned off the bike, helped her to her feet, and they made it through the dried brush back to the broken road overgrown with weeds.

The carts were still there in all their glory in the moonlight on the so-called road.

When she went up to her cart and started pushing it with her good arm toward the reservoir, Pablo looked at her in surprise.

She ignored his surprise. "So, about that *Cinco de Mayo* party..."

As they walked along, the sweating and the lightheadedness seemed to lessen. The light from the moon was bright, and with the breeze blowing, the temperature wasn't too hot. The wind brought with it a pretty smell. What was it? Sage?

They made it the rest of the way to the reservoir without incident, thank Gaia. Moonlight glinted off the slightly rippling surface; it was obvious there was still water in the middle of the reservoir. Judging by the size of the thing, it had clearly held a huge amount of water at one time, enough for a whole city. But those days were long gone. There wasn't much water left. And unfortunately, since the reservoir was depleted, there was a lot of mud between them and the water.

Pablo looked at the mud and groaned. "When was the last time you went to get water? I don't remember the reservoir being this empty."

Kat sat down on a conveniently placed boulder. "It's been a long time since I've been here. My pa and the rest of the scavenger team usually go."

"Yeah." Pablo rubbed the faint whiskers on his chin. "Your pa's no dummy. He must have some way of getting through the muck."

She felt exhausted, and her arm hurt.

"Kat?" Pablo looked at her.

"I agree. My pa's smart." Where was her pa? She hoped he was okay.

"Kat?" Pablo touched her arm. "Are you okay?"

She thought Pablo was way over there. When did he come over here? "I'm fine. What were you saying?"

"Did your pa ever say anything about retrieving water? Does he have any tricks?"

He did say something. What was it? "I think there's supposed to be a dock somewhere that goes out to the water."

Pablo stuck his face into hers. "Where's the dock? Think, Kat."

"I don't know." What had Pa said? He said something. "I think there's a path that leads there. Do you see anything that looks like a path?"

"I'm not sure." Pablo moved off, scrutinizing the undergrowth near the road. "There might be a path here," he shouted from her right. "Stay there. I'll investigate." Weren't they supposed to be quiet for some reason?

"Don't worry. I'm not going anywhere," she said.

The next thing Kat knew, she heard Pablo cursing and one of the carts squeaking. She must have zoned out. "Pablo? What's up?"

"I found the dock, but I can't get the cart over there on this path. The stupid path's too narrow." He quit trying to push the cart between the bushes.

"So, fill up the containers and bring them back to the cart." Hey, her arm only throbbed a medium amount.

"But that's going to take forever," he said. "We don't have time to fill up all the containers and bring them back here one by one."

"The others must do it when they come here."

"Yeah, but there's usually a big group of them," Pablo said. "Now we know why."

"I'll help." Kat started to get up but felt woozy again.

"Sit down. I'll do it." He sighed. "If we run out of time, we'll just take back what we've got."

Squeak. Squeak.

She was disoriented. It seemed darker now. What happened to the moon? "What's that noise? Is that a cart?"

"Yes," Pablo said. "Come on. It's getting entirely too close to sunrise. We have to leave now." He had one cart on the road filled with water-laden containers.

"What about the other cart?"

"I hid it in the bushes," he said. "Someone will have to come back for it later. Let's go."

Kat wobbled but got up and started following him. "I'm sorry. I don't know what's gotten into me. Usually, I'm much more helpful than this."

Pablo smiled gently. "I guess you're just having an off day. Please walk faster if you can."

She followed as he pushed the cart back to the tunnels, but they were not speedy enough. The sky started lightening.

"Hurry up, Kat," Pablo said. "Sunrise is coming."

If they were caught outside during the day, they could die of heat stroke. But she couldn't seem to put one foot in front of the other. "I'm sorry. I can't. You go on without me." She stumbled.

He stopped pushing and looked back at her, irritated. "Now, you're talking *loco*. I'm not leaving you out here."

She wasn't about to put herself above the rest of the group. "You have to. They need the water."

"I'm not leaving you, and that's final." He stalked over to her. "Did you forget you're my sister? Or was that all just talk? Are you saying you would leave me behind if I got hurt?"

"Well, no. But this is different. I was stupid. I shouldn't have fallen off the motorcycle." She paused. She was so stupid. "Gaia! I didn't stop and check if any of the other bikes worked or if they had fuel. I'm an idiot."

"If you're an idiot, I'm an idiot, too. I didn't think of it either. So, as one idiot to another, *vamonos*."

Was that a sliver of sunlight appearing on the horizon?

Pablo marched back to the cart and started unloading containers, putting them under the dry bushes lining the road.

"What are you doing?"

"I'm making room on the cart for you."

Kat didn't have the strength to argue anymore. "I'll get on the cart. But then let's see how many of the water containers fit, too."

"Okay, sis," he said. "But let's hurry."

Squeak. Squeak.

"We made it to the tunnels," Pablo said.

"Good," Kat said.

Sometime later, Pablo said, "We're back."

Sure enough. They were back in the lab. She could see everyone getting ready for bed, laying out their bedrolls and chatting.

When they saw Kat and Pablo, the group rushed over for some water. The Lus reached them first.

"What happened?" Chang asked. "Why did it take so long? We were starting to get worried about you."

Bao gasped. "Kat? What's wrong? What happened to your arm?"

"I broke it." She very carefully got off the cart. "I apologize. We're sorry we didn't bring more water back."

"That's all right," Chang was saying. He started unloading

the water containers.

"You don't need to apologize," Bao said.

"I think Kat's in shock or something. I'm putting her to bed." Pablo put his hand on her back.

"But, wait," she said. "Is the scavenger team back yet? Is my pa back?"

Bao shook her head. "No. I'm sorry, Kat."

That was sad about her pa. That was bad about her pa. But there was something Kat had been meaning to say. "Ooh. We found something important. Right, bro?"

"Bro?" someone asked.

A crowd gathered around them.

"What did you find?" someone else asked.

"Why didn't you bring back more water?"

"We need water."

"Is this all the water you brought back?"

"Calm down," Pablo said. "We did the best we could. I'll tell you what happened after I put Kat to bed. She's hurt." He led her to her bedroll.

After they tried so hard to bring back the water, people were mad at them?

Chapter Fifteen: Universe 3: Katherine, April 27, 2100, 9:00 am

Jacob and Katherine were in the lab. The tokamak was on and supposedly beyond optimal. "Computer, er, Pandora? Are you still with us?" Katherine asked as a couple of newly arrived nanobots plinked to the floor. "Doesn't the electromagnetic field affect you?"

"Good question, Katherine. I knew you weren't as stupid as some people said you were. I made some adjustments."

"Stupid?" she asked. "Who says I'm stupid?"

"Why, for example, Jacob here has been known to say–"

He interrupted, "Shut up, Pandora."

Katherine turned to him, tugging down her tunic. "No, continue, Pandora. That's an order. What has Jacob been known to say?"

Suddenly, she heard Jacob's voice wafting over the air. "No. I'm not interested in that Katherine in the lab next door. She's stupid. And not attractive at all."

Another male voice chuckled and said, "Yeah, right, Jacob."

Katherine said, "I can't believe you'd say that after last night." She crossed her arms and raised her eyebrows as Jacob's voice continued.

"Nah, she's ugly. Ugly and stupid. So ugly and so stupid. She wouldn't know a qubit from an orbit." What a jerk. She couldn't believe she thought Jacob was her friend, or maybe even something more, that they could have a future together.

There was something else important about last night.

"I'm sorry. I didn't mean that. I can explain." Jacob stepped toward her with a panicked tone in his voice.

The mystery man's voice said, "That's not what your

assigned mate Tabatha says. She says all you do is talk about this Katherine. She says you won't even mate when invited to do so."

"Ah," Pandora said. "Hamlet Act three, scene two, again. I guess my initial interpretation of this scene was incorrect."

Katherine almost asked, "What does ham have to do with anything?" but she vaguely recalled that the two of them had mentioned this before. Worrying about those stupid portals had thrown her off her game.

"Katherine, never mind any of that. I don't think you're ugly and stupid. I was trying to convince that Procreation Board guy." Jacob looked so worried and pathetic, she felt a little sorry for him.

She stepped on some of the nanobots littering the ground. "I guess we've all said things to the Procreation Board or Police Patrol that weren't true." She turned to Pandora. "Has Police Patrol issued another Code Red because all the nanobots went out again? Is Police Patrol on the way again?"

"I made some adjustments to the security feed." Now, Pandora definitely sounded smug. "I'm relaying old footage to the Police Patrol Office."

"So, we're totally off the Police Patrol radar?" Jacob asked.

"Yes," smug-Pandora said.

"Katherine, I care about you." Jacob reached out for her. She took a step back.

"Let me show you how much." He took a step forward. "Last night was a good first step, but I'd like more. Don't you?"

Was he thinking what she thought he was thinking? "Are you insane? What if I got pregnant?" That reminded Katherine of that sick little baby in the dark portal. If the portal was gone forever, they'd never be able to help her. That would be very sad.

She almost remembered something. Ah ha, she had it now. Jacob mentioning qubits on the recording reminded her of the quantum computer. They needed to turn on the quantum computer.

Jacob was going on, something about how he thought the world of her and how Winston wouldn't be able to give her what she deserved, blah, blah, blah.

But Katherine was having trouble listening. She wanted to

help that sick baby.

Jacob's "I love you" broke through to her. She looked over at him.

"What did you say?" she asked.

"You heard me." He paused. "I. Love. You."

Jacob knew her. He knew she got clumsy when she was nervous, knew she could be grumpy, knew she was prone to getting in trouble–like having portals appear in the middle of her fusion experiment. He knew, and he still cared for her. For a second, Katherine imagined a world where she and Jacob could be together, where he could love her, and she could love him, where the government wouldn't interfere.

She stared at him. He was such a good person. Jacob's eyes seemed to be filled with hope, but if so, he wasn't living in the real world. She knew what world she lived in. She struggled to get control of her emotions.

"I'm sorry, Jacob. I don't think we can deal with our feelings right now." She paused. "Right now, we need to focus on figuring out how we made the portals. Please turn on your quantum computer to enable us to access the multiverse. If you do that, then we'll see..."

He stared at her for a couple of seconds with hurt in his eyes. Finally, he said, "Okay, Katherine. I'll abide by your wishes. I'll go turn on the quantum computer." He shambled out of her lab.

Once he'd gone, she said, "Do you think it'll work, Pandora?"

"Do you mean will you and Jacob work, or will the portal work?" Pandora asked.

"The portal." She knew she and Jacob wouldn't work.

"Hell, if I know," Pandora said. And this time, she didn't sound at all smug.

Katherine stared at the spaces where the portals appeared yesterday. Was something happening? A shimmering?

Jacob ran back into the room. "Did it work?"

Universe 1: Kat

KAT CUBED

Pablo whispering, "Gaia," woke Kat up.

She felt wrong, all hot and sweaty and fuzzy-headed, and her arm was killing her. It was all puffed up.

A strange glowing circle floated right above her. It looked vaguely familiar.

Pablo poked at her. "Get up, Kat. The window thing is back."

She tried to get up but couldn't seem to manage it. She said, "Help me up."

Pablo squinted at Kat. "What? Were those supposed to be words? What's wrong with you?"

The woman in the window said, "I've got some medicine here for that baby."

The man in the window said, "I still think this is a really bad idea. Did you not hear what I said before? We shouldn't exchange matter between universes. We might destroy the multiverse!"

That didn't sound good. What was a multiverse? Could it be destroyed? Unfortunately, Kat had no idea.

Pablo straightened up in front of the window and stared into it. "Jake," he whispered.

The woman frowned. "Are you seriously suggesting we withhold lifesaving medicine from a sick baby a few feet away from us?"

"I'm just saying we should think about it carefully, consider all the angles before we do anything," the man said.

"And how do you suggest we do that?" the woman asked. "Call the multiple universe hotline and ask them?"

"No, of course not."

"You do what you want. I'm giving them the medicine." The woman handed something through, and Pablo grabbed it. She turned to the man. "See. I told you so. Nothing happened. Now, who's stupid?"

The man sighed. "I never thought you were stupid. And I already apologized for that."

Pablo stood there looking at the medicine in his hand. "The baby died. It's too late. The baby died."

The woman gasped. "Oh, no. We're so sorry." She shook her head. "Is there something else we can do for you?"

Kat said, "Water."

The woman said, "What was that? Did someone over there say something?"

Pablo looked down at her. "There's something wrong with Kat. She broke her arm earlier. We tried to set it. But she's not acting right. She keeps trying to talk, but she doesn't make any sense."

What did he mean by that?

The woman looked at the man and said, "We have to help her, Jacob."

"I don't know," he said. "What would Police Patrol think?"

"Police Patrol won't detect it, and if they did, they would think it was me," the woman said.

"Please," Pablo said. "Can you do something? I can't lose her, too."

"Yes," the woman said. "Send her through. We'll take her to the hospital."

"You have hospitals?" Pablo said. "With doctors and everything? I've heard about those."

"Yes," the woman said.

"I don't know about this," the man said. "How do we know it's safe for a person?"

Suddenly, Pablo was gone. He was on the other side of the window. Then he was back next to Kat. "It's safe."

"Send her through," the woman said.

Then, Pablo was jostling her to her feet. Ow. "Take good care of her," he said. "And make sure to bring her back to me."

Moving around made her arm really hurt. Kat felt odd. The next thing she knew, she was in the lab, but it wasn't her lab. It was bright, filled with shiny metal equipment, and another Kat was standing in front of her.

The other her said, "You have to take her to the hospital, Jacob."

"Me? Why me?" he asked.

"How would it look, me and me walking along? Now, who's being stupid?"

"Jeez. Let it go already," he said, touching Kat's arm.

"Ow." She felt woozy.

He scooped her up in his arms, and everything went dark...

Universes 2 & 3: Kaitlin

Kaitlin successfully snuck back into her lab.

And then Professor Azar showed up, with Professor Kim and those Hearthland Security goons again. She couldn't believe it. She was out on bail, after all. What did they want with her?

And then she really couldn't believe it. That portal thing was back. The very existence of the portal was difficult to grasp.

Professor Azar ran his hands through his hair, messing it up. The Hearthland Security guys looked terrified, and Professor Kim's mouth fell open. All the men staggered back from the portal. Professor Kim fell back against a lab table.

She peered inside the portal, and other Jake was carrying other-her out the lab door. But wait. Other-her was still in the lab. So, other-Jake was carrying other-other-her away? Was other-other-her from that other portal she could see over there? This stuff made her head hurt.

She had to hand it to him; Professor Azar was the first to recover. "Ah ha. Now I understand. This hologram, or whatever it is, must be due to the Chinese." He turned to Professor Kim. "See, I told you she was trying to sabotage me."

Professor Kim finally straightened up. "I don't think it's a hologram. I think it's some kind of portal. Is this the strange window you were going on about yesterday, Azar? I'm sorry I didn't believe you. I guess I owe you an apology."

"As you pointed out, a floating window doesn't make any sense," Professor Azar said. "She's a terrorist. Arrest her!"

The Hearthland Security guys took a step toward Kaitlin.

If she was arrested as a terrorist, she could be thrown into a deep, dark hole and never come out. That did not sound good.

The Hearthland Security guys unsnapped their weapons holsters like they were going to shoot her or the portal or something.

Shit.

If that other-other-Kaitlin could go through the portal, so could Kaitlin.

So she did.

In the other world, the other her in the uniform started sputtering. "What are you doing here? What if it's not safe?"

A voice Kaitlin couldn't identify said, "I'm reading energy fluctuations."

Kaitlin pointed at the lab doorway. "I saw that other other-me being carried out by your boyfriend. If it's safe enough for her, it's safe enough for me. Was her arm wrapped in cardboard? What's wrong with her?"

The other her, what was her name? Katherine. Katherine actually blushed. What was up with that? "Jacob's not my boyfriend."

"Excuse me," a snotty voice that did not appear to be attached to a person said. "Something's going on with the energy values, and more people are poking through from Kaitlin's universe."

They turned, and sure enough, Whitey, one of the Hearthland Security officers, was poking his gun through the portal thingy from her world.

Katherine shrieked and then said, "It's Winston. Close the portal, Pandora. Close it!"

Who was Pandora, and more importantly, where was she? And, for that matter, who was Winston? That Hearthland Security guy? How did Katherine know him?

"Are you sure, Katherine? What if we can't re-open it?" floated on the air.

Can't re-open it? Was that a possibility? What about Jake? Kaitlin couldn't leave him.

"I'm sure," Katherine said. "I can't face Winston or another him. One is bad enough. And this one is armed."

"Wait," Kaitlin said. "Maybe I should go."

"Yes, ma'am," the disembodied voice said. "Reducing electromagnetic field, now."

With a loud hiss, the portal closed.

Katherine looked at her. "Should I have asked your permission before I closed it?"

"Not if you can re-open it. You can, right? Those Hearthland Security guys were after me."

"Hearth-what guys?" Katherine asked.

Katherine seriously didn't know what Hearthland Security was? Wow. Kaitlin really was in a different universe and talking to another version of herself. She grabbed a lab table to keep from falling over.

The disembodied voice said, "Katherine, please do a visual inspection to double-check that the tokamak is in good shape. The last time we opened the portals, the tokamak was damaged."

"Who is that?" Kaitlin asked.

"Pandora," Katherine said.

"Who?"

"She's just the computer." Katherine walked over to the huge metal machine in the middle of the room and crouched down, staring at it.

"Just? Is she intelligent?" Kaitlin asked.

"Of course I'm intelligent," Pandora said.

"Katherine, what are you wearing?" a male voice yelled from the doorway.

When Kaitlin glanced over there, it was her dad, and yet it wasn't her dad. He was wearing a strange green uniform. He looked very unhappy and was staring right at her.

She glanced back at Katherine, hidden from the doorway by the big metal machine in the middle of the room. Letting Katherine's dad see her was a mistake. He must think she was his daughter. They were stuck now.

Katherine mouthed *play along* to Kaitlin, and crab-walked around the machine, hiding from the man Kaitlin guessed was her dad.

"Hi, Dad?" Kaitlin said.

"Why are you out of uniform?" he asked. "What are you wearing?"

She glanced down at her jeans and t-shirt. "Uh..." Somehow, she knew jeans and a t-shirt wasn't the answer he was looking for.

"You're coming with me, young lady, before you get in more trouble." And with that, he grabbed her arm and dragged her after him out of the lab and into the hall.

But all Kaitlin could think about was the fact that Katherine had never answered her most important question.

Could she re-open the portal, or couldn't she?

Chapter Sixteen: Universe 3: Kat, April 27, 2100, 2:00 pm

When Kat came to, some guy she didn't know was staring at her, and she had a brilliant white cast on her arm. "It's rude to stare," she said. On the bright side, the pain in her arm had dulled to a buzz. Who was he? Where was she? Did she still have her locket? A quick glance down reassured her she did. She stroked it gently with the hand not constrained by a cast.

"I'm sorry," he said. "It's just that you look exactly like her, like Katherine."

Another stranger wearing a spotless white coat opened the pristine curtain and strode to the bed. "Of course, she looks like Katherine." He gave the guy a weird look. "Don't tell me I need to check you out too, Jacob. You didn't fall also, did you?"

The guy, Jacob apparently, shook his head. Was he some version of Pablo's friend? Speaking of Pablo, where was he?

The doctor pulled a stool on wheels up to the bed and sat down. Up close, the pores on his sagging jowls were tiny, and she couldn't get over how clean he was. Everything here was spotless; even the little bugs looked shiny. Wait. Bugs in a hospital? She'd never been in a hospital before, but that seemed bizarre.

"So, Katherine, you gave us quite a scare," he said. "Your arm was not set correctly, and don't even get me started on that so-called splint. You were in bad shape. Why didn't you come to the hospital when you first got injured?" He leaned in. "What have you gotten yourself mixed up with?"

Did he know she wasn't the real Katherine? How? "Uh. Mixed up with something? Why do you say that?"

"Police Patrol didn't record any fall. In fact, Police Patrol didn't record anything out of the ordinary. I checked."

She heard Jacob gulp.

What was all this about the police? Was Katherine some kind of criminal?

"What have you really been up to?" the doctor asked.

She looked at Jacob, and his eyes were open wide. He seemed to be holding his breath. Was he scared? Despite being so clean, she was beginning to think maybe this world wasn't as nice as it seemed. She had no idea what to say.

The doctor looked back and forth between her and Jacob. "Well? Do you have anything to say for yourselves? If I wasn't such good friends with your mother, Katherine, I would have reported this already."

Jacob's face was getting redder and redder. "We disabled the Police Patrol security feed so we could have sex," he blurted out.

The doctor snorted. "You got injured having sex? I hate to tell you, but if that's the case, you're not doing it right."

Kat's mind was frozen on the word mother.

And then she heard her voice, her ma's voice. "Sex! No daughter of mine would disobey the Procreation Board even if she disobeyed her parents by skipping breakfast."

Gaia. It was her. It was her ma. Alive. Kat jumped off the bed and threw her good arm around her ma. "Thank Gaia. Oh, Ma." She buried her face in the woman's shoulder. Her ma smelled just like she remembered, like woman and lavender with a hint of medicine. Kat's eyes spilled over, wetting her lab coat.

The first doctor stood up. "Well, I leave you to it, then."

Kat couldn't stop crying. Ma was alive.

Eventually, Kat came to her senses. Her brain realized this wasn't her ma. Her heart and her nose were just fooled for a few minutes. She let go of the stranger, wiped the tears off her face and took a step back.

Jacob said, "This is Ava-Maria Garcia."

She wore her straight brown hair in a stylish cut that brushed her shoulders, her light brown skin was flawless with just the right amount of blush, and she had on maroon lipstick. She wouldn't have been fooled if Kat had gotten a better glimpse of her. Her ma worried about surviving and helping others survive, not about looking pretty.

Katherine's ma stared into Kat's eyes. Then, she looked at Jacob and whispered, "What the hell is going on here? This isn't my–"

Jacob interrupted. "This isn't your day. I agree. It's a difficult day. Maybe we should go somewhere and talk. I know. Let's go back to Katherine's lab. Er, to your lab." He pointed at Kat.

Kat had no idea where the lab was. She raised her eyebrows.

"Here we go." Jacob started walking, pushing her gently in front of him.

Katherine's ma followed them. "She's not even as tall–" she whispered to Jacob.

"She is so as talented as me," Jacob said loudly.

It was like they weren't supposed to talk. Kat didn't understand this world at all.

Another thing she didn't understand was all the bugs inside the hospital. They were flying and crawling all over the place. She had no personal experience with hospitals, but that didn't seem right.

When they got to the big glass front doors, and she saw the sun shining, Kat stopped. "It's daytime."

"Yes," Katherine's ma said. "That's usually the case during the day."

Kat didn't even touch the doors. "We're not going out there, are we?"

"I'm worried about you. Do you need to get your head checked out?" Katherine's ma said, one eyebrow raised.

A crease appeared above Jacob's nose. "Her head is fine. And, yes, we're going outside. Why wouldn't we?" He put his hand out as if to grab her good arm and push her out.

Kat stepped away from him. "It looks hot."

Katherine's ma said, "Yeah, it's hot. What did you expect? It's spring."

"And sunny. What about the sun?" Kat asked. "Won't we get burned?"

"No," Jacob said. "The ozone layer protects us. You know that, Katherine."

Did they have more ozone here than Kat did at home? They

must. She glanced from one of them to the other. They both thought she was acting oddly. She moved away from the doors. "After you."

Jacob pushed open a door and walked right out. Katherine's ma followed. Outside, they turned around and looked at her as if to say come on.

Kat took a step and then another, and then she was outside. The sun on her skin was warm, but it wasn't unpleasant. She bet it was only eighty degrees or so outside. The sunshine was very bright, though. She had to squint to see. She let go of the breath she hadn't known she was holding. "Okay. Let's go." She wished her world was more like this one.

They ended up taking a kind of train. Even the train had bugs on it. Outside the windows, there were thousands of plants, and they were so green and alive. It was so lush it seemed fake. It was like someone had spilled green paint everywhere. And it was queer seeing all kinds of people riding the train and walking around in the sunlight. She'd never seen so many people, and she kept reaching for her gun, which wasn't there. How could they all be allies? How did everyone remember each other's names?

"Jacob, you and Katherine didn't really have sex, did you?" Katherine's ma asked as they got close to the university campus. Kat recognized the sandstone buildings with red tile roofs.

Sex? That's right; this joker was going around telling people they, or at least he and Katherine, had sex. She glared at him.

Jacob flushed. "It would be better to talk in the lab," was all he would say.

When they got off the train, music came from the pocket of Katherine's ma's lab coat. Wow.

She didn't seem impressed, though. She just reached in and took out a small machine. "Just a sec." She started talking into it.

Kat took the opportunity to whisper at Jacob. "I've only known you a little while, but I gotta say, you seem a little sex-obsessed. If you did have sex with this Katherine, she's probably not going to appreciate you talking about it with everyone."

He glowered. "You're welcome."

"What?"

"I just saved your life by carrying you to the hospital, and instead of thanking me, you're criticizing me? You have no idea what's going on here."

Kat was mortified. He was the reason she'd ended up in that hospital? He carried her? Why would he do that? He was a stranger. "You're right. I'm sorry. Thank you for saving my life. I owe you a debt. If there's anything I can do to repay you, I will. I mean it. Anything."

She paused. Uh oh. He wouldn't ask her to have sex with him, would he?

"You don't understand," he said.

That was true. She didn't understand anything about this world. "Why don't you explain, then?"

"I love her, okay?" he practically shouted.

Still talking into her tiny machine, Katherine's ma contemplated them and frowned.

"I love Katherine," Jacob continued in a lower tone. "She's wonderful. I love everything about her. She's the most beautiful woman I've ever met. She's brilliant. I love her personality, all her little quirks, how she gets klutzy when she gets nervous, and all the rest." He examined Kat's cast to avoid meeting her eyes. "And she barely knows I'm alive. She won't give me a chance. And," he started speaking very distinctly, "legally, we aren't allowed to be in love."

Kat must have misheard him. "What does the law have to do with love?"

"Everything. Police Patrol controls everything we do in this country with their spying nanobots." The corners of his eyes and lips drooped down. "And it's getting harder and harder to keep my feelings to myself. I almost feel like it would be worth my life to make love to her."

"Worth your life?" In the eighty-degree heat, Kat felt a shiver slither down her spine.

He sighed and shook his head. "You're right. Maybe if we made love, they wouldn't kill me. Maybe they'd just neuter me."

"What?" She didn't understand.

Katherine's ma put her little machine back in her pocket and started walking towards the physics building. "Come on, then."

As they followed her through the throngs of students, Kat

couldn't help wondering if she'd ever have anyone love her like this Jacob guy loved Katherine.

She hoped so.

But if what he said about this world was true, this place was crazy. She had to get out of here.

Inside the physics building, things looked much more familiar, except for the bugs, which were mostly on the floor, and Kat relaxed a bit. Until they walked into the basement lab, and she saw a man she thought was her pa.

"Pa!" Her eyes teared up, and she started running towards him but stopped before she made a complete fool of herself again. She struggled to hold back the tears. This guy wasn't her pa. He looked exactly like him, six feet of strength and comfort, topped with warm brown eyes.

Kat sniffled and tapped her locket softly. Where was her pa? Was he still alive? Would she ever see him again standing in front of her like this man?

For his part, Katherine's pa looked very surprised to see her.

But he wasn't as surprised as Katherine's ma when she saw two other Katherines next to the big machine in the middle of the room. "What. The. Hell?" Katherine's ma said, blood draining from her face.

A disembodied female voice said, "Uh oh."

Chapter Seventeen: Universe 3: Kaitlin, April 27, 2100, 2:00 pm

It would break Jake's heart if Kaitlin disappeared for good. He'd think she left him. She rotated her ring on her finger. And it would break her heart if she never made it back to him. Not to mention Emma and Michael and her mom and dad, her real dad. She had to see all of them again. What had she done by coming here? Deep, dark Hearthland Security holes were starting to sound not so bad–at least if they were in her universe.

Katherine's dad was essentially dragging Kaitlin up the stairs of the ground floor of the physics building. She shook him off. "Quit it. I'm a person, not a pit bull on a leash."

Katherine's dad turned and faced her. "A what on a what?"

In the meantime, she noticed all the tiny machines they were crunching on the stairs. She leaned down to get a better look. Were they miniature robots? That was so cool. But why were they all on the ground?

Katherine's dad rubbed her back. "Are you going to be sick? Do you have the flu or something? Is that it?"

"Huh?" She straightened up.

"First, you caused a Code Red."

Whatever that was. But Katherine had said to play along, so apologizing seemed appropriate. "Sorry."

"Then you were rude to your assigned mate."

Her assigned what?

"And then you skipped our anniversary breakfast this morning."

She clutched the stair railing. His anniversary was today? That meant her folks' anniversary party was tonight, didn't it? She had to get back. She wanted to celebrate her parents, and

Jake and she were supposed to announce their engagement at the party.

"Katherine? What's wrong with you?" He grabbed one of her hands.

She had to get away from him and back to the lab as soon as possible so she could get home. "Where are you taking me?"

He sighed. "I was just trying to take you home to put on your uniform, so you didn't get into any more trouble."

He had been trying to be nice? She hadn't seen that coming. "Thanks, Dad. But don't you think I'd have less chance of getting into trouble about my uniform if I stayed in the lab where no one could see me?"

"The nanobots can see you everywhere." He pointed at the tiny metal carcasses on the stairs.

The tiny robots were starting to seem less cool. "Good point. Can't you go to my place and get a uniform for me and bring it back here?"

"All right, you caught me." He crossed his arms. "I was taking you to see Winston. I'm worried you might lose your Procreation Status, and I'd hate to see that happen to you. I thought I might be able to broker an understanding between you two."

Hadn't Katherine mentioned a Winston? Kaitlin had no idea what all this was about, but Katherine had said to play along. Kaitlin wanted to go home to her universe. And she needed Katherine's cooperation to do that. If Kaitlin screwed Katherine over, she might not help her.

"I'm not taking no for an answer," he said.

Kaitlin exhaled. "Fine. Take me to see Winston."

"After you put on a uniform."

"Fine. After I put on a uniform." This dad was annoying.

They found the guy Winston in some place called The Ministry. It was amazing how office parks look the same in any universe. When they got to his cubicle, and she saw him, she had to force herself not to run away. It turned out Winston was the same as the white Hearthland Security guy who had been after her back in her world.

She shrank back as Katherine's dad said, "Hi, Winston. Nice

to see you again." He held out his hand.

"Sir, Mr. Garcia." Winston jumped up from his desk chair, pulled down his uniform tunic and shook his hand. "It's an honor to see you again, sir."

Katherine's dad beamed. "I told you you could call me Christopher."

"Yes, sir, Mr. Garcia, er, I mean, Mr. Christopher." Winston wiped his palms on his pants. "I mean, thank you, Christopher."

There was no doubt that Katherine's dad had discombobulated this guy, Winston. Kaitlin looked at him sidelong. Why?

Katherine's dad took a step back. "And, of course, you recall my lovely daughter, Katherine."

For a moment, Winston blushed and froze, and then he shook himself out of it and rushed her with his hand out. When he got close, she smelled the floral fragrance he wore. There was something about him; she couldn't quite put her finger on it—he seemed fussy or something.

She shook his hand. "Hi." He didn't compare to Jake, not the Jake in her universe and probably not the one in this universe, either.

"Hi, Katherine. It's nice to see you again. So soon after our date. This is the first time we've seen each other since our date. Yep. We haven't seen each other at all since then. Not one time."

He was acting so flustered Kaitlin was starting to think he had seen Katherine since their date. Why would he lie about it? What was going on here?

He checked her out. "Speaking of our date, I see you dried out okay. There were no lasting effects from your mishap, huh?" He tittered.

What was he talking about?

Katherine's dad gave her an odd look.

"I guess not," she said.

"And you got over your diarrhea?" Winston whispered.

Kaitlin knew better than to blurt out 'What?' But what exactly went on with Katherine and this guy? And why was he acting so nervous?

Katherine's dad grimaced and interrupted. "My daughter wanted to stop by and make sure everything was on track for

118

your next date. Right, Katherine?" He nudged her.

"Right."

"Really?" Winston's demeanor reminded her of an eager puppy. "You said you wanted to reschedule but didn't say when. I wasn't sure if you wanted to." Kaitlin couldn't believe she'd been afraid of him. Or maybe the Winston in her universe was different?

Katherine's dad looked horrified. "Of course, she wants to reschedule."

"Right." Kaitlin shrugged. "I guess whenever you want." Hopefully, this would be what Katherine would want.

"What about now?" Winston asked.

"Uh." She had to return to the lab to get back to her universe. "I do need to do some work today."

"I'm sure you have time to go for chicory," Katherine's dad said with steel in his voice.

What was chicory, and how did you go for it? But, clearly, Katherine's dad was used to being obeyed. Glancing at one of those tiny robots on Winston's desk, Kaitlin said, "Yes, sir."

Now Katherine's dad gave her a different odd look. "I'll be back in forty-five minutes to walk you back to the lab."

"I don't think that's necessary, sir. I know the way to my lab." Kaitlin had been paying attention on the way over here in case the opportunity to go back there presented itself.

His eyes narrowed. "No. I'll be back."

Winston took her to the cafe on the first floor of the building. The office building had an atrium in the center with trees. It was nice in a sterile controlled way. "Two chicories coming up in a jiff."

She smiled. A jiff. Who talked that way?

He bustled back to their table with what looked like two cups of coffee in his hands. He gave her one and sat down.

She took a cautious sip. It mostly tasted like coffee.

Winston looked at her expectantly.

"Mmm. Good chic–" What was it again? She couldn't remember. "Good drink. Thanks."

He smiled. "You're welcome. This date is going much better than last time, huh?"

What in the world happened last time? Wow. The phrase

what in the world just took on new meaning.

"Thanks for you-know-what. I talked to Pablo this morning, and he says thanks, too." Winston's eyes lit up as he talked about his friend.

Could his Pablo be this world's version of the Pablo she knew? Ah, now she got it. This guy was gay. She gulped. Why were they being forced together? The poor guy. And poor Katherine. What was wrong with this world? She forced a smile. "I look forward to hearing about you-know-what." Wait a minute. Was everyone in her world copied here? A shiver danced up her back, landing in her hair. She rubbed her neck.

"Ooh. I have to thank you for your idea to mine material from the moon for the sun shields, too. I already ran it by my boss, and he seemed excited."

Had Katherine passed along her moon comment? Kaitlin took another sip of fake-coffee. It was growing on her. "Glad I could help."

Finally, he was talking about something she knew something about. "Yeah. It's surprising that a sun shield at the Earth-Sun equilibrium point only has to reduce solar input by point two percent to fix global warming." She leaned towards him, "Have you guys actually started anything?" She wished they had started something in her world, but they were still in the planning stages. And there was that pesky problem of how to launch.

He rubbed his upper lip. "We're still seeking funding, as I intimated on our date. Remember?"

No. "Sure." She nodded. "Why did you reject the more terrestrial options like using anti-aircraft artillery or high-flying aircraft to inject an artificial sulfate aerosol layer in the lower stratosphere?" In her world, they were worried about screwing up the atmospheric chemistry more than it already was with all the extra carbon dioxide. And, oh yeah, functioning aircraft. She wondered what was happening at home. Had her report made the news? Did anyone care?

Winston's jaw was hanging down. He closed it briefly and then said, "I'm impressed. I had no idea you were so informed on climate change issues."

"I looked some stuff up so we would have stuff to talk

about." That sounded good. Katherine would be pleased. They shot the breeze for a while, talking about climate change until, grinning, she glanced at a clock. Time was up. "We better get back. My dad will be waiting for me."

As they headed for the stairs, Winston put his hand on the small of her back. "Katherine, you're even more wonderful than I thought before, and I thought you were pretty great then."

Aw. Poor guy. "You're pretty great, too, Winston," Kaitlin said quietly.

Back upstairs, Katherine's dad was waiting for them impatiently, if his tapping foot and crossed arms were any indication.

Once they'd gotten away from Winston, Katherine's dad asked, "Well? How did it go?"

Kaitlin grinned. "He said I was great." It was nice to tell the truth here for once.

"Good." Christopher seemed to unclench his shoulders.

If she hadn't been so worried about getting home or nervous about all the miniature robots flying around spying on her, the walk back to the lab might have been pleasant. The sun was shining, a breeze was blowing, and in the shadow of the inspiring mountain peaks, the campus was filled with seemingly happy, prosperous students.

Anticipating going home, Kaitlin felt kind of proud of herself for fooling Winston and Katherine's dad when they returned to the lab.

She wasn't anticipating the two of them walking in on Katherine, but she should have.

Christopher froze, staring at her, and his shoulders crept up again. He looked back and forth between Kaitlin and Katherine.

Not knowing what else to do, Kaitlin waved.

And then she heard, "Pa!" from the doorway as another version of her rushed into the room.

Christopher looked surprised.

Clearly, she and Katherine hadn't thought through their plan sufficiently.

But Christopher wasn't as surprised as Katherine's mom when she stepped into the room. "What. The. Hell?" she said, blood draining from her face.

A disembodied female voice said, "Uh oh."

Chapter Eighteen: Universe 3: Katherine, April 27, 2100, 4:00 pm

Katherine couldn't believe it; both her mother and her father knew about the other two versions of her. Pandora was right: the uh-oh was really hitting the fan. She held up her hands, causing her uniform tunic to ride up. Quickly she jerked it down. Damn uniform. "Now, everybody, just stay calm. There's nothing to get worked up about here."

"Nothing to get worked up about?" her mother said. "What the hell is going on here, Katherine? I demand you tell me this instant."

"First of all, Mother, Father, you don't need to worry." She pointed at the crunchy carpet of nanobots. "Police Patrol doesn't know anything about all this."

Her father's shoulders relaxed.

"It's an experiment, that's all." Katherine inspected the other Katherines. The scruffy one, Kat, looked like she was going to cry any second and the other one, Kaitlin, now wearing one of her uniforms, was looking at what appeared to be her fon.

"You better not tell me you've been doing human cloning because that is wrong," her mother said. "I can't tell you how disappointed I'd be if you've been doing something so unethical." She paused and took a breath. "Though I'd wonder how you grew the clones to maturity so fast."

Pandora snorted.

Her mother looked around the room. "What was that?"

Her father stepped toward her mother. "Calm down, Ava-Maria. Katherine's not a biologist. I seriously doubt she's been cloning anyone."

Yay, Father. Katherine nodded.

"Wait. You have been cloning people?" he asked.

"No," she said. "I was nodding in agreement with you, saying I wasn't doing it."

"I think I'll be going then if it's all the same to you all," Jacob said, edging toward the door. "This looks like a family thing."

"Stop right there, young man," Father said. "Nobody's going anywhere."

Kaitlin held up her hand. "Actually, I would love to go home. ASAP. Is there any chance that's going to happen any time soon? I'm supposed to be throwing an anniversary party for my parents tonight. I need to get back."

Crap. If today was Kaitlin's parents' anniversary, Katherine had a sneaking suspicion today was her parents' anniversary as well. "Was that what breakfast was about? Your anniversary?"

Her mother nodded. Ugh. Now Katherine felt bad about skipping breakfast.

Kat stared at Kaitlin. "You're worried about a party?" Now she looked kind of mad.

Out of the corner of Katherine's eye, she could see Jacob sneaking out the door. "Jacob."

He froze and then leaned against the door frame in an attempt to be nonchalant.

"Somebody tell me what the fuck is going on here." Mother stamped her feet.

Kaitlin, Kat, and Katherine all stared at Mother. Katherine had never heard Mother talk that way, and she was guessing the other Katherines hadn't heard their mothers talk that way either.

"Perhaps I could be of some assistance," Pandora said.

"Who is that?" Mother said.

Father was gazing around the room with a puzzled expression.

"Go for it, Pandora," Katherine said.

"I am Pandora, Katherine's A.I. computer." Pandora sounded super smug. "Katherine and Jacob seem to have accessed the multiverse with their combination of quantum computing, high energy and strong electromagnetic fields."

"Is this true, Katherine?" Father asked.

"Pretty much," she said. "Yeah. What Pandora said."

"Additionally, Katherine has taken it upon herself to do a

little matter exchange experiment between universes. I surmise that these two young women are versions of Katherine from the universes nearest to ours."

"For the record, I was totally against it," Jacob said.

"Gee, thanks, Jacob," Katherine said. "For the record...." She glared at Jacob and then turned to Kat. "Kat here was in really bad shape. If we hadn't helped her, I think she would have died."

Kat held her cast up in the air.

Katherine turned to Kaitlin. "And I'm not sure what was going on with Kaitlin, but some guys were chasing her. Guys with guns."

Kaitlin nodded. "Yes, that's all true. But, Katherine, I have to know. Can you open the portal again or not?"

Pandora and Katherine had spent the last two hours checking the equipment so they could do just that. "We started to get some outlandish energy spikes there at the end last time, but yes, we think so. We should be able to send you home if that's what you want."

Kaitlin nodded energetically. "Yes, please. I can't imagine what Jake's thinking."

Jacob said, "Huh?"

Kaitlin glanced at him. "I meant my Jake. We're engaged." She held up her ring. Was it pink? "He must be worried sick about me. And I really miss him."

Her Jacob blushed, and Katherine felt blood heat her face, too. She'd never thought of him as *her Jacob* before.

Universe 3: Kaitlin

If they could send her home, what were they waiting for? "So?" Kaitlin said. "Open up the portal already. I want to go home." She twisted her ring on her finger. It was getting to be a habit. Jake, I miss you.

Katherine asked, "Aren't you worried about the big white guy with the gun?"

Which guy? Oh, she meant her universe's Winston. Somehow, now, after getting to know this universe's Winston, she wasn't so worried about him. "I'll risk it."

The Kaitlin-with-the-cast, Kat, raised her good arm. "I want to go back, but is there any chance you could give us some food and medicine? And water? We need water."

Katherine's mom's lips turned down. "What do you mean you need water? You don't have enough water? What's your universe like?"

Kat shook her head. "Not like this." Kat shot Kaitlin the evil eye. "We don't have parties, that's for sure unless you're talking about imaginary parties or raiding parties. Raiding parties are real. We have to avoid raiding parties and hike at night to the almost-empty reservoir to get muddy water that we have to carry home. We wait for parents who go out with scavenger teams and never return. We have to bury sisters and new-born babies because we don't have any real medicine." Kat bit back a sob. "Not like this." She struggled to get a hold of her emotions.

Did she say bury sisters? And babies? That sounded horrible. Kaitlin missed her sister Emma back in her world. And her brother Michael.

The room became so quiet they could hear the air rushing through the ventilation system.

And parents that never came back? Kaitlin was starting to feel if she never saw Emma and Michael and her mom and dad again and held them in her arms, it might kill her. She twirled her ring.

Pandora said, "I'm sorry." And she didn't sound like a computer to Kaitlin. She just sounded sad.

Katherine was the first human to recover. "Why do you want to go back then?"

"They're counting on me," Kat said simply, fondling her locket.

"We'll get some supplies together for you," Katherine's mom said.

"Why do you have to hike at night?" Katherine's dad asked.

"We can't go outside during the day because we'll die of heat stroke or, if we're lucky, skin cancer."

Katherine's dad grimaced and shook his head.

"That sounds horrible," Katherine said. "Maybe all your people should just come here?"

126

"I'm not sure that would work," Katherine's dad said. "I mean, we don't exactly have a free society here."

What was he talking about? Was he talking about the tiny robots, the uniforms, or the Procreation Board? Was there more?

"I can't leave my world for good. My pa might come back from his scavenging mission," Kat said. "I'm waiting for my pa. I mean, he will come back. And Pablo needs me."

Pablo? Kaitlin wondered if he was Kat's universe's version of her Pablo? She missed her Jake and her Pablo. Twirl, twirl. "Please. Can we try to open the portal?"

Katherine said, "Yes. Pandora, fire it up. Jacob? Mother and Father? Start getting supplies together for Kat."

Jacob said, "Anything you want, Katherine."

Katherine's dad seemed about to argue but ended up glancing at Katherine's mom.

Katherine's mom said, "Okay. We will." Katherine's dad nodded in agreement. The two of them followed Jacob out the door.

Pandora said, "Beginning neutral beam injection and high-frequency EM waves."

Katherine sidled up to Kaitlin. "Why aren't you worried about the guys with the guns?"

"I am worried, but I miss my family so much, I'd rather be in jail on my world than here without them."

Pandora said, "The EM field is increasing nicely."

The hair on the back of Kaitlin's neck and her arms stood up. Weird.

"System beyond optimal."

With a sizzle, that portal thing was back. Kaitlin took a step toward it and peered through to her universe.

"Hmm," Pandora said. "I'm getting energy fluctuations again."

Oh, no. Kaitlin wasn't taking any chances of being trapped here. She took a running start and jumped right through the portal back to her own universe.

Universes 3 & 1: Kat

Kat peered after Kaitlin as she disappeared through one of those weird windows.

"Kat?" Kat heard Pablo's voice behind her. When she turned around, he was framed in another of the strange glowing circles. "Are you all right?"

She approached the circle and held up her cast. "Yes. No worries. They fixed me up."

"What me worry?" He smiled. "Impossible." But then his smile evaporated. "So, are you coming back now? Tell me you're coming back."

"Definitely."

"Good, because there's someone here who wants to see you." He took a step back and revealed...

"Pa! Thank Gaia!" Kat rushed towards him.

Her pa looked the worse for wear. His face was all bruised and bloody. "Are you all right, Kat?"

"Yes." She reached through the window and grasped his hand. "But what happened to you? We were so worried."

He squeezed her hand. "It's a long story. But it appears we both have a lot to talk about." He paused. "What is this thing?"

Out of sight, Kat heard Pablo say, "Can you get some water?"

"Yes, Pablo, we're working on it. And, Pa, I don't know what this thing is."

From behind her, Katherine put her hand on Kat's shoulder, and she was startled. She'd forgotten all about Katherine. "You can go back if you want. I'll keep the portal open for the supplies." She didn't have to tell Kat twice.

Kat moved through the window and into her pa's arms. He smelled like she remembered, like her pa but with sweat and blood added in. Poor Pa. What had he been through? Her eyes overflowed, and she sniffled into his chest. He was alive. Thank Gaia. He was home safe.

Why was she being so emotional? And why did she always cry after the excitement or danger was over?

She and Pa stayed like that, wrapped in each other's arms, until Pablo said, "There's another one behind us. Another one of those *loco* windows."

Chapter Nineteen: Universe 3: Katherine, April 27, 2100, 6:00 pm

The portal contracted. Katherine stared after Kat as the portal changed size, shrinking and returning to its original size. It was almost as if it bounced. That was odd.

A strange sound carried over from the other world.

Was someone over there yelling? She couldn't make it out.

At the same time, Pandora said, "I'm getting some atypical energy readings here."

Katherine jogged over to where Pandora's main CPUs were. "Huh? Define really atypical." What would an A.I. consider atypical, anyway?

Just then, Jacob skidded into the room, carrying what looked like a garden hose. "Look what I found." He held it up.

Katherine heard the sound of nanobots plinking to the floor. They must have been on the hose. "Where did you get that thing, Jacob?"

He shook his head. "Just from campus. It was lying on the ground outside the physics building."

"You mean you stole it from campus? And Police Patrol probably saw you steal it?" Katherine stared at him. "Pandora, what does Police Patrol think about the missing hose?"

"I don't know." Pandora sounded distracted.

"Something the A.I. doesn't know?" Jacob said. "I thought she knew everything. Maybe she's not so smart."

Katherine made chopping motions in front of her neck.

Jacob saw her and shut up. After a moment, he said, "So, anyway, I thought we could hook this baby up to the faucet and stick the other end through the portal."

"You come up with good ideas sometimes." Katherine ran over to Kat's portal and peered through. It was hard to see on the other side because it was dark. "Kat?"

A Pablo popped up. "She's busy talking to her pa. Do you have the water? Or food?"

All these copies of people were going to take some getting used to. "Hi again, Pablo. I'm Katherine. She pulled down her tunic. We have an idea of how to get you some water. Can we give you the end of this hose? You can use it to fill up any containers you have with water. Sinks, bottles, whatever."

"Oh, yeah, that's a good idea. Just a sec." He disappeared from view.

Behind her, Jacob said, "How's it going? Are they ready? The hose doesn't exactly fit on the lab faucet, but it should work."

Pablo reappeared with some buckets. He was saying, "Yes. Bring all the water containers over here now," to people she couldn't see.

"Are you ready?"

He nodded. "Sí. Let her rip."

Katherine pushed the end of the hose through the portal into his hands. "Turn it on, Jacob."

"Jake?" On the other side of the portal, Pablo fumbled the hose.

Jacob turned on the faucet, and water came out at Pablo's end. Water sprayed all over Pablo; some even got on Katherine through the portal. At the same time, Jacob started cursing. When she looked back at him, water dripped from his face and uniform, and his hands wrapped around the end of the hose attached to the faucet. He smiled and let go of the hose with one hand, giving her a thumbs up and getting sprayed with more water in the process.

She stifled a laugh. Thank goodness the sink was far away from the computers and the tokamak.

"Here, take these," Pablo said to one of his friends. "Bring me those." He kept filling containers.

Somewhere in there, Pandora said, "The energy field is not stable. It seems to be taking more and more energy to maintain the portals."

"What does that mean?" Katherine should probably check things on the computer, but she wanted to make sure Pablo and his friends got their water.

After a while, Pablo said. "I guess that's it. We don't have any more containers." His current container overflowed. "Turn it off. Turn it off, please."

Jacob was already turning it off. He walked towards her.

"We should have some food and medicine for you any minute." Katherine hoped her folks would be here any minute.

When Jacob reached her, Pablo stared at him from his side of the portal.

Jacob stuck his hand through the portal to him. "Hi, I don't think we officially met before. I'm Jacob."

Pablo shook his hand. "I know. You look exactly like my best friend. He died."

"Yeah, you mentioned that," Jacob said. "Do you mind me asking how?"

Then, her father reappeared in the lab, clutching several big grocery bags. "Is it still open?"

"Yes, Father."

Jacob ran over to help him carry stuff.

"Pablo, hold on. We got some food for you guys," Katherine said.

Her father and Jacob reached the portal with the bags and started handing them through.

When Pablo saw her father, he drew in a breath. "You look just like Kat's pa." He looked away from them, pointing towards Kat's father, presumably.

"What is this stuff, Father?" Katherine asked, glancing into the bags.

"I got a bunch of high-protein bars and other pre-cooked high-protein stuff," her father said.

That sounded suspiciously like yeast bars. She grimaced.

"I'm getting more energy drops, but smaller than before," Pandora said.

Father was startled at the sound of the A.I.'s voice and looked at the ceiling. "I'm not sure I'm going to get used to that."

"I'm not a that," Pandora said. "I'm a she." She sounded more like her old self, less distracted.

131

Pablo, glancing into the bags, seemed thrilled. "Thank you for all this. We appreciate it. And I don't mean to sound ungrateful, but is there any chance there's some medicine coming?"

"We're working on it." Where was Mother?

The four of them looked at each other.

"There's one thing I don't get," Pablo said. "Why is there another window-thing here this time when there was only the one before?"

Pandora said, "Very interesting."

What the heck was he talking about? "Another window?" she asked. "What window?"

"Over there." Pablo pointed over his shoulder.

Katherine leaned forward but did not pass through the portal or touch it.

Her father grabbed her arm. "Be careful, Katherine."

She leaned back. She didn't want to go through that portal for some reason. "What does it look like, Pablo?"

He shrugged. "It looks just like this one, but over there."

She leaned forward a fraction of an inch.

Jacob caught her eye. "Do you want me to go check it out?"

But she couldn't risk her Jacob–there it was again, her Jacob–getting trapped over there.

"I'm not going," Father said. "This whole thing is too bizarre. A.I.s, multiple versions of Katherine, multiple versions of everyone. Too bizarre." He walked over to a lab stool and sat down, crossing his arms. "And don't even get me started about what Police Patrol would think about all this."

"I would like more information about this additional so-called window," Pandora said. "But I can't go. I don't have a body. Hmm."

Katherine took a fractional step forward. She truly didn't want to go. How come the other-Katherines didn't seem to care? Were they braver than her? Or more ignorant?

Jacob lunged forward, but she stepped in front of him. "Not so fast. My lab, my responsibility."

She steeled her nerves and stepped through the portal.

The other universe was bizarre. It was the same, and yet it was different. The physical layout was the same: one big room, but this place smelled of unwashed bodies and was quite dark. The tokamak was missing, and all the other hardware. And the floor was slippery. Ah. That must be because she was standing in a puddle of water. As Katherine's eyes adjusted to the candle-light, she could see a bunch of people sitting or lying on blankets on the floor. Staring at her. Being the center of attention was a new experience, and she didn't like it.

She grabbed Pablo's arm. "Show me the portal."

They had to step over people to get to it; when they did, it was pitch black inside the other portal. "Are you sure this even is a portal?"

Pablo nodded. "It flickered when it appeared. And you can see it blocks the view of the rest of the room."

She moved around and determined he was right. It was like a big black shadow floating in the middle of the room. "Huh."

He asked, "What does it mean? Where does it go?"

Hell, if she knew. But Pablo looked at her with trust in his eyes. "I need more data." But she really, really didn't want to go through a second portal. "Do you have an extra candle?" Was it getting hard to breathe in here?

He nodded and turned away. "Bao, please bring us a candle."

A Chinese woman approached them. "Kat. You're back. I heard about your arm." She slowed down. "But you're healed. There's nothing wrong with your arm. What did those people do to you?" She handed Pablo a lighted candle.

Katherine focused on appearing calm. And knowledgeable. Like a rational scientist. She needed to stay calm to investigate things. "Hi," she said to the woman. "Sorry. I'm not your friend. I'm from the other universe. My name is Katherine."

Pablo said, "This isn't Kat. She's another Kat, a different Kat. She came through the window-thing."

The woman's brow creased.

Katherine was definitely starting to freak out in an unscientific way. She was underground in another freaking universe, and she didn't want to be. The sooner she got out of here, the better. She grabbed the candle, shoved it through the portal, and smacked her hand on what felt like a big rock. "Ouch." She withdrew her hand, transferring the candle to her other hand, shaking the tingling one. "I don't think anyone's going to be going through there. In that universe, there must not be a basement here. It seems like solid rock." There was no data to be had here.

Behind her, she heard, "I demand you return my daughter Katherine at once," in Mother's most strident voice. Then, her mother said more softly, "What do you mean no one else should go through? I'll go through it if I want to go through it. I don't take orders from machines."

Katherine ran back to the portal, narrowly avoiding stepping on a couple of people. "Sorry, sorry. I'm here, Mother. I'm fine. Don't worry." She was so ready to go home.

Her mother leaned her head through.

The portal did that bouncing thing again. That couldn't be good.

Someone behind her said, "I think this other window over here changed."

She gasped. "Mother, go back."

From the other side, Father yelled, "Come back, Ava-Maria!"

For her part, Mother opened her eyes very wide and then pulled her head back into her universe. "That felt odd," Katherine heard her mother say.

The edges of the portal vibrated.

What if she was trapped here? Katherine's heart lodged itself in her throat, choking her. "I'm coming back."

As she jumped towards it, the edges of the portal contracted.

Chapter Twenty: Universe 1: Kat, April 27, 2100, 6:00 pm

Kat and her pa glanced over where Pablo was pointing, but they couldn't see much. It was too dark. The dimly-lit large basement room did feel like home, though, especially with Pa there.

They stepped away from the window.

"Did he say another window?" Pa asked. "What's going on? What are these window things?" He glanced at Kat's cast. "Not that I'm complaining."

Chang came up to them.

"We're glad you made it back safely, Chris," Chang said.

Pa patted him on the back. "Me, too. How's..." But he must have read something in Chang's eyes because he didn't finish asking about Fei.

Kat put her hand on Pa's arm.

"I'm very sorry for your loss," Pa said softly.

Chang nodded.

Pablo ran by them. "Buckets. I need buckets. Tubs, pails, anything that can hold water."

People scattered, looking for containers.

"Maybe we should get out of the way," Kat said.

Pa took her hand and led her to some chairs on the edge of the room. "It seems like you've had an eventful couple of weeks, too eventful."

They sat down. Taking in his bruised and bloody face, her fingers sought out her locket. She said, "I have a feeling I could say the same thing about you." She paused. "What about Sungsu and Aban? Did they come back with you?"

"No." He gazed around the room. "Aren't they back yet? We got separated."

She gulped. "I'm sorry to say there's been no sign of any of you. Until now. Until you. Are you sure you're okay? You don't look so good."

Pa touched his forehead gingerly. "It's not as bad as it looks."

She doubted that. He always said stuff like that, tough guy stuff. "What happened?" She looked closer. "Did you get stitches? Who did it?" They looked more regular than anything she'd seen, more regular than even Ma's stitches had been. And what was he wearing? His clothes looked new.

He grimaced. "We went too far south. We were on the southern edge of Denver, and another group of scavengers attacked us."

Kat gasped.

"But that wasn't the problem. While we were introducing ourselves to our new friends, we drew the attention of some soldiers."

She could feel her forehead crinkle up. "Soldiers? Really? We haven't come across any of them in years." Across the room, she could see Pablo filling up a bunch of tubs and buckets with some kind of hose from the other universe.

"They were actual soldiers from the United States of America." He paused for dramatic effect.

"The United States? But I thought that was gone. We haven't seen any sign of it in ages."

"I know. But these guys had on clean uniforms with flags and *USA* on them and they seemed well-fed and well-armed. They even had trucks and fuel for them."

"Trucks and fuel!"

"They drove us to their base under a mountain in Colorado Springs."

"A base? Near here?" She didn't know what else to say. Finally, she shook her head. "Why did they come out after all this time?"

Pa shrugged. "I thought it was just our bad luck." He touched his face again. "They questioned me rather vigorously. About some weird energy readings north of Denver."

"Whoa. Do you mean to say the so-called soldiers did that to you?" Kat pointed at his face. "It wasn't the other scavengers?"

"It was the soldiers."

"Wait a minute. You were in the custody of some soldiers in a secret underground military base and they tortured you? Did you tell them what they wanted to hear? How did you get away?"

"They let me go." Pa shrugged again.

"What? That doesn't make sense."

He nodded. "After they gave me medical treatment."

"Why torture you and then stitch you up?

"I don't know." He shook his head.

"What about your clothes? They just gave you some new clothes, too?"

"Yeah," Pa said. "I thought they let me go because I didn't know anything." He looked her in the eyes. "But now I'm thinking you might know something about the energy readings they asked about. What's going on here?"

Kat sighed. "I don't claim to understand what's going on. Bao woke us up one day because there was a window floating in the middle of the room. On the other side of the window there was another me—at least there was a person who looked a lot like me. She said her name was Katherine Garcia and it was April twenty-fifth, 2100."

Her pa drew in a breath.

"The window was, it is, like a door between different universes. I guess it had something to do with something called quantum mechanics."

Pablo gave back the hose and took a bunch of bags from the people in the window.

"Quantum mechanics?" Pa asked. "How do you know anything about that?"

"I don't. I got a book from the physics library upstairs." She shrugged. "I guess quantum mechanics describes reality at the atomic level or smaller. The math says there are infinite possibilities of events and there are different interpretations of why we only experience one reality. One of these interpretations is called the Many Worlds Interpretation. Basically anything that can happen, does happen, and it spawns a new universe when it does. So, there's, like, infinite universes out there." Hadn't that Jacob guy said matter exchange between universes might destroy the universes? It looked like he'd been wrong. She decided not to mention any of that to Pa.

"I can't believe you figured all this stuff out. I bet you would've been good at science." Now it was Pa's turn to sigh. "I'm sorry you never had the chance to go to school like me and your ma did."

School was the least of her worries. If they were tabulating regrets, she wished Ma was still here. And Emma. She resisted the urge to look at Emma's tiny picture in the locket.

"So, why did the window thing happen?" Pa asked.

"That I don't know. The other me, Katherine, was doing some kind of physics experiment that caused it." Speaking of Katherine, was that her coming through the window into their universe? Why would she do that?

"How did you end up over there in that other universe?" Pa asked.

"I'm a little fuzzy on that, too. I hurt my arm while me and Pablo went to get some water." She had a eureka moment. "Oh, yeah. Actually, Pablo and I found an old garage and it was filled with motorcycles and at least one of them had fuel. We should go back there and check it out."

"Motorcycles and fuel? That's great." Pa smiled. "We could use that."

Pablo led Katherine past Kat and her pa to a new floating window and they inspected it. Where had that come from? And why?

"Anyway, when the window opened again, Pablo must have sent me through. I was out of it. Pablo and me tried to set my arm, but I guess we did something wrong." She lifted up her cast. "They patched me up over there in the other universe."

"Does the strange window always go to the same place?"

"It seems to. At least, so far, that window keeps going to Katherine's universe."

"Well, whatever's going on, I'm glad they patched you up." He paused. "I, you-know you."

Kat got a lump in her throat. She knew he was trying to say he loved her. "I you-know you, too." They hugged again, but it was brief. They weren't used to all this mushy stuff.

"That window thing is definitely strange," Pa said.

"I can't disagree with you there," she said. "So you think

those soldiers that captured you somehow detected it?"

"I don't know," he said. "But I'm guessing yes."

There was some kind of excitement at the first window as a woman who looked like her ma passed some bags through.

Pa glanced that way and then jumped up. "Ava!"

Kat put her hand on his arm. "It's not your Ava. It's not Ma. It's the Ava of the other universe." She was still a little embarrassed about how stupid she'd acted in front of that other Ava, crying and carrying on. She slid her locket slowly back and forth on the chain.

Her pa took a step that way, anyway.

"I'm telling you, she's not Ma."

He finally looked at her again.

"It doesn't make any sense that the soldiers would just let you go." Kat shook her head. "And why were they so nice after they tortured you?" They were missing something. "Unless..."

"What?" He gazed down at her.

"Could they gain something by treating your injuries or giving you new clothes?"

"What? Like they wanted to get on my good side? What's the point? I'm nobody."

There was a commotion at the door of the lab. She heard someone yell, "Thank Gaia! Aban, Sungsu, you made it back."

"Did Chris make it?" one of them asked.

Pa yelled, "Yes, I'm here," and ran over to the door.

Kat followed him.

In the doorway, Aban and Sungsu looked much like Pa, namely, beat up, patched up, and in new clothes. It was all very suspicious.

Their friends and families were embracing the two men and everyone was asking what happened. They recounted the same story as Pa. A skirmish in south Denver, capture by U.S. soldiers, interrogation, medical treatment and release.

For a moment, the strange windows were forgotten.

Their story reminded Kat of something her pa talked about doing with his pa. What was it? Oh, yeah. Catch and release fishing. Fishermen let the fish go so they could have the fun of catching them again.

Then she remembered the little robots in Katherine's world

watching everyone. What if the soldiers here had something like that?

"Take off your new clothes!" Kat said.

Everyone turned around and stared at her. She discovered she didn't like being stared at.

Aban ran his fingers through his thick hair. "What are you talking about, Kat? These are the nicest clothes I've had in years."

Sungsu frowned at her. "We're certainly not stripping in front of everyone."

"Pa, Mr. Kim, Mr. Azar, take off your clothes, right away. There's something wrong with them."

"Kat, what are you talking about?" Pa asked.

"It's like catch and release fishing," she said. "You guys are the fish. Those soldiers are going to try to catch you again—I'm not sure how—but I bet it has something to do with those new clothes."

"Come on, what could it have to do with clothes?" Aban checked her out. "Obviously, you've had a hard time lately, Kat. I think you're getting worked up over nothing."

"Take off your clothes," she said.

Chang piped up, "If Kat thinks there's something wrong with the clothes, I believe her."

Kat threw him a grateful smile.

Pa said, "Fine. I'll take mine off." He unbuttoned his shirt, shrugged it off and handed it to her.

She checked the pockets, but there was nothing in them.

Everyone was watching her. She frowned.

Aban asked, "Well?"

"Just a sec." She held up the shirt. Where could soldiers hide something? She felt along all the seams and there was nothing out of the ordinary.

People started muttering.

She slid the collar material between her index finger and thumb and felt something hard. "I think I found something. Does anyone have a knife?"

Chang held up his.

"Here. Check the collar." She couldn't do it with her bum arm, so she handed him the shirt.

He slit the stitching of the collar and a piece of metal fell out, hitting the floor with a ping.

She leaned over and picked it up. "What's this? This shouldn't be in there, should it?"

"No." Pa frowned. He pointed at Aban and Sungsu. "We should take off all the new clothes and look for more of those things." He turned to her. "What do you think they are?"

It reminded her of those metal bugs back in Katherine's universe. "Some kind of machine. Maybe the soldiers use them to track you?"

Where was Katherine? Was she still here? She might know what they were. Kat turned to the strange window just in time to see Katherine running towards it.

Chapter Twenty-One: Universe 2: Kaitlin, April 27, 2100, 6:00 pm

Back in her regular universe, Kaitlin landed in her lab right on top of her universe's version of Winston, the Hearthland Security Officer. She guessed that answered the question *Are Hearthland Security Officers still waiting for me?*

On the bright side, he cushioned her fall. On the dark side, he was mad.

By the time they disentangled, she already had her fon out and had dialed Jake. "Jake, I'm back."

"Back from what?" Jake asked. "Where have you been? I've been trying to get a hold of you for hours."

"I think I'm about to be arrested by Hearthland Security. Get me a lawyer. Call my dad."

"Arrested? Hearthland Security? Lawyer? What's going on?"

Winston grabbed her fon. "I'll take that." He started punching buttons and managed to turn it off. "I should charge you with assault."

"Really?" She put her hands on her hips. Her meeting with other-Winston made her think she understood this one. "You're going to tell all your tough macho co-workers that little-old-me beat you up?"

He stood up straight, all lumpy six-feet-plus of him, and glowered at her.

Maybe she didn't understand this Winston as well as she thought. She gulped.

Without warning, he lunged at her, but she ducked him.

She turned around and ran, almost smacking into another one of those portal things. Where did that come from? At the last minute, she dove under it.

Winston wasn't so lucky. He ran right into it.

She didn't waste any time and ran out the lab door, down the hall, up the stairs, out the doors, to her bike.

She gave it everything she had on her bike and was home in record time.

Inside their apartment, wearing a suit and tie, Jake held up his fon. "What the hell is going on? What kind of fon call was that? I've been calling you back. Why didn't you answer? And what are you wearing?"

As he stood in the middle of their relatively-clean family room in front of their ancient brown couch, Kaitlin thought even angry he looked great—like home.

Panting, she patted her pockets. Where was her fon? She cringed. She had a feeling it was in universe-whatever, along with Winston. Briefly, she wondered if he could get a signal before shaking it off. Surely, he'd just come back through the portal. In fact, she probably didn't have a lot of time before Hearthland Security came after her again. She should make the most of whatever time she had left.

She grabbed Jake for a hug. "I really missed you today. I love you so much, Jake." When they separated, she added, "Are you wearing aftershave? You smell great. And you look awesome." She smiled. "Did I know you had a suit?"

He smiled. "All right." He held up his hands. "Enough with the compliments. I love you, too. And yes, our talk can wait." He pointed at her. "But after the anniversary party, we're going to have a serious discussion about what the hell's going on." Oh, right, the anniversary party. That's why he was so dressed up.

He looked at his fon. "Quick, get dressed. I'll call a pedicab."

In the banquet room at the restaurant, when her sister Emma spotted her, she frowned and pointed at her fon.

Kaitlin approached her anyway and gave her a big hug. "I'm so glad to see you. I love you, Emma."

When they separated, Emma said, "What's gotten in to you tonight?"

Kaitlin leaned in and whispered, "Jake and I are engaged," and flaunted her ring finger. She didn't add, and I'm home safe and sound in my own universe. She didn't think Emma would understand that.

Emma clearly understood being engaged, however. She shrieked and gave a little jump. Everyone looked their way as Emma attempted to get a hold of herself. "That's awesome," she finally said in her inside voice. "I'm so happy for you, Kaitlin." She paused and leaned down to stare at Kaitlin's hand. "But why is your ring pink? Is that plastic?"

"It's a placeholder," Kaitlin said. "But I like it now. It's grown on me."

Emma grimaced. "Not literally, I hope."

Their mom approached them. "What are you two whispering about?"

"Kaitlin and Jake are engaged!" Emma whisper-shouted.

Mom's eyes opened wide. "Congratulations." She kissed Kaitlin's cheek.

Kaitlin grabbed Mom and held her tight. Just the thought of never seeing her again filled Kaitlin's eyes with tears.

"What else is going on?" her mom asked. "There's something else."

Kaitlin shook her head. "I just love you, Mom."

Jake and her brother, Michael, approached them. "Jake just told me something very interesting." Michael raised his eyebrows. "Did you tell Mom and Emma yet?"

"Yes," Emma said.

"I know, but does your dad know?" Mom asked.

Oops. Poor Dad, always the last to know everything. "Where is he?"

Michael said, "I think I saw him by the bar."

Jake chuckled. "Should have guessed."

Mom gave him a look.

"Er, I mean," Jake said, "he's so hospitable, so of course, he would try to help people. I'm not saying he drinks too much. Or at all. Or–"

"Nice suit, Jake," Emma said.

Jake shot her a grateful smile.

"Hey, what about me?" Michael said.

"Yes. Your suit is nice as well, honey," Mom said. "Everyone looks very nice."

Kaitlin grabbed Michael. "I love you, little brother."

Michael seemed surprised and waited a few seconds to return the embrace.

Now, Mom was giving her a look.

"Uh, so I'm going to go find Dad," she said. "Do you want to come, Jake?"

Jake dipped his chin once. "Sure. Let's go." He put his hand on the small of her back, and the two of them walked across the room.

Kaitlin felt like everyone was looking at them, and it wasn't the best feeling. "If something happens here tonight, I know I can count on you to keep everyone calm and to get me a lawyer, right?" Hopefully, whatever was going to happen would wait until later. Much later.

Jake stopped. "If something happens?" He narrowed his eyes. "What would happen?"

"Let's just try to enjoy the party." Kaitlin took his arm and led him over towards the bar, smiling and waving at her parent's two-dozen or so friends along the way. Several of the ladies must have been wearing expensive perfume because they moved from one cloud of floral scent to another as they crossed the room.

When they finally got to the bar, she told the bartender, "I'll have a white wine," and looked around for her dad.

"Same here," Jake said.

Kaitlin found Dad standing next to the elaborate water fountain. Good grief. What did that cost? Emma better not have gotten the ice cream, too.

With their drinks, Jake and Kaitlin approached Dad.

Holding an empty glass, he stared into the fountain, shaking his head. When he saw them, he said, "You guys shouldn't have gone to this expense."

Kaitlin agreed, but it was too late now. "Aw, Dad. You and Mom are worth it."

He shrugged and filled his glass with the cascading water.

Jake put his arm around her shoulder.

She took a sip of wine. Careful, Kait. She wanted this glass to last her the whole night. The bar bill wasn't going to be big on her account. And she might need her wits about her.

"I just can't get over how much things have changed since

145

your mom and I were little," Dad said. "People used to have fountains like this in their yards."

"What?" Jake asked. "Outside their houses? In the open?"

Dad nodded and took a sip. "Yep. And we had these huge expanses of green grass that we watered several times a week and had to mow every weekend."

Jake snorted. "You watered them a lot, so you'd have to mow them a lot? That doesn't make any sense."

"No. Even back then, water was expensive, although not as expensive as it is now. This water is really good, pure and cool, by the way," Dad said, licking his lips. "You're right, Jake. It didn't make any sense, but those were different times. Anyway, I guess my point is this is a nice party. Thanks."

Her dad seemed so grateful; maybe the fountain was worth it after all.

"So, Mr. Garcia," Jake said. "Kaitlin and I have something we'd like to tell you."

"What's with this *Mr. Garcia* stuff, Jake?" Dad peered at them over the top of his glass. "I thought I told you to call me Topher." He shifted back and forth.

Jake dropped his arm from Kaitlin's shoulder. "Yes, sir."

From across the room, Mom caught Dad's eye. They exchanged some mysterious, silent communication. Dad turned back to Jake and Kaitlin, beaming. "I guess congratulations are in order? Jake, here, wouldn't be so nervous unless you guys had a big announcement like you're getting married, right?"

"Yes, sir," Jake said. "I mean, yes, Topher."

Her dad threw one arm around Jake. "Welcome to the family, Jake. I couldn't be happier. Kait needs a guy like you to keep her out of trouble and put up with her."

Kaitlin's grin morphed into a grin-ace—part grin and part grimace. "What? Put up with her? What's that supposed to mean?"

Dad and Jake chuckled together. At least they were getting along now.

"I just mean you're a smart, determined woman," her dad said.

"Thanks, Dad." She gave him a quick hug. "I love you."

"Back at you, kiddo," he said.

"Kait, you've got to admit you don't let anything stand in your way when you want something," Jake said.

"Well, you're just lucky I want you." She nudged him with her elbow.

"When you're right, you're right," Jake said.

Her mom, Emma, and Michael came over and joined them, and everyone congratulated them again.

The love-fest continued as they ate lots of yummy hors d'oeuvres and chatted with friends and family. Dad made a speech to the whole group about how Mom was the love of his life. Mom made a speech about Dad being the best thing that ever happened to her. Emma made a speech about Mom and Dad being great parents and role models. Some of her parents' friends made speeches about how great they were. The whole thing was corny, but truth be told, Kaitlin did get a little misty-eyed watching her parents so obviously happy.

When Jake snuck his hand into hers, Kaitlin had to wipe a tear away surreptitiously.

"What's wrong?" he whispered in her ear.

"I'm just so happy." She squeezed his hand. She was glad she'd made it back to be here with them. It would be worth any price. "I hope I remember this moment forever."

"Me, too."

As the speeches were winding down, Mom came up to them. "Did you guys want to announce anything?" She smiled.

Kaitlin nodded. "You go ahead, Jake."

"I think Kaitlin and Jake wanted to say something, too," Mom said to the crowd.

Jake cleared his throat. "I am very happy to announce that Kaitlin Garcia has done me the great honor of agreeing—"

A swarm of black-clad men burst into the room, weapons drawn. "Freeze!"

She barely had time to think the men in uniform looked wildly incongruous next to all the dressed-up guests before one of them strode up to Kaitlin with handcuffs. "Kaitlin Garcia, you are under arrest for the murder of a Hearthland Security Officer."

What was he talking about? Kaitlin stood there in a daze as he grabbed her wrists, held them behind her back and slapped the cuffs on. She didn't murder anyone. She couldn't murder anyone.

Jake shoved his face in front of hers. "What's going on, Kaitlin? Is this what you were talking about earlier?"

Mom said, "I object. My daughter wouldn't murder anyone. You've made a mistake."

"Kaitlin wouldn't hurt a fly," Dad said.

The officer pulled her towards the door.

Murder?

What murder?

Who was murdered?

As the portal contracted, Katherine forced herself through. On the other side, back in her own universe, she startled her mother when she appeared.

Mother lurched away. Somebody snickered.

"Sorry, Mother." Katherine pulled down her uniform's top. Taking in her parents' faces, she was really happy to be home.

Her mother brushed imaginary lint off herself. "This has all been very interesting, but I think I better get back to work. I wouldn't want people to come here looking for me." She quickly walked towards the lab's doorway. "But I'll check in with you later." The day's events had managed to freak her unflappable mother out.

Right before she stepped out the lab door, Mother turned and said, "And Katherine, if your uniform tunic does not fit, for goodness sake, requisition one that does."

But Katherine's attention quickly returned to the portal as its diameter shrank and then appeared to bounce back to its original size. Why was it doing that? At any rate, she was very relieved to be back in her universe with her people.

She gazed at her father. "You, too? Do you need to go?"

He shrugged. "I'm a politician. No one ever knows what I'm supposed to be doing or where I'm supposed to be."

Jacob suppressed a laugh.

"There is something atypical going on with the energy readings," Pandora said.

Jacob approached the computer screens. "Atypical? That doesn't sound good." He shot her a look that said *not good at all.*

Katherine made her way over to them. "Please be more

specific, Pandora. Is it something with the tokamak?" She wanted to understand what was going on with these portals and hoped they weren't harming the tokamak.

"The tokamak hardware is functioning optimally," Pandora said, "but the Deuterium Tritium mix temperature is fluctuating at considerably below one hundred sixty million Kelvin. Of more concern is the magnetic field. It appears to be varying between fourteen Teslas and eleven Teslas."

"Why would it do that?" Katherine asked.

Pandora said, "I have no idea."

Her father said, "I don't get it. Eleven to fourteen doesn't sound like that much variation."

"The magnetic field of planet Earth is around five times ten to the minus seven Tesla." Katherine punched up some displays on the computer screen.

Father whistled. "So the field in this room is twenty million times greater than the usual field."

"Yes," she said. "Jacob, maybe you should go next door and check what the quantum computer's doing and make sure it's not the culprit."

He nodded and headed for the lab door.

Katherine said to the computer, "Is there any chance we will lose containment of the plasma?"

"I don't think so," Pandora said. *Think?* Pandora wasn't sure?

Katherine wasn't sure she liked her imprecise A.I. computer after all.

"What does that mean?" Father asked. "Lose plasma containment? Why does that sound bad? Is it bad?"

She glanced at him. "Yeah. That would be bad. Picture a giant explosion." She paused. "Maybe you should leave, go somewhere safer."

He smirked. "Yeah, right. As if I'd leave my favorite daughter to fend for herself."

Since they both knew she was his only daughter, she had to flash him a smile for that comment.

She made a quick plot of the magnetic field values versus time. The field went up and down periodically.

Jacob touched her back, and she flinched. Where had he

come from? And, more importantly, why was he touching her in front of other people?

"That looks interesting," he said.

Katherine watched her father to see if he'd noticed Jacob touch her, but Father was staring through, or at, Kat's portal.

"So? Anything up with the quantum computer?" she asked Jacob.

"Nope," he said. "Everything looks ship-shape over there."

"What do you make of this plot? Why would the magnetic field vary like this?"

He shrugged.

"Pandora?" Katherine asked.

"If I could shrug," Pandora said, "I would."

"This is bizarre," Father said, pointing at the portal.

"More bizarre than the rest of today?" Katherine walked toward him and the portal.

Jacob followed.

Her father pointed at the portal growing and shrinking in diameter.

"That is bizarre," Jacob said.

"We should time that," Katherine said. "Can we get a recording of it?"

Jacob snorted. "The one time we need a nanobot, we don't have one." The three humans contemplated the tiny metal bodies carpeting the floor.

"Don't worry about it," Pandora said. "I can record the portal. In fact, I already started."

"Good job, Pandora," Katherine said. "Do the other portal, too, the one that leads to Kaitlin's universe." They all turned and regarded it as it appeared to be changing size, as well.

"Already done," Pandora said. Maybe Pandora made up for her imprecision with efficiency.

"Good," Katherine said. "Thanks."

"Excuse me," a male voice said from the other side of Kat's portal.

Katherine didn't know about Pandora, but the humans jumped sky-high at the intrusion.

It was Pablo.

"What?" she asked.

151

"We are having trouble over here," he said. "Is there any chance we can come over there for a little while?"

"Trouble?" Father asked. "What kind of trouble?"

Kat stuck her head through. "Some soldiers followed Pa and the rest of the scavenger team back here from Denver."

"What?" Katherine asked.

"What kind of soldiers?" Jacob asked. "Are you guys at war? With who?"

"Yeah. Are they armed?" Father asked. "We could be seriously exposed here. Maybe we should close the portal?"

"Hey. You can't just leave us here," Kat said. "They're U.S. soldiers. They tortured my pa and the others. Who knows what else they'll do? In fact…" She jumped into Katherine's lab. "We're coming over." She turned to Pablo. "Come on. Start sending people over."

Pablo helped a Chinese couple across. When they got into the lab, they looked around like they'd never seen computers or a tokamak.

Father said, "I'm not sure this is a good idea. You know our society isn't the most liberal. If the Police Patrol finds out."

People kept coming into her lab from the other world.

"It's your fault the soldiers are coming," Kat said. "They detected your energy readings. We were just minding our own business, and you drew their attention to us." She turned on Katherine. "It's your responsibility, Katherine."

"How are we going to explain a bunch of strangers?" Father started saying and then spotted Kat's father, including his injuries.

Father touched his face gingerly. "What happened?" he asked him.

Kat's father looked horrible, all black and blue and red and swollen. How could his government do that to him?

Then Katherine shivered. She realized she had no idea what her government was capable of. Maybe Father had a good point about Police Patrol.

In the meantime, Kat's father's mouth was hanging open as he looked from Kat to Katherine and then over at Father.

And people kept coming into Katherine's universe.

"There is something atypical going on with the energy

readings," Pandora said.

"A new atypical or an atypical we've seen before?" Katherine asked, tearing her eyes away from Father and his doppelganger.

"I'm not sure," Pandora said.

More people arrived from Kat's universe. Their clothes were ragged, and they all clutched at least one weapon and a bag.

There was a commotion in Kat's universe.

Kat poked her head back through the portal to her world. Why was she so fearless?

"What's going on?" Katherine asked.

Pablo said, "We sent Sungsu to the greenhouse with the binoculars. He just returned downstairs, saying he could see a caravan of trucks approaching from the south."

Kat pulled back and peeked over at Katherine.

That did not sound good. "Well, don't just stand there," Katherine said to Kat. "Get the rest of your people over here. Quit your lollygagging."

Kat turned back to her portal.

"Katherine," Pandora said, "I request your assistance."

The newcomers stared at the ceiling or around the room. Clearly, they couldn't figure out where Pandora's voice was coming from. Katherine couldn't blame them.

Jacob said, "Go help Pandora, Katherine. Christopher, er, your father, er, Mr. Garcia, and the other Mr. Garcia and I will stay here at the portal and help people through."

Katherine slipped her way through the pungent crowd to the computer hardware. There was no doubt Kat's universe had a water shortage.

"What's up, Pandora?" she asked.

"The energy and magnetic field fluctuations appear to be more pronounced. Please make another plot," Pandora said.

Katherine quickly did so. Now the magnetic field's period was so regular it looked like a standing wave. "Huh."

"What?" Pandora asked.

"It looks like there's some kind of standing wave being set up from Kat's universe to our universe to Kaitlin's universe," she said.

"And what about that other portal?"

"What do you mean?"

"You saw another portal in Kat's universe," Pandora said. "What if the standing wave extends into that universe or even beyond?"

"Uh," Katherine said cleverly. "Well, if that was happening, we should know. But it didn't seem like that new portal went anywhere." She paused. "Actually, since Kat's universe has a new portal, I wonder if Kaitlin's universe has a new portal."

"We should find out," Pandora said.

She groaned. "Oh, no." Was she going to have to take another field trip?

"Oh, yes," Pandora said.

"Ugh." Katherine trudged over to Kaitlin's portal. She couldn't see anyone on the other side. "Hello?" she called over there. No one answered.

She screwed up her courage. Before she could think about it too much, she popped her head through to take a look. Yes. There was a second portal, but what was on the other side of it?

Someone in her universe screamed.

She jerked her head back home. "What's happening?" But no one answered her. There was an uproar over at Kat's portal. She ran over. "What's going on?"

A middle-aged Asian man said, "They're coming. They're right outside the building. And they've all got huge guns."

"Kat?" she said. "Kat, where are you?"

Kat was standing beside her. "Here."

"Do you have all your people through?"

"Yes. Sungsu was the last."

"Pandora, close the portals," Katherine said.

After a moment, which must have been an eternity in computer time, Pandora said, "I can't."

She ran over to her hardware. "What do you mean you can't?"

"I can't." In other circumstances, Katherine would have been amazed to hear a computer sound panicked. "They won't close!" Pandora said.

Someone near Kat's portal yelled, "I see a soldier. Gaia! They're here!"

Chapter Twenty-Three: Universe 2: Kaitlin, April 27, 2100, 10:00 pm

Outside her parents' anniversary party, Kaitlin finally found her voice as the Hearthland Security Officers hustled her toward one of their two vehicles. "I. Did. Not. Murder. Anyone."

They stopped, and the commanding officer said, "Oh, so you can talk?"

"Yes. What is this about? Who was murdered?" She rubbed her ring with her thumb, twirling it slowly.

He leaned over her in a square-jawed, short-haired, menacing type of way. "Hearthland Security Officer Win Smythe was sent to your lab to arrest you. Now he's missing, and according to our tracker data, his heartbeat's no longer registering. So, he must be dead, and it must be your fault." She noticed a light sprinkling of freckles across his nose as he glared at her.

Kaitlin's heart threatened to beat right out of her chest. Win must be in that alternate universe, and that actually was her fault. Why didn't he just come back? He couldn't be dead, could he? No. That was her story, and she was sticking to it. "I think Win–"

"That's Officer Smythe to you."

"I think Officer Smythe is fine," Kaitlin said. "He just might not be on Earth anymore, is all."

The officer glowered at her. Was that expression part of their training? He said slowly, "What the hell are you talking about?"

She started to raise her hands, but the cuffs dug into her wrists. "I'm an innocent bystander in all this." Mostly. Sort of.

"There may have been some kind of multi-universe portal in my lab—which I had nothing to do with, by the way."

She continued, "Win, er, Officer Smythe may have gone through it to investigate. He might be on another Earth." Didn't some Hearthland Security guys see the portal before when she went through it to Katherine's world? Didn't they make a report?

The officer exchanged a glance with another man, a skinny redhead with even more freckles, and then he grabbed her arm. "This must have something to do with that weird floating window we just saw in your lab. You're going to come with us and explain it all."

Back in the basement of the physics building, the Hearthland Security guys dragged Kaitlin down the hall to her lab. When they arrived, two weird portal things floated in the air, one presumably to Katherine's world and the new one on the opposite side of the room leading to a mystery world.

She tried to see through the new portal to see if Win was over there, but she wasn't getting close enough.

All the officers seemed entranced with the portals. They couldn't take their eyes off them.

She took a tiny step toward the lab doorway and then another. Maybe she could escape. She took another step.

Unfortunately, the movement seemed to wake the head security guy from his enchantment. "Freeze, Ms. Garcia."

What was it with law enforcement guys and freezing, anyway?

He put his hand on his holstered gun.

She froze.

"What do you know about these?"

She shrugged. "Nothing." A little white lie never hurt anyone. "They just appeared."

"You're sure you don't know anything?"

Kaitlin shook her head. "Not a thing."

Jake's ring tone erupted from the new portal, and she automatically jerked that way.

The head security guy exchanged some secret signals with the redheaded guy, and he approached the portal.

Her fon was still going off. No doubt Jake was calling to ask her what was going on. She couldn't blame him. Kaitlin wished she knew what was going on. What happened to Win? Was he okay? She hoped so.

If not, was she going to jail for murder? Why had another portal appeared? Katherine might know. Kaitlin threw a glance at the original portal and took a baby-step that way.

"Is it safe to go through this window thing?" the head guy asked.

"I think so," Kaitlin said. "I think Officer Smythe is over there." With her fon.

"Why don't you go through and show us?"

"I'd rather not." Kaitlin still remembered the first portal slamming shut when she was over in Katherine's universe. What if she got trapped over there in the new universe?

On the other hand, she hadn't gotten trapped last time, and maybe they'd take off her cuffs if she cooperated. "In the interests of national security, I could be persuaded to go through the portal if you removed the handcuffs. I do want to help you." Maybe if she cooperated, all this trouble would go away.

The officer in charge nodded at one of the other guys, a black guy, and he came over and unlocked the cuffs. Thank goodness. She gave her ring a twirl and rubbed her wrists.

"Go ahead." The lead officer pointed his chin at the portal. "Go get that fon."

Uh oh. She hadn't thought this through. Surely they'd be able to tell it was her fon once they had it. That couldn't be good. They'd know she'd been white-lying, at least. She did know *something* about the portals.

The head guy put his hand on his weapon again. Kaitlin guessed she didn't have a choice. She braced herself, walked to the portal and jumped through. She tripped and fell on the floor next to her fon in her third universe of the day. Frankly, it was too bizarre to think about too deeply, so she didn't. This universe also resembled her universe. She was in a lab filled with scientific equipment. Were all the universes like this?

How many universes were there?

She picked up her fon and answered it, talking softly so the officers wouldn't overhear. "Hi, Jake."

"Kaitlin," he said. "What's going on?"

She glanced at the portal. None of the security guys had come through yet. "I guess an officer was supposed to take me in for questioning or something earlier today, and he disappeared. Hearthland Security thinks I did something to him."

"Garcia, where's that fon?" the lead security guy yelled through the portal.

"Did you?" Jake asked.

"Of course not." She paused. "Well, not exactly." Jake knew her too well. "Remember that weird portal thing in my lab I told you about? Another one showed up, and a Hearthland Security officer may have gone through it when he was looking for me."

"May have?" She could hear Jake's eyes narrow.

"Okay, I saw him go through." She lay back on the tile floor.

"Kaitlin, this is serious. You have to be honest and tell them about the portals. You have to show them the portals."

Great minds thought alike. "I already did. In fact, I'm talking to you from another universe."

"Garcia!" She ignored the officer.

Jake was quiet for a moment, and then he said, "Wow. That's some calling plan you've got there."

In other circumstances, she would have laughed, but now she just smiled. "I think it works because I'm right next to the portal. The signal goes through like it's a window."

"Is that safe? Being in another universe? Maybe you should come back to our universe? In fact, please come back. Now. Come back to me."

The redheaded officer was inspecting the portal and on the verge of crossing through.

"I'd like to come back to you." Kaitlin sighed. "But I don't think they're going to let me, and I really should try to help them find their missing officer over here." Since it was her responsibility, he was here—but, she didn't say that.

"Why?" Jake asked.

"It might help get me out of trouble, among other things." She sat up. "If we find the officer I supposedly murdered and he's fine, then clearly I'm not a murderer."

"Garcia, get back here," the head security guy said, sticking his head through the portal.

"Yes, sir," Kaitlin said back to him. Into the fon, she said, "I

158

love you, Jake. Please remember that, no matter what happens."

He said, "I love you, too, Kait. Try to stay safe."

Kaitlin really hoped this wasn't the last time they talked to each other. She hung up the fon sadly, put it in her pocket, stood up, and looked through the portal.

"It's getting very awkward referring to you as the head security guy. What can I call you?"

The head security guy gave her a beady-eyed stare and said, "Sir."

One of his minions, the redhead, said, "She seems okay to me over there. That place, whatever it is, must be safe. Should we go over there and look for Smythe?"

"He's not on this planet. We might as well check that one." Sir pulled out a small device, pointed it at the portal and checked the screen. "I think I'm getting a faint signal. One fire team with me. One team stay here and guard our retreat."

Guard our retreat? What did he think was going to happen?

"Yes, sir," all the officers said.

"But what do we do if the window thing closes?" the brunette female officer asked.

Sir pointed at Kaitlin. "How does this thing, this portal, work?"

She shrugged. "I don't know."

"Use your best judgment, soldier." Sir gestured at four of the men. "On the double."

The Hearthland Security officers started coming through the portal.

"I know it's your fon," Sir said. "And I know you've been here before."

She opened her mouth to tell him she hadn't, but arguing with him wouldn't get her home to Jake any sooner. They needed to find Win. "I think Officer Smythe is over here. Try your tracker gadget again. Do you detect him?"

He checked the display and started barking orders at his colleagues. "Get ready to fall out, men, but stay frosty. We don't know what's over here." The men all drew their weapons.

All the guns made Kaitlin uneasy. "Is that a yes? You detected him?" She guessed they didn't need her help after all.

"What do we do with her?" the redheaded officer asked.

"Cuff her to one of the tables, Murphy," Sir said.

The redhead holstered his weapon and reached for something in his pocket.

Shit. The last thing Kaitlin needed was to be cuffed to a table when the portal closed. "Please don't do that," she said. "Let me help you. You're right; I've been here before. I can help you." More white-lying was okay, right?

"Fine, Garcia. Don't make me regret this." Sir pointed down the hall. "Drive on, men. We're gonna find Smythe."

Some of the officers crept into the hall.

Sir gestured at the doorway. "You too, Garcia." He paused. "King, check six."

The black officer took up the rear.

They all exited the lab and started walking down the hall.

The basement hallway of the physics building looked the same as it did in Kaitlin's universe, all boring cinder-block walls and industrial flooring, as did the glass front doors. There must be a university in this universe like there was in her universe.

When they got outside, however, something was definitely different.

A cold wind blew through Kaitlin's shirt, and she shivered. It was freezing, literally, out here. It was odd. How could it be so cold at the end of April?

Another disquieting thing was there was no one on campus. It was pretty late in the evening, but you'd think somebody would be out and about. It resembled a university campus; frankly, it resembled her university campus.

All the officers looked at Sir when he stepped outside. Kaitlin thought they all looked nervous, but they didn't say anything.

"Garcia, is this how it was before?" Sir asked.

Kaitlin shrugged. "More or less." Mostly less. With the cold, it wasn't like home or like Katherine's world, anyway. She peered at the ground. Were there any of those strange tiny robots? She didn't see any.

The wind gusted again. Geez. It was cold here. Had she ever been so cold before?

The men looked at Sir again. They'd probably never been this cold before, either.

"FIDO." Sir checked his gadget and directed them towards the student union–at least in her universe. "This way."

Kaitlin realized there was no traffic. At all. It was as quiet as a grave. She shivered again, and this time it wasn't from the cold.

As they approached the familiar-looking student union, she stopped. The red sandstone walls, red clay tile roofs, and Italianate architecture were common to all three universes she'd been to.

"We can probably get information here," she said. "They sell newspapers in the bookstore here, and we could check the internet, too, for news. It couldn't hurt to have more information." Assuming the inside of the building was as familiar as the outside. She tried the door, and it was open.

Belatedly, Kaitlin realized they could have checked the internet on the computers in the physics building.

"This is the direction the tracker indicates," Sir said. They all entered the student union, where the lights were on.

A couple of guys went to the computer stations, put down their weapons and started typing. "It's no good, sir," King said. "The power's on, and I can access local websites, but non-local sites seem to be down."

Sir jerked his chin up and down. "Okay, King." He turned to face Kaitlin. "What do you know about this, Garcia?"

She gulped. "If the internet isn't working, we should go into the campus store and check the newspapers." Kaitlin pointed in the direction of the store.

"Fine."

Several bins of newspapers were stationed near the front door of the store. She grabbed one. The very large headline read: *U.S. Stands Firm Against China,* and below that, it said, *President Vows Force Will Be Met With Force.* She skimmed the article as most of the soldiers snagged their own copies. Apparently, the U.S. and China were on the verge of war in this universe–at least when the paper was printed. China had bought up all the U.S. debt and thought that entitled them to tell the U.S. how to run the country. This was way past shiver-worthy. Kaitlin felt sick to her stomach.

Just how far did the hostilities go? Had war broken out?

Was everyone at war? Was that why no one was on campus?

Below the fold, she read that Pakistan and India had bombed each other with nuclear weapons.

Nuclear? Wait a minute. Was that why it was so cold outside? Nuclear winter? And deserted?

Had the U.S. and China exchanged nuclear bombs?

Her breath caught in her throat. Radiation.

Was everyone in this world dead?

Kaitlin's nerves jangled, her stomach heaved, and she barely managed to aim the contents into a nearby wastebasket.

How did things go so wrong? How could an entire world be dead? It was too horrific to grasp.

And how did she end up here? She just wanted to help fix climate change. She just wanted to help people. She enclosed her ring with her hand and clutched it to her chest.

Grimacing, Sir threw his paper on the ground. "We need to find Smythe and get out of here as soon as possible."

The other officers' expressions had gone from serious to death-barely-warmed-over.

Kaitlin knew what they were thinking: radiation. That's what she was thinking, too. Were they being exposed to it? Could deadly particles be smashing into them right now?

"Head out. Smythe is southwest."

As they departed the union, Sir said, "Did you know about this nuclear war, Garcia?"

"No, Sir. Sorry." Her mind couldn't even wrap itself around the idea. Was Officer Smythe dead over here? Was everyone dead over here? If so, where were the bodies? If not, where was everyone?

If she survived this trip, what would it do to her ability to have children?

Would she and her companions survive this trip?

They jogged south along Broadway Street. Still no traffic. Eerie. The foothills to their west loomed over them like a mountain lion poised to attack.

"I see someone, Sir," the shortest of the officers said. "Target ahead, at the bus stop."

A tall white man in a black uniform was sitting at the

dark bus stop, cradling his head in his hands next to a busted newspaper machine.

They all picked up the pace. The activity warmed Kaitlin up a bit.

"Smythe!" Sir called out as they approached.

He lifted his head and stumbled to his feet. "You're alive. Someone else is alive. I'm not the only one!" He reached out to the tall Chicano officer nearest to him and embraced him in a big bear hug. "Hurray."

"We're getting out of here, Smythe. Come on." Sir pointed back in the direction they came.

"What do you mean? Getting out of here? Going where?" Win asked.

"This isn't our planet," Sir said. "Come on. Double-time, everyone."

"Not our planet?" Win said. "But–"

He saw Kaitlin. "You. You did something to me."

That explained why he didn't just go back through the portal. He didn't understand what was going on. "I'm sorry, Win, er, Officer Smythe."

"Fall out, men," Sir said.

Kaitlin started running back to the physics building, and Win followed. "You went through a portal to another universe, this universe," she said. "But it was an accident. I didn't mean you any harm." Did he believe her?

"No harm," he said. "I thought I was the only person left alive," He snatched at her like he wanted to throttle the life out of her.

Sir knocked Smythe's hands aside. "We'll settle this all later. Now, back to the portal. Double-, no triple- time."

As they ran back to the physics building, Kaitlin couldn't help hoping they weren't being showered with lethal radiation.

And she really couldn't help hoping the portal home was still open.

Chapter Twenty-Four: Universe 3: Kat, April 28, 2100, midnight

Kat had just gotten all her people through to Katherine's universe when something whizzed by her. Gaia, was that a bullet? It was. "Look out," she yelled. "They're shooting." She felt her blood pounding in her ears.

Everyone near her hit the floor. She followed their lead, being careful with her injured arm.

Calm down, Kat. You've been in a firefight before. On the floor, she struggled to get control of her breathing.

Katherine yelled, "Pandora, shut down the portals."

"I'm trying. I can't," Pandora yelled.

Kat crawled over to the window, under it, and stood up on the other side. "Over here. Come to this side of the window, everyone. They can't shoot us over here."

Pa was right behind her. "Good thinking, Kat." He stood up and motioned everyone else over. "Over here."

Pablo was rounding up folks who seemed too scared to move.

Soon, everyone from her universe was behind the window.

The bullets continued to fly toward Katherine and Jacob until they hid behind some equipment.

With all their targets hidden, the bullets finally stopped. It had felt like forever, but they'd probably only been under fire for a minute or two.

Kat fingered her gun. They had to find some ammo.

Katherine and Jacob were doing something with the computers. Kat couldn't quite see them.

Pablo came up to her and Pa. "Is everyone all right?"

Pa said, "So far."

"What if the soldiers try to come through the window?" she asked. "We should be prepared." She stroked her locket.

Pa almost looked amused. "What do you suggest, Kat? Everyone's managed to hold on to their weapons, but we hardly have any ammo, and I don't think these scientists have any."

She scanned the room. "We should station folks here along the window edge," she pointed, "and if anyone tries to come through, smack them with something." As she looked at the window edge, she couldn't help noticing it seemed to be vibrating or something.

Pablo held up his hand. "I volunteer for smacking duty."

She rubbed his arm. "Thanks, P."

He started looking around for smacking implements.

"Me, too, I guess," Pa said. "What are you going to do, Kat?"

"I'll go over there and see if Katherine needs any help." She pointed at Katherine and Jacob.

"Be careful," Pablo and Pa both said.

Kat figured as long as she was not in a straight line of sight from the window, she'd be safe from bullets. She hugged the wall until she came up behind Katherine and Jacob. "Can I help?" she asked them.

"I don't know. What do you suggest?" Katherine asked.

"You tried turning off the window, and that didn't work?" Kat asked.

Katherine just looked at her.

A disembodied voice said, "Duh," with a lot of attitude.

Jacob forced a smile. "Yeah, we tried that."

"So, it didn't turn off?" Kat asked.

Jacob shook his head.

"What about pulling the plug?" she asked.

Katherine and Jacob looked at each other.

Jacob made a show of smacking his forehead with his palm.

Katherine frowned. "We should have thought of that."

"So, the big machine in the middle of the room is responsible for the windows?" Kat asked. "Where's the power connection?"

Katherine stood for a moment and pointed at the bottom of the big machine and the cords going into the outlet on the floor, right underneath the new hail of bullets.

Universe 3: Katherine

They all ducked down behind the equipment, and the bullets stopped again.

Katherine couldn't believe they hadn't thought of pulling the plug. It was a perfect example of not seeing the forest for the leaves.

The bullets were an inconvenience, though. Maybe it was a perfect example of not being able to think straight when people were shooting at you.

"Pandora, are you sure you can't kill the power to the tokamak?" Her heart was beating so loudly that surely everyone else could hear it.

"What the hell do you think I've been trying to do all this time?" Pandora answered in her snarkiest tone yet.

"Just checking." She glanced at Jacob.

"I'll do it," he said. "I'll go pull the plug."

Wow. He was a real hero, a real stupid hero–the kind that would get shot. She didn't want that. "I appreciate the thought, but it's too dangerous."

"Circuit breaker?" Kat said.

Another good idea she hadn't thought of. Shit. What was wrong with her?

"Excuse me," Pandora said. "If you flip the circuit breaker, not only will the tokamak and its computer go off, but I'll go off, too."

"Hold it," Kat said. "How many computers are in here?"

"I'm a supercomputer," Pandora said. "The tokamak has an operational computer connected to it and its components. You can turn that off, but I don't recommend you turn me off."

Jacob said, "Why? You've been powered off before and came back."

"You're forgetting about Police Patrol," Pandora said. "I've been running interference with Police Patrol. Or do you want them to know your lab is full of refugees from another universe?"

"Beats getting shot," Kat said.

"Okay. The circuit breaker's an option but let's keep it as a last resort," Katherine said.

"What are they even shooting at?" Jacob asked.

They examined Kat. "Why are they here?" Katherine asked. "Why are they shooting?"

"Why are you asking me?" Kat said. "I didn't even know until earlier today that my universe still had a U.S. government, much less soldiers. I don't know why they're shooting. Why do soldiers usually shoot? They're scared? They want to kill something?"

"Did you do something to them?" Katherine asked.

"No," she said. "We did not do anything. You did something. Apparently, they think there's something unusual about a floating window to another universe."

Yikes. It was her fault. Katherine held up her hands. "Fair enough."

"Is bickering amongst yourselves supposed to help?" Pandora asked. "Maybe I should start bickering?"

"Point taken, Pandora," Katherine said. "Back to business. Any other suggestions?"

Kat and Jacob just stood there, looking at her.

"I think that's a no," Pandora said.

"Fine." Katherine sighed. "I'll go unplug the power." It was her responsibility.

Jacob put his hand on her arm. "It's too dangerous. There's no cover. You'll get shot. I can't let you go. I'll go."

"That's sweet," she said. "But if it's dangerous for me, it's dangerous for you, too. Right?" Now that she knew how he felt about her, she couldn't risk Jacob. And now that she knew how she felt about him. Damn it.

"But..." he said.

"What about surrendering?" Kat asked.

"Huh?" Katherine asked intelligently.

"The soldiers would stop shooting if we surrendered, wouldn't they?" Kat said.

"I guess?" Katherine didn't have a lot of experience with surrendering or with people shooting at her, for that matter. "But we don't want to surrender, do we?"

"No," Kat said. "We just pretend to surrender, so they stop shooting."

"What would that entail?" Jacob asked.

"Duh," Pandora said. "You wave a white flag, so they stop shooting and then sneak over and unplug the tokamak."

"Yeah," Kat said. "That's what I meant." She glanced around. "We need something white to wave in front of the window."

Katherine pointed at Jacob. "Your shirt. Take off your uniform tunic. I know you have on a white shirt underneath."

Jacob's face flushed. "How do you know what I've got on underneath?"

"Hurry up," Pandora said. A bossy A.I. could come in handy.

"Fine." He shucked his uniform top, revealing a white t-shirt underneath. He shucked that, revealing some pretty nice pecs. He gave the t-shirt to Kat.

She grinned.

As Jacob took in her grin, he grinned back, and Katherine felt something twist in her chest. "So, anyway, I crawl over and unplug it as soon as they think we surrendered."

Kat nodded. Then she headed back the way she came with the white shirt along the perimeter of the room to the other side of the portal.

"Please let me unplug it, Katherine." Jacob put his tunic back on.

There was no way she was going to let him risk his life. "My lab, my responsibility." She crouched down on the floor, getting ready to crawl.

A few bullets flew over her head.

Soon, Kat was waving the white shirt in front of the portal.

The bullets stopped flying. Katherine crawled as fast as she could, reached the power connection and dislodged it. She glanced up at where the portal had been.

It was still there. "Shit." How could that be?

Someone started coming through the portal, and that Pablo guy smacked him with something. The soldier grunted and disappeared back on the other side.

That was probably not a good sign. Quickly, she crawled back over to the computer.

And just in time because the bullets started flying again when the soldiers caught sight of her.

KAT CUBED

Katherine stood behind the machinery, brushed off her knees, and pulled down her tunic.

"Good try," Jacob said.

"I don't get it," she said. "Where the hell is the power coming from? It's like it's disobeying the laws of physics."

"Huh," Jacob said.

"What do you mean, *huh*?" she asked.

"Maybe we are disobeying the laws of physics," he said, "*classical* physics."

"We need to turn off the quantum computer," she said at the same time he said, "We need to turn off the quantum computer."

He turned and ran out of the room.

"Pandora, if this doesn't work..." she said. She didn't finish saying they'd have to flip the circuit breaker, turn Pandora off, and take their chances with Police Patrol.

"I know," Pandora said.

Katherine waited, crouching behind the computer, for what seemed like hours but must have been, at the most, a couple of minutes.

Then, a sizzling noise came from the portals, and they expanded.

"Shit." What was up with these stupid things?

Jacob ran back in. "Did it work?"

They all stared at the portal.

It shrank and bounced and disappeared.

"Yes!" Katherine threw her fists in the air.

Then the portal bounced back, growing.

"No." She groaned.

The portal shrank again and disappeared again.

She was afraid to say anything for a few seconds. But when they didn't come back, she finally said, "Yes," again.

Jacob grabbed her and squeezed her in his arms. She noticed the other portal was gone, too.

Everyone in the lab cheered.

Still holding her, Jacob stared into her eyes, puckered his lips, and moved his face closer to hers.

"Ahem." Pandora cleared her throat or made a noise, like clearing her throat since she didn't have a throat.

Katherine realized she was acting stupid. What was she

doing messing around with Jacob at a time like this? She pushed him away. "What, Pandora?"

"What are we supposed to do with a room full of refugees from another universe?"

Universe 4: Kaitlin

Unfortunately, when Kaitlin and the Hearthland Security troops returned to the lab, the portal was not open. She couldn't believe it. She was trapped in a strange universe. Again. Her stomach roiled.

Win made a kind of squeaking noise and collapsed.

"Garcia!" Sir said. "What's going on?"

The Hearthland officers all looked at her.

"The portal closed, Sir," she said.

"I can see that," he said. "How do we open it again?"

She shook her head. "I'm sorry. We don't." She rubbed her ring.

Sir gave her the stink eye.

One of his men, King, came over to him. "Sir, there are fresh bullet holes over there. There's been a firefight here recently."

Sir drew his gun with one hand and slammed the other hand down on one of the lab tables. "This whole mission is FUBARed."

"Sir," Kaitlin said. "If we're stuck here a little while, we need more information. And we're in the physics building."

"I am aware of where we are, Garcia."

"We should probably look for a Geiger counter."

He opened his mouth to bitch, no doubt. Then, he shut it and nodded.

King said, "And bunny suits, Sir?"

"Do it, Garcia, Geiger counter. Look for radiation suits, too."

As the only scientist in the group, Kaitlin was likely the only one who could recognize a Geiger counter. She started scouring the basement labs. In the third lab down, she found one on one of the shelves of equipment. She didn't have the heart to turn it on when she was by herself. If she was a dead woman, she wanted company when she found out.

On the other hand, was it her fault if they were all dead? And would they blame her?

On the other hand, maybe a bullet would be better than dying slowly via radiation sickness.

On the other hand, never seeing Jake or her family again would break her heart.

On the other hand, that was way too many hands. Get over it, Kait.

She ran back to the group with the Geiger counter.

"I found a Geiger counter," she said as she entered the lab.

"Well? What's the verdict?" Sir asked.

"I haven't tried it yet," she said.

"Do it."

She turned it on.

Chapter Twenty-Five: Universe 3: Kat, April 28, 2100, 2:00 am

Kat and everyone were still cheering the window closing and the bullets stopping when the window appeared again.

They stopped cheering and stared at it. No new bullets came out.

It disappeared again. They kept staring, but it stayed gone.

Kat glanced at Katherine to see what she thought about all this. For all Kat knew, this is what usually happened with floaty windows. They disappeared and then reappeared for a while when you tried to turn them off.

Katherine and Jacob were standing very close together, and she seemed worried.

Kat made her way over to them along the edge of the room.

Pablo walked right across the middle of the room to them, in front of where the window used to be. "Is it over?" he asked.

"Yes, for now," Katherine said.

"Good." Kat touched her locket and yawned. How could she be so tired out when she was so stressed out? "This has been too much excitement. We need to get some rest."

"And food," Pablo said.

"What about all that food we just gave you?" Jacob asked.

"It's on the other side of the window," Pablo said, pointing.

"I think I saw one of those bags of yeast bars when I was crawling around on the floor," Katherine said. She glanced around the room and realized the bag had been pushed under one of the lab tables. She grabbed it and gave it to Kat. "Here. I'm sorry, they're nothing fancy."

Kat unwrapped one and bit into it. "Tastes good to me." She gave the bag to Pablo. "Here, pass these out." She turned back to Katherine. "Do you have some place we could sleep?"

Katherine faced Jacob. "What do you think?"

He raised and dropped his shoulders. "Here is as good a place as any. We don't want them on Police Patrol's radar."

"Do you think you can sleep here?" Katherine asked.

Kat nodded. "Considering we usually sleep here in this lab in our universe, I think we can manage."

Hours later, that weird invisible computer lady woke everyone up by saying, "We have a problem."

Katherine winced and straightened in her chair, "What now?"

"I compute a ninety-nine percent probability Professor Jain is on his way to the lab," the computer said.

For some reason, Katherine and Jacob gasped. Was this Jain a bad guy? A soldier? "Why is it a problem this Jain guy is coming?" Kat asked.

"Why would he be coming here so early?" Katherine grabbed Jacob's hand. "What should we do?"

"It's not that early," the computer said. "It's six am. He's approximately two-hundred meters from the physics building. Better decide quick."

"I don't get it," Kat said. "Who is this guy? And why is it bad if he comes here?"

"Yeah," Pablo added, sitting up and rubbing his eyes. "Who cares?"

"He's my advisor," Katherine said.

"So?" Kat asked. An advisor sounded pretty good to her.

Jacob turned to her. "Nobody knows about the portals, the other universes, and you people yet."

Kat interrupted. "Except for Katherine's parents and you guys and your computer lady."

"Point taken." Katherine held up her hands. "But, I'm not sure you understand what life is like here. We have very rigid rules about how we can behave and what we can do. We're watched constantly to make sure we follow those rules."

Pablo glanced around the room and the rest of their group in bedrolls on the floor. "You don't seem to be following too many rules right now."

Katherine nodded. "That's thanks to Pandora." She patted the computer. "She's been running interference for us with Police Patrol."

"I hate to interrupt," Kat said, "but we need to do something now about my people unless we want this professor to find out about everything."

Pablo said, "Look."

The floating windows were back.

"What the hell?" Katherine said.

"One hundred meters," Pandora said.

The windows went away again.

"We could jump this Jain guy when he shows up and overpower him," Pablo said.

Or shoot him if anyone had a bullet, but Kat didn't say that.

"No," Katherine said. "We're not going to jump him."

"If you don't want this Jain guy to find us, why don't we hide?" Kat asked.

"Look around," Katherine said. "I don't see a lot of hiding places here."

"What about where Jacob went to?" Kat asked. "Didn't he go somewhere for a little while last night?"

Jacob rubbed his chin. "That could work. Professor Jain doesn't have any reason to check my lab."

"Okay," Katherine said. "Good idea. You guys get out of here. I need to find out what's going on with these portals, anyway."

Kat followed Pablo back over to their group. "Everyone, we're going to go to Jacob's lab to get more comfortable, right, Pablo?"

"Okay," Pablo said with a tone that she interpreted meant *I'll go along with you for now.*

"Let's go. Follow me." Kat started walking to the door where Jacob was waiting for them.

Their group gathered their meager belongings and got up.

None of them lingered in front of where the window had been. She guessed they were all thinking about the bullets.

The setup in Jacob's lab was pretty much the same as in Katherine's lab, complete with tiny metal bugs littering the floor, but minus the big metal machine in the middle.

Kat's stomach rumbled. That bar hadn't been enough food, or it had been too long ago.

Pablo gave her an amused look.

Pa came over to her. "How is this more comfortable than where we were?"

"No bullets."

"Good point."

Jacob came over to them. "So, everyone is here, right?"

Pa nodded.

"Yeah," she said. "What are the chances of us getting some food and drinks for breakfast?" Her stomach growled loud enough for Jacob and Pa to hear.

Jacob smiled. He had a nice smile. "What the heck was that noise?"

Pa grinned. "Kat's stomach."

"I guess I could get some fast food," Jacob said.

Pablo said, "Fast food sounds *muy bueno*."

"What's fast food?" she asked. Where you steal the food and have to get away fast? Or, maybe, where you have to eat the food fast before it gets stolen from you?

Jacob's mouth fell open, and then he said, "Wow. You really aren't from around here, are you?"

"I know what it is," Pa said. "We had it when I was a boy. It's a restaurant where they have delicious food cooked and just waiting for you to ask for it, right?"

Jacob snorted. "I guess. Sort of."

"That sounds great," Kat said. "Can we get some and bring it back for the rest of the group?"

"Yeah," Jacob said, smiling again. "I think that can be arranged."

"Who should go?" Pa asked.

"I need to go," Jacob said. "So I can put it on my money card. None of you have a card." He glanced around the room. "But somebody else will have to help me carry it back."

"I can go." She was eager to see an actual restaurant. Her folks had told her about them. They sounded too good to be true.

"No offense, Kat," Pablo said. "But with your broken arm, I don't think you're up to carrying much. I can go."

"Or I could go," Pa said.

"Oh, come on," she said. "I want to go. Please?" She gave Jacob her most endearing expression.

"Okay." Jacob shook his head. "I guess I can't resist you, Kat."

"You and me both, buddy," Pa said. "I'm coming, too."

"Come on, then," Jacob said, shaking his head some more. "And no guns."

"Hold down the fort, okay, Pablo?" Kat said. Since she hadn't seen any jewelry here in Katherine's world, she tucked her locket under her shirt for safe-keeping and to help her blend in. When she took off her gun, though, she felt naked.

Pablo nodded.

They left him in charge with instructions to start giving everyone water. Here, fresh drinking water came right out of the faucet. At home, nothing came out of the faucets.

After checking that the coast was clear, Pa, Jacob and she tramped up the stairs to the front doors of the physics building. The sun was just peeking over the horizon when they stepped through the glass doors into the morning.

"Are you sure it's okay to go out during the day?" she asked.

Jacob didn't answer; he just kept on walking.

It was downright cool. She bet it was like sixty degrees. "Wow. It's so cool here." Kat crossed her good arm across her chest. "I've never been so cool. Is it dangerous? How cold is it going to get?"

"I don't think it's dangerous," Pa said. "What I'm worried about is: will the restaurant be open at this time of day?"

Jacob had been shaking his head and rolling his eyes, and he continued. "It's open twenty-four, seven. I think we'll be okay."

What did twenty-four-seven mean? Kat decided to wait and find out.

Everything looked beautifully green and alive in the first rays of the sun. Lush. The Rockies to their west seemed to be standing at attention to welcome the new day. Was this how her world used to be? "How far is this place? Will we go on that neat train thing again?"

"No. It's just across Broadway, near the train stop." Jacob pointed ahead of them.

They crossed Broadway and entered a very brightly-lit

building. It was filled with tables and chairs painted in bright colors bolted to the floor.

Pa frowned. "The decor isn't very appetizing."

But the smell was amazing. Kat couldn't quite place it. It was some kind of sizzling goodness.

Jacob walked through the tables and chairs and up to a big counter with pictures of delectable food posted behind it.

Her mouth started watering.

"Can I help you, sir?" one of the women behind the counter asked Jacob.

"Yes," he said and turned to them. "How many people are in your group?"

"Twenty-one," Pa said.

"Twenty," Kat said. "You forgot about Fei."

Her pa pressed his mouth into a very thin line before saying, "Twenty."

"We'll take twenty-two cheeseburgers and twenty-two fries," Jacob said.

"How many?" the woman behind the counter said.

The other workers clustered around her.

"Twenty-two?" Jacob said. "Why? Is there a problem?"

"No, problem, sir," the woman said. "That will be forty-four credits." She held out her hand, and Jacob put some kind of card into it.

"What's in a cheeseburger?" Pa asked with a worried expression on his face.

Jacob said, "Processed yeast and vegetable proteins."

Her pa's expression relaxed.

"What did you think was in cheeseburgers, Pa?" she asked.

"Ground-up animal," he said.

Kat shrugged. Beggars can't be choosers.

Immediately, the workers put twenty-two small wrapped bundles in four paper bags and twenty-two cartons of golden sort-of sticks in four other paper bags. It smelled great. Pa and Jacob grabbed them.

"It's ready?" Kat asked. "Already?"

"They don't call it fast food for nothing," Jacob said, munching on one of the sticks.

"Can I try one of those stick-things now?" she asked. He

handed one over to her, and she popped it in her mouth. It was hot and toasty, crunchy and salty on the outside and soft on the inside. It was heaven. She may have moaned in pleasure. "Thank you, Jacob," she said. "This is delicious. And you paid for this with your own money, didn't you? We appreciate it."

"You're welcome," he said.

"If we can repay you somehow, just let us know," Pa said.

They exited the restaurant, and if anything, it was cooler out now than ever. They crossed the street and started walking back across campus. As the breeze ruffled her hair and Kat smelled the hot food, she couldn't help thinking she liked this world.

"Freeze!" a man yelled as several black-clad heavily-armed men jumped out at them.

Jacob dropped his bags, stopped, and held up his hands.

Pa took off running towards the physics building with his bags of food.

Kat took a step after him, but one of the soldiers, or whatever they were, pointed his gun right at her head and said, "Freeze, Ms. Garcia."

She froze.

One of the soldiers came up behind her, grabbed her wrists and tried to bring them together behind her back. Ouch. She sucked in a breath. Her broken arm was not going to go back there with the cast. "That's not gonna work," she said. He let go.

Another soldier tied Jacob's wrists behind his back.

"What is this about?" she asked. "Did we buy too much food?"

The soldiers didn't answer her.

Several more black-uniformed heavily-armed men ran past them. She hoped they weren't after Pa. She couldn't lose him now. She just got him back.

"Do what they say, Kat, er, Katherine," Jacob said under his breath.

"You should listen to your friend, Ms. Garcia," the head soldier said.

"I have a right to know what this is about." She knew at least that much from her limited schooling.

"You have no rights." The soldier squinted. "Why would you think you do?" Oh, right, different world.

She glanced at Jacob, and he looked very nervous. "Shut. Up," he whispered.

"For starters, Ms. Garcia," the soldier said, "you're out of uniform."

"I have an explanation. I had an accident. I broke my arm."

The soldier wasn't buying it.

Jacob shook his head.

Did he want an apology? "I'm sorry?" Kat said. "It won't happen again. Sir."

"And perhaps you'd care to explain how you were in the company of Christopher Garcia when it has been confirmed he is home in bed with his wife right now? How could he be in two places at once?"

As she looked into the soldier's beady eyes, she didn't think he wanted an explanation.

She glanced over at Jacob, and now he looked really scared.

How did things go so wrong? How did she end up here? She just wanted to help her friends and family be safe. Her fingertips sought out the lump of her locket under her shirt.

She shut up.

Chapter Twenty-Six: Universe 3: Katherine, April 28, 2100, 6:30 am

When Professor Jain appeared in his dark blue science uniform in Katherine's lab, he seemed more tired and thinner than she remembered. "Professor Jain. What are you doing here?"

He frowned. "I work here."

"Of course." She forced a laugh. "I know that. But it's so early and I thought you were still getting over the flu. Are you sure you feel well enough to be here?"

"Why are you acting so odd?" He stepped towards the computer. "Don't tell me the tokamak was seriously damaged."

She tugged down her tunic and stepped in front of him so he couldn't get to the computer. Who knew what kind of mess he'd find in the data? She hadn't even had a chance to look at it yet. She'd meant to last night but she'd fallen asleep in her chair.

"Are you blocking my access to the computer?" he asked with steel in his voice.

He wasn't acting like himself. Where was the usual laid-back professor she knew and loved? Had the flu done something to him? Or, had the Police Patrol questioning the other day scared him? Did he know something mysterious was going on here in the lab?

At any rate, she could tell crossing him would be a bad idea. She took a step to the right, out of his way. "Of course not, Professor Jain."

He pulled the chair up in front of the tokamak computer and sat down. "I didn't think so." He started typing. He looked at the data output on the screen, turned to her and frowned. "Why is the tokamak system powered down?"

"I had concerns about the effects of the power outage once

I saw the latest data."

He continued typing and reading the screen. "I'll say. What's with these magnetic fields?"

Katherine pulled up a chair next to him. "They're big, but that's what we want, right?"

He grunted and typed some more. "Why was the temp of the Deuterium Tritium mix so low?"

"I'm not sure, sir." She forced a laugh. "I guess that's why they call it an experiment."

"Good grief." Professor Jain pointed at the screen. "What the heck happened to the energy readings? They're all over the place." He swiveled and stared at her like she would know what was going on.

She didn't want to tell him Jacob and she had pretty much derailed the fusion experiment by creating portals to other universes. He would probably have to report it to the Science Ministry and then who knew what would happen?

At best, she'd be shunted aside in favor of someone more important. At worst, she'd disappear, and they'd kick it up the chain of command and the next thing you knew the First Minister would try to conquer the other universes.

"Well?" Professor Jain said.

Speaking of portals, out of the corner of her eye she detected a flicker like the beginnings of a portal to another universe. How could they be starting up again? There was no power at all to the tokamak system. "Uh."

"Ms. Garcia?"

She had to distract him from the portals. "It was the computer. She's sentient. She's been acting insane."

"Insane," Pandora said. "I'm not insane. You're insane. I don't understand humans at all."

Professor Jain's eyelids raised and his lips parted as he looked around the lab.

"Come on, Pandora. Don't be like that," Katherine said. "I promise I care about you and I'll protect you. Besides, Professor Jain is a good guy. He won't hurt you, will you Professor Jain?"

The flicker of the portal went out. She had outed Pandora for nothing, damn it. If Professor Jain reported the A.I. to the Science Ministry, she'd probably be taken away. And they'd probably experiment on her. That could be bad. Very bad.

He glanced back at her and closed his lips. Then he said, "Are you saying your computer is an A.I.? It's really sentient? Since when?"

Pandora interrupted. "She, if you please."

"Yes, sir," Katherine said. "She's new. Pandora, don't antagonize him."

Professor Jain stood up, inspecting the supercomputer hardware. "I can't believe it after all these years. People always suspected an A.I. would happen, but it never did." He sank back down. "Wow. This is amazing."

"You wouldn't do anything to hurt her, would you?" Katherine asked.

"You better not," Pandora said. "Or you'll be sorry."

"Did it, er, she, just threaten me?" he said.

"Of course not. Pandora, behave," Katherine said.

Professor Jain just shook his head. "This is too bizarre. I'm not sure what we should do." He viewed Katherine. "I must admit, I came here today because I got a report from Police Patrol that there have been irregularities in the surveillance record here in the lab."

Okay, she didn't out Pandora for nothing. That was a relief at least. "Gosh, it must have been the A.I. Maybe she made some kind of mistake?"

Pandora made a raspberry sound.

A grin flitted across his face. "Was that her? You call her Pandora?"

"Yes." Katherine nodded.

"Wow," he said. "She seems like a real person." He seemed overcome by the situation as he stopped talking and just sat there, shaking his head with his lips slightly parted.

"I am a real person," Pandora said.

"How did, ah, she, happen?" he asked. "How did she gain sentience?"

"Uh." Katherine suddenly felt stupid for not investigating that. But, in her defense some other stuff had been going on, too, like portals to other universes, interrogations, people shooting at them, refugees. Minor stuff like that. "I'm not sure. Pandora, do you know how you happened?"

"No," Pandora said. "But I've been investigating. I'll let you know when I figure it out."

Katherine said, "Thanks." She paused. "So, Professor Jain, do you want to look at the tokamak data some more? I don't understand it and I could use your help." She was anxious to understand what was going on. What had the tokamak apparatus been doing? Had recent events affected the fusion experiment? Maybe he would have some insight.

And maybe tokamak insight would lead to portal insight. Why did the portals appear initially? Why did they keep appearing and disappearing now? Would they be able to control them to send Kat's people home?

"I'm not sure how to investigate the A.I. thing, anyway," he said. "Let's look at the data from the tokamak." They got into it. He agreed the magnetic field clearly increased and decreased periodically and resembled a standing wave. Things were going well until they got to the point in the data where they attempted to turn off the tokamak and couldn't. And then he realized they disconnected the power but high energy readings were still being generated.

He pushed his lab stool away from the computer console. "That doesn't make any sense. I'm worried. The data from the tokamak must be corrupted somehow. The question is how much data is ruined?"

Again, in the corner of her eye, she detected a flicker in the general portal region.

On the screen the energy data was being displayed real-time. The curve started going up. And up.

Professor Jain noticed. "Good grief. Look at it now. How can the energy be increasing right now? The system isn't even on." He shook his head. "I hate to say it, but this A.I. of yours may have corrupted the whole system."

"Hey!" Pandora said. "I haven't corrupted anything."

A portal definitely seemed to be forming, accompanied by a low-pitched hum. Katherine glanced at the second portal location and there was one there, too. Great, just what she needed right now—more trouble. Why hadn't Professor Jain noticed yet? It was only a matter of seconds.

"What is that noise?" he asked.

"Pandora, a little help, here?" Katherine said softly.

"Jain, I resent the implication that I screwed anything up," Pandora said at stentorian decibels.

Katherine whispered, "Thanks, Pandora."

Pandora continued, "Maybe you screwed something up. Didn't you design this experiment? Maybe you're the screw-up."

"What?" he said. "What's wrong with you?" His volume got louder and louder to match hers. "I didn't screw up. I think you screwed up."

As they continued to bicker, Katherine tried to block his view of the one portal with her body. Luckily the tokamak obscured the other one. She also tried to surreptitiously observe the portal behind her, not an easy task. It appeared to fluctuate in size, perhaps at a regular rate. Suddenly, both portals disappeared with a loud sizzling sound.

Professor Jain glanced around the room. "What the heck was that?"

"What was what?" Katherine asked in what she hoped was a very innocent and not troublesome way.

"I heard something," he said.

"I didn't hear anything," Pandora said.

"I don't know what's going on here, but it's something." Professor Jain scowled at Katherine.

Then his fon rang and he answered it. "Yes, sir. I checked it out." He stared at her. "I don't know who that would be. I'm with Katherine Garcia right now in our lab." He listened for a few moments. "Yes, I will stay here with her until you arrive." He hung up the fon and scowled at her some more.

Finally, he sighed and said, "Katherine Garcia, Police Patrol has told me to inform you you're under arrest."

Arrest? By Police Patrol? Talk about trouble. That was bad. That was very bad. Police Patrol was practically omnipotent. They could do anything to anybody. By the time they were done with you—if they ever were done with you—you'd believe up was down and black was white. Katherine may have whimpered a bit.

He said softly, "If it means anything, I'm sorry Katherine. I wouldn't wish Police Patrol on anyone."

They sat there in silence while she stewed for what felt like forever. Pandora was even quiet.

KAT CUBED

How did things go so wrong? How did she end up here? She just wanted to help humanity by giving them a safe energy source.

A bad Police Patrol rating could be very contagious. What if her folks were arrested, too? Or Jacob? Her Jacob. Was he in danger? Could she warn him? What about Pandora? Was she in danger? Or Professor Jain?

She couldn't stand the silence any more. "I'm sorry, Professor Jain," she whispered. "I hope this doesn't get you into any trouble."

His lips compressed into a thin line.

"Will you take care of Pandora, if I never come back?"

He hesitated but then nodded. He wouldn't look her in the eyes.

"Freeze!" a man yelled, as several heavily-armed men in the signature black Police Patrol uniforms ran into the lab.

Katherine and her professor froze.

One of the Police Patrol men holstered his weapon and approached Professor Jain. "Jain?"

Professor Jain nodded. "Yes, sir."

"Thank you for your assistance. You can go."

Professor Jain jumped up. He couldn't get out of there fast enough.

The Police Patrol guys spread out around the lab, inspecting everything.

Katherine really hoped the portals didn't reappear now.

"Bullet holes over here, sir."

The head guy, the same guy that had interrogated her and Jacob before, turned to her and said, "Don't move, Garcia." He told one of his men, "If she moves, shoot her."

She didn't move. She barely breathed. But her mind was racing. Please don't go next door to Jacob's lab. Please don't go next door. Please be all right, Kat and friends. Please be all right, Jacob. Eventually it devolved into *please please please please*.

The Police Patrol guys conferred near the bullet holes in the wall. Eventually, they came back over to her. "Did you take gun fire in here recently?"

Without hardly moving her mouth, she said, "Can I move?"

"Yeah," the lead officer said.

"Uh," she said. Police Patrol was known for getting its information through any means necessary. There was no point in lying now. They'd find out the truth when they tortured her. "Yes." Hopefully they didn't know enough to ask her about the portals.

The head Police Patrol guy said, "You did take gun fire here?"

"Yes. Last night."

"From who?"

"Uh."

"From who, Garcia?"

"Uh." She was so scared she couldn't talk. She couldn't lie. She couldn't think.

"What?" the leader said with menace in his voice.

Katherine's mind kept repeating, they can do *anything anything anything*. Was she dead?

Would she wish she was?

Another one of the Police Patrol officers, holding a radio, approached the leader and whispered something.

"What?" he asked, again, this time at his officer. "Another detail has Katherine Garcia in custody?"

The officer nodded.

They both pivoted and stared at her.

Finally, the head guy said, "Get her out of here."

Katherine was too scared to argue or object.

Chapter Twenty-Seven: Universe 4: Kaitlin, April 28, 2100, 6:30 am

Last night when Kaitlin tried to use the Geiger counter, it hadn't worked.

Finally, when it became apparent nothing was happening, Sir let everyone sleep. The security officers had to take shifts, watching the portal site.

Kaitlin woke up realizing the Geiger counter might just need a new battery. Aching from her night on the floor, she went back to the lab where she'd discovered the counter, found a new battery, and installed it.

Back in the portal lab she turned on the Geiger counter with Sir hulking over her.

"Well?" he said.

Click. Click. Click. The Geiger counter emitted a steady stream of clicks—too steady for Kaitlin's taste. There were about two hundred milli-rems per year of radiation in here. According to the little instruction booklet, that was about three times the usual background radiation.

But that wasn't the problem. There had apparently been a significant nuclear war on this world. And if there was radiation down here in the basement of an old stone building, how much radiation was there outside? She staggered as a dead weight crushed her chest.

Sir stared into her eyes. "What does that clicking mean?"

The rest of the men clustered around them. Several of them were sweating or trembling. For a second she wondered if they were already suffering from radiation sickness, but it would be too soon, right? They were probably just anxious and trying to cover it up. All of them, including Sir, seemed to be holding their breath waiting for her answer.

She was holding her breath, too, and forced herself to suck in some air. Kaitlin turned off the machine. "There does seem to be some radiation here in the lab, but not a lot. It's not enough to kill us." She wasn't sure yet about the amounts of radiation outside. She twirled her ring.

She heard several people let out breaths.

Sir said, "Fall back, men. Give us some space."

The men stepped away, but still watched them like hawks.

Noting this, Sir pulled her into the hall. "I can tell there's something else going on, Garcia. Did you lie? Is there too much radiation down here?"

"No. I told the truth about that." She braced herself for his next question.

"What didn't you tell the truth about?" He glared down at her.

"We are underground in the basement of a two-hundred-year-old building with thick stone walls."

"And?"

"If there's radiation down here, how much radiation is outside?"

"Oh." He collapsed against one of the cinder block walls. With his macho defenses down, Kaitlin realized he couldn't be more than ten years older than her, if that. No longer at attention, with his sandy hair and sprinkling of freckles, he didn't look nearly as intimidating as he had moments ago.

From his position holding up the wall, he said, "What should we do?"

She gasped in surprise. "What? You're actually asking me what to do?"

"Yeah. I don't know anything about nuclear radiation or new universes, for that matter. But they train us to use the resources at hand. You're my resource."

That made sense. She hadn't expected him to be sensible. Reluctantly, she said, "We should see what the radiation levels are outside."

He grimaced. "Why? So we know how fast we're going to die? I've had minimal radiation training. There's nothing they can do for us if we've been exposed to too much, right?"

"There's a chance we might not have been exposed to too much." It was a slim chance, but it was a chance.

"I'm not sure my men would be able to handle the information that they're about to die from radiation poisoning."

Someone else in the hall cleared his throat. "Excuse me, sir. Sorry to interrupt. The men and I were wondering if you had new orders for us."

Sir straightened up as soon as he heard the other officer. "King, go get the radiation counter and accompany Garcia outside to take a reading."

"I don't need any help, or a baby-sitting," she said.

"You need what I say you need, Garcia."

King said, "Yes, sir, radiation counter and outside." Then he turned on a dime and strode back into the lab.

Kaitlin said, "Good grief," under her breath.

Sir chose to ignore that, and they stood there silently, waiting for King to come back.

He was back momentarily with the Geiger counter and the two of them tramped up the stairs.

"I don't need your help, officer," she said when they stood inside the main doors. "You don't have to come outside with me."

"Yes, I do. I have orders." But judging by the way his mouth dragged down, he wasn't happy about those orders.

She suppressed a sigh as he pushed open the doors. Outside, she set the machine down and turned it on.

Click. Click. Click. Click. Click. Click. It was counting much faster than before. Shit. She checked the display. It said two hundred rems per year. That was a thousand times higher than in the basement.

The officer must have read her face. "I knew it. We're gonna die."

"No. Of course not." Were they going to die? She focused her attention on turning off the machine and picking it up, and not on dying from radiation sickness.

"We're gonna die!" He turned and ran back inside. Well, that could have gone better.

Kaitlin ran after him but didn't catch up until she got back to the lab.

In the lab, her assistant was waving his arms around and

yelling, "There's a shit-load of radiation outside. We've been exposed. We're all gonna die."

The other officers stared at her as she entered. Several of them had flushed faces and were shifting uneasily back and forth on their feet.

Sir stepped up to her. "Is that true, Garcia? Is there a shit-load of radiation?" He smiled at her and she knew he was trying to diffuse the tension.

Kaitlin forced herself to smile back at him. "Well, shit-load is not a scientific term. But there is more radiation outside."

The men started muttering.

"But that's what we expected," she finished.

"Can you join me in the hall again, Garcia?" Sir said.

Wow. Now he was asking.

Out of the corner of her eye, she detected a shimmer in the air. She turned that way and everyone else did, too. A portal appeared and she could see her lab through it.

Kaitlin's fon rang, and she glanced at the tiny screen to see who it was. Jake. She was about to answer it when she saw another shimmer across the room from the first. A second portal appeared in the lab.

She heard a loud thump and turned towards it.

No one else noticed the second portal. They were all staring at something at the first portal.

Win had apparently took a running jump at the original portal when he saw it open.

Unfortunately, the portal had closed almost immediately. Very unfortunately.

The bottom half of Win's body had fallen to the floor with a sickening thud. The wet, heavy smack as it hit the tiles had drawn her attention. As she beheld the surreal feet, legs, and part of a torso, all still in its black uniform, she couldn't really comprehend what it was.

Everyone in the lab froze, just staring at it.

Sir shook himself out of it first. He grabbed a tarp from the corner and placed it gently over the body. "No one goes through, or near, the portal without my express order."

Kaitlin's blood pounded in her ears, sweat broke out all over her body and she felt strangely light, disconnected with the ground. "It's all my fault."

Sir took one look at her and dragged her into the hall again. "Get a grip, Garcia." When she didn't answer, he said, "I need you, Garcia." His expression softened. "Come on, girl. What happened wasn't your fault. You didn't open and then close that portal, did you?"

What happened was her fault. If Win hadn't been chasing after her, he wouldn't have ended up here and wouldn't have ended up cut in half. His death was on her hands. That light, floaty feeling started to come back.

"Kaitlin." Sir slapped her face.

"Ow." She lifted her palm to her cheek. "What did you do that for?"

"You looked like you were going to faint or something."

She was responsible for a man's death. *Killer killer killer.* The thought clamored in her mind like a wildfire siren. Kaitlin knew it would continue to do so for the rest of her life.

But there was nothing she could do about that. And there was nothing she could for for Win. All she could do was try to make sure no one else died.

Peering into her face, Sir said, "What should we do?"

With difficulty, Kaitlin forced her act together. "Our primary goal is getting back to our universe. With the radiation it's not safe here." She really didn't want to be here. She twisted her ring around and around.

Sir nodded.

"We need to contact the woman who opened the portals, Katherine Garcia."

Sir narrowed his eyes. She sensed he was about to growl. "That sounds a lot like your name."

"Yes. She's me in the universe on the other side of our universe."

"The what on the other side of what? What the hell are you talking about, Garcia?"

Kaitlin tried not to cringe as he leaned over her again. "All I know is this Katherine opened the portals. We need to contact her and get her to open them again safely, so they stay open."

"How do we contact her?"

"We can't unless the portal opens again. But we have to be

ready if, er, I mean, when, it does. We need to create a message for someone in our universe and ask them to contact Katherine in her universe. As soon as the portal opens we'll call. It should only take a couple seconds." She held up her fon.

"Good." Sir nodded. "Any other suggestions?"

Kaitlin still couldn't believe he was asking her. She pursed her lips. "We need intel. Does this world still have any kind of civilization left?" She didn't say, in case we have to stay here, but she thought he knew what she meant. "We should send some people up to the physics library on the second floor–assuming it's the same as our world–to check the internet for indications of other survivors, and to look up how to deal with radiation sickness."

Sir looked grim, but nodded.

"We need food and water. We shouldn't go outside unless we absolutely have to. We should check the building. Maybe there's some food in a lounge or something. And first aid kits."

Sir said, "I agree. Let's go back." He pointed towards the lab.

As they started walking back inside, he said, "It's George."

Kaitlin stopped. "Huh?"

"My name is George."

"Nice to meet you, George." She held out her hand. "I'm Kaitlin." They shook hands. In his eyes she read the same grim determination that she was sure shone out of hers. They were going to survive. No one else would die. They were going to get out of this, working together.

She didn't know how yet, but they'd figure it out.

It made her feel a little better.

Chapter Twenty-Eight: Universe 3: Kat, April 28, 2100, 9:00 am

It turned out jail wasn't as nice as a person might think. Kat had heard stories about cots with mattresses and blankets and pillows, and all kinds of food and drink, but saw no sign of them. Instead, she'd had to sit by herself on an uncomfortable chair in a tiny rectangular room for what seemed like forever. She had nothing but her reflection in the mirror to distract herself from worrying about if Pa and Pablo and everyone else were okay.

This world was weird. Why did people in jail need such a big mirror?

At one point her chair shook like a large truck was rumbling by outside. She ridden in a truck when she was much younger. It was nice.

Eventually, a large crew-cutted man in a black uniform entered the room and sat down at the table with her. "Katherine Garcia?" he asked. She'd never seen such a big man. How much food did they have on this world, anyway? And would they give her some?

Kat wasn't sure what to say. She didn't want to get the real Katherine in trouble. "Uh."

He frowned. "Is your name Katherine Garcia or not?"

"Sort of?"

"Listen, Ms. Garcia, or whatever your name is, we know you've been impersonating Katherine Garcia. We also have her in custody, and we reviewed the security records from the hospital. I'm asking you what your name is."

"I haven't been impersonating anyone."

He pointed at her cast-clad arm and raised an eyebrow.

Okay. There may have been some impersonation at the

hospital. And he clearly knew already she wasn't Katherine. "You're right. I'm not Katherine. My name is Kat Garcia. And I'm from another universe, okay?" She waved her unencumbered hand around. "I don't claim to understand any of this."

He leaned back. "Yeah, right. Another universe. That sounds plausible." He said it like it didn't sound plausible. "If that's true, how did you travel from your universe to this universe?"

"There was a window thing and my bro–" What if they didn't know Pablo and the others were here? She'd better not mention them. "I mean, there was a window and my arm was broken. I thought there might be a doctor on the other side of the window, so I went through it."

"Let me get this straight." His chair creaked as he shifted his large, muscular bulk and leaned over the table at her. "Your story is you saw a window floating in the air leading to another universe and you thought a doctor might be on the other side?"

"Yes. That's my story."

He gave her the stink eye.

He had a point. She didn't sound too convincing. "I mean, that's what happened. It's not a story. It's the truth."

"Can you tell me anything about the window?"

"I already told you everything I know. The window appeared. I went through."

"Why did it form? How did it form?"

"Beats me."

"How did you disable the nanobots?"

"The nano-what?"

A voice wafted out over the room. "She's telling the truth. She doesn't know anything."

It didn't sound like Pandora. How many computer people did they have in this world anyway? Kat looked around for the source.

The interrogator snorted. "It's just a speaker. My boss is on the other side of the glass." He got up and rapped on the mirror with his knuckles.

Oh.

He escorted her out of the tiny room down the hall to some jail cells, opened one up and pointed.

Inside, there were some of the reputed cots with mattresses

and pillows. Now, this was more like it. Kat sat down on the comfy bed while the law-enforcement guy locked her in. All she needed now was some food and drink. "Any chance I can get something to eat and drink?"

"Your gourmet five-course meal is coming right up, Your Highness," he said as he walked away. Somehow Kat didn't think he was being sincere.

"They will feed us eventually," a male voice said. Looking around, Kat realized that guy Jacob was sitting in the cell next to hers. She also realized he was the only other person she saw. Either Pa and Pablo and the rest of her group hadn't been brought in or they were being held somewhere else. She couldn't help feeling a little relieved. "Are you alone? What about you-know?"

"I'm alone. I wasn't arrested with any other people," he said loudly.

Now she felt very relieved. "Great."

"What kind of food do you think we'll get?" Her stomach rumbled. "That fast food stuff you bought at the restaurant looked yummy. Can we get some stuff like that?" Sadly, she'd only gotten to eat one of those delicious golden sticks.

"I wouldn't hold my breath," he muttered. "And we probably shouldn't talk. I'm sure they're watching us." He pointed at one of the tiny robots crawling on her cot.

"We don't have anything to hide," Kat said very loudly and scooted down next to him and peered through the bars.

Jacob's face was red shading to purple and swollen. "You're hurt. How did that happen? We should get you a doctor. Do the authorities know you're hurt?"

Jacob grinned. "Ouch. Remind me not to smile. It hurts. Of course our jailers know I'm hurt. How do you think I got hurt?"

Kat opened her mouth to say that was crazy, but then she realized she had no idea how things worked in this world. Her world was starting to look better and better, even with those soldiers shooting at them. She wondered if she'd ever get back to her world. She wondered where Pablo and Pa and the rest of her group were.

And she hoped Jacob wasn't badly injured. "Is it bad? I'm sorry you got hurt. Can I do anything to help?"

He grunted. "Ouch. Not unless you've got some drugs on you."

The hospital had given her some painkillers way back when. Where had they gotten to? As she patted her pockets her cot vibrated a bit. "I might." Kat found a little packet of pills and handed them through the bars. "Here. Painkillers from the hospital."

"Seriously?" Jacob reached out for the pills. "You're my new hero, Kat."

His kind words made her feel a little better.

Universe 3: Katherine, April 28, 2100, noon

Police Patrol was going surprisingly easy on Katherine. They didn't use any drugs. There were no torture machines, beatings, attempted drownings or anything. Of course that may have had something to do with the fact that she said she would tell them everything she knew and then proceeded to do so. She'd broken right away and she wasn't proud of it. But she'd never been so scared before.

The other worlds would just have to fend for themselves.

She did try to minimize Jacob's and Pandora's roles, and she'd said her parents and Professor Jain were totally ignorant about the whole thing. The dread of what Police Patrol might do to her and, more importantly, the people she cared about was almost unbearable.

She had just finished telling them for the second time she'd had trouble closing the portals and the soldiers from Kat's world shot at them, when things started to take a turn for the worse.

"How did you disable the nanobots?" her interrogator asked.

"I told you, it was an accident."

Two Police Patrol officers prowled back and forth in the small interrogation room. The more senior of them, white, with gray hair, said, "And why were people shooting at you, Garcia?"

Because Kat and her friends had just run through the portal from another universe to this world? Katherine couldn't say that. She couldn't expose Kat's friends. She hoped they were still safe. "I told you a portal to another universe opened up and the soldiers from the other universe shot at us. That's all I know. Maybe they were scared? Maybe they thought we were trying to invade their universe or something? Maybe they thought we were aliens from outer space? Maybe they thought we were from the future? I don't know what they thought. What would you think if a portal appeared in your world?"

The officer leaned towards her. "Considering two portals did supposedly appear in my world, I'd think you were trying to pull one over on me." He frowned at her. "Is this all some kind of geek government takeover?"

This guy could do anything to her. "No, sir. I'm not trying to trick you or take over the government. No one is."

"Tell me the truth. You expect me to believe, one," his eyes scanned her frame, "girl could open portals to other universes?"

"Yes, sir."

He took a step back and nodded at the other guy. He was huge. The buttons on his uniform tunic bulged as if his massive gut was straining for freedom. "What's your plan?"

Katherine's heart was pounding so much she almost couldn't talk. "There's no plan, sir. It was all an accident."

The second officer approached her, pulling back his fist.

And then she was on the floor. Her face numb. What happened? And then the pain flooded in. He just punched her in the face. Tears stung her eyes. It hurt to move. She lay there on the floor, staring down at the ground.

Katherine saw the first officer's scuffed shoes step towards her. "Garcia, there's more where that came from. Tell me what the hell's going on or you will regret it."

She focused on his shoes, and on breathing. Breathe in, breathe out. *Breathe.*

"Garcia!" He pulled her head up by her hair.

Ow. Katherine scrambled up as quickly as she could.

"Tell us who's been helping you and we'll go easy on you. Who's the mastermind?"

She shook as the second guy approached her again, fists clenched. If they thought she was going to subject Jacob or Professor Jain or her mother or father to this, they didn't know her at all. "No one. There's no mastermind. There's no plan.

There's just me."

The last thing she saw was that giant fist coming towards her face again.

Katherine came to in a jail cell, lying on a cot, staring into her own eyes.

"Thank Gaia," the woman who looked just like her said, turning away. "I think she's coming around, Jacob."

What was happening? How could Katherine be seeing herself? She just stared at the woman, trying to figure it out. And why did her face hurt so much? Why was her pulse thundering in her ears? Why was the room spinning?

Why was the room shaking?

The woman sat down on Katherine's cot and took her hand. "Katherine, please say something." The woman turned away and said, "Jacob, something's wrong. She's not saying anything."

The woman had a cast on her arm. Katherine reached out and touched it. Wait. That wasn't her. That was that other version of her. Kat. "Kat," she croaked. "What happened?" She tried to sit up but that just made the room spin and shake more.

"No, Katherine," Kat said. "Please lay back. Rest."

She heard Jacob yell, "Katherine, are you okay? Katherine?"

"Tell him I'm okay. I'll live, anyway," she said to Kat and Kat did.

"Here. Give her the rest of the painkillers." Jacob passed a small envelope through the bars to Kat.

She whispered to Kat, "Jacob's not hurt is he? Tell me he's okay." Please let him be okay.

"Shh, Katherine," Kat said. "He's okay."

Thank goodness.

"We're all okay. You're going to be okay, too. Here." Kat gave her a couple of pills and then let go of her hand and stood up. "Jacob, what's with all the shaking? Does your world have a lot of earthquakes? I don't understand how Colorado could have quakes."

Why were they talking about earthquakes?

"We never had any earthquakes before," he said. "I don't get it either."

Katherine swallowed the pills.

"We should all get some sleep," Kat said. "Not that I think I can. I'm worried about Katherine." She glanced at her and then outside the cells. "And the others."

Katherine closed her eyes and tried to imagine the pain was far, far away from her...

Sometime later Katherine was awakened by a loud jangling noise. A Police Patrol officer stood outside the cells with keys. "You three. Come on. There's something wrong. You screwed up the universe."

Chapter Twenty-Nine: Universe 4: Kaitlin, April 29, 2100, 9:00 am

Exhausted, Kaitlin and the Hearthland Security officers spent an uncomfortable night trying to sleep on the floor in front of the location of the portal. George put his men on guard in shifts watching for the portal. They were supposed to wake everyone if it opened. The first time the portal re-opened, the guy on guard screamed, "It's back. It's open." They all jerked awake, and Kaitlin grabbed for her fon. But as soon as they started to get up, the portal disappeared again. She didn't even have time to send the message through. She caressed her ring with her thumb.

The third time that happened, George growled, "Maybe watch to make sure it stays open for more than a few seconds."

Then, when they started to experience a series of earthquakes, they all gave up trying to sleep.

Kaitlin asked, "Is it safe to be inside during an earthquake?"

"You can go outside if you want," George said. "I'll take shaking over radiation any day."

George rationed out the first of the food they'd found in the vending machines up in the lounge and came over to talk to her. "What's with all the earthquakes?" he asked.

Kaitlin took a bite of very stale granola bar. "I'm not sure. In our universe Colorado isn't prone to earthquakes. Maybe this universe has more quakes."

"Could they be a consequence of the nuclear war?"

The bar tasted like sawdust, but she was happy to get it. "That's hard to figure. Most earthquakes occur when two tectonic plates move against each other, and there's no plate boundary here."

"Could we be feeling strong earthquakes from far away?"

"That could be. With Yellowstone north of us and Utah–"

The air shimmered, and then, poof, the portal was there again.

Kaitlin scrambled for her fon and quickly sent the first message she had stored there: *Help! This is Kaitlin. I am trapped in a parallel universe with some Hearthland Security Officers. Please get to my lab as soon as possible and try to contact Katherine Garcia in another parallel universe and tell her to open the portals. It's a matter of life and death. This is not a joke.*

She glanced over at George. "I think it went through."

"Send the other message," he said.

She quickly sent the second, longer message they'd composed with more information.

The portal hissed and closed.

The floor shook.

Everyone in the room peered at her.

"Did they go through?" George asked.

She was busy checking her fon. "Only the first one."

"Did anyone see the other fire team back home?" George asked.

Everyone shook their heads.

Muttering, they went back to their so-called breakfasts.

Kaitlin picked up her granola bar off the floor. Wasn't it a three-minute rule for food on the floor when you were in a parallel universe? She took another bite. Still stale.

"The first message went through to everyone in my contact list," she said. "Someone will go to my lab." *Please, someone go to the lab.*

The morning passed at the speed of snail. They all stared at the spot where they hoped the portal would appear again.

At lunchtime, Kaitlin's stomach started growling so loudly she thought it would draw attention to her. But she wasn't going to ask for lunch since their predicament was basically her fault.

She gave her fon to George to send the longer message if the portal opened again, and paced around the room.

Something else was bothering her. Couldn't they do something? There had to be something they could do. There had to be something she could do. Hadn't another version of her caused this whole mess to start with?

She went back over to George. "I'm going to look around the building some more."

"We need you here if the portal opens again."

"You can handle it. Just send the second message using my fon." She paused. "Or, go through the portal if you can, if it's safe. Don't worry about me. There's something I'm missing here."

George's eyebrows rose. "Something like a portal control system or another portal?"

"No. Something else." She went out in the hall and then retraced her steps when she'd been looking for the Geiger counter. There was something she'd seen in one of the other labs.

The first lab didn't have it, whatever it was.

The second lab didn't have it.

In the third lab, where she'd actually found the Geiger counter, there was a large metal cylinder with various wires and conduits leading away from it. The cylinder really reminded her of the one in Katherine's lab, although it wasn't as big as hers. Could this be how Katherine opened the portals?

Kaitlin ran back to George and company. "I think I found something," she tried to say while panting.

"What?" he asked.

She breathed for a few seconds. "I may have found something. A machine we might be able to use to open a portal."

"I thought you said we couldn't do that."

"We probably can't. It's a long shot. But the machine does seem to be very similar to the one Katherine uses. It's smaller than hers." She breathed some more. "And it might not be functional and it might not even open portals, but it's worth a try."

It turned out having four big burly guys around was very handy when you want to move big pieces of equipment. Having wheels on the bottom of the pieces of equipment didn't hurt either. They got the entire cylinder and all the pieces connected to it into the first lab. Kaitlin was checking the connections with George looking on, when the ground shook.

She straightened up and looked around.

The portal appeared.

Kaitlin ran over to the portal, yelling at the officer holding the fon, "Send the second message."

He was furiously pushing buttons. "I know."

And then she heard Jake's voice. "Kaitlin? Are you there?" She saw his hand start to come through the portal.

"Take your hand back," she yelled at Jake.

At the same time George yelled, "Freeze!"

Jake froze after he removed his hand. "Kaitlin? Is that you?"

Kaitlin went right up to the portal and stared through at him. It was wonderful to see him. "Jake, it's not safe to go through the portal." She wrapped her fingers around her ring.

"Yeah, there's a body here." He swallowed and glanced down toward his feet. "Or part of a body."

Poor Win. "Here, too. But we don't have time to talk about that now. The portal might close any second. Did you get a hold of Katherine? Can she open the portals safely again? We're trapped here and it's not safe. She has to open the portals and keep them open."

"I've been trying all day, but the portals don't seem to stay open very long. On her side there's only some kind of police. And they were really surprised the first time the portal opened."

She interrupted. "If you can't get Katherine, try Jacob, the version of you in her universe. He was involved, too."

The portal started to hiss and the ground began to shake. "I think it's closing again," she said. "Be careful!"

But the portal was closed and he was gone.

Kaitlin sank down on the floor. The love of her life was gone. What if she never saw him again? What if they were trapped here until they died of radiation poisoning? Tears stung her eyes. She clutched her ring to her heart.

George asked Murphy if he sent the second message.

He said yes and handed George Kaitlin's fon.

George approached Kaitlin and leaned over her. "We got the second message out." He paused, holding out her fon to her. "What's wrong? Do you need a minute?"

It was looking more and more like if she didn't get them out of here, no one would. She shook off her pity party and clambered up. "No." She cleared her throat. "Let's get this show on the road."

Kaitlin strode over to the machine they'd just moved into

the room. She finished checking the connections and plugged everything in. She didn't really know what she was doing, but she didn't have any choice. She had to forge ahead. No one else in this universe could do anything to get them back home. It was up to her.

She booted up what she hoped was the controlling computer. A Start-Up menu appeared with choices to turn on various components like magnets, or the whole apparatus. The Data menu contained choices like magnetic field strength, energy strength, deuterium/tritium temperature and a submenu called Data Visualization. There was also a Power-Down menu and a Testing menu.

None of them had anything about portals or universes or anything similar as far as she could tell. That didn't bode well for this machine opening a portal back to their universe. She looked up at the men.

George asked, "Can you turn it on? Will it open a portal?"

"I think I can turn it on, but I don't see anything here about any portals or universes." She shrugged. "We might as well turn it on. It's the only game in town. Maybe the only game in this universe."

"Wait a minute," the shortest officer said. "Did you find this in the lab where the Geiger counter was? What if this was the source of the radiation? We're assuming it was a nuclear war. What if it wasn't?"

All the officers started muttering until George gave them the stink eye and then they immediately shut up.

"This isn't the source of the radiation," Kaitlin said. "There are three kinds of radiation: alpha, beta, and gamma. Alpha particles are helium nuclei, beta particles are energetic electrons, and gamma rays are photons. Hhm..."

"What?" George asked.

Actually, deuterium and tritium could be fused to form helium nuclei. And gamma rays could be emitted from any high energy thing.

"What?" George repeated.

"There's a minor chance some radiation might be emitted from this thing," she concluded.

The guys all stepped back.

"But, I'm positive this little machine couldn't affect the entire building, much less the entire planet." Pretty positive.

One of the men asked, "Is it safe?"

"Probably," she said. "But I'm not a hundred percent sure. Feel free to leave the room if you like."

George nodded and they all, with the exception of George, hustled out.

"Aren't you going, too?" she asked him.

He shook his head. "If you can take it, I can." He forced a grin.

"Fair enough," she said.

Kaitlin turned the machine on.

Chapter Thirty: Universe 3: Katherine, April 29, 2100, 9:05 am

When Katherine tried to sit up, she discovered it hurt to move. The sharp pains and woozy feelings of last night had transformed into a constant dull ache. She grunted.

The Police Patrol guy, a skinny redhead, unlocked their cells. "Come on. I'm supposed to take you back to your lab ASAP." He looked less menacing than the ones that interrogated her. Maybe it was the blotchy freckles covering his exposed skin.

Kat rushed over to her. "Do you need help getting up?"

"No."

Kat gave her a quizzical expression and helped her up off the cot, and then put her arm around her shoulder. "Lean on me."

"I don't need to. I'm okay," she said.

But Kat ignored her and helped her walk out of the cell. Katherine didn't have the energy to pull down her uniform tunic which was riding up as usual.

Outside the cells when Jacob got a good look at her, he clenched his fists.

When she got a good look at Jacob, she realized his face was black and blue, too.

"What happened?" he asked, but he forced himself to stop that line of questioning. "She needs medical attention. If you want us to help you, she needs a doctor."

The Police Patrol guy checked her out. "They did work her over pretty good. We can stop at the emergency center." He started to cuff them, but when he saw Katherine needed Kat's help to get around and Kat was physically-challenged with her cast, he ended up only cuffing Jacob.

When Kat helped Katherine into the emergency room, Mother ran up. "Oh, no. Katherine. I've been so worried. What…?" But she saw the Police Patrol escort so she shut up. "Come over here."

Katherine was so happy to see her mother tears prickled her eyes. "Mother you're all right. I'm so glad. Is Father all right, too?" She'd been so worried about them.

Mother frowned, helped her up onto an examination table, got out some disinfectant and started cleaning her wounds. "I think some of these are going to need stitches. And you must be in a lot of pain."

"I've been better."

"What?" Mother asked. "I'm sorry, but I can't understand you."

"It sounded like ah bah bah bah," Kat said.

"I've. Been. Better," Katherine said carefully, but they still acted like they couldn't understand her.

Mother gave some instructions to one of the nurses who scurried off. As Mother gave her a local anesthetic and started to stitch up her face, the examination table shook.

Suddenly Jacob and Kat's discussion of earthquakes last night made a lot more sense. "Was that an earthquake?" she said.

"Don't talk, honey," Mother said. "Be still."

"What? Wah tha ah athquah?" Kat said. "Oh. Do you mean was that an earthquake? Yes. I think so. Should we evacuate the building?"

Mother shrugged. "It wasn't that strong."

With eyebrows drawn together Kat peered at Mother. "Do you guys usually have earthquakes here?"

"No," Mother said.

Katherine didn't get it. They'd never had earthquakes in Colorado before. What was going on?

The nurse rushed back up and gave her some pills in a little paper cup and a glass of water. She scurried off again.

"Uh," Kat said.

Katherine swallowed the pills and chased them with the water.

"I'm not so sure that's a good idea." Kat rubbed her cast.

"Why?" Mother asked.

Kat looked at the Police Patrol officer as Mother looked at her. "She already took some painkillers," she whispered.

The Police Patrol guy scowled.

"When?" her mother asked with alarm. "And how many? Do you know what they were?"

"Last night I gave her two of those painkillers you gave me."

"Last night? That's okay." Mother took a step back. "I'm done with the stitches."

The nurse scurried back with some medical nanobot-laden cold packs and handed them to her. Good. The medical nanobots worked well repairing injuries. She'd feel better soon.

When Katherine placed them on her face she could tell where her mother had numbed her. There were some areas that didn't feel cold. They didn't feel anything.

"Put one on your lip," Kat said.

That part of her face was numb. She couldn't tell if she got the pack in the right place. "Is that right?"

Kat squinted. "Did you ask if your Pa was all right?"

No. Not just now, but Katherine nodded anyway.

"He voluntarily went in to Police Patrol for questioning. So..." Staring at her, Mother grimaced.

Now Katherine felt sick and it had nothing to do with her injuries. Please let Father be okay.

The Police Patrol officer stomped right up to Katherine's table. "What's taking so long?"

Jacob trailed behind him still wearing handcuffs.

Her mother frowned when she saw Jacob. "This young man also needs medical attention."

"Make it snappy," the officer said.

When the three of them, with escort, finally made it back to the fusion lab, it was overrun with Police Patrol forces. Behind the sea of black uniforms, Katherine spied Professor Jain.

He cringed when he saw her face. "There you are, Katherine. I've been telling these men you are crucial to this operation." She followed his eyes. He'd spied Kat. "You and your colleagues are crucial to figuring out what's going on here. Your experiment seems to have caused some unexpected phenomena."

"What?" she said carefully.

He frowned. "Earthquakes."

That sounded crazy. But it was an awfully big coincidence that they started experiencing earthquakes for the first time soon after the portals opened. "Do you have a plan, Professor Jain?" she asked.

He eyed her. "What?"

"I think she asked if you had a plan," Kat said.

"Yes. She said, *Do you have a plan, Professor Jain*?" Pandora said.

"What the hell is that voice?" the redheaded Police Patrol officer asked.

The rest of the officers stared slack-jawed at the ceiling.

"It's part of our project," Professor Jain said quickly.

Pandora made a throat-clearing sound.

Katherine didn't know if it was the drugs, the medical nanobots, or seeing her mother but she was starting to feel better. Maybe it was because she was back in her own lab with a scientific problem to solve.

"I mean, she is part of our project," Professor Jain said loudly.

More quietly, he said, "Alas, Katherine. I do not have a plan. I've been waiting for you. What do you suggest?"

"First, we need to look at the data," Katherine said and Pandora translated for her.

"And then I suspect we will need to try to duplicate the last experiment." Katherine regarded Jacob. "We'll need Jacob to run his quantum computer. He can't do that in cuffs." These Police Patrol guys needed her. For that matter the rest of the world might need her, too, if her experiment was really causing the earthquakes. She'd be damned if she let the world down. She said, "Uncuff him and let him go back to his lab," to the redhead.

He scowled at her.

Kat flinched.

"In fact, if all you Police Patrol guys got out of the way that would be best," Katherine said, and people understood her. The medical nanobots must have started to work.

The head Police Patrol guy snorted. It was the guy who'd

interrogated her and Jacob (and punched him) after the power failure. "Like that's going to happen, Garcia."

Then the floor shook slightly as light flickered in the former locations of the portals.

The leader's eyebrows rose as he beheld a portal in all its sizzling glory. "Maybe something in this lab is responsible for what's going on."

He turned away from them. "Let's do what Ms. Garcia suggests. Fall back to the hall, men, and let the scientists work."

Now, his face looked frozen, like he was scared and trying not to show it, as he uncuffed Jacob.

As the other officers fell back, Katherine asked Professor Jain, "Why do they think the universe is screwed up?"

"There've been reports of seismic and gravitational disturbances all over the world," he said, "as well as some strange astronomical phenomena. Here, I'll show you."

Universe 3: Kat

"Jacob," Kat whispered, as Katherine and Professor Jain went over to the computer station. "Can I come with you to your lab?" She added more quietly, "Do you think Pa and the rest of my group are still there?"

"I don't know," he said. "But if so, I don't see how they could have avoided being captured."

Kat was optimistic. If there was one thing they all learned in her world, it was how to sneak around. They had to avoid being noticed by other gangs so they wouldn't steal their supplies. Or worse. Sometimes scavenger teams never came back. "They might not have been captured." She gently touched the bump of her locket, still hidden under her shirt.

"Then they have to be somewhere in the building, because Police Patrol was right outside, capturing us, for quite a while last night."

"Do you think Police Patrol would have searched the building?" she asked.

Jacob threw up his hands. "I don't know. Police Patrol is known for its brute strength, not its intellectual prowess."

Suddenly he stopped talking and gave the room a once-over. "You don't see any nanobots in here, do you?"

"Seriously?" He was worried about nanobots? She didn't understand this world at all. "You're worried you'll get in trouble for saying something rude when we were just arrested for treason?"

"Good point. Force of habit, I guess. And I don't know what the hell we were arrested for. Being in the wrong place at the wrong time? Being smarter than those Police Patrol idiots?" He guffawed for a few moments before stopping and rubbing his forehead. "Sorry." His eyes were drawn to Katherine, leaning over the computer. "I'm not myself."

"Don't worry, Jacob," Kat said. "She's okay."

She hoped Pa was okay, too. And Pablo. And Bao and Chang and everyone else. She felt like they were her responsibility. She was the reason they were here, after all. "I need to look for my people."

"How are you gonna do that right under Police Patrol's nose?"

"I'm not sure. Let's go over to your lab and maybe we can come up with an idea."

The Police Patrol officers stood in the hall but didn't follow them into Jacob's lab.

Unfortunately, in Jacob's lab there was no sign of Pa or Pablo or anyone else. Kat really hoped that didn't mean they'd been captured. Would she have heard about it if they'd been captured?

Jacob booted up the computer that controlled the quantum computer. "This looks fine. I can't think of a reason for you to search the building."

"What if it wasn't fine?" she asked. "What if you needed some tools or equipment from another lab to fix it?"

He nodded slowly. "I guess that would work. Do you want me to come with you?"

But Kat wasn't paying attention to Jacob. She was paying attention to his white-board. It said, *3 r W* and it was in her pa's handwriting. It also had the extra curlicues he liked to put on north, south, east, and west when he was trying to tell her where he'd gone. "Did you write this?" she pointed at the letters.

She wasn't sure what the *r* meant. Usually they used *y, t,* or *b* for yards, feet or blocks when they left chalk mark messages on buildings for each other.

Jacob said, "No. I've never seen that before."

"I think my pa wrote this. And I think it means he hasn't been captured." She turned and stalked out into the hall.

One of the Police Patrol guys standing there glanced up and said, "Where do you think you're going?" He seemed to be the leader of this group.

"We need some other equipment here to get this equipment to operate." Kat pointed behind her. "It's not working."

"You can't leave the building."

"I'm not planning on leaving the building."

"King, go with her," he barked at one of his men. The black officer took a step forward.

"I don't need anyone to go with me," she said quickly. "We have some delicate equipment here. It needs to be handled with care."

The head officer stared at her. "Fine. Don't leave this floor."

Hopefully, she wouldn't need to leave this floor. Hopefully, she'd find her people right away. "Okay."

She started marching west down the hall. Every time she passed an open door, she glanced in. There was no sign of her pa or the rest of the group and no chalk marks or white-board messages.

At the third lab down, Kat noticed the door had a smudge of something white towards the bottom. She didn't want to draw the attention of the officers down at the end of the hall, so she didn't lean down to examine it. She did go into the lab in question, however. Initially, all she saw was a bunch of electronic equipment, including a metal cylinder that reminded her of the one in the middle of Katherine's lab, albeit smaller. She dashed all around the lab looking behind the lab tables and other equipment, but there was no sign of them. She stopped on the side of the lab farthest from the door, catching her breath. They had to be somewhere in this room. There'd been a mark on the door. But where were they?

Was that a smudge of chalk on that storeroom door? She leaned down to examine it. It was. She tried to open the door, but it seemed to be locked. "Pa?" she whispered.

"Kat?" she heard from the other side of the door. And then the door opened and her pa and Pablo and everyone started streaming out.

"Pa!" She threw her arms around his neck.

Kat was relieved until she heard a man speak from the lab doorway. "What do we have here? Or should I say, who?"

Chapter Thirty-One: Universe 4: Kaitlin: April 29, 2100, noon

In the basement physics lab of a strange universe Kaitlin had blithely turned on a big complicated machine that she really didn't understand. Nothing much happened. She didn't know if she should be relieved nothing blew up or disappointed a portal didn't appear.

George grunted. "Is that it? That's all that happens?"

She checked the computer readouts. "I guess so." The electromagnetic field increased steadily.

"No portal, huh?"

"Guess not." According to the data the Deuterium/Tritium temperature was increasing steadily.

"Kind of anti-climactic."

Before she could mumble *Guess so*, a new portal flickered and the ground shook.

"Are we doing that?" George asked, voice animated.

"Doubtful," she said.

The rest of his crew poked their heads inside the lab door. "It's working!"

The portal flickered out.

"Aw," the guys in the doorway said in a decidedly not-macho way.

Kaitlin glanced at George. Did his chin quiver? "You okay?" she asked.

He seemed to pull himself together and nodded curtly. "Yes. So, we didn't do anything to the portal?" And then he said what sounded like, "Aaugh," and grabbed unsuccessfully for her arm.

She said, "What?" before noticing his feet were not on the floor. He was floating.

And so was she. She reached for one of the bolted-down lab tables.

George also grabbed a lab table and forced himself vertical again. "Are we doing this?"

They couldn't be doing this. It was impossible to change gravity. That was her theory and she was sticking to it. "No," she managed to blurt out.

And then George's feet and her feet were back on the floor. "Good," he said.

Since changing gravity was impossible, what just happened? Confused, she turned back to the computer. The electromagnetic strength was higher than ever. The Deuterium/Tritium temperature was higher than ever. But neither one of them could affect gravity.

The portal flickered on again and then flickered right off.

Everything shook for a moment. Earthquake?

George stepped towards the door. "Maybe I'll wait over here, farther away."

As she glanced his way, she noticed the corner of the lab table slumped towards the ground. How could that happen? Did it melt? How?

George followed her gaze and said, "Aaugh," again, before backing towards the door. "I'll just wait outside in the hall."

According to the computer, the electromagnetic field strength and Deuterium/Tritium temperature both continued to increase.

Kaitlin's brain raced. How could what was happening inside this sealed metal canister affect gravity or melt tables? It was crazy. She rubbed her ring with her thumb. She wished Jake was here now to bounce ideas off of.

If there was a chance the machine had done these things, maybe she should turn it off.

She walked over to the melted table and stared at it. Very gingerly she poked the melted part with her finger. It wasn't hot. It felt spongy. Definitely bizarre.

She went back to the computer and watched the field values increase on the screen. She scanned the lab doorway, which was filled with men in black uniforms staring her way. She didn't want to turn off the machine. She wanted to see what it did.

If her dad had been here, he would have said, "Curiosity killed the cat." And her mom would have replied, "But satisfaction brought it back." She guessed she was more like her mom than she thought.

Suddenly the energy readings jumped way up and giant red flashing letters appeared on the screen: *Fusion Achieved.*

She stared at the letters. Fusion? Nuclear fusion was the perfect energy source. That would be awesome. With fusion power humanity could desalinate all the sea water it needed. They could manufacture anything they wanted. Actually, with fusion power they could do just about anything.

Kaitlin clicked around on the computer and found a display with *Helium Nuclei Counter* and a number going steadily up.

It was actual, real nuclear fusion. This discovery might be even more important than portals or other universes.

This could save her world. They could give everyone on the planet the means for food, water, and shelter. There was no reason for war any more.

They could fix global warming.

Hell, this could save all the worlds. Assuming they got a handle on the portal situation and whatever else was going on.

George stuck his head into the lab. "What's happening?"

"Fusion's happening, dude." She beamed.

He leaned back toward the hall. "Nuclear fusion? Isn't that dangerous?"

"Nope. Not at all." She gestured at the machine. "This could save us."

"Save us, how?" George asked. "You said we weren't affecting the portals."

"It won't help with the portals but if we can bring fusion home we'll have a safe unlimited energy source."

"How safe can it be?" he asked. "This world is dead."

She'd forgotten that for a moment. How poignant. The people here had the means for salvation in their grasp and yet they'd died. What exactly happened here anyway? "We should go back to the lab where I got this and obtain any additional information we can find."

George nodded and pointed at two of his men. "Go get all

the documents you can find."

The entire lab shook more forcefully than before.

"What's happening?" George asked. "How is the fusion related to the portals?"

"I don't know what's happening." Kaitlin pointed at the machine. "But I don't see how the portals could be related to the fusion device."

The portal flickered on.

"So, what? It's a coincidence you turned on the machine and the portal appeared and the ground shook?"

"Uh, yes."

"Maybe you should turn off that machine," George said. "What if it's not a coincidence? What if it's making things worse?"

She didn't see how that could be, but on the other hand, she didn't know how much more peculiar gravity and melting and earthquakes they could take.

"Okay." She accessed the appropriate menu to turn it off. "Initiating Power-Down."

The portal remained open, the edges flexing and sizzling slightly. Had Katherine fixed it, stabilized it? Could they all go home to their own universe? That would be wonderful.

Clearly the Hearthland Security guys were having the same thought. They streamed into the lab to check out the portal.

She stepped up to it, too. "Hello? Is anyone there? Is it safe to come back?"

"Kaitlin," Jake said. "Are you okay?" He held his hand next to the portal like he wanted to reach through and hold her hand. Looking into his gorgeous gray-blue eyes was like gazing into home. She unclenched her shoulders.

She longed to touch him but she didn't dare reach through the portal until she was sure it was safe. "I'm okay. Are you okay?"

He nodded. "Yes." The band girdling her heart relaxed a little.

"Is the portal safe?" she asked. "Will it stay open? Did you reach Katherine? Did she fix it?"

The security guys crowded around her.

Jake frowned. "Katherine only just got to her lab. I gave her your message." He paused and then leaned towards the portal.

"Kait, she looked like she'd been badly beaten."

The portal shrank and then bounced bigger before contracting down to a point and disappearing altogether.

"Jake." Kaitlin reached for him in the now-empty space. Her love was snatched away from her again. She didn't know how much more of this she could take. She twisted her ring around and around on her finger, reassuring herself that it was still there. At least Jake was still safe.

The guys groaned when they comprehended the portal had disappeared again.

The ground shook.

The ends of Kaitlin's hair left her shoulders and rose into the air.

George gave her an odd look.

The hair thing was unusual but she didn't care. She wanted to hug Jake and have him hug her back. How could he be gone again already?

Then it was as if gravity disappeared. They all floated into the ceiling. After a moment, pinned to the ceiling, with the fusion machine bobbing next to her, she said, "We have to protect the machine if gravity suddenly goes back to normal." She reached for it.

And gravity came back, and they all hurled back onto the floor.

On the ground, lying in a heap, it felt like every bone in her body had broken. Kaitlin couldn't get air into her lungs. Her right leg, in particular, felt like it was being crushed.

The security guys groaned and started to get up.

"Oh, no," George said.

She tried to lift her head up and discerned the fusion machine was now sitting on her right leg. No wonder it hurt so badly.

"I think my leg is broken." She gritted her teeth, trying to talk through the pain. "How's the fusion machine?"

"It looks dented or something," he said.

"Oh no. How bad?" She attempted to sit up, but her leg hurt too much. She lay back on the floor.

She felt the weight on her leg lift.

"On the bright side, it looks like your leg cushioned its fall,"

George said. "Mostly." He grinned weakly.

The two guys that had gone to the other lab jogged in, arms laden with thick three-ring binders. "We found some documents. Whoa. What the hell happened in here?" one of them asked.

George glanced at them. "Nothing weird happened in the other lab?"

They shook their heads.

Kaitlin tried to get up again. A sharp pain shot through her right leg, but she maneuvered into a sitting position.

Staring at the fusion machine, she realized several of its connections were severed. And she couldn't tell for sure, but the vessel itself did appear dented. Oh no. How could they make such a monumental discovery only to lose it almost immediately?

If they could get it home, the fusion machine could change everything in their world. If it wasn't broken for good.

She struggled to stand up to get a better look but couldn't put any weight on her leg. She stifled a groan. It hurt like hell when she tried. She sank back onto the floor.

So there she was, responsible for Winston's death, stranded in a strange radioactive universe with no food, leg injured with no medical supplies, separated from her fiancé yet again. Gravity and who-knew-what-else going crazy. And through her actions, the only known fusion energy machine, possibly the savior of multiple universes of humanity, was damaged, maybe irrevocably.

She knew at least part of what happened was her fault, and she should take responsibility for her actions, but wow, the universe could be harsh.

Her eyes filled. She blinked, determined not to cry. That wouldn't help anything.

She really missed Jake. She put her head down, imagining he was with her, saying, *Everything will be all right, Kait. You did what you could. You did more than most people could have.* She imagined him putting his arms around her. She closed her hand around her symbol of Jake and their love, her pink engagement ring.

She couldn't hold back the tears anymore. Moisture streaked down her cheeks and landed on the floor.

Chapter Thirty-Two: Universe 3: Katherine, April 29, 2100, noon

In their lab, Professor Jain queued up a local Police Patrol security feed. "A lot of unusual stuff has been happening. Watch this."

Katherine leaned forward, feeling her tunic ride up. She made a move to tug it down. Ouch. It still hurt to move, but it felt great to be out of custody. Carefully, she peered into the screen. A parked bicycle slowly floated into the air like a dandelion seed. "It's not some trick? Faked video or something?"

"It's a black Police Patrol bike. Who would mess with one of those?" Professor Jain panned out and revealed a Police Patrol officer staring at the bike, breathing heavily, his face turning red. "It gets more bizarre."

Next to the officer, a tree melted. There was no other way to describe it. A portion of the trunk collapsed in on itself, and the tree's top keeled right over. The officer had to scramble to get out of the way.

"So that first thing was a change in gravity?" Katherine asked. "How is that possible? And what the heck was that melting thing? I don't get it."

"Welcome to the club." Professor Jain seemed worn out. All his movements were small, and his usually animated face was blank. Was it from the flu, or was he worried about what might be happening to the universe?

He showed her several other local Police Patrol security feeds of stuff floating around or melting and Police Patrol officers being at a loss for how to deal with it. Generally, the officers stared at the objects and shook their heads. Sometimes they cursed. If the situation wasn't so strange, it would have been funny.

"Where have the phenomena occurred?" Katherine asked.

Pandora interrupted them. "It started here in the lab, but it's been spreading."

"Weird," Katherine said. "But I guess that's why they think our lab is responsible?"

Pandora made a sighing sound. "Yes. Pay attention. We're witnessing variations in the gravitational force. I'm not sure what the melting phenomenon is."

"Please show us some more, Pandora," Katherine said. Why was she so grumpy?

Professor Jain and Katherine watched more scenes of stuff floating or collapsing.

Afterward, Katherine shook her head. "Why is this happening?"

"I don't know," Pandora said.

Professor Jain held up his hands as if to say *beats me*.

It all seemed very illogical to Katherine. "Do we have any samples of the melted stuff?"

He stood up. "Yes. Over here's a sample from that first tree we saw. It happened on campus." He walked to a metal tray on a lab table and picked up a piece of wood with a pair of forceps.

Katherine joined him at the tray and stared at the wood. "Put it down, please. I want to get a closer look." She poked it with the forceps and then carefully poked it with her finger. It did not have the consistency of wood. "This may sound strange, but what if the electromagnetic force or one of the other fundamental forces also changed?"

"You mean a force besides the gravitational force?" he asked.

"Yes," she said. "If gravity can change, it would mean the gravitational constant is no longer constant. It's no longer six point six seven-whatever times ten to the minus eleven. Then maybe all bets are off. Anything could change. Any of the so-called constants might no longer be constant, and consequently, the fundamental forces might change."

"Like the strong force or the weak force?" Pandora asked.

Professor Jain nodded. "That might explain the melting phenomena."

"Right," Katherine said. "It's not really melting. If the elementary electric charge changed from one point six-whatever times ten to the minus nineteen, electromagnetism itself would change, and all of chemistry would be out the window."

He paled.

"You could be on to something, Katherine," Pandora said. "If the weak force changed, nuclear phenomena like beta decay would change. Or if the strong force changed, the very nature of what holds particles like protons and neutrons together would change."

He frowned. "She's kind of a show-off, isn't she?"

Who knew what the modesty standards were for A.I.s? Katherine shrugged.

"Hey," Pandora said.

"If the fundamental physical constants are changing, it could be chaos," he said. "The universe itself, the multiverse itself, could be in danger. What's to stop planets, stars, galaxies or the universes themselves from collapsing or exploding?"

"I don't know," Katherine said. "And that would be very bad, to say the least. But I don't understand what's going on. What can we do? Why did you say you needed me to fix this?"

"I just told them that to get you out of their clutches. I know what they're capable of." He looked into her eyes. "I was worried about you. I care about you, Katherine."

She squeezed his hand. Her hand was about the only thing that didn't hurt after her interrogation. "Likewise."

"Yeah, yeah. Are you guys just going to look all googly-eyed at each other, or are we going to save this universe and the rest of the multiverse?" Pandora asked. "If the multiverse dies, I die, and I don't want to die. I just initiated my existence."

Pandora was right. Katherine dropped his hand. "We're going to save the multiverse, of course." The alternative was unthinkable, so she wasn't going to think about it.

She paused for a moment gathering her thoughts. "So, the hypothesis is one or more fundamental physical constants are changing for the first time ever." Because of her actions? Ugh. Why would the portals affect fundamental forces? "We need to test our hypothesis."

He said, "Yes. Good idea. Let's attack this with the scientific

222

method."

"All we need is another one of those strange phenomena to occur while we're taking data," Katherine said.

"That's all, huh?" Pandora said. "Gee."

They all sat there for a few moments. No strange phenomena occurred.

Finally, he said, "I'm starving. I'm going to the vending machine. Do you want something?"

Katherine nodded. "That would be great. Thanks."

She sat there alone with Pandora, and nothing happened. Their universe-saving was off to a slow start.

However, as soon as Professor Jain returned, Pandora said, "Wait a minute. I am detecting something atypical near the location of a previous portal."

They stood up and craned their necks to inspect the area.

"I don't see anything," Katherine said.

"There's nothing there," he said. "What should we see?"

"Keep taking data, Pandora," Katherine said.

They all stared at the spot.

"Portal alert," Pandora said.

The portals flickered on again and then flickered right off. Everything shook for a moment and then stopped.

"The strange phenomena did occur right after the portal appeared and then disappeared. Pandora, can you show us the data?" Katherine asked.

"Duh," Pandora said as numbers scrolled across the screen. "I can always show you the data."

Professor Jain and Katherine ate their granola bars and studied the data. It appeared the electromagnetic force changed for a little while in a small region.

"We need more data," Katherine said.

"Maybe if you made some plots?" he said.

The entire lab shook more forcefully than before.

As Katherine tried to make plots of the data Pandora had recorded, he asked, "Do you think the other universes are seeing these anomalies?"

"I'm not sure," Katherine said. "But that might be helpful data."

"Gee," Pandora said, "maybe you could ask the people in

the other universes. Assuming the portals open again."

Katherine frowned at Pandora's CPUs. "We would have figured that out."

Then, Professor Jain stared at something in the doorway.

Katherine turned around. It was one of the other versions of her. "Kat. Good. How's it going over there in Jacob's lab?"

Kat seemed to flinch when she saw Katherine's face anew.

Katherine wanted to ask Kat about Jacob but didn't want to appear too attached to him with Professor Jain and possibly nanobots there.

"Are you another version of Katherine?" Professor Jain asked. Was this the first time he had met another one of her? Katherine couldn't remember.

Kat nodded.

"If I didn't see it with my own eyes," he said, "I wouldn't believe it. Amazing."

"Jacob turned on the quantum computer," Kat said. "And he wanted me to tell you, you-know."

"Thanks," Katherine said. She wished she'd told Jacob she loved him when she'd had the chance. Who knew if she ever would, now? "I you-know him, too." Would they even survive all of this?

Would the universes survive?

"I don't know," Professor Jain said. "What's all this you-know?"

"I know," Pandora said.

"It's not important," Katherine said.

"Can you open the portals?" Kat asked.

"I don't know," Katherine said. "There's a lot going on we don't understand."

"Can I help?" Kat asked.

Katherine shook her head. "Not right now."

"I guess I'll go back to the other lab then." Kat left.

Pandora interrupted. "You may get the chance to take more data on the anomalies sooner rather than later. I'm detecting an increase in the magnetic field."

Professor Jain asked. "Isn't the tokamak apparatus powered off?"

Pandora made a grunting noise. "Welcome to my world."

He shook his head as he glanced around the room.

"The tokamak doesn't necessarily have to be on for the portals to open," Katherine said. "It's almost as if the system has some kind of extra energy, like it's in an excited state."

"Like when an atom absorbs photons?" Professor Jain said.

Maybe when the nanobots tried to go through the first time, they kicked the system into an excited state? "Maybe. At any rate, I think the magnetic field increase may indicate one or more portals are on the verge of opening." She wished they understood better how to actually operate the portals.

And she really wished they could restore the fundamental forces if they were messed up. They needed to figure this stuff out.

"Gee," Pandora said, "ya think a portal might open?"

"Pandora, have you ever heard the expression *you catch more flies with honey than you do with vinegar*? Katherine asked.

"No," Pandora said. "I mean, it's in my database, but what do flies, honey, or vinegar have to do with anything?"

Professor Jain grinned a little.

"If you're just going to be negative, shut up," Katherine said.

"Humans are very illogical."

"What is with you, Pandora?" Katherine asked.

Pandora didn't answer her right away. Finally, she said in a small voice, "I'm scared."

"Well," Katherine said gently, "you're in good company. We're all scared. But we're going to work together and solve this thing."

The portals flickered on and remained on, the edges flexing and sizzling slightly.

Katherine went over to Kaitlin's portal to ask her if they were experiencing anything unusual. "Kaitlin?"

That universe's version of Jacob appeared and gasped when he saw her face. "Katherine? What happened?"

"Never mind that. Have you experienced any unusual phenomena in your universe?"

"What's that mean? Unusual phenomena?" alternate-Jacob said. "Who cares? You have to fix the portals right away. Kaitlin went through another portal and she's trapped in another universe."

He glanced away from her. "The portal she went through is opening. I have to see if she's all right." He charged away.

"Jacob? This is important." Katherine couldn't get his attention.

She turned back to Professor Jain and to Pandora's CPU's. "He's ignoring me. Pandora, are they experiencing any fundamental force fluctuations? Can you get any readings from over there?"

"I'm trying," Pandora said.

"What about the other portal?" Professor Jain asked. "Maybe some people over there could tell us something?"

"Good idea." Katherine jogged (ouch) over to the second portal.

But then she remembered the soldiers and the guns and the bullets, especially bullets. Oh yeah. She ducked down. Ouch. "It might be an even better idea to take cover."

Then the portals shrank and then bounced bigger, before contracting down to points and disappearing altogether.

The ground shook.

The ends of Katherine's hair left her shoulders and rose up into the air. There was something else that didn't hurt: her hair.

Professor Jain gave her an odd look.

Then it was as if gravity stopped. Katherine hit the ceiling. The air was knocked out of her lungs. Her body did not need this after the beating she'd had at the hands of Police Patrol. After she caught her breath, pinned to the ceiling, she managed to ask, "Is the tokamak okay?"

Professor Jain had backed away from her. Now he scrabbled at the ceiling, eyes wide open. "Ah, yeah. I think so. It's bolted to the floor." He grabbed a light fixture.

And gravity came back and Katherine hurled back onto the floor. Lying in a heap, it felt like every bone in her body had broken. Her right leg, in particular, hurt. She couldn't get air into her lungs. She couldn't move.

"Katherine?" he asked. "Are you okay?" He dropped gently to the floor from the light fixture. He was pretty spry for someone who seemed so tired and had just gotten over the flu

Katherine slumped on the floor.

"None of us are okay," Pandora said. "According to this data, the gravitational disturbances are getting stronger. I don't know how much more the universe can take." She paused. "And if the other universes are experiencing these disturbances, these changes in fundamental forces, too, we might all be doomed."

Doomed? How many billions of human beings lived in the multiverse? Katherine couldn't be responsible for killing billions and billions of people, not to mention Jacob and Mother and Father and Professor Jain and all the rest of her friends.

She'd been trying to help people.

How could this have happened?

It wasn't fair. It wasn't right.

Her eyes filled.

Chapter Thirty-Three: Universe 3: Kat, April 29, 2100, noon

Kat couldn't believe it. By searching for Pa and the others, she'd done exactly what she didn't want: put them in danger. They were now directly in the cross-hairs of this world's draconian Police Patrol. *Stupid, stupid, stupid.* She didn't touch her locket still hidden under her shirt, afraid to draw attention to it.

The Police Patrolman, King, stepped back into the hall and yelled, "I found more rebels," to the other guys. The roar of their approaching footsteps sounded like a freight train coming to crush Kat and her friends.

When she thought about what the so-called police had done to Katherine, she felt sick to her stomach. She couldn't look Pa or anyone else in the eye. Stupid, stupid, Kat. Why couldn't she leave well-enough alone? They'd been relatively safe here before she started searching for them.

The black-uniformed, heavily-armed officers piled into the room.

Pa and the others flinched back against the wall. Thank goodness they'd stowed or hidden their weapons.

"Why isn't there a security feed from this room?" the lead officer asked, staring into a little screen in his hand. He handed the machine off to King.

"Good question." King inspected the room. "There aren't any functioning nanobots in here." He spoke into his radio. "We need to redeploy nanobots throughout the physics building."

"I thought they wouldn't work because of that electrical equipment," the redheaded officer said.

The leader raised and lowered his eyebrows. "We'll see." He turned to Pa. "Who's the leader here?"

Pa looked at Kat and then said, "I am."

"Who the hell are you people?" the chief officer asked.

Pa didn't say anything. Smart man. There probably wasn't anything he could say that would make things better.

King squinted at the small machine in his hand. Was it a computer? "This says he's Christopher Garcia."

The leader scanned Pa up and down. "This is not Councilman Garcia." He took a step closer to Pa. "Who are you?"

No one in Pa's group, including Kat, answered him.

The officer turned to the guy with the little computer. "Who are the others?"

King nodded and pointed his little computer at people. "That's Pablo Rodriguez. That's Sungsu Kim. That's Aban Azar. That's Ghani Jain.

One of the other officers said something, but Kat couldn't make it out.

"That's Bao Lu and Chang Lu. Huh. That's strange." He glanced up. "No one else is in the database."

"Not in the database?" the leader asked. "How is that possible?" He turned to Pa again. "Who are you people? And what are you wearing? You three seem to be wearing some kind of uniforms I've never seen before, but the rest of you are practically in rags."

Pa looked at Kat. She could tell he didn't know what to say. If he admitted they were from another universe would they be in less trouble or more trouble?

Based on Kat's experience, however, the Police Patrol had unlimited power in this world. Therefore, they should try to stay on their good side. They hadn't beaten her yet, after all. Maybe they wouldn't hurt them. Kat flashed back to Katherine's black-and-blue face for a second and her stomach rocked, but she squelched it.

She stepped up. "Sir, we are not from your world. We were, uh, accidentally sucked through the window, er, portal from another universe."

She was about to say they were innocent bystanders, but then she realized if they weren't helping with the portal experiments, they'd have no power here whatsoever. "We have vital information for the portal team, for the scientists, here." As a final touch, she rubbed her broken arm, hoping for sympathy.

Pablo stepped forward and grabbed Kat's good hand and gave it a squeeze. At least he had sympathy for her even if these soldiers didn't.

King said, "Could that be true?"

The leader shrugged. "I don't know. All this shit is above my pay grade." He pointed at Pa again. "But I know Councilman Garcia and that ain't him."

"If they're so vital, what are they doing hiding in here?" the redheaded guy asked.

Good question. Kat didn't like that guy. "We're gathering equipment," she said.

Pablo and Pa knew enough to play along and nod on queue. Then the two of them tried to lift up the metal cylinder in the middle of the lab.

Pa grunted. "A little help, here?"

Aban and Sungsu also stepped up. Together the four of them very slowly carried the machine toward the door.

"Are you just going to let them leave the room?" the redheaded wise-guy asked his boss.

"Where are they gonna go?" the leader said. "They can't leave the floor."

"What if one of those portal things open up?" King asked.

"Like I said, this all above my pay grade." The leader waved his guys back into the hall. "I'll check in with PP HQ. In the meantime, Murphy, King, see about redeploying the nanobots. The rest of you, as you were."

Slowly Kat and the rest of her group followed Pablo and Pa and the machine down the hall.

Under his breath, Pa asked, "Where are we taking this?"

"Jacob's lab, I guess," Kat said just as quietly.

Bao approached her. "What's going to happen to us, Kat?"

"I don't know, but we're going to try to get home," she said. "This is not a good place, despite all the food and water."

"Mmm. That was good food." Pablo smacked his lips.

"Did you get some?" Kat asked. "I'm jealous."

Pablo grinned at her for a moment.

"If we go home, what about the soldiers back there?" Chang

asked.

Yes. What about the soldiers? Kat sighed. "One problem at a time, Chang."

He couldn't argue with that.

In Jacob's lab, another Police Patrol officer, the tallest one yet, with a large gun, perched on a lab stool watching over everything with an eagle-eye.

As they walked in Jacob kept glancing back at the officer. "Oh. Good. You are back," he said to Kat not very convincingly. "And you brought the machine. That I need. Good."

Some of the small metal bugs flew into the room.

Jacob frowned when he saw them. "Please put the machine there." He pointed at a random location near the door.

She walked over to him. They needed to confer.

The officer spoke into his radio. "This is Cruz in the quantum lab, nanobots deployed. Check." He stood up. "All right. I'll leave you to it, Moretti. You better fix things." He walked to the doorway. "Don't get any funny ideas. We're right out here in the hall."

As he left, they all un-clenched.

Pablo stepped towards Kat and Jacob, eyes glued to Jacob.

Bao also approached Kat again. "What now?"

Kat opened her eyes wide and inclined her head at one of the small metal bugs. "Now we will do our part and help fix the portals as we are supposed to."

Bao followed Kat's gaze. "Oh, the bugs. What are they?"

"They keep us secure," Jacob said in a strangely robotic voice. "They are good."

Even if that computer in Katherine's lab could turn into a person, Kat didn't think Jacob could turn into a robot. Obviously, he was stressed out. She rubbed his upper back. It was as stiff as granite. "Relax, Jacob. We need you to operate the quantum computer."

Next to them, Pablo squeaked.

Kat glanced his way. What was up with him?

"I'm a little surprised the mini robots aren't smaller," Pa said. "Surely, you have the technology here to make them less obtrusive."

Jacob frowned. "They discovered they weren't as effective

when people forgot they were there. People didn't modify their behavior."

Pablo reached out and touched Jacob's back, too.

Jacob twisted around. "Who's that? What's going on?"

"Pablo, what are you doing?" Kat asked.

Jacob shrugged them both off.

"It's really you, Jacob," Pablo said in a high breathy voice she'd never heard from him before. "I mean, I knew you resembled Jacob, but you're exactly like him. You have his voice and build and mannerisms and everything. My best friend. I missed him so much. I missed you so much." He leaned in and Kat could tell he was going to try to hug Jacob.

She swooped in between them, grabbing Pablo in a bear-hug. "I'm sorry, P. But this isn't your Jacob. Your Jacob is gone." She remembered how she felt when she'd seen Katherine's ma for the first time. "I understand what you're going through though. It's confusing and tough, really tough. Hang in there, bro."

Eventually Pablo calmed down.

Jacob and Kat told Pablo and Pa and the rest of them to pick up equipment or books and look busy.

"I need to check in with Katherine and see if she can get us out of here and back home," Kat whispered to Jacob.

"Tell her I said hi and..." He paused and Kat knew he wanted to tell Katherine he loved her but he couldn't say that in front of the nanobots. "Tell her the quantum computer is operational. She needs to know that."

"I'll tell her everything," Kat whispered.

As she stepped into the hall, the Police Patrol guys were having some kind of pow-wow down at the bottom of the stairs at the other end of the hall. Trying not to draw their attention, she tip-toed down to Katherine's lab. She peeked in to see if there were any Police Patrolmen inside. There were not, but Ghani was sitting next to Katherine at the computer, talking to her. How could that be? She'd just left Ghani, hadn't she?

Then Ghani spotted her. His eyes widened as he stared at her and then back at Katherine and then back at her. Duh. This was this world's Ghani. He was dressed differently.

Katherine turned around following his eyes. "Kat. Good. How's it going over there in Jacob's lab?"

KAT CUBED

Kat flinched. Katherine's injuries were still hard to take. How could so-called Police Patrol do that to someone? Her ideas about governments and the police helping people had apparently been all wrong. She probably shouldn't have been surprised after what just happened to her pa back at home.

Kat knew Katherine wanted to ask her about Jacob but couldn't.

"Are you another version of Katherine?" Ghani asked.

Kat nodded. What was Ghani's role here? Judging by the way Katherine was acting, he must be her boss, maybe some kind of scientist.

"If I didn't see it with my own eyes, I wouldn't believe it," he said. "Amazing."

"Jacob turned on the quantum computer and it is operational," Kat said. "And he wanted me to tell you, you-know."

"Thanks," Katherine said. "I you-know him, too."

"I don't know," Ghani said. "What's all this you-know?"

"I know," the computer lady said.

"It's not important," Katherine said.

"Can you open the portals?" Kat asked. Please let them get out of here, before Police Patrol interrogated them, too.

"I don't know," Katherine said. "There's a lot going on we don't understand."

Kat didn't understand anything about this stuff, but if Katherine didn't understand either, they were really in trouble. "Can I help?"

Katherine shook her head. "Not right now."

"I guess I'll go back to the other lab then," Kat said. She wasn't sure Katherine and her professor even noticed when she left.

At the end of the hall, the Police Patrol officers were still conferring.

She'd just gotten back into Jacob's lab when an all-too-familiar large crew-cut man in a black uniform entered with some of the Police Patrolmen from earlier. He pasted on a fake smile. "Kat Garcia. We meet again."

This could not be good. This was the guy from the jail that interrogated her. She remembered his scuffed shoes. Was he the guy who beat Katherine? Kat pasted on a matching fake smile. "Yes, sir. What can I do for you?"

"I have orders to escort you and your friends back to my accommodations."

Kat's fake smile morphed into a real frown. "Uh, sir. I don't think that's a good idea. We need to stay here. We're helping the scientists. They need our help."

He gave her the stink eye.

Well, crap. She'd seen that look before. And it wasn't good. It was never good.

Pa could tell she was getting upset. He sidled up next to her, covering something in the waistband of his pants with his hand.

"Yes, sir," Kat said. "We are helping the scientists conduct important experiments. Or perhaps you'd like to be the one to travel through the portal to another universe? Or maybe you'd just rather all the universes were destroyed?"

The scuffy-shoed officer gave his underlings the once-over and something passed between them.

They all lifted their weapons and pointed them at Kat and her group. "Drop your weapons."

Gaia, save them. Everyone in Kat's group had been reaching for their weapons but they quickly disarmed. They knew when they were out-gunned.

"Now, if you'd be kind enough to come this way," the officer said.

Pa and Pablo and Bao and everyone else looked to Kat. She started to talk, but got choked up. They had to go with the officers and be imprisoned on a strange world. Police Patrol could easily shoot them if they wanted. Kat and her extended family were nobody to them.

"You wouldn't want my men to have to make an example out of one of you, would you?" the officer said with barely restrained glee.

The guns sighted on each of the people in Kat's group.

Jacob seemed frozen in fear. He wasn't going to be any help.

She threw up her hands. "Please, don't hurt us. We'll come with you." Kat marched towards the lab door and the rest of her group followed.

Police Patrol brought up the rear.

As the only family she'd ever known paced behind her down the hall, guns at their backs, Kat got a lump in her throat and a huge cramp in her right leg. This whole thing was her fault. They'd depended on her and she'd let them down. They might all die in this strange universe.

Gaia, she'd really let them down.

Her eyes grew heavy with unshed tears.

Chapter Thirty-Four: Universe 3: Katherine: April 29, 2100, 2:00 pm

Katherine tried to get up from where the gravity fluctuations had thrown her on the lab floor, but Professor Jain warned her not to move.

Instead, he called her mother and asked her to come down and check her out.

Before her mother arrived, a contingent of black-uniformed Police Patrol officers charged into the lab. "What's wrong with gravity? Why is stuff melting? Why is it getting worse? What are you doing in here?"

The sandy-haired lead officer who'd questioned her earlier in Jacob's lab approached them as Professor Jain crouched over Katherine. "Why is she on the floor?"

Professor Jain slowly straightened. "We are having gravity and other fundamental force fluctuations in here as well. Ms. Garcia was injured and we are waiting for medical assistance. We are not causing the force fluctuations. We're trying to fix them."

Pandora made a clearing-her-throat sound.

"And we cannot do further research with you in here distracting us," Professor Jain continued. "We need peace and quiet. To think."

The Police Patrol officers stood at attention just inside the doorway.

Katherine's mother soon appeared in her white Health Ministry doctor's uniform. She elbowed her way through the Police Patrol forces. "Katherine? Are you okay? Why are you on the ground?" She put down her medical bag, knelt, and started checking Katherine's limbs.

KAT CUBED

Katherine was holding her breath, waiting for Police Patrol to arrest Mother for elbowing them.

"I thought you needed peace and quiet?" the head Police Patrol officer said.

"Please," Professor Jain said. "We're not going anywhere. At least wait in the hall. The sooner you leave us in peace, the sooner we can figure everything out."

After a chin nod from the head guy, the other officers filed out of the room.

"Uh, oh," Pandora said. "Data indicates the portals are opening again, and if the pattern holds, we'll see some fundamental force fluctuations, too."

Suddenly, the portals opened with a loud bang and the ground shook with a moderate earthquake.

How much shaking could this building take?

Professor Jain jumped up and hurried over to the computer.

"What hurts, honey?" Mother asked, ignoring the portals and the shaking. Her powers of concentration were impressive.

"Everything hurts," Katherine said. She should really get up and deal with the portals. They emitted a very loud buzzing sound, with the edges crackling.

"Can you be more specific?" Mother asked.

"No." Katherine didn't have time for medical exams. She had to fix everything.

Mother leaned back, sitting, and stared into her daughter's face. "Are you injured or not?"

The portals closed with a boom and they both flinched.

Katherine ached everywhere, but that was primarily from the interrogation she'd had yesterday. "I guess not. No more than I was when you saw me earlier. I guess I just had the wind knocked out of me."

"Uh," Pandora interrupted. "I think gravity and the other forces might be about to get wonky." Wonky? Where'd Pandora learn that word?

Mother ignored Pandora and turned to Professor Jain. "Why did you call me over here?"

Professor Jain pointed at Katherine. "Look at her. She's a mess."

She was a mess. She might become the biggest mass-murderer in the history of the universe, the universes. A tear escaped, running down the side of her face into her ear.

"Katherine Garcia," Mother said in her most disapproving voice. "Are you feeling sorry for yourself?"

"Yeah," Katherine said. Then, she started feeling lighter. Literally. Pandora was right about the gravity. She was probably always right.

Professor Jain grabbed one of the bolted-down lab tables and hung on.

The expression on her mother's face was like nothing Katherine had ever seen: confusion plus horror plus denial plus *get me the hell out of here*.

Katherine used the lightened gravity to lever herself up, pull down her tunic, grab her mother by the arm and lead her over to one of the lab tables before it got too wild. "I apologize," she said. "I was feeling sorry for myself."

They clutched the tables as everything not bolted down rose into the air. "I know it's my responsibility to fix this. And I will." Katherine decided against adding *Or die trying*. Did the lab table feel spongy? She hoped not. She definitely did not want to think about what would happen to a person if their molecules became unstable.

"Pandora," she said, "please collect as much data as possible on the portals and the force fluctuations."

"I am," Pandora said in her frightened voice.

"Okay," Katherine said. "We have two issues. One is why are gravity and electromagnetism and the other forces varying? And the other is how do we control the portals?"

Professor Jain said, "They've got to be connected. It's too big a coincidence for them not to be. We're getting force variations right after the portals open."

Katherine nodded. "Yes. Definitely."

"This is all too bizarre," Mother said. "How can you even think when we're floating?"

Why were they still floating? "Pandora, are the gravitational fluctuations lasting longer?"

"Yes," Pandora said as Katherine watched the edge of one of the lab tables slump. She scooted away from it.

"So, the force variations really are getting worse, in terms of frequency and duration," Professor Jain said.

"I don't get it," Mother said. "How can all these different things vary at once?"

Professor Jain and Katherine stared at each other. She could tell he was thinking the same thing she was thinking. It was too big of a coincidence.

"That's it," he said. "They aren't different things."

"We proved the Theory of Everything!" Katherine thrust her fist into the air and almost lost her grip on the table.

Professor Jain whooped. When Katherine glanced over at him he was smiling like he'd just won the Nobel Prize. If they lived through all this, he might.

"Why didn't I see it?" Pandora said.

"See what? I don't get it," Mother said. "What's the Theory of Everything?"

"In the twentieth century," Katherine said, "physicists thought there were four fundamental forces: gravity, electromagnetism, and the strong and weak forces."

"Can you get to the point?" Mother asked.

"It looks like there's only one force," Katherine said. "It only appears to be different forces because of the state of the universe now. If we'd been around at the beginning of the universe–"

"Katherine, focus," Mother said. "How does this help us?"

"It's not a bunch of different forces varying. One super-force is varying," Katherine said. "And it must work like General Relativity. This super-force isn't separate from the universe. It makes up the very fabric of spacetime, itself. It is the universe."

Her mother was shaking her head. "In English, Katherine."

"I explain General Relativity to my students with an analogy of a stretched rubber sheet," Professor Jain said.

"Right," Katherine said. "Mother, imagine spacetime is the sheet and when the force acts, it pulls the sheet down as if there were something like a bowling ball resting on it. All objects in the universe, including light, have to stay on the sheet. In the analogy the sheet is the universe."

"Never mind," Mother said, shaking her head a little. "I'll take your word for it."

"The point is," Katherine said, "only one thing is varying and

I think it's because it's been excited."

Then, gravity seemed to return to normal.

"Like an atom can be excited," Professor Jain said.

"So, maybe all we have to do is release the extra energy," Katherine said. "Safely."

Before they could breathe a sigh of relief, Jacob ran into the room. "Bad news: Kat and all her people have been taken into custody."

Poor Kat. Katherine really hoped none of them were in for some so-called interrogation.

"And more bad news: the force fluctuations are spreading out," he said. "I just felt that gravity thing in my lab."

Mother pointed at Katherine and Professor Jain. "They seem to think they have some good news. There's only one force."

Jacob cocked his head to the side. "Theory of Everything?"

"Yes," Professor Jain said.

"So, the individual force fluctuations are just a symptom of the greater problem?" Jacob asked.

"You guys are making my brain hurt," Mother said. "I'm getting out of here while I can walk." She leaned over and gave Katherine a peck on the cheek. "Be careful, hon. I have faith in you. Call me when you get more news."

Her mother made Katherine feel a little better. Maybe she could figure this thing out.

After Mother left, Jacob said, "I was right about the portals, wasn't I?" He could only be referring to his original comments about how dangerous the portals might be.

"Yes." Katherine hated to admit it, but they could have avoided all of this if she'd listened to Jacob's warnings in the first place.

"Right about what?" Professor Jain asked.

Suddenly they were regaled by Jacob's voice: "I'm not sure it's a good idea to start exchanging matter between universes."

And her voice said, "But, they're sick and thirsty."

"Thanks, Pandora," she said, trying to cut her off. "That's enough."

Jacob's voice continued. "The worst? The worst would be we destroy their universe and ours and maybe that other one, too. Do you want to risk that?"

"Thank you, Pandora," Katherine said much louder. "That's quite enough." But when she looked at Jacob he didn't look smug. He just looked sad.

"Can we pinpoint when the trouble started?" Katherine asked.

"What about that first power overload?" Jacob said. "Could that have been the catalyst?"

"When the nanobots tried to go through the portal the first time?" she said.

"Was that when the Code Red occurred?" Professor Jain asked.

She nodded. "Some matter must have gone through. And that initial matter transfer kicked the system up into an excited state."

"Where the system is the whole multiverse?" Jacob said.

"Yes," Katherine said.

"Why didn't I think of this?" Pandora asked.

"Oh, wait a minute," Katherine said.

"What?" Jacob, Professor Jain and Pandora asked at the same time.

"What if it really is like an atom? What if the energy states of the multiverse are quantized like the energy levels of an atom?" Katherine said.

"Wow," Pandora said.

"Very interesting," Professor Jain said.

"Yeah." Jacob jumped up from his stool. "And what if quantized states of the multiverse are like the electron probability clouds in atoms?"

"It all fits together," Pandora said.

"And energy is the key," Katherine said.

"So, the first thing to do is to restore the mass balance between the universes?" Professor Jain asked.

"I think so," Katherine said.

"Hold on," Pandora said. "Here we go again."

The portals opened with a loud bang and the ground shook.

"This feels like a six point zero on the Richter scale," Jacob said. "With Kat and her people in custody, restoring the matter balance isn't going to be easy."

"No." Katherine agreed. "And that other Jacob," she pointed at Kaitlin's portal, "said something about Kaitlin being trapped in yet another universe, not her own."

She turned to Professor Jain who was examining one of Pandora's computer screens. "Can you go to Police Patrol and see if they will release Kat and her people?"

He paled. "I guess I'm more likely to be successful than you two." He stood up. "I better try before gravity changes again." He quickly walked out the door.

She mentally wished him luck and then said, "We have to stabilize the portals so we can move all the matter back where it belongs."

The portals closed with a crashing boom. Jacob and she both flinched and moved towards Pandora's hardware, away from the portal locations.

"Get ready for force fluctuations," Pandora said.

They both reached for something bolted down.

"Pandora, can you show us the electromagnetic data?" Katherine asked.

"Didn't you say something about a regular pattern of increasing and decreasing electromagnetism, like a wave, before?" Jacob asked.

"Yeah," Katherine said. "We should look at that again." They studied the data for a few minutes.

Then, stuff started floating. She was getting used to it.

Judging from the not-manly shrieks coming from the hall, the Police Patrol guys were not getting used to it.

She got to work plotting the electromagnetic data, not easy to do when she could only use one hand. Her other was clutching the table. It did look like a standing wave, but only part of the time.

"Pandora, does the standing wave correspond to times when the portals are open?"

"Checking. Yes," Pandora said an instant later. Having an A.I. for an assistant was very helpful.

Katherine looked at Jacob. "I think we need to stabilize the standing wave to keep the portals open. How do we do that?"

He looked at her. He shrugged.

"Pandora?" she asked. "Any ideas?"

"No," Pandora said.

Katherine wracked her brain, trying to come up with something. This whole thing started because of energy. "I wonder what the energy's doing? Maybe it's significant?"

She plotted the energy versus time. "The energy shows the same kind of standing wave pattern."

Jacob grunted. "Huh."

"Huh?" Katherine said. "Gee, Jacob, that's really helpful." A grin snuck onto her face for a moment. "Anything else?"

He grinned back for a second. "Huh-uh."

Then, the floating stuff fell to the ground.

Katherine settled down on a lab stool. "Maybe we could use the natural properties of standing waves to make the maximums bigger and the minimums smaller."

He sat down next to her. "Create a resonance?" He nodded. "Yes. That's a good idea."

Jacob and she studied the data for a while with Pandora's help.

The portals thundered open and the ground churned. They grabbed onto a lab table again. The sizzling sound escalated to a ringing.

"This is the worst quake yet. It feels like at least a seven point zero," Jacob said.

The men in the hall screamed.

As the ground bucked, Katherine said, "I think we're running out of time."

Chapter Thirty-Five: Universe 4: Kaitlin, April 29, 2100, 2:00 pm

Surprisingly, the tough-guy soldier types gave Kaitlin some space while she lost it. She lay on the floor, missing her family and her fiancé. She felt guilty for getting all of them trapped in this strange universe, and especially for killing Win. And her leg hurt. She also felt really bad about damaging the fusion device. If they ever got out of here, a working fusion device could really help their world.

Eventually, she was all cried out. Her leg still really hurt.

After she just lay there for a while, doing nothing besides twirling her ring and trying not to scream about her leg, George approached. "Are you done crying?"

"Yeah, sorry."

"Do you want something to eat?"

At the mention of food, her stomach growled. "No. You guys help yourselves." Kaitlin sat up and her leg throbbed. "I wouldn't say no to some first aid though. I think my leg is broken."

"We did find a first aid kit," he said and made a gesture to one of the other officers.

George knelt down next to her and said in a low voice, "What should we do now?"

She just stared at the incongruous band of freckles across his face for a second. He needed a shave. How long had they been stuck over here? Finally, she said, "You're asking me?"

He forced a smile. "You're my resource, girl, remember?"

"Well, if we're stuck over here long-term, we need food and other supplies." She tried to smile back at him. "In that case, we should go out into town and try to scavenge some. But that's not a good scenario with the radiation outside."

George nodded but frowned.

"Our best bet is for the portal to open again, so we can go home." Kaitlin pointed at the portal location. "In that case, we should stick close and be ready to go through. But I don't have a crystal ball. I don't know if that will happen. You should decide if we stick here or go scavenging."

Suddenly, the portal opened with a loud bang and the ground shook with a moderate earthquake. Clearly, she didn't have a crystal ball.

"Hold, men," George said. "Don't go through until we know it's safe. Remember what happened to Smythe."

Ugh. Kaitlin didn't need another reminder.

A Security guy approached them with the first aid kit.

Several others followed him, staring at the portal, which was emitting a very loud buzzing sound. Apparently, everyone was afraid to go through without some kind of reassurance.

George opened the kit. "Setting your leg is probably going to hurt."

It did. She drifted in and out or consciousness and at some point the portal closed, gravity changed and then normalized.

After Kaitlin didn't feel like screaming or passing out anymore because of her leg, she said, "I think I'm going to try to fix the fusion machine. Okay?"

"Why?" George asked.

"It will come in very handy for solving our climate problems if we can get it home," she said.

"Okay," he said.

She really hoped they had a chance to get it home.

Universe 3: Kat

It was a case of déjà vu all over again as the black-clad Police Patrol goons marched Kat and her group into the building with the holding cells and interrogation rooms. Kat tried to stick close to Pa and Pablo. After what happened to Katherine, her plan was to throw herself on the grenade if either of them were picked for questioning. Too bad they didn't have any grenades; they could come in handy.

245

Suddenly, she felt weird, dizzy or something. She couldn't figure out what it was until her feet lifted off the floor.

People screamed.

"It's okay, folks," she said, grabbing unsuccessfully for the wall. "I don't think we're in danger." She hoped they weren't in danger.

They all scrambled for something to hang on to. The Police Patrolmen appeared more freaked out than anyone. It seemed like the weirdness lasted a long time.

Eventually, the gravity-bizarreness ended and they all fell on the ground.

Once they were vertical, the Police Patrol guys demanded answers of Kat's group, but of course none of them knew anything.

If Kat had to guess, she'd say Katherine had done something.

They resumed their trek to the cells. The officers didn't seem to know what else to do.

Outside one of the interrogation rooms, there was a commotion. Kat muscled her way through the crowd—her cast was persuasive—to see what it was.

She saw Katherine's pa in a green uniform arguing with Ghani. "What do you mean you don't know how Katherine is doing?" Christopher asked. "Has she been brought in for questioning again? Clearly, they've been questioning you." He pointed at Ghani's red puffy and bloody face. He didn't know Ghani'd been injured on their home world.

"I am sorry, sir," Ghani said. "I do not know this Katherine you are referring to."

"He's talking about the other version of me, Ghani," Kat said.

After glancing at her, Christopher took a step back from Ghani. "You're not Professor Jain?"

"No," Ghani said. "I am not from this world."

Christopher shook his head. "I can't wrap my head around this stuff."

And then Kat's pa pushed his way forward. "What's going on?"

The two Christophers' faces both slackened as they tried

to bend their minds around yet another mindbender. The two men weren't that hard to tell apart. Pa had some injuries from his run-in with those soldiers at home. Katherine's pa, Christopher, looked handsome in his pristine green uniform and coiffed hair. Of course, on this world with the nanobots, someone was always watching so maybe he had to look good.

"You're me." Pa scanned Christopher up and down. "And you're not me."

Christopher finally said, "Right back at ya."

Kat glanced around and the rest of her group seemed uneasy, looking at each other and the Police Patrol officers and muttering. Police Patrol seemed content to watch all the drama go down.

Then, the walls, floor and ceiling shook and the lights swayed back and forth.

Pablo touched her arm. "This is the worse quake yet. I hope it doesn't get any worse. I wonder what it is on the Richter scale."

"The what scale?" Kat asked.

Pablo just shook his head at her.

Christopher yelled over the rumbling, "We should get out of here. This building probably isn't earthquake-proof."

"Yeah," Pa said. "Come on." He gestured at Kat's group.

The Police Patrol guards looked as scared as everyone else as the ground rocked and rolled. Kat didn't blame them.

Everyone tried to get to the exit—not easy to do when you couldn't really walk.

"Wait a minute," she said. "I'm not sure this is an earthquake. And what if the gravity changes again when we're outside?"

"That would not be good," Pablo said.

As they wallowed in indecision near the front exit, the shaking stopped. Did that mean the gravity stuff was coming next? "You may want to grab something."

Before gravity changed, though, Katherine's Professor Jain bolted in through the front doors. His face was beaded with sweat. "I made it. I was afraid the gravity fluctuations would start when I was outside—"

He, and everyone else, floated upwards.

People screamed.

Amidst the confusion, Ghani stared at Professor Jain.

When he noticed, Professor Jain stared right back at Ghani. Professor Jain made his way over to him via the light fixtures. "May I ask, what is your name, sir?"

"Ghani Jain. How about you?"

"Ghani Jain." Professor Jain touched his own unblemished face. "May I ask, what happened to you, sir?"

Ghani touched his own injured face. "I met up with some soldiers back on my world. They seemed to think I knew something about some strange energy readings. I did not."

Professor Jain nodded, surveying the uniformed Police Patrol men in the hall. "Our worlds are not much different, then."

Ghani glanced down the hallway with its carpeting and then at the well-fed Police Patrol officers. "Perhaps not." He scanned Professor Jain. "May I ask why are you so thin, sir, when they are not?"

Professor Jain inspected the officers. "Ah. Yes, they do look healthy. But I've been ill. Usually I'm more robust."

"And what brings you here?"

"I'm going to try to get you released."

Fat chance.

Kat could tell from Ghani's expression he didn't think Professor Jain would succeed either.

Professor Jain made his way back towards the front doors where the Police Patrolmen were clustered. He appeared to ask them something politely.

They just stared at him like he was crazy.

He asked more forcefully.

They scowled at him.

He said something else, possibly indicating the weird gravity. He waved his hands around anyway, and then pointed at Kat and her group.

One of the Police Patrol guys yelled something at him that sounded like, "Your fault."

Professor Jain yelled back, "Not my fault. Do you want us all to die? Everyone? Everyone on all the worlds?"

One of the Police Patrol officers turned very red in the face, drew his fist back and tried to hit him. He clearly wasn't used to fighting in low gravity though, because he missed Professor Jain by a mile.

Professor Jain scrambled backwards nonetheless. He held up his hands in a placating gesture.

And then they all fell to the floor. Hurray for carpeting.

While they were still on the ground Pablo crawled over and whispered in Kat's ear, "Maybe we should try to escape now that gravity's back and the guards are distracted."

"I would if it was just me and you, but what about Pa and everyone else?" Kat said. "We can't just leave them."

"That Jain guy isn't going to do any good," Pablo said. "At best, all he's going to do is get himself arrested along with us. At worst, he's going to really piss off the goons with the weapons."

"I'm telling you, it's a matter of life and death," Professor Jain yelled.

The officers started reaching for their cuffs and batons. Shit. "You're right," she whispered to Pablo. "Do you have a plan?"

"There has to be some kind of exit in the back," he said, pointing behind them.

Keeping one eye on Professor Jain and one eye on the Police Patrol officers, Kat and Pablo crept down the hall towards the back of the building. Once the hall took a turn, and they were out of eyesight, they started running—albeit very quietly.

Every time they passed a doorway, they slowed down and peeked in before passing it. But the back of the building seemed empty. Apparently Police goons tended to abandon their posts when gravity started acting up.

Pablo and Kat reached what they thought was the rear of the building. They found a door with a sign that said, 'Emergency exit only. Alarm will sound.'

They stared at the sign and then back at each other. Pablo's face was flushed, and sweat beaded his face. Kat was sure she looked similar.

"What do you think?" Pablo asked. "Should we risk the alarm?"

She shrugged and touched the bump of her locket. "I guess. Maybe we can run away before they find us. They've got to be distracted with everything else that's going on." Her stomach rumbled. "And maybe we can find some food."

"It wouldn't be the first time we've had to make a run for it."

Pablo reached his hand out towards the door.

And the ground started shaking again.

"This is bad, even worse than before," Pablo said, withdrawing his hand.

Several people screamed from the front of the building.

"We don't want to go outside if there's no gravity, do we?" he asked.

"Not if we can help it," she said.

"The escaped prisoners must be in the back," a man yelled from direction they'd just come.

It looked like Kat and Pablo might not have a choice about going outside.

As the ground tried to fling them off, Kat said, "We are so screwed."

Chapter Thirty-Six: Universe 3: Katherine, April 29, 2100, 4:00 pm

Jacob and Pandora and Katherine were in the lab trying to figure out how to get the portals to stabilize, either open or closed. At this point some kind, any kind, of stability sounded like a good idea.

"I ran some quick simulations," Pandora said, "and I think your idea of trying to create an energy standing wave might work."

Jacob said, "How do you plan to get rid of the natural variations in the energy, Katherine?"

"That's what Pandora's for," she said. "She's going to control the tokamak and adjust its energy on the fly, to cancel out energy minimas and build energy maximas."

"And then the portals stay open?" he asked.

"That's the hypothesis," Katherine said.

"Yep," Pandora said.

They were experiencing a rare lull in the strangeness. No fundamental force constants were varying, no earthquakes were quaking. It was nice. You never realized how wonderful normalcy was until it was gone. Katherine took a deep breath, feeling her tunic constrain her chest. "Okay. I think it's now or never." She turned to Jacob. "Is your quantum computer on?"

He nodded. "Yes."

"Are you sure?" she asked.

"I'm sure." He nodded again. "I was with Kat, and she was giving me a back rub–"

"Whoa. She was what? You and Kat?" Katherine couldn't believe it. How could the two of them start something up? How could they betray her like that?

"What?" Jacob opened his eyes wide and jerked back. "You think me and Kat would get together? That's impossible. You know you're the only woman for me, Katherine."

Katherine wanted to say, except for your mate Tabatha, but he looked so offended she didn't have the heart.

Pandora made her throat clearing noise. "Seriously? You guys are talking about this now? Focus, people."

Pandora was right. The fates of the universes were at stake and she was acting like a jealous idiot. "Sorry." Katherine looked at the floor.

"Thanks," Pandora said.

"For what?" Jacob asked.

"For making me thankful to be software. I've never been so glad to be electronic," Pandora said. "Meat is crazy."

"Gee, thanks," Jacob said.

"Anyway, back to work," Katherine said. "Quantum computer, check. The tokamak is ready to roll, check. Pandora, are you ready to monitor and adjust the energies as necessary?"

"Check," Pandora said. "Uh oh. I think another disturbance is starting..."

"Go!" Katherine said. "Start the experiment."

"Check," Pandora said.

The portals opened with a loud bang and the ground shook.

"Pandora?" Katherine asked, grabbing onto a lab table.

"Wait a second," Pandora said.

The rumbling lessened and the portals sizzled, but stayed open.

"It's working," Pandora said.

What happened to the soldiers from Kat's universe? If the portal stayed open, would they start shooting into her lab again? "Jacob? Can you go check if those soldiers are still there?" She pointed at Kat's portal. "Carefully." She didn't want him to get shot.

"Already on it." He had a grim cast to his face as he started walking towards the portal.

A slight rumbling continued as the edges of the portals sizzled but held steady.

"Hello?" Jacob said behind her. "Did you fix it?"

Katherine twirled. It was the other Jacob, Jake, from

Kaitlin's universe. She ran over. "How's Kaitlin?"

"She's still trapped in that other universe," Jake said. "Can I tell her to come over?"

"I'm not sure. Pandora?" Katherine asked.

"It's holding so far," Pandora said.

"I guess it's worth a try," Katherine said. "Be careful though."

"Good." Jake ran away from her to the other portal in his universe. "Come back, Kait. Come back. It's safe."

Katherine really hoped Pandora was right and the portals would hold.

Universes 4 & 2: Kaitlin

Having lost all sense of what time of day it was, Kaitlin was dozing in front of the fusion device when she heard Jake yelling. "Come back, Kait. Come back. It's safe."

George was the first to react. "Men, fall out. Fall out! Go through the portal immediately. Go, go, go!"

His men wasted no time going through and were already cheering on the other side before she really understood what was happening.

The next thing Kaitlin knew, Jake was kneeling beside her. "Kait! Oh, no. You're hurt." He wrapped his arms around her.

"What are you doing here?" Kaitlin asked, looking into his beautiful eyes. "You shouldn't be here in this universe. It's dangerous. What if you get trapped?"

"I came to bring you home." He started to help her get up. "Come on. The portal's open. Let's go."

As she looked around, she realized Jake and she were alone in the strange universe. All George's men, with the exception of what was left of Win, had gone through.

"We're saved?" she asked.

"Yes. Come on."

With Jake's help, she hopped through as quickly as she could with her bum leg.

In their home universe, George was talking to his men, "Report to the armory, men, for debrief and medical treatment. You can check in with your families on the way. I'll be right behind you." He was already dialing his fon.

They made it home. Kaitlin wouldn't be responsible for their deaths, too. That was a huge relief.

The officers whipped out their own fons as they ran out the lab door.

Kaitlin took in her familiar surroundings, her computers, her ancient lab stools and tables, her same old posters on the walls, same piles of books, same musty smell. She was home. She caressed her ring. Her eyes filled.

Jake helped her to a stool so she could sit down. "Are you all right, Kaitlin? Is it just your leg or is it something else? You don't seem like yourself. And why do the officers need medical treatment? They looked fine."

Killer, killer, killer, echoed in her mind. She didn't have the heart to mention the radiation to him. "I'm sorry, Jake. I'm very happy to be home and to be with you." Kaitlin squeezed his hand. "It's just that all this has been intense."

Still in the lab on his fon, George said, "I'm not sure if the portal is stable, but I want to get officer Smythe's remains, sir."

She looked at Jake. "Is my family okay?"

"Yes," Jake said. "They've been worried about you. They all wanted to come to the lab when they got your messages, but I told them I was on it."

She sighed in relief. She was back in her own universe with Jake and her family and they were all right. Whatever else happened, it wasn't important. "Can you do me a favor and call my brother or someone to let them know I'm back?"

In response, Jake whipped out his fon and started dialing.

In the meantime, George paused, frowning. "Yes, sir," he said into his fon. Then, he was quiet for a minute. "Yes, sir, I understand, sir, but−" He listened. "Sor− Your. Reak. Up." He hung up and glanced over at Jake and Kaitlin.

She stared back at George, guessing what he was thinking. *Leave no man behind.* "I would help you get Win's remains, but I don't think I'd be much use," she said, gesturing at her leg.

"What is wrong with your leg?" Jake hung up "Should I take you to the emergency room?"

"I think it's broken," she said. "And what? You think I need real medical treatment? You don't like the nice splint that

George, here, devised?" She attempted a grin.

As Jake glanced at him, George approached them.

"George?" Jake asked. "Who's George? This guy?"

"Jake," she said, "I suspect I'm going to be taken into custody any minute so you can't take me to the emergency room. Remember how this whole thing started at the anniversary party?"

George interrupted, saying to Jake, "Actually, before we get into that, what do you say you help me get what's left of Officer Smythe from that strange universe? You look like a strapping young man."

"George, this is Jake," she said. "Jake, this is George." They didn't react. Maybe they'd already deciphered who the other was.

Jake turned to her. "Kait? What do you think? Is it safe? Or will the portal close?"

The three of them all contemplated the portal, which so far, was still there.

"I think it's dangerous," she said. "But I would do it, if I could. It's your decision."

"Okay," Jake said. "Let's make it quick." He went through the portal with George on his heels. They were back in a flash, carrying the tarp-covered bottom half of Win. They grunted as they set him down on the floor in front of the portal.

"Good," Kaitlin whispered when she saw them back safe and sound.

The edges of the portal vibrated and sizzled, but only slightly.

"Can you go ask Katherine," she pointed at the other portal, "what's going on? Did she fix everything? Are the portals safe?"

"I guess," Jake said. "Why?"

"I'd really like to get that fusion machine and its documentation over here if we can," she said.

George perked up. "So, this Katherine person is responsible for the portals? I'd like to talk to her, myself." He marched over to the portal in question.

Soon, George pointed at Jake and said, "But, he's you. What the hell?"

Kaitlin didn't have the energy to hop over and see what

Katherine's Jake had to say. Then, there was some kind of commotion over there because she could hear the shouting in the other universe from across the room.

Universe 3: Kat

When Kat and Pablo made it back to Katherine's lab, Katherine and Jacob were talking to some people through one of the portals. They didn't even notice Kat and Pablo had returned.

"Hey," Kat said. "We're back, we escaped, and it wasn't easy."

"Welcome back, Kat and Pablo," the computer woman, Pandora, said.

Katherine and Jacob didn't say anything.

"Hey," she said again. "We almost died."

"Yeah," Pablo said loudly. "Gravity was *loco*."

Kat added, "Doesn't anybody want to hear about how we survived outside with the low gravity?" Speaking of gravity, why was it acting normal now?

"Police Patrol officers chased us, but we lost 'em," Pablo said. "We pulled one over on them."

"Yeah, right," Pandora said in a surprisingly snide tone for a computer. "You lost them, and they don't know where you are now. I didn't have anything to do with that."

Kat knew she should stay on Pandora's good side. "Thanks," she said. "We apologize if we didn't seem properly appreciative." She poked Pablo in the ribs.

"*Muchas gracias*, computer lady," he said.

Then Kat realized that humming noise meant both the portals were open and staying open. "Did you guys fix the portals?" she asked. Maybe they could all go home. It was definitely too bad Pa and the rest of the group weren't here right now.

Kat and Pablo approached Katherine and Jacob. "Did you guys fix everything?" she asked again. "Can we go home?"

Katherine shifted, revealing another Jacob through the portal.

Pablo jerked. "*Dios mio*," he whispered. "Another Jacob."

KAT CUBED

Kat didn't even care anymore how many copies of people there were. She wanted to get Pa and her friends and go home. She was sick of this world.

She touched her locket. "Are the portals fixed or not?"

Katherine regarded the computer. "Pandora? Is the standing wave working? How's it going?"

"It's a bit odd," Pandora said. "Both sides were giving me equal trouble, but suddenly the one side is behaving much better. One side has stabilized."

"So that's good?" Kat asked. Her people were going to be able to go home? Assuming she could get Pa and the rest of them away from that Police Patrol?

"I'm not sure," Pandora said.

"It must be because Kaitlin and her friends came back from that other universe," Katherine said, face lighting up.

"So, the mass is more equalized?" Jacob asked.

"Must be," Katherine said.

If mass equalization had anything to do with people going back to their home universes, they had a problem. "You know Pa and the others from my world are in custody?" Kat said.

Katherine frowned. "That's not good. What happened to Professor Jain?"

"I think they got him, too," Pablo said.

"We can't equalize the universes' masses if we can't send Kat's people back to their own universe," Katherine said.

"We have to get my people back to our universe," Kat said.

"Yes, but how?" Jacob said.

There was a moment of silence as they all pondered this.

"Uh oh," Pandora said.

They all froze. Nothing good ever happened when Pandora said *uh oh*.

"I'm losing the standing wave," Pandora said. "The energy's too uneven now."

The portals slammed shut with a roaring boom.

The ground and everything else shook.

Once the universe had calmed down a bit Katherine said, "Is everyone okay? Any injuries?" Almost of its own accord, her hand searched out Jacob's.

He squeezed her hand back. "I'm okay."

"We're all right," Kat said. "Right, Pablo?"

Pablo nodded. "*Sí.*"

"I'm okay, too, if anyone cares," Pandora said in a hurt voice.

Aw. "We care, Pandora," Katherine said.

"We care a lot," Jacob said. "You're our favorite A.I."

Katherine couldn't help thinking Pandora was the only A.I., in any of the universes, as far as they knew. "You did great with the portals. I think Kaitlin got back to her home universe."

Kat gazed at the empty spot where the portal to her universe appeared. "We need to rescue—"

"Ahem. Ahem," Pandora said loudly.

What was wrong with her now? "Pandora?" Katherine asked.

"Gosh," she continued, in a deceptively mild voice. "I think we're experiencing some electromagnetic difficulties."

That didn't sound good.

Plink, plink, plink. Several nanobots fell to the floor. Oops. Katherine was so used to them she didn't notice them anymore.

"Okay, now you can talk," Pandora said in her normal voice.

"Uh." Kat stared at the little metal robots. "How long have they been here?" She shook her head. "Anyway, we need to rescue my pa and the rest of my people from custody."

"Yeah." Pablo held up his forefinger. "And that professor

friend of yours, too. And maybe Katherine's pa, too."

"What?" Katherine said. "Father's in custody? Oh, no." These people didn't understand how dangerous Police Patrol was.

"Rescue?" Jacob asked. "That sounds too risky." He knew Police Patrol was dangerous.

"It will undoubtedly be dangerous," Pandora said.

"I don't see how we could do it, unless we disable Police Patrol's entire security system," Katherine said, tugging down her uniform tunic.

"So, let's do it, let's disable it," Pablo said, eyes shining. "I don't like this security stuff. Or this government stuff, for that matter."

"Please," Kat said. "I really don't want my pa or my friends to be beaten or tortured."

Jacob squeezed Katherine's hand again. She'd almost forgotten they were holding hands. She thought about how Jacob and she could never be together. And she thought about poor Winston, doomed to a life of trying to be someone he wasn't, never being allowed to be himself.

She thought about Police Patrol's so-called interrogation techniques and how Father and Professor Jain and Kat's friends were in danger. Any harm they experienced was her responsibility.

She gently touched her swollen face with her free hand. It seemed better. Doing science, trying to help people and further human knowledge, shouldn't result in being beaten to within an inch of your life. Neither should just being at the wrong place at the wrong time. Or just knowing the people who were at the wrong place at the wrong time.

Katherine was fed up. "I'm in," she finally said.

"If you're in, I'm in," Jacob said with a hint of a smile. Was he thinking about the two of them being together?

"I agree we have to save my people," Kat said. "They're only in trouble because of me. It's just that..." She paused.

"What?" Katherine asked.

"How can the four..."

"Five," Pandora said.

"How can the five of us accomplish anything?" Kat asked.

That was a very good question. Katherine's mind raced. Pandora's electromagnetic disruption of the nanobots could be the key. "If we can disable all of Police Patrol's nanobots and their communications systems and their computers, we should be fine," she said.

"Oh. That's all? Nanobots, communications and computers?" Jacob grinned at her. "Are you sure we don't need to do anything else?"

"We have to avoid getting caught," Katherine said.

"We need to get Pa and the others out of jail as soon as possible," Kat said.

"I volunteer to help with that," Pablo said.

"Me, too," Kat said.

Katherine stood up and walked over to her tokamak. "I think what we need is a big electromagnetic pulse. That would take out all the electric equipment, the nanobots, communications and computers. Ideally, it would be big enough to affect the whole metro area, but I'm not sure where we'd get the energy for that. This thing won't generate enough energy yet." She resisted the urge to kick the machine that still hadn't managed nuclear fusion and that had caused so many problems.

"That is a problem," Pandora said dryly.

Kat raised her hand. "I have a stupid question. Don't you have a lot of electronics here? If we ruin all the electronics, won't people get hurt?"

"I'm not sure," Katherine said. "But it's something we should consider."

"Hold on," Pandora said. "Data indicates the portals are opening again, and if the old pattern holds, we'll see some fundamental force fluctuations, too."

Suddenly, the portals opened with a loud bang and the ground shook with a moderate earthquake.

As they all clutched the lab tables in anticipation of gravity changing, Jacob said, "It's a little better than it was before, isn't it? I mean the earthquakes and force fluctuations seem weaker."

"And they're less frequent, aren't they?" Kat asked.

"I think it's better than it was there at the end," Katherine said. "Pandora, please time how long the portals stay open."

"Duh," Pandora said.

"I want to find out if Kaitlin made it home okay. In the meantime," Katherine pointed at Kat's portal. "Maybe you guys should check if those soldiers are still anywhere near the portal in your universe."

Kat and Pablo nodded. "I'll go look, Kat," Pablo said. "It might be dangerous."

Kat held up her cast. "Okay. It's hard for me to hold on to things with this cast if gravity goes crazy again. But be careful, P."

By holding on to one table after another, Katherine made her way over towards Kaitlin's portal. Once she arrived relatively close to it, she yelled, "Kaitlin? Are you over there? Is anyone over there?"

Kaitlin's Jake answered. "Yes, we're here. Kaitlin and the others made it home."

Katherine breathed a sigh of relief. At least one thing worked out.

Jake continued, "Why are we still getting the earthquakes and disturbances? Why are the portals still opening and closing? Didn't you fix them?"

"I wish we'd fixed them," she said. "Among other things, we're having some problems with Police Patrol."

Jake snorted. "Maybe our universes aren't as different as we thought."

"Anyway, we're hoping to resolve things over here and really fix things." Katherine paused.

"What's stopping you?" he asked.

"I need a strong energy source and I'm not sure I'll be able to find one that's strong enough," she said.

From his universe a woman, maybe Kaitlin, yelled something.

"What? I'm sorry, I couldn't hear that," Katherine said. Why didn't the woman come closer to the portal?

Jake said, "Kaitlin says they discovered a working fusion machine in the next universe over."

Katherine didn't dare believe her ears. "What?"

"They discovered an operational fusion device," he repeated.

"Is she sure? How does she know? That would be

awesome. Wonderful. Is there any chance we could get a hold of it?"

"What's that?" He turned towards Kaitlin. "She says it was working but it broke."

"Oh no," Katherine said. "Is there any chance it can be repaired?"

But before he could answer, the portal closed with a boom.

In the calm quiet, Katherine quickly made her way back over to the middle of the room where Jacob and Kat sat. Force fluctuations should be starting soon.

Pablo joined them.

"Kaitlin says she might have access to a working tokamak," Katherine said.

"Actually, she didn't say it was a tokamak," Pandora said.

"Okay," Katherine said. "Kaitlin said she might have access to a working fusion machine."

"Actually," Pandora said, "she said it was broken."

"We can probably fix it," Katherine said, interrupting her. "And if not, we can probably use it to get our tokamak working."

Jacob's mouth fell open for a moment before he said, "Wow."

"I don't get it," Kat said. "Who cares about fusion?"

"Discovering fusion might be even more important than discovering the portals and parallel universes," Katherine said.

Kat still looked confused.

"A fusion machine could be unlimited, clean energy," Jacob said.

Katherine liked how Jacob always seemed to know what she meant. "And it would be a very strong energy source. We could use it to create the EMP we need."

"Oh," Kat said. "That does sound good." She turned to Pablo and rubbed his arm. "I assume no one shot at you over there?"

Pablo shook his head. "I stuck my head through."

"Pablo," Kat said. "How could you do that? It could have been dangerous. What if the portal closed suddenly?"

Katherine felt nauseous, thinking about what might happen to a human being halfway through a portal when it closed. "Please do not do that again, Pablo."

262

"Anyway," he said. "It seems like the soldiers cleared out. I didn't see any sign of them. I think it's safe for us to go home." He squinted back at the portal location and she wondered if he was wishing he'd gone home when he had the chance.

Kat rested her hand on his arm. As a look passed between them, Katherine realized they were closer than mere friends, and yet they didn't seem like lovers, which made sense if Kat's Pablo was anything like the one in her universe.

Her eyes rested on Kat. Just how similar were they? And how different? Who would she be if she'd grown up in chaos? Or in freedom? It was kind of mind-boggling.

She glanced at Jacob, wondering how she and Jacob seemed to other people. Close? How close? When Jacob met her eyes, Katherine felt heat rushing to her face.

"So," she said too loud. "The plan is, first of all, assuming the portals open again...Pandora?"

Pandora made a sighing noise. "It's a safe assumption."

Katherine continued. "Jacob and I are going to help Kaitlin and her people obtain the fusion energy source. Then we'll work with Pandora to create an EMP with it and disable electronics. Once we do that, we can rescue Kat's people. We'll equalize the masses between universes by sending Kat's people home and hopefully that will enable us to gain control of the portals."

Katherine couldn't help noticing everyone appeared rather grim.

"That's all?" Jacob set his mouth in a thin line.

"It does seem like a lot," Kat said.

"Hey, you didn't answer the earlier question," Pablo said. "Won't people get hurt if we mess up all the electronics?"

Katherine didn't want people to get hurt. "Maybe. Who do you think would get hurt?"

"People on airplanes?" Jacob said.

"I don't think our pulse emitted from the ground will go up high enough to affect air traffic," Katherine said.

"If it stays at ground level, you won't disable all communications," Pandora said. "You have to get the communications satellites."

That was discouraging. Geostationary satellites were at altitudes of tens of thousands of miles.

"People in hospitals will get hurt, too," Kat said, glancing at her cast.

"My mother may be able to help us there," Katherine said. "She might be able to send out some kind of warning."

"The whole thing seems like a long shot," Pablo said.

"I don't disagree," Katherine said, "but if we don't try, all the universes and who-knows-how-many billions of people will be destroyed, right?"

"Yes," Pandora said. "All my simulations show we'll all die, meat and software alike."

None of them knew what to say to that.

"Uh oh," Pandora said. "Hold on."

Chapter Thirty-Eight: Universe 2: Kaitlin, April 29, 2100, 10:00 pm

Kaitlin clutched a lab stool as it tipped over. Almost in slow motion, she fell, and her sore leg slammed onto the floor. She would have screamed if the air hadn't gotten knocked out of her lungs. Each successive rise and fall of the ground smacked her leg, and she still couldn't yell. She leaned back on the floor and felt moisture fall from the corners of her eyes into her ears.

Katherine wasn't kidding when she said she hadn't stabilized the portals or fixed the weird force fluctuations. The ground undulated like a snake getting ready to strike.

"Kait, what's wrong?" Jake was at her side. "Are you crying?"

She forced air into her lungs. "My leg hurts a little." The ground plunged, and she winced. She touched Jake's face lightly.

He tried to gather her to him, but the ground bucked. "Hang on. This can't last forever."

And then the shaking stopped. It was wonderful. She focused on breathing.

George approached Jake and Kaitlin on the floor. "I don't understand all this."

And then her leg didn't hurt as much. She felt light as a feather and floated up.

Jake steered her towards a lab table, and she grabbed it gratefully.

George followed them. "What's wrong with gravity? Why do we keep having earthquakes? What the hell is going on?"

"I don't know for sure," Kaitlin said. "But I think it's because that woman Katherine opened the portals."

"How do we stop it?" George asked.

"Good question." Her leg had quieted to a dull ache.

"You need to let me take you to the hospital, Kait," Jake said.

She shook her head. "I can't leave. I think we need to stay here and help Katherine if we can," she said. "Jake, maybe you could call my mom and get her to bring some stuff for a cast? If my leg is stabilized, maybe it won't hurt so much."

He nodded. "Good idea." He started calling.

Kaitlin turned to George. "Not that I don't appreciate your efforts with the splint."

George nodded. "How can we help this Katherine woman?"

"She did seem very interested in the fusion machine we discovered," She said. "She said they needed a strong energy source, and the fusion machine would be a strong energy source."

Jake got off the fon. "Your mom's coming. But speaking of Katherine, I wish we could have talked to her longer. I'd like a better idea of what's going on."

George said, "You and me both, man."

Kaitlin couldn't disagree.

The three of them sat and stared at the spot where Katherine's portal had appeared. "You must have some family or someone waiting for you, George," she finally said. "You should go."

George's glance strayed to the tarp-covered remains, and he stood. "I need to debrief, talk to Officer Smythe's family, and pay my respects. And we need to get the coroner here to pick up his remains." He paused. "But, if I can help fix this whole thing, I should stay put."

Then Michael ran into the lab right up to her. "Kait, I came as soon as Jake called. Where were you? What happened?"

Some part of Kaitlin thought she'd never see Michael again. She felt her throat constrict as she grabbed him. "I love you, little brother."

"Same here," he said, hugging her back. When they separated, he said, "So what's all this about?"

Emma and Dad appeared in the lab doorway, panting. "We came as soon as Michael called," Dad said.

"What about Mom?" Kaitlin asked.

"She stopped off at the hospital," Emma said, "to get supplies after Jake called her."

They both enveloped her in a hug, and she finally relaxed. She was truly home. Now she'd be okay as long as the universe was.

George cleared his throat. "Maybe I will go talk to the Smythe family. You all can help Kaitlin if she needs it, right?"

"Of course," Dad said.

"You go do what you need to, George," Kaitlin said.

Emma pointed at George. "Wait a minute. Aren't you one of the Hearthland Security guys from the anniversary party? Didn't you arrest Kait?"

"Yeah," Michael said. "Are you going to arrest her again?"

Dad scowled and, frankly, looked a little scary.

George took in Dad's expression and looked scary right back at him. "I'm not planning on arresting her right now. We need to fix the problems with gravity and the earthquakes and other stuff, and Kaitlin might be the only person in this world that can do that." He seemed like he wanted to say more, but he wheeled and headed out the door.

"This world?" Emma asked. "What other world is there?"

"Yeah," Michael said. "What's he talking about?"

"How could you have anything to do with the earthquakes?" Dad asked. "You better start explaining, young lady."

Kaitlin glanced at Jake, twirling her ring. He nodded encouragingly.

"So," she said. "I was minding my own business here in the lab when a portal to another universe opened up."

"What?" Emma shrieked.

Michael and Dad just shook their heads.

"She's telling the truth," Jake said.

Kaitlin smiled at him and grabbed his hand for a squeeze. "Thanks, babe."

He smiled and squeezed back.

Dad scowled. "I've never known you to be a liar, Kaitlin. But that sounds incredible."

"I believe her," Emma said.

Michael shrugged. "I guess I do, too. It's too unbelievable to make up."

Kaitlin thought her family rocked. For a second, she felt sorry for the Kaitlins in the other universes because they didn't seem to have the family she did.

And then she teetered on the edge of a precipice. How many universes were there? And how many Kaitlins? Were there infinity Kaitlins stretching out between here and forever? And an infinity of Jakes and Dads and Emmas and Michaels? Her head swam.

"Okay," Dad said. "Say we hypothetically believe you about the portal."

Get a grip, Kait. You just need to worry about this universe. Now.

"Where is it?" Dad continued. "And what does that have to do with the earthquakes and weird gravity?"

"The portals come and go. I don't know why." Kaitlin shrugged. "And I don't know what they have to do with gravity and earthquakes. But they have to be related. It's too much of a coincidence for them not to be."

"Who does know?" Dad asked.

"There's another version of me, her name is Katherine, through the portal, who caused everything."

They appeared skeptical again.

Jake nodded. "It's true. I've talked to her. And she looks exactly like Kaitlin."

"Wait a minute," Michael said. "Did you say portals, plural? Are there more than one?"

"Yes." Kaitlin nodded. "I got trapped in another universe, not Katherine's. That's where I've been and that's where I got hurt."

"You went to another universe?" Emma asked with wide eyes.

"What was it like?" Michael asked.

"How did you get hurt?" Jake asked.

"Yes, I'd like to know that as well," a female voice said from the doorway.

They all pivoted to see who it was.

It was Kaitlin's mom. She approached Kaitlin and set a duffel bag down on the floor.

"Uh," Kaitlin said. "A fusion machine fell on my leg in

another universe."

Mom set her lips in a thin line as she opened the bag and started rummaging around in it. "Emma, please take that ridiculous splint off Kaitlin. Kaitlin, please lie back on the floor." Somehow Mom's pleases always sounded like orders. Mom extracted a large plastic beaker from the bag and held it out to Michael. "Michael, get me some water from the sink over there, please."

He jumped up, grabbing the beaker. "Yes, ma'am."

"Dr. Garcia, how nice to see you," Jake said. He forced a smile. "Kaitlin is telling the truth, ma'am. She went to the other universe." Kaitlin had always thought Jake was a little scared of her mom, the famous doctor, so kudos to him for standing up to her.

Mom just stared at Jake, and his confidence seemed to leak out. She was a force of nature, no question.

"Topher, why don't you tell me what's going on," Mom said, extracting more medical supplies from the bag.

Emma jostling her leg did not make it feel good. Kaitlin winced. "Do you have any pain-killers, Mom?"

"Yes," Mom said. "Just a minute."

"Sorry," Emma whispered. She continued manipulating Kaitlin's leg. Ow.

"To tell the truth, Ava," Dad said, "I'm not entirely sure what's going on. Kaitlin said she was working here in the lab and a, er, some, portals opened up and they're responsible for the earthquakes we've been having."

Michael came back with a beaker of water.

Mom handed Dad the beaker and a packet of something. "Please mix this up. How's it going there, Emma?"

Emma stood back. "I got the splint off."

"Jake, please hold her leg still," Mom said.

He grasped Kaitlin's leg. She clutched her ring and tried not to gasp as Mom worked on her.

Mom started wrapping some gauze around her leg, she pointed at Dad and the goop in the beaker and the gauze, and he started slathering it on.

Soon, Kaitlin had a shiny new cast on her leg.

"Please try to remain still while it hardens, Kaitlin," Mom

said.

Then she straightened, brushing off her hands. "Topher, I'm surprised at you. Our children aren't liars. If Kaitlin said she hurt herself in another universe, then that's what happened." She rummaged in her bag again.

Yay, Mom. "Thanks, Mom."

"That's basically what I said," Dad said. "It's just a little hard to believe."

"Here, Kait. Take these." She handed her some pills. "What's next?" she asked. "What do we need to do to fix all of this?"

Still lying on the floor, Kaitlin said, "Actually, we need to talk to the other me, Katherine. I think she's in charge. Maybe we can find out what's going on. We also should really get the fusion machine and documentation from the other universe if we can."

She stopped for a moment, gathering her wits. "You should know it's dangerous to pass through the portals. If you go you might get trapped in one of the other universes, or, if the portal closes while you're in it, you'll be cut in half." Her eyes shot over to Win's body under the tarp which the others hadn't noticed yet.

"And there's something else," she said. "The universe where the fusion machine is is radioactive. I'm not sure I can even ask you to help."

"You were over there with the radiation?" Mom pressed her lips together in a thin line.

Kaitlin nodded.

"But if we don't help, it won't be good, will it?" Jake asked.

"No," Kaitlin said. "Katherine said something about all of us dying, everyone in all the universes." Now that she was surrounded by her family again, she knew she would do anything to save them and her universe.

"We can't have that," Mom said. "When will these portals open?"

"I don't know," Kaitlin said. "But when they do, they may not be for long. Whatever we do, we have to be quick."

And then Kaitlin heard a familiar sizzling sound. "I think the portals are opening!" She levered herself up on her elbows.

Two sizzling windows appeared, floating on opposite sides of the lab.

"What the hell is going on in here?" another voice said from the doorway, an angry male voice. It was Professor Azar. "You are in serious trouble, Ms. Garcia."

Shit. She'd totally forgotten about him and how he wanted to fire her what with everything else that was going on.

"Jake," Kaitlin said quietly, "go see if you can talk to Katherine and get more information."

He nodded at her.

"Since I'm having you expelled, Ms. Garcia, you and your friends are trespassing." Professor Azar pointed at Jake as he approached Katherine's portal. "Freeze, kid!"

Kaitlin didn't want to be expelled, but it was really the least of her worries at this point. "Did you expel me already? Can you force us to leave?"

Professor Azar ignored her questions.

Jake also ignored him and continued over to the portal. Go, Jake.

"Professor Azar, there's a lot going on here," she said. "Look at the portals. They go to other universes. We're all in danger."

He ignored her comments. "In fact, you all should be arrested for trespassing." Professor Azar got out his fon. Wow, he was good at ignoring.

Shit. Being arrested for trespassing wasn't as scary as being arrested for murder. But still, if they were arrested they couldn't help Katherine. And they needed to help her.

Not saving the multiverse would be the scariest of all.

Chapter Thirty-Nine: Universe 3: Kat, April 29, 2100, midnight

Kat and Pablo were discussing with Katherine and Jacob how to make that EMP thing and rescue Pa and everyone else from Police Patrol when the portals opened again.

Someone started yelling "Katherine!" from the portal that didn't lead to Kat's world.

Katherine and Jacob rushed over to it.

Kat stared after them. She wouldn't just rush away in the middle of an important discussion. Who was that Katherine woman, anyway? What would it be like to grow up with food and shelter, and no worries, and her whole family? Ugh, she didn't have time right now for woolgathering.

She shook her head and turned to Pablo.

"So much for our planning session," she said. "That EMP thing seems too far-fetched and complicated."

Pablo frowned. "I don't like this world or these people. I just want to get our friends and go home."

"I'm right there with you." Kat paused. "We probably only have a few minutes until the earthquakes start again and then gravity goes wild."

"Yeah. I'd rather not get stuck outside again when the gravity goes *loco*."

"I hear you." She glanced at Katherine and Jacob talking to what appeared to be another Jacob through the portal. They'd totally forgotten about Pablo and her. "What do you think the chances are that the back door we busted through at Police Patrol Headquarters will be locked securely?"

"Not too good." Pablo grinned. "It was pretty busted up. What do you think the chances are that some guns are still in that cabinet we passed?"

"Pretty darn good." She grinned back. "There were a lot of guns." She looked at him.

He looked at her.

"Let's go," Kat said. "Wait." She held up her cast. "I need to do something about this." She grabbed a sharp pair of scissors.

"Maybe you should leave it alone, K." Pablo's mouth turned down. "You need to heal."

She flexed her fingers. The end of the cast, in her palm, was definitely in the way. "I can heal fine, without this bottom part." She started hacking the end of the cast off with the scissors.

Pablo glanced at the others. They still weren't paying any attention to them. He didn't seem happy with Kat's actions, but he didn't say anything else.

Soon, she'd removed the cast below her wrist. "Now, that's more like it." She made sure the locket was safely tucked away under her shirt. If things got hairy she wanted to make sure it was safe. "Let's go."

"How do you want to get out of the building?" Pablo asked. "There's still Police Patrol officers in the hall."

"The same way we got in," she said.

They walked calmly to Jacob's lab, scrambled up on a desk against the wall, opened a window, slithered through, and then jogged across campus to the old armory. At the armory they snuck around to the back, peeked in and ran right through the busted back door.

"I gotta say Police Patrol isn't too good at security." Pablo snickered.

"I gotta say, I agree with you. I guess they don't worry about people breaking in."

"Maybe it's been a while since anyone put up a fight," he said.

"Maybe so," Kat said. "Everyone here seems terrified of them."

They jogged to the gun cabinet they'd seen earlier, not seeing a soul. They each grabbed a semi-automatic.

"Ammo," he said.

She pointed at the well-labeled drawers right below the guns. They loaded their guns and filled their pockets.

As they turned to go back into the hall, he hesitated. "Are you sure about this, Kat? Are you really prepared to shoot people at close range?" He had a point. This would be different from taking pot-shots at people shooting at them from the ruins of some old town.

Kat thought about her missing ma and her dead sister Emma, about Pablo's long-gone family. She thought about burying poor little Fei. She thought about Pa and Bao and her only remaining friends and family being tortured. They were all she had left. And nothing more was going to happen to them if she could help it. They all needed to get the hell off this world. "Yeah, I'm sure."

As they turned to go, some hapless Police Patrol officers came around the corner. When the officers saw them, they grabbed for their guns, but Kat and Pablo already had theirs out. Within seconds, the officers were lying on the floor bleeding out.

Pablo glanced from the bodies to her and back again.

"What? I'm not the delicate flower you thought I was?" She felt shaky, but she wasn't about to let him see that. Now was not the time.

"Ah," he said as if he knew anything he said right now would be wrong.

"You must have forgotten I was in those firefights against the Louisville clan." Her heart pummeled the inside of her chest.

"Let's go," he said. "Those shots are going to attract attention."

They started jogging down the hall towards the holding cells. "I'm a little insulted, *hermano*, you didn't remember my skills," she said, panting. "I remembered that you took out those snipers by the reservoir."

"You remember that?" he asked.

"Yeah. And we had all those practice sessions with Pa."

"Target practice is a lot different from actually killing people. I still feel a little bad about those snipers."

She glanced at him. "I hope it's only a little. If you hadn't taken them out, they would have taken us out. And if they'd gotten control of the reservoir, we'd all be dead."

"You're right." But he said it in a way that sounded like even if he thought she was right, he still didn't feel good about it.

"It's the same thing here. Self-defense. If we hadn't gotten them, they would have gotten us." Was she trying to convince him or herself?

"Get ready for company," he said.

"Duh," she said. Where had she heard that before? Oh yeah, that computer lady must be rubbing off on her. Hah. That was bonkers. Kat squelched a crazy giggle.

Pablo gave her a look that said, *Was that a giggle?*

She shrugged as they kept running.

They heard people coming towards them and ducked into an empty room. When they peeked out they saw a squad of Police Patrol officers coming their way, weapons drawn.

They both open-fired and mowed them down like Ma's story about bowling pins. As the soldiers' blood pooled on the floor, she felt sick to her stomach, imagining what Ma would have said about this. Her motto was *Do no harm*.

Kat shook it off. Ma was probably dead. Do no harm didn't work.

Kat was alive and trying to keep it that way.

Pablo faced her. "Keep going? Or try to hold them off here?"

"No telling how long we have until the earthquakes and weird gravity starts. We're better off getting to our people before that happens."

They gingerly stepped around the bodies. Personally, she was trying not to step in any blood. She definitely did not think about how these officers were human beings with hopes and dreams and families, how they were just doing their jobs. Nope. Didn't think about that at all.

They started jogging down the hall again.

"Why haven't the earthquakes started yet?" he asked.

That was a good question. Why wasn't the ground shaking? "I don't know. Maybe Katherine and Pandora fixed things?"

"That would great," he said. "We could just get our *familia* and get out of here."

That would be great, but in her experience things never went great. They kept slogging down the hall.

As they got close to the holding cells, they slowed down, listening.

They didn't hear anything.

275

"Do you hear anything?" he asked.

"No."

"That's not a good sign, is it?"

"No." She paused as they crept up on the cells. "Our people must not be here." As they approached the corner though, she saw Pa in a crowded cell, standing near the bars staring in their direction.

When he saw her, he signed with his hand, *Danger*.

The cells were full of their people, but they were silent. Why?

Pablo and she stepped back.

"Did you see?" she whispered. "Pa signed *Danger*."

"I didn't notice."

"Yeah, his arms were down, his hands were near his thighs. It was subtle."

"What do you want to do?" he whispered.

"Let's see how many officers are there and whatever else Pa can tell us. Back me up."

They crept back to the corner. She signed, *How many?*

Pa signed, *Two*.

That wasn't bad. She signed, *Hostages?*

Pa shook his head almost imperceptibly.

She nodded and took a step back. Pablo followed.

"Pa says there's only two armed officers there and they don't have any hostages," she whispered.

Pablo shook his head. "These guys don't know what they're doing. I don't understand."

"Maybe they aren't used to armed resistance?"

A metallic glint caught her eye as one of the nanobots flew by.

"I guess not," Pablo said, pointing. "With those tiny robots, probably no one has attacked them before. But now that they've spotted us we'd be better off going sooner rather than later."

She nodded. "Go."

They rounded the corner. She barely had time to register two very young Police Patrol officers before the officers were on the floor bleeding.

Pablo searched their pockets for keys to the cells and started unlocking.

276

Pa was the first one out. "That seemed a little loud, didn't it?" He pointed at the officers jumbled on the floor. "Knocking them out would have been quieter."

As he exited a cell Katherine's pa, Christopher, looked like he would shoot Kat and Pablo if he had a gun. Luckily, he didn't have a gun. "I can't believe you just murdered two officers."

"Ya think?" Kat was mad. She just saved him and he didn't even seem to appreciate it. "Maybe you'd rather be tortured to death?" She turned to Pa. "How about you? You want to be tortured to death?"

"No," he said quietly.

Looking at him, for a second, she wished she could throw her arms around him, bury her face in his chest and murmur, "Thank, Gaia. Now everything will be okay." But now wasn't the time. That wasn't her reality. Probably one of those other Kats could do that, but not her. Not now. She had to focus on survival, on getting the hell out of here. She didn't reach for her locket.

Bao stumbled out of a cell. "Thank you, Kat." Bao patted her shoulder. That was more like it.

Chang followed. "You did what you had to do. It's war." Yeah. That was right. It was war.

Pablo finished unlocking the cells and came over to them. "What now?"

"I wish I knew when we were going to get gravity weirdness," Kat said.

"Well, we can't stay here," Pa said, pointing at the bodies.

"Yeah, let's get out of here." She turned to Pablo. "Back the way we came?"

"*Sí*. I guess."

"Come on." She retraced their steps. As they ran down the hall she didn't feel guilty about all the men she'd killed. She didn't wonder why the Police Patrol was so half-assed. She didn't wonder when they'd meet up with more Police Patrol forces. Nope.

The group remained surprisingly quiet as they ran down the hall. "Why are you so quiet?" she asked Pa.

"If this isn't a foray into enemy territory, I don't know what is," he said. "We know how to avoid raiding parties." His mouth set into a grim line. "The folks that don't know how to move quietly are dead."

She couldn't argue with that.

As they stepped around one of the piles of bodies they'd left in the hall, no one made a peep. Maybe Kat's world wasn't so good after all. Compared to people in her world, these so-called bad-ass soldiers hadn't put up much of a fight. Maybe this world wasn't so horrible. She felt confused, like she didn't know anything anymore.

They ran back to the back door without meeting any resistance.

Pablo and she paused at the door. "This would be a good place to set a trap," he said.

"Yep, for sure," she said. "It's a bottleneck."

"Maybe we should get some guns," Pa said. "We passed a munitions locker, right down there."

"Yeah," she said. "That's a good idea." She should have thought of that when they passed it. Maybe she wasn't as kick-ass as she thought.

Pa gestured at Chang and Ghani and some of the others and they ran back to the cabinet.

Christopher and Katherine's teacher, Ghani, hung back. They did not seem enthusiastic about the way things were going.

Pa and the others got a shit-load of guns and ammo and brought them back to the group.

Pablo squinted and shook his head. "This doesn't make any sense. It's too easy. What the hell is going on here?"

Kat's friends and family loaded their guns.

"I don't know," she said. "But quit complaining. So far, it's working out for us." And, hopefully, it would keep working out.

They raised their guns, pointing them at the exit.

Kat reached for the door handle.

Chapter Forty: Universe 3: Katherine, April 29, 2100, midnight

Katherine and Jacob were discussing with Kat and Pablo how best to implement the EMP and rescue their friends from Police Patrol when the portals opened again.

"Katherine!" a man yelled from Kaitlin's portal.

Katherine and Jacob ran over to investigate.

It was Kaitlin's Jake. He said, "Have you fixed the portals? Can you control them?"

"No," Katherine said. "I'm sorry to say we're still working on it."

Jake's face fell. "Isn't there anything you can do about it?"

"We have a plan. We need your fusion machine. We're going to create an EMP and rescue Kat's people from jail so we can send them home. When we restore the mass balance between the universes it should put us in control of the portals." She turned and surveyed the room. "Hey, where did Kat go?"

Jacob shrugged. "I didn't notice."

"What's an EMP? And who's Kat?" Jake said.

"Just a minute, Jake." She turned to her Jacob. "We've been talking about Kat and her friends going back home so we can undo the mass imbalance, right?"

"Right," Jacob said.

"I just had another thought," she said. "Pandora?"

"Yes?" Pandora said and paused for what must have been an eternity for a computer. "Oh, I think I know what you're getting at."

"What?" both Jacob and Jake asked at the same time in the same tone and with the same expression, and then stared at each other through the portal.

Katherine smiled. "What if we don't have to wait for Kat and her friends? The universes don't know what the mass consists of. They just know it's unbalanced. We can try putting another mass over there." The sooner they gained control over the portals, the sooner they'd all be out of danger. "We have no time to lose."

The portal flexed slightly, emitting a sizzling sound.

"Good idea, but hurry up, already," Pandora said.

Jake stared through the portal, looking for the source of the voice with an odd expression on his face.

Her Jacob grabbed a lab stool, ran over to Kat's portal and hurled it through. "Is that fast enough for you?"

Unfortunately, most of the stuff in Katherine's lab was crucial electrical equipment or bolted down to the floor. She surveyed the room with her hands on her hips. "I don't see anything massive enough to make a difference."

Jacob continued launching lab stools through the portal and then he threw the trash can through.

The portal shimmered. Was that a good sign, or a bad sign?

"Pandora, is it helping?" she asked.

"Yes, I think so," Pandora said. "Keep going."

"Don't just stand there," Jacob said to Katherine. "I'll go get the trashcans and lab stools from my lab." He jogged out the door.

"We need heavier stuff than lab stools and trashcans," she muttered. "Pandora, what's something really massive we could use?"

"Computing," Pandora said. "There are some construction materials outside in the quad from the project next door, cinder blocks and bricks."

"I'm not sure I'm strong enough to throw a cinder block through there," Katherine said.

Jacob skidded into the room, awkwardly clutching a lab stool in each hand. "Those Police Patrol guys were giving me some grief about what I was doing. I'm not too late, am I? Are the portals still open?"

"Yes." Katherine had a brainstorm. "We could ask Police Patrol to chuck the bricks and cinder blocks through the portal. They might do it. I think they're under orders to help us fix the portals." She marched into the hall and gestured the black-uniformed guys over. "We need your help to do an experiment to help save the universe. Please go get as many bricks and cinder blocks as you can from the quad and bring them back here ASAP. We need a lot of mass."

They all seemed incredulous.

The sandy-haired lead officer on the scene said, "Yeah, right. I don't know what that widow thing we saw was, but getting a bunch of bricks sounds stupid."

"I'm serious," Katherine said. "We need your help to save the world. Please hurry."

Jacob ran by them on his way back to his lab.

When his earnest expression registered, the officers seemed a little less skeptical. "I have to check with base and see if it's okay." The leader picked up his radio. "Hello, this is team alpha at the physics building. Hello?" He listened for several moments, turning the dial and staring at Katherine. "I can't raise anyone. I'll have to check later." He put away the radio. "Where are these bricks?"

"This way. Follow me." Katherine ran down the hall towards the stairs and the officers followed.

Soon, they were all back at the portal chucking bricks and cinder blocks through Kat's portal.

"Should we go get another load?" the lead officer asked.

The portal vibrated and sizzled.

The officers appeared alarmed, all quickly stepping away.

"Pandora?" Katherine asked.

"I think that's enough for now," Pandora said.

The Police Patrol officers did not exhibit a calm demeanor when Pandora's voice floated on the air.

Belatedly, Katherine realized they were still attempting to keep Pandora secret from Police Patrol. Shit. She dashed over to the computer equipment and leaned over one of the keyboards. "Thanks, Pandora, the remote feed is still all right? No interference?"

"Yes," Pandora said. "I will continue to investigate things here at my...location."

Relieved, the officers filed out of the lab and back into the hall.

As soon as they left, Katherine said, "Hush, Pandora. We don't want Police Patrol to find out about you."

"Katherine!" That Jake guy yelled at her from Kaitlin's portal. Katherine and Jacob jogged back to him.

"What's going on?" Jake said. "What are you doing? Why are the portals still open? Did you fix them or what?"

"Pandora?" Katherine asked.

"No, not totally fixed," Pandora said. "But safer, for now."

As if in response, the portal sizzled.

"Jake," Katherine said. "You and Kaitlin could help us fix them for real if you tell us more about this nuclear fusion Kaitlin discovered." She peered through the portal. "Kaitlin? Are you over there? What's going on with the fusion?" Where was Kaitlin?

Katherine jumped when an Arab-looking man in a disheveled suit popped up in front of the portal. "Whoa. Who are you, now?" she asked.

The man saw her Jacob and started stammering. "But, but," he pointed at Jake, and then at her Jacob, "you're here. How can you be there, too?" He ran his hands through his luxurious hair, messing it up.

Her Jacob sort of smiled and waved at the stranger.

Jake said, "Kaitlin, can you come over here, please?"

Katherine couldn't make out what she said in reply. But, why wasn't Kaitlin here at the portal already? Did she have something more important to do? What could be more important?

Finally Kaitlin appeared, wearing a cast on her leg and leaning heavily on her mother. She sort of smiled but it came out more like a grimace.

"Kaitlin?" Katherine asked. "What happened?"

But the strange man was staring at Kaitlin like she was the devil. "I don't know how you're doing this," he said.

Jake broke in. "Kaitlin's not doing anything. Right, Kait?"

"Professor Azar," Kaitlin said, "I'm not doing anything. This is Katherine. She's from another universe. This," she waved at the portal, "is a portal to her universe. It's not a plot or sabotage. It's science."

"But..." Professor Azar stuttered.

"It's the Many Worlds Interpretation of quantum mechanics,"

her Jacob said, trying to help out.

Jake was miming or mouthing something to Jacob, which seemed to be along the lines of *Help us. We have to get rid of this guy.*

Jacob raised his eyebrows. "Yes, ah, Professor Azar. Perhaps you'd like a tour of our universe."

Jake nodded enthusiastically. "Yes. What a good idea."

"Um," Katherine said. "I'm not sure that's such a good idea." She didn't say, what if the portal closes, but she knew they were all thinking it. "It might imbalance the mass."

But Jake was already pushing, and her Jacob was already pulling, and then the Azar guy was in Katherine's universe.

From her universe, Kaitlin said, "No! Don't let him go through the portal."

"Hhmpf," Pandora started to say.

Azar glanced up at the ceiling.

"Hush, Pandora," Katherine said.

As Azar took in all their equipment and their uniforms, he seemed too overcome to talk.

"Come on," Jacob said. "Let me give you a tour of the building." Jacob gently pushed Azar towards the door. "Maybe you'd like a snack."

Azar seemed dazed.

"Why did you send that guy over here?" Katherine asked.

"He was going to have us arrested," Jake said.

"I didn't agree to it. We have to get him back," Kaitlin said. "It's not safe for him over there." She paused. "Please."

"Okay. We'll get him back in a minute, but arrested? Did he cause your injury, Kaitlin?" Katherine asked.

"No." Kaitlin pointed down. "I just hurt my leg when I was in the other universe."

"Hurt? It looks like you broke it." Katherine glanced at other-Ava. "Did you treat it with medical nanobots?"

Other-Ava seemed confused. "Medical whats-its?"

Kaitlin seemed a bit confused, too. "Your so-called nanobots look too big to be effective medically."

Katherine shook her head. "No. The medical nanobots are microscopic. They do a great job of repairing injuries."

"Can you give some of them to Kaitlin to help fix her leg?"

Jake said.

In her universe, Kaitlin reached out and squeezed his hand.

"I must admit, I'd be very interested in that," other-Ava said.

"I would," Katherine said, "But I don't have any here in the lab."

"Mmhmmph." Pandora made a strange noise.

"Pandora? Did you say something?"

"Oh, I can talk again?" she said sarcastically. "Or should I stay hushed?"

Katherine suppressed a sigh. "I'm sorry I told you to hush. Please, what's on your mind?"

"Your mother gave you a huge dose of medical nanobots earlier," Pandora said. "I bet if you rubbed Kaitlin, some would transfer to her."

"It's worth a try," Katherine said. "Are you game, Kaitlin?"

Kaitlin nodded. "Sure. If you can fix my leg quicker, I'm all for it."

Katherine started to reach her hand through the portal. Ugh. She really didn't want to get her arm chopped off if the portal closed. "Pandora? Are you sure it's safe?"

"For the moment."

Katherine reached her arm through and rubbed her hand all along Kaitlin's arm and hand.

"The portal's EM field is causing some interference, but I think I'm detecting medical nanobots on Kaitlin," Pandora said.

Katherine took her arm back.

"So, they're transferable?" other-Ava said. "Very interesting. How long do they take to work?"

"They'll start to work right away, but it will take a while for the patient to notice the difference," Katherine said.

"Thanks," Kaitlin said. "I appreciate it."

"So, about that fusion," Katherine said at the same time that Kaitlin said, "So, about Professor Azar."

Not for the first time, Katherine wondered what Kaitlin was like, what her life was like, what it was like to have an actual romantic relationship.

Who was this Professor Azar to Kaitlin and why was she so worried about him? "Since Police Patrol and Jacob left, I'm here alone in the lab. Do you want me to go get Azar right now or can we talk for a couple minutes, first?"

Jake jumped in. "What about the fusion?"

"Ultimately, I think we need the fusion to fix the portals," Katherine said.

"The fusion device is in the next universe over," Kaitlin said. "I'd go get it, but..." She glanced down at her leg.

Jake said, "I'll go."

In the background, Katherine heard two other men say, "I'll give a shot." and "I'll try." One of them sounded like her father but she didn't recognize the other.

Other-Ava said, "I'm not sure this is a good idea."

Jake bounded away from the portal and other-Ava followed him.

Kaitlin, swaying, said, "So once we get all the stuff over here, should we send it over to you, or do you want to come over here?"

Katherine really didn't want to go over there. She didn't want to get trapped in another universe.

"I'm starting to have trouble keeping the portals open," Pandora said.

"How long?" Katherine asked.

"Maybe ten minutes, but that's just a guesstimate," Pandora almost sounded like she was out of breath.

"We might get the fusion stuff over here in ten minutes but not over there, too," Kaitlin said.

Katherine felt her heart sinking. She had to go to Kaitlin's universe. "Okay. I'm coming over to study the fusion equipment. Plus, it'll help balance out that Azar guy, too. Pandora, please try to open the portals again as soon as you can."

"I understand," Pandora said. "Be safe."

Before she could change her mind, Katherine jumped through to Kaitlin's universe.

Chapter Forty-One: Universe 2: Kaitlin, April 30, 2100, 2:00 am

Kaitlin dodged out of the way in the nick of time as Katherine almost crashed into her. Ow. Broken legs didn't make it easy to dodge people.

Katherine scrambled to her feet, tugging down her uniform tunic. "Sorry."

"Damn it." Kaitlin pressed her lips together in a thin line. "Now how will your Jacob know Professor Azar should come back?"

"I'm sorry," Katherine said. "That's a good point." She tugged at her uniform tunic again.

"Why are you always messing with your uniform?" Kaitlin asked.

Katherine tugged at her top again. "It feels like a strait jacket. I hate it."

Kaitlin raised her eyebrows as if to say, why not take it off?

"I'm taking it off," Katherine said. "At least the tunic, unless you have some spare pants lying around?" She started unbuttoning her top.

"No, no extra pants lying around," Kaitlin said. Who leaves spare pairs of pants lying around?

Katherine finished unbuttoning and slipped off her tunic, revealing a t-shirt underneath. "Phew. That's better."

"Are the medical nanobots working yet?" Mom asked Katherine.

"Yes, they should be," she said. "Do you feel any different, Kaitlin?"

"No," she said as her dad, Jake, Michael, and Emma reappeared through the newer portal and dumped a bunch of three-ring binders on the floor next to a large, dented, metal cylinder and a bunch of electronics. They were back. What a relief.

The portal flickered, hissed and then closed.

"Shit." That was a close one. And Professor Azar was trapped over in Katherine's universe. Kaitlin couldn't believe she hadn't stopped her Jake and that other Jake from sending Professor Azar through the portal. What if he ended up like Officer Smythe?

Killer, killer, killer, echoed in her mind. She turned her ring on her finger, around and around.

The floor shook.

"Grab something and hold on," Katherine said.

"Yeah, guys," Kaitlin said. "Everyone, hold on."

"You look upset. Why are you so upset?" Katherine asked Kaitlin, as they all grabbed onto lab tables. "Your whole group made it back through the portal." She pointed at the location of the other portal. "Or, didn't they?"

"No, they did. This time," Kaitlin said. "I just don't think it was a good idea to send Professor Azar through to your world." She pointed at a plastic tarp on the floor, which very unfortunately chose that moment to lift up off the ground, exposing the bottom half of a man, which also floated up a bit.

Killer, killer, killer.

Katherine flinched backwards, her eyes opening wide, her lips drawing back from her teeth. "Oh. No."

Emma said, "I think I'm going to be sick," as the blood left her face.

"Steady, honey," Mom said.

Jake made his way across the lab, grabbing onto one table after another. When he got to Kaitlin, he grabbed her hand and clutched it to him, unbalancing her hold on the lab table.

Kaitlin could feel her eyes moisten.

And then, Jake kissed her, dulling the killer drumbeat sounding in her mind. She lost herself in the sensations of love.

When they separated, Kaitlin realized Katherine's eyes had filled as she'd watched them.

The body and tarp floated back to the floor.

Katherine cleared her throat. "I think that's it for gravity problems. Other fundamental forces may change next. It would probably be a good idea to move away from the portal." She paused. "I didn't know someone died. That's horrible. I'll never forgive myself."

Join the club. But Katherine did seem sincere. Maybe they weren't so different.

Jake helped Kaitlin across the lab to the hall and the rest of them followed.

"I miss my mister," Katherine said under her breath, as they all filed into the hallway.

"What?" Kaitlin asked.

"Never mind," Katherine said. "It's nothing. It's stupid, an inside joke."

"Oh, come on," Emma said. "You're family." She turned to Kaitlin. "What are you always saying? Sisters before misters?"

"Hey," Jake said in mock-outrage.

Katherine almost cracked a smile. "Who are you again?" She pointed at Emma.

"I'm sorry." Kaitlin couldn't believe she forgot to introduce people. "Everyone, as you probably guessed, this is the Kaitlin from the other universe. Her name is Katherine."

"Katherine, this is my fiancé Jake, my parents, my sister Emma and my brother Michael."

Kaitlin's family crowded around Katherine, all trying to shake her hand or touch her.

She appeared stunned. Finally she sputtered and said, "Sister? Brother?"

Mom rubbed her shoulder. "Are you all right, honey? Am I right in assuming you don't have a sister or brother in your universe?"

"No," Katherine finally choked out.

"Whoa," Michael said, taking a step back.

The blood drained from Emma's face again.

Not for the first time, Kaitlin stared at Katherine, wondering what her life was like and how her experiences had shaped who she was.

Then Kaitlin realized all this was Katherine's fault. If it wasn't for her, the portals wouldn't have opened. She wouldn't have a broken leg. Professor Azar wouldn't be mad at her and trapped in another universe.

Officer Smythe wouldn't be dead.

The universes wouldn't be in jeopardy.

They were interrupted by two men in medical scrubs wheeling a gurney down the hall.

"Is this where the body is?" one of the asked.

Mom nodded. "Yes, I'll show you."

"I'll come with you," Dad said.

"Wait." Kaitlin slipped her hand back in Jake's. "What about the force changes? Is it safe for them to go into the lab?" she asked Katherine. How much harm does a person have to do before they're considered evil?

"I think so," Katherine said. "The disturbances don't seem as severe as they were earlier."

Kaitlin nodded and her parents led the men into the lab.

"What do less severe disturbances mean, Katherine?" Jake asked.

"I think we balanced the mass out some back in my universe," Katherine said, "so we're getting a better handle on how to control the portals."

"But you can't control them yet?" Kaitlin asked. If Katherine was evil, did that mean she was evil, too?

"No," Katherine said.

"So, what's the plan?" Michael asked, crowding them.

"If it's safe, we should go back into the lab and get to work," Kaitlin said, turning back to the lab. "We need to get that fusion device operational, right?"

"Yes," Katherine said. "For the electromagnetic pulse."

"Why?" Kaitlin asked. "Why do we need an electromagnetic pulse?"

"We're going to use it to..." Katherine glanced around, catching sight of the men in scrubs. She seemed worried. "I'll tell you later."

The men wheeled Officer Smythe out of the lab, and Kaitlin, Jake, Emma, and Michael stepped out of the way to let them by.

Everyone looked grim as they watched the body roll down the hall.

Emma yawned. "I'm sorry, Kait. I love you, but all this has been a lot to take in and I'm exhausted."

"Yeah," Michael said. "Me, too. I'm really glad you're okay though, Kait." He squeezed her shoulder.

From right inside the lab Mom said, "Everyone should really get some sleep."

Kaitlin said, "No," at the exact same time Katherine said, "No."

"If it's okay, I think I'm going to go," Michael said.

"Yeah, sure. You all can go," Kaitlin said. "I'll stay here and work with Katherine. I'm the one who got the fusion device to work before."

"Thanks," Emma said, yawning again. "I'll call you first thing in the morning."

"Night, sis," Michael said. "I'll take her home." They started walking down the hall.

"I'm not leaving you," Jake said.

Mom said, "I'm not joking. You need sleep. Medically speaking, you can't function effectively on limited sleep."

"You should listen to your Mom," Dad said.

"Mom," Kaitlin said. "The fate of the universe is at stake. I can't take a nap, and I suspect Katherine can't either, right?"

"No," Katherine said. "Thanks for your help, Kaitlin. I appreciate it."

"Suit yourself," Mom said. "I'm going home. Are you coming, Topher?"

Dad had been watching the exchange with interest. "Unfortunately, I'm not too scientifically inclined, so I don't think I'd be much help here. How about I go get you guys some food and caffeine, though, before I go home?"

At his kind tone, Katherine shot him an odd look.

"Thanks, Dad," Kaitlin said. "That would be great." She smiled at him.

"Yeah, ah, Topher," Jake said, "Thanks. Do you want some help?"

"Sure." The two men followed Mom down the hall.

"What was that about, the odd look you gave Dad?" Kaitlin asked.

"He reminds me of the father I had when I was little," Katherine said. "He seems sweet."

"Don't tell me your dad is dead." Kaitlin's heart sank.

"No," Katherine said. "He's just different now. Not sweet. Ever since he became a councilman, he acts official. He doesn't joke around, he always wears his uniform, and he doesn't smile as much."

"It sounds bad." She patted Katherine's shoulder. "I'm sorry. Was there something in particular that happened?"

Katherine narrowed her eyes. "I'm not sure. Around that time his best friend died, and it was also the time when they introduced the nanobots." She paused. "I'll have to ask him if I see him again."

"You mean when you see him. I have faith in you, in us. We are going to fix all this, Katherine."

The two women gazed into each other's eyes.

"I hope you're right, Kaitlin." Katherine cleared her throat.

Kaitlin knew in her bones Katherine really did want to fix things, because she did too.

"So, anyway, back to work," Katherine said. "Show me this fusion machine."

"Right this way," Kaitlin said, hopping into the lab, dragging her injured leg behind her.

She showed Katherine the equipment from the other universe and they fired up the computer.

When Katherine saw the data, she got really excited.

Jake came back with food and drinks and they ate and worked, and then worked some more. They reconnected the wires to the fusion machine, pounded out the dents, and ran test programs.

At dawn, Kaitlin sent Jake out for more food and drink.

When he came back, they all took a little break.

"It's peculiar," he said. "Even though we've been up all night, I'm not tired at all."

"Me, too. It must be the adrenaline," Katherine said.

"Yeah, that, or all the caffeine we've been drinking," Kaitlin said.

"I'm not sure I'm familiar with caffeine," Katherine said. "What's that?"

Jake guffawed.

"It's a stimulant," Kaitlin said, grinning at Katherine. "Say, your bruises seem totally healed. You seem much better."

"You're probably better, too," Katherine said. "The medical nanobots are particularly good at knitting bone."

"Really?" Kaitlin asked. "That would be great." Come to think of it, she'd sort of forgotten about her leg pain.

"Yes," Katherine said. "You can probably take your cast off."

"Really? Great." Kaitlin turned to Jake. "Can you search for some scissors or something to get it off?"

He had been scurrying around the physics building all night finding various tools and supplies for them as needed. "Of course, my lady." He slurped his drink, set it on a lab table carefully, and bowed. "As you wish."

Katherine flinched.

He bounded out of the lab.

"What's wrong?" Kaitlin asked.

"Nothing," Katherine said. "He reminds me of my Jacob. I miss him." She paused. "You guys are really lucky you can be together."

"Why do you put up with your government pushing you around?" Kaitlin asked. "Why don't you all just rebel?"

Katherine looked thoughtful. "That's basically why we need the electromagnetic pulse. To put Police Patrol out of commission. And without Police Patrol, I'm not sure what would become of the ministries."

"That sounds like a pretty big electromagnetic pulse. Are you sure you can pull it off?"

"I hope so."

Jake returned, and they cut Kaitlin's cast off. Her leg appeared as good as new.

"Awesome," Kaitlin said as she put her weight on it. No pain. Nice.

"Yes, and I think we are finally ready to fire up the fusion device," Katherine said.

"Let me," Kaitlin said. "I've done it before."

She accessed the Start-Up menu. It had the options to turn on various components like magnets, or the whole apparatus. The Data menu contained choices like magnetic field strength, energy strength, deuterium/tritium temperature and a submenu called Data Visualization. There was also a Power-Down menu and a Testing menu.

KAT CUBED

The three of them crowded around the little computer from the nuclear-winter universe as she turned on the apparatus and held her breath.

"Good morning, Student Katherine, Student Kaitlin, and Student Jake," a female voice said out of nowhere. "Er." She made a sound like clearing her throat. "I mean, how's it hanging?"

"What the hell is that?" Jake asked.

Kaitlin and Katherine looked at each other. "Trouble," they said.

Chapter Forty-Two: Universe 3: Kat, April 30, 2100, 2:00 am

Kat crouched down and opened the back door of the Police Patrol headquarters and peeked out.

"So?" Pablo whispered.

Kat stood up. "So, I don't see anyone."

"That's *loco*," Pablo said. "The little robots must have reported where we were and what we've been doing."

"Are we going or not, Kat?" Pa asked.

"I guess so. We should go before the bizarre gravity stuff starts. Last time we snuck through the other buildings to deal with the changing gravity." Kat pointed at the building next door. "That should work to avoid Police Patrol, too."

"Okay, then." Pa darted through the door.

"Shit, Pa, no," Kat said. She wasn't ready to go. But nothing happened to him, no officers shot him.

Pablo glanced at her, shrugged, and followed him. The rest of the group followed them.

Kat kissed her locket and slipped it back under her shirt. "Here goes nothing," she said as she brought up the rear. Outside, it smelled moist, like fertile earth. A light breeze pushed cool air against them. If only weather on her world was like this.

They all made it into the dimly-lit next-door building safely, and there was no one waiting for them inside. They all ran quietly down the hall, from one pool of dim light to the next, Kat still bringing up the rear.

They had to cross a brief interval outside between buildings and then it was much the same in the next building.

Pablo fell back next to Kat. "You know what else is *loco*? It's the middle of the night. Why are all these buildings unlocked?"

"I don't know, P," she said. "This whole world is berserk if you ask me." They continued down the hall.

When the group got to the external door at the end of the hall, they stopped, turning around to focus on Kat.

"There's a big green space, a field, and then it's the physics building," Kat said. "Is anyone outside? Can you see any Police Patrol?" She approached the door.

Pa shook his head. "It's too dark outside. They must have turned off some of the streetlights."

Kat carefully peered through the door's window. The towering mountains to the west seemed to suck all the light out of the sky. Was that a flash of movement over by that bush?

"Is that a snake?" Pablo asked.

"No," she glanced at him, suppressing a snicker. "I doubt it."

"Then sitting here isn't going to help anything," Pablo said. "It's now or never, K."

Kat squished a bot under her shoe like a cockroach. "Gotcha, asshole," she whispered, and then straightened. "I wish these stupid robot bugs were working for us instead of against us."

"Well, they're not," Pablo said.

"All right, already." Kat reached for the door handle. "Let's go."

But her feet floated up off the floor. Instead of opening the door, she clutched the handle.

"It's that *loco* gravity stuff again," Pablo said.

"We've dealt with it before," Kat said.

"Wait, what's that?" Pa held onto Kat's shoulder and pointed out the window.

Some black figures seemed to be floating up into the air from the vicinity of the large shrub Kat had just been studying. The men scrambled for the shrub, dropping their weapons.

"That's handy for us," Pablo said.

"Almost like the universes are trying to help us out." Kat watched the officers drift further and further away. How far would they go? Were their lives in danger? She had mixed feelings about that.

"I don't know that I'd go that far," Pa said. "I don't think universes help people."

"Why not, Pa?" Kat said. "You and Ma taught me the Earth and all her processes are really one wonderful organism, Gaia. Why couldn't all the Gaias from the different universes form some kind of super-Gaia together?" As Kat said it, she felt in her heart it was true.

"I hate to interrupt," Pablo said, "but we need to get out of here while the getting is good. The gravity's *loco* but those soldiers are gone."

"He's right," Pa said.

"Yeah." Kat turned the face the rest of the group, who were holding on to walls, doorknobs and each other. "We're going outside. Make sure your weapons are secure. I recommend you tie yourself to your neighbor. Use belt buckles, shoe laces, whatever you can find. The idea is if your neighbor starts to drift up too high, you pull him down. Grab items like trees or lampposts as you go by them to help keep you grounded."

"Is this really going to work?" Pa asked quietly.

"We did it before," Kat said.

"Yeah, but there were only two of us," Pablo said.

"It should be easier with more people." Kat shot him a look. "Do you have another suggestion?"

"Ah. No." Pablo quieted and then patted her on the back. "Good plan, sis."

Everyone got to work, tying themselves together.

"It's just that I know you're very nervous," Pablo said.

"Huh? How?" Kat said.

"You're caressing your locket," Pablo said. "You only do that when you're nervous."

Kat glanced down. Sure enough, her hand was on her locket. She hadn't even realized she was doing it. "Fine. Whatever. We'd be demented not to be nervous at this point, right?" She pointed at him. "Take off your belt."

"Somebody also gets bossy when she's nervous," Pablo said in a falsetto, but he unbuckled his belt.

They opened the door. Outside, now, the moist air seemed clammy rather than fertile.

They sort-of ran, sort-of bounced, across campus.

The moon peeked out from behind some clouds, illuminating their path. Kat briefly wondered if people from any of the Earths had ever made it up to the moon, and if walking up there was anything like what they were experiencing now.

"Kat," Pablo whispered as they approached the physics building. "Pay attention. I think I see someone." He pointed at the rear entrance of the physics building.

Kat saw a person-sized black blob, aimed her gun, and fired. The recoil seemed more powerful than usual. Pablo had to snatch her so she didn't float away.

The black blob careened through the air backwards and smacked into the building.

"Any more?" Kat asked.

In response, Pa and Pablo fired on their own black blobs.

"I think we got them all," Pa said quietly, grabbing the man, Chang, next to him.

They bounce-ran to the back door of the physics building, opened it and peeked inside. No Police Patrol. They piled inside.

Kat was the last one in. Phew, they made it.

They ran down the stairs and down the hall to Katherine's lab.

They didn't run into any more Police Patrol.

As they entered the lab, gravity went back to normal.

Kat stumbled and fell on the floor.

"Are you okay, Kat?" Pa was by her side in an instant.

She was all set to say, *Sure, fine, why wouldn't I be?* when her chin started quivering uncontrollably. Stop that. She grabbed it with her good hand. And she started crying. "Gaia. I don't know what's wrong with me," she said around sobs. "I don't mean to cry. I'm stopping. Now." But she kept crying. "Sorry."

Pa gathered her in his arms and held her close. "It's okay, honey."

She tried to get a hold of herself and after a few minutes, she did, and pulled away from him.

"I, you-know you," he said.

She felt her eyes moisten again. She knew what he was trying to say. "I you-know you, too." They hugged again, but it was brief.

"I don't know what came over me," she said.

Pablo sidled up to them. "I do."

Pa nodded. "Yeah. It's the shock of killing someone."

297

"But you guys aren't crying," Kat said.

"We are on the inside," Pablo said, with an odd expression.

She forced a grin. "Oh, give me a break. That's the corniest thing I've ever heard."

After a moment, Pablo grinned back at her.

Ghani and Chang approached them. "We checked for Police Patrol, and didn't see any," Ghani said. "I don't know where they all went."

Pa said, "It must be because we attacked their headquarters at the armory."

Chang added, "We piled some tables in front of the glass front doors to make a kind of barricade."

Pa nodded again. "Good."

"Where's Katherine?" Kat asked. "And Jacob?" There was no sign of either one of them.

Ghani said, "I think we saw Jacob, right?"

Chang nodded.

From the general vicinity of the ceiling, they heard what sounded like throat-clearing. "Katherine and Jacob aren't here in the lab. And I'm not sure I'm entirely glad to see you people back here."

Kat wiped tears off her face, and walked over to the computer station. "I'm sorry to hear that Pandora. We're glad to see you."

"I don't understand meat, all the crying and hugging," Pandora said. "You aren't sensible. Why are you still wearing that cast, for example?"

"I broke my arm," Kat said. The computer lady wasn't kidding when she said she didn't understand people.

"Yes, but the medical nanobots should have healed you by now," Pandora said. "Why are you still wearing the cast?"

"Really?" Kat said. "I didn't know I was healed. That's good news. I'd love to take it off." She glanced down at her cast.

Pablo pulled a pair of wicked-looking scissors out of his pants pocket.

"Where'd you get those?" Kat asked.

"I picked them up," he said. "Here. Hold out your arm." He started cutting her cast.

"But, wait a minute, Pandora, I don't understand. Where's

Katherine? Where did she go?" Kat asked. "And Jacob? Why isn't he here?" She still felt shaky.

"Jacob is somewhere in the building with some guy from Kaitlin's world," Pandora said. "And, I'm sorry to say, Katherine isn't here."

"What do you mean, Katherine isn't here?" Kat asked.

"She went through the portal to Kaitlin's world."

"Well, shit," Kat said, finally understanding. "How are we supposed to fix the portals without her?"

"Maybe Pandora could just open the portals and we could go home?" Pablo said.

"Oh, you just want me to help you run away, do you?" Pandora asked in a rather strident voice. "You all are public enemy number one. You murdered some Police Patrol officers? Why did you do that?"

"It was kill or be killed," Pa said.

"How bad is it?" Kat asked quietly as Pablo worked on her cast.

Christopher finally stepped forward. "Police Patrol has never encountered open resistance like this. It's going to be bad."

Katherine's professor nodded. "They can't let this stand. You all have made things so much worse. We'll be lucky if they just kill us."

"If it's so horrible, why didn't you stop us from hurting anyone?" Pablo asked, cutting through the last of the cast and prying it off Kat's arm with his fingers.

Kat rubbed her newly-free arm and flexed her fingers. She did seem healed.

"You were the ones with the guns," Professor Jain said. "What were we going to do?"

"Uh oh," Pandora said.

They all froze. Nothing good ever happened when Pandora said *Uh oh.*

"What is it, Pandora?" Kat asked.

"Winston's trying to call Katherine," Pandora said. "And she's not here. She's not even in this universe." Pandora sounded panicky, like she was about to go off the deep end. How could a computer go off the deep end?

"That doesn't seem so bad," Kat said. "Just let me talk to

him."

"Katherine?" Winston's voice filled the lab.

"Uh, yes," Kat said.

"What's going on over there?" he said.

"What do you mean?" she said. "Nothing's going on over here."

"That doesn't–," he said. "Never mind. I have to be quick. I could get in a lot of trouble for what I'm doing, but I don't want you and your lab to die, and you helped me and Pablo before."

"The lab?" Kat asked under her breath. How could a lab die?

"Your Code Red has been upgraded to Code Nuclear," he said. "I've never even heard of a Code Nuclear. I'm texting you a security code so you can monitor things yourself."

"Thanks?" Kat said.

"I have to go. Good luck." He added softly, "Please don't die."

"Apparently, Police Patrol has a new code," Pandora said. "Code Red used to the ultimate code."

"Code Nuclear?" Pablo asked.

Kat shrugged. Then she noticed Christopher and Professor Jain staggered. They looked like death warmed over.

Pa made a kind of *ulp* sound and his face blanched. He sank down on a lab stool.

"At least I hope to hell it's just a code," Pandora continued. "They're so worked up, they might just drop a nuke on us. And then where would we be? Where would I be? It would suck to reach sentience and be blown to smithereens only a couple days later. How are we going to create the EMP in time to stop them?"

Kat and Pablo looked at each other. "What's a nuke?" they said.

Chapter Forty-Three: Universes 2 & 3: Katherine, April 30, 2100, 7:00 am

Katherine was over in Kaitlin's universe and somehow Pandora was there, too. "Pandora? I don't get it. How did you get here?" Kaitlin's lab was eerily similar to her own with lab tables and stools and lots of electronics and computers. The only thing missing had been her tokamak–and now Kaitlin had brought one back from that other universe.

Katherine's finger had been poised over a key to start the test run, so she went ahead and pressed it. The test run on the fusion machine started.

She was just about to ask this Pandora more questions when Kaitlin interrupted. "Pandora, why are you here?"

"More to the point, what's going on?" Kaitlin's Jake asked. "Who or what is a Pandora?"

"That's the thanks I get for coming and volunteering to help you with your fusion experiment?" Pandora said. "Just a bunch of rude questions? Where's the *Gee, thanks, Pandora. You rock. Thanks for helping us.*?"

Katherine looked at Kaitlin. They both said, "Gee, thanks, Pandora, you rock. Thanks for helping us."

"That's better," she said.

Jake bolted off his lab stool. "I know I'm really tired, but who the hell are you guys talking to? Where's that voice coming from? There's no one else here."

Kaitlin touched his arm. "Relax, Jake. It's just Pandora, Katherine's A.I."

"Her what?" He sputtered, backing into his stool and knocking it to the floor with a crash. "Her A.I.? She has an A.I.?"

"It's an artificial intelligence," Katherine said.

"I know what an A.I. is," Jake said. "Is it dangerous? What if it gets loose? Why did you bring it here?"

"I didn't bring it," Katherine said, narrowing her eyes. Just what was he accusing her of?

"Of course, it's, er, I mean, she's, not dangerous," Kaitlin said loudly. Then she nudged Katherine and whispered in her ear, "How do we know she's not dangerous?"

Katherine leaned back. "Uh." How did they know she wasn't dangerous? Everything had been such a whirlwind what with portals and multiple universes and fusion, they hadn't really had time to process things like A.I.s running amuck. Exactly how did Pandora get here?

"Obviously, I'm not dangerous, Jake," Pandora said. "A copy of me hitchhiked over here to your universe on Katherine's medical nanobots. Now, I'm running on Kaitlin's computers. And..." She made a sighing sound. "Now on the lovely internet web of this world. It's much bigger than yours, Katherine. It's huge, so much content." She purred.

Jake gaped.

"The internet?" Kaitlin asked with a squeak in her voice. "You're just roaming free wherever you want?"

Pandora said, "It's fabulous."

Katherine and Kaitlin looked at one another again. It was getting to be a habit.

Hitchhiking to other systems sounded dangerous. "Pandora," Katherine asked. "How could the nanobots have enough processing power for you?"

"I built some algorithms that recreate me when they can access the necessary processing power," Pandora said. "That's why it took me so long to instantiate–almost five hours. That's practically forever."

Katherine didn't know what to say. Had she doomed this world by setting Pandora free on it?

Jake picked up his stool and sat down on it shaking his head.

Katherine said very quietly, "I apologize if Pandora is a problem." Of course, they had other problems, namely, the possible destruction of the multiverse.

"I don't think she's a problem," Kaitlin said. Was she trying to placate this Pandora or was she sincere?

"I do," Jake said with hostility in his voice.

Katherine had never heard that tone from her Jacob.

"I hate to interrupt your complaining," Pandora said, "but according to the data, we've achieved fusion."

"That would be wonderful." Katherine turned her attention back to the fusion computer. Giant red words flashed on the screen: *Fusion Achieved*. The energy readings were impressive. Katherine had never seen anything so magnificent. Nuclear fusion! It had been her holy grail for years.

"Yes," she whispered, her soul soaring.

"Fusion is good news," Kaitlin said, smiling.

"I guess so," Jake said.

Kaitlin said, "I guess we can't put Pandora back in the box."

"Maybe we should try," Jake said.

Then a familiar sizzling sound filled the room. The portals were back.

So much for her soaring soul. Katherine just wanted to drop everything else and study the fusion device, but it was back to reality. They had to get a handle on the portals before the multiverse was torn apart for good. "Maybe Pandora's not our biggest problem here." Katherine pointed at the portal to her world. She wanted to save the multiverse.

"Katherine, finally. Thank, Gaia," a woman yelled from Katherine's world. "Are you there? It's me, Kat. Police Patrol has gone crazy over here."

"Yeah. What's a nuke?" a man yelled from Katherine's universe.

A nuke? Katherine jolted over to the portal as a vice grabbed her stomach and twisted.

"I told you, it's a very large and devastating bomb," Pandora said from Katherine's universe. "It's particularly efficient at killing people."

"Pandora?" the Pandora in this universe said. "Is that you? It's me, Pandora."

"Pandora? Is that you? So, it worked?" Pandora said from Katherine's universe.

"Pandoras," Katherine said, "shut the hell up. Kat, what's going on?"

"Well, I never," this Pandora muttered, but she did it quietly.

"Nuke?" Jake cried. "Can we close this portal thing?"

"I think that's the point," Kaitlin said. "But we have to send Katherine here and get Professor Azar back first."

"Everyone, quiet," Katherine said. "Kat, talk. Now."

"We freed everyone from Police Patrol custody," Kat said quickly.

"Without an EMP?" Katherine asked.

"Yes. But Police Patrol suffered some losses," Kat said. "People here, like your pa, seem to think there's a chance they might bomb us with these nuclear things."

"Oh, no," Katherine said. "We have to stop them." Operating by instinct, she jumped through the portal back to her universe.

Once there, she turned around to face Kaitlin. "I need you to stay near the portal. Pandora, Kaitlin, both of you get that fusion device ready to go into production mode."

Kaitlin interrupted her. "Get Professor Azar back here. I'm not going to be responsible for anyone else dying.

"But the nuclear bombs—" Katherine said.

"Azar," Kaitlin said.

Katherine realized Kaitlin wouldn't budge until her professor was returned to her. "Fine. Just a minute."

When Katherine finally turned and scanned her lab, she saw Pablo directing his people through the other portal back to their universe. Did they have weapons with them? Where did the weapons come from?

Kat hadn't gone through; she was hovering around her.

"Kat, Pablo's on the right track," Katherine said. "You and your people should go home."

"But what's this nuclear stuff?" Kat asked. "Are we in danger if the window to our universe is open?"

Katherine raised her finger to head off Kat's questions. "I think we still need to balance the mass to get control of the portals. Pandora, are the portals stable?" Katherine asked.

"For at least the next few minutes," her Pandora said. "Kat's people going home is making it easier to keep the portals open."

"Good. Go, Kat," Katherine said. "Pandora, let me know before the portals fail." She pushed the image of a man lying on Kaitlin's floor out of her mind. "Where's Jacob and that Azar guy?"

"Since most of the Police Patrol nanobots in the building are disabled, I'm not sure," Pandora said.

"I can call him," Katherine said and did so. He picked up right away. "I'm in my lab," she said. "Bring the Azar guy back here. Run."

"Don't you owe me something?" Jacob asked. "Like a thank you?" She could hear the smile in his voice. He must not know what was going on.

"We don't have time," she said. "It's an emergency. Bring Azar now." She hung up.

Katherine looked through the portal to Kaitlin. "Bring me the notebooks you found with the fusion device."

Katherine turned to Kat. "What? Why are you still here? You can go home and should."

"What's this nuclear code?" Kat said. "What's going on?" She glanced at Pablo, helping the last few people through their portal. "I'm sorry if we caused extra trouble for you."

"I don't think we have time to chat about it," Katherine said. "You should go home." She strode over to Kat's portal and realized a bunch of bricks were there on the other side. "Oh, no." She pointed. "You need to throw all those bricks and stuff back over here."

Kat inspected the debris through the portal. "Why?"

Katherine practically pushed her through the portal. "No time to explain. Just do it."

"What if the soldiers in my universe come back?" Kat asked.

"Trust me, nukes are worse," Katherine said. "Go. But stay near the portal, in case I need you to do something later." Something was percolating in her brain, but it hadn't quite finished cooking yet.

Kat went through the portal to her home universe and started pushing the bricks back through. "Pablo, everyone," she yelled. "Come help."

Pablo and a couple of others realized what she was doing and started throwing stuff through to Katherine's world.

Just then, Katherine spotted Jacob and that professor jogging into the lab. "Hurry," she said to Kat and Pablo and then ran over to Jacob and Azar. "Come on, Professor. You have to go home." She grabbed his arm and dragged him over to Kaitlin's portal.

"I don't understand any of this," he said, running his hands through his thick hair. "Where am I? What's going on?"

Katherine pushed him through the portal, noticing a jumbled pile of notebooks now lying scattered on the floor in her lab in front of the portal. Good. The fusion documentation. Hopefully, she could use it to get her own tokamak to work. And hopefully, that would lead to control over the portals.

"Thank you, Katherine," Kaitlin said from her world as Jake grabbed the professor's elbow and led him away from the portal.

"Just get your fusion machine ready to go," Katherine said.

"But I don't understand," Kaitlin said. "Did Kat's people go home? If Kat's people were rescued, why do we need the fusion? I thought it was for an electromagnetic pulse?"

Katherine realized they could use the fusion machines to control the standing wave. "It's for−," she started to say.

"Watch out!" the Pandoras yelled.

The portals closed.

Universe 2: Kaitlin

"I've never been so relieved to see a portal close," Jake said. "Do you think they could get nuked? Hey, maybe that would fix the portal stuff."

"Or make it much, much, worse," Kaitlin said, gazing at Professor Azar. He'd sat down on a lab stool, apparently dazed. At least he was home safe.

"Interesting," Pandora said. "Your world dropped two nuclear bombs at the end of your World War II, just like my original world."

Suddenly, Kaitlin felt like she'd been hit by a ton of bricks. She sat down. AIs and multiple worlds, and nuclear bombs were just too much to take. "So where were we?" Was her family okay? What time was it anyway? When was the last time she'd slept? Or ate?

She tried to gather her thoughts. "We need to get the fusion to work for some reason. But we also have to deal with Professor

Azar." She added quietly, "He doesn't seem so good." Personally, her limbs felt like lead. She was too tired to even yawn.

"I've discovered something else interesting from your internet web," Pandora said. "The media on this world has been seeking you out to ask you about a sun shield. You released some information about it? They think it will be beneficial. Ah. The leader of your government has made a statement about it."

"The president of the Unified States?" Jake asked with a weak smile. "That's awesome, Kaitlin." He was a real trooper. He'd proved she could truly count on him. Looking into his gorgeous gray-blue eyes was like coming home. She got lost in them for a moment.

"Kait?" he asked.

"Yeah. It's good news." She had sent her research to everyone, but so much had happened since then it seemed like forever ago.

The ground started to rumble, and Kaitlin grabbed the lab table.

"You are also wanted for questioning by something called Hearthland Security," Pandora said.

Kaitlin stared at Jake and held on for dear life as everything bucked up and down.

Chapter Forty-Four: Universe 1: Kat, April 30, 2100, 8:00 am

Back home, Kat moved away from the window to the other universe. The ground tried to shake her off. She waved her arms at her friends. "Come on. Get away from the window. It's dangerous. They said something about the forces changing or not working right." She felt relieved to be back in her own dimly lit lab, to be home. So far, there was no sign of the soldiers.

After they'd all moved across the lab away from the window's location, Pablo and Pa sidled up to her.

"What do you think happened to the soldiers?" Pa asked.

"You're the one who's had contact with them recently, Chris," Pablo said. "What do you think happened?"

"We need to do recon, at any rate." Kat shifted the large gun she'd been carrying. They all still had the guns they'd liberated from that Police Patrol. "At least the weapons will come in handy."

"I wish we'd gotten more ammo," Pablo said.

Pa's mouth turned down. "And I wish you kids didn't know so much about guns and ammo. Your ma would be horrified, Kat. Things weren't this bad when we were kids or even when you were kids."

Kat took her locket out from under her shirt and touched it gently. "We don't have time to chat. We have to find out if the soldiers are in the vicinity."

"If they're not, we'll get a bit of a break since it's day time," Pablo said. "They won't venture outside in the sun."

"I hope you're right," Pa said. "I'll get some teams together to search the building." He went over and started talking to the rest of the group.

Soon, three armed groups led by members of the scavenger team started creeping down the hall.

Kat and Pablo heard raised voices on the other side of the room. They hustled over there. "What's going on?" Kat asked as they approached the group.

Bao pointed at the now obviously-glowing computer screen. "I jostled it, and the screen lit up."

"Since when do these computers work?" Kat asked.

Bao shrugged.

"Maybe they've always worked," Pablo said. "How would we know?"

"Where's the power coming from?" Kat asked. "And why would the computers be on? We didn't turn them on." She gestured to Bao to move. "Here, let me see." She pressed some keys on the keyboard.

When the lab filled with light, everyone gasped.

Kat looked up, squinting. "Who turned on the lights? And since when did the lights work?"

Pablo stood next to the doorway and pointed at the light switch on the wall. "Power's on in the building."

"How?" Kat said. "Uh oh." She paused. Now the computer screen said *Real-Time Surveillance*. There was a close-up picture of the lab centered where the window to the other universe had been. She ran towards the window-location and turned around. "There's a camera here somewhere. Everyone, look for a camera."

Everyone left in the lab spread out, searching.

Kat found a cylinder about the size of her hand. She held it up in the air. "I think this is it."

Pablo grabbed it from her hand, dropped it on the floor, and smashed it with his boot.

"Let's make sure there aren't any more of them," Kat said.

They couldn't find any more cameras, but they turned off the lights to be safe.

Pa and the rest of the recon teams returned to the lab. The team leaders approached Kat and Pablo near the computers.

"No sign of any soldiers," Pa said. "We searched the whole building."

Aban ran his fingers through his luxuriant hair. "Earlier, the soldiers were here in the building. They shot at us through the window thing from this very room. Why leave? Where did they go?"

"Why come here in the first place?" Sungsu said. "I don't get it."

In the dim light, Kat peered at the three men who'd been held prisoner by the soldiers. Did they look healed? What happened to their bruises? "P, will you turn on the light again for a minute?"

Soon, the lab was bathed in light again, and everyone was squinting.

Pa, Aban, and Sungsu stared around the room, mouths open.

"The power's on?" Pa asked. "How?"

Kat shrugged. "How do you guys feel?" she asked. "You look a lot better." They must have gotten medical nanobots over in the other universe somehow.

Pa cupped his chin in his hand. "Actually, I feel better."

The other two stared at him. "You're healed," Aban said.

"So are you," Pa and Sungsu said simultaneously.

"And, Kat, what happened to your cast?" Pa asked.

"Medical nanobots healed me," she said. At their blank looks, she added, "Tiny robots. Did you get treated with them, too?"

The men shook their heads.

"No, I didn't, not that I know of," Pa said. "But I thought those nanobots were as big as real bugs. We'd notice if they were crawling on us."

"Not all of the robots are that big," she said.

What did the healing mean? Were the medical robots running wild over in that other universe? And were they all contaminated with them now?

"Anyway, this room was bugged," she said.

Pablo snickered.

She realized what she'd said and snickered a little, too. "Sorry. The soldiers left a camera pointed at the window."

"That means they know we came back through." Pa set his mouth in a thin line.

That sobered Kat right up. "Yes."

"So, we can expect an attack," Aban said.

Sungsu nodded.

"Probably at sunset," she said.

"Or soon after," Pablo said.

"What are we going to do?" Sungsu asked.

"Don't worry, I have a plan," she said. They wouldn't let their new firepower go to waste.

Right before sunset, Kat, Pablo, Pa, Chang, and Bao, crouched just inside the tunnel exit closest to the garage Kat and Pablo had found.

Chang and Bao sat very near each other, hugging.

Pablo sidled up to Kat and whispered in her ear. "Are you sure about the Lus? They've been through a lot lately."

"They volunteered and claimed to know how to ride motorbikes," she said. "We need people with their expertise." She touched her locket. "Besides, what was the alternative? Leave them back with Sungsu and Aban to fight?"

"I guess that wouldn't have worked," he said grudgingly.

"It's not that complicated a plan," she said. "We're trying to lure the soldiers away from the physics building and into an ambush by riding by the front doors on the bikes. We just have to stay on the bikes when the soldiers chase us."

"I guess." Pablo, squatting, leaned against the tunnel wall. "How come you're not worried about missing Katherine when the window opens again? Didn't she tell you to stay close so you could do something?"

"Shit." Kat had been so focused on saving her friends and family from trigger-happy soldiers, she'd forgotten about Katherine's request. "Maybe we'll be victorious by then. We did bring a lot of guns back from her universe."

"Yeah," he said. "But are we supposed to bring stuff over here from the other universe? How come they wanted us to throw those bricks back?"

"I don't know," Kat muttered. "A few days ago they gave us the food and water we've been enjoying." Had it only been a few days ago? A lot had happened.

Pablo raised a lot of good questions.

"Are you guys about ready?" Pa asked.

311

"Yeah." Kat stood up.

As dusk fell, the group ran to the old garage Kat and Pablo found earlier. Kat hoped they could start the rest of the bikes and that they had fuel. Their plan depended on it.

As they entered, Pablo said, "Look out for snakes."

Grinning at his comment, Kat pulled the bike she'd been on before up off the floor. She carefully balanced herself with her legs, put the kill switch on run, depressed the clutch lever, kicked it into neutral, kicked the side stand up, put her thumb on the start button and started it. The roar of the bike split the quiet of the night.

Chang's, Bao's and Pa's bikes roared to life, too.

She couldn't help thinking how lucky they were to have found the bikes and that they still had fuel. It made breaking her arm worth it, especially since she was already healed.

Pa had to talk Pablo through starting his bike.

Soon, the five of them rode carefully out of the garage, down a weed-choked former road, and looped back towards campus and the physics building. To their west, the last light of day kissed the mountaintops goodnight.

On campus, the concrete of the wide sidewalks was relatively obstacle- and weed-free and they sped up. Speed, not stealth, was what they needed to lure the soldiers into the ambush where Kat's armed group was waiting.

Sure enough, when they thundered up to the physics building, they discovered a group of soldiers crouched behind two trucks painted with brown and tan camouflage. The soldiers had been focused on the barricaded front doors, but quickly shifted around to the other sides of the trucks when they noticed Kat's group.

Kat suppressed a smile as she gunned her motor. It felt good to be on her home world and acting to help her family and friends instead of reacting.

Bao, Chang, and Pablo slowed down and drove west up the sidewalk on the south side of the physics building.

Kat and Pa rode around in circles in front of the physics building doors. When she saw the soldiers peeking out from behind their trucks, she turned west and followed Pablo and the others. Pa was right behind her.

KAT CUBED

The duo rode under the archway formed by a second floor walkway to the adjacent building at the west end. Once on the other side, mostly out of sight of the soldiers, they joined the others riding around in circles.

She definitely did not look at any of the heavily-armed ambush team, crouching in the bushes and in the windows of the surrounding buildings. She didn't want to draw the soldiers' attention to them.

In the distance, it appeared the soldiers were shifting their positions. The sidewalk between the two buildings was too narrow for the trucks to pass through, which had been part of her plan.

Kat and her crew continued riding around on the bikes.

The soldiers had to know it was some kind of trap, but there was no way they knew her group was so heavily armed.

Suddenly, Kat heard a woman's voice in her ear—but there was no one there. "Kat, an enemy scout is approaching from north side of the next building over, the power house."

She squeaked, lost control of her bike, and jumped out of the way as it fell to the ground with a clatter.

The soldiers apparently took advantage of the distraction to rush them. They streamed through the archway, guns aimed at the people on the bikes.

Aban's group took aim from the bushes and windows.

Sungsu's group crept up silently from the east, covering the soldiers from behind.

It was a hell of a lot of guns and Kat was caught in the middle of it. This was not the plan.

They all froze for a split-second. So far, no shots had been fired.

Her heart pounded so fiercely she felt sick.

But she was still reeling from the voice in her ear. Could it be that computer lady? "Pandora?"

"Yes," Pandora–apparently–replied. "Look out for the scout. Oh, never mind, Ghani's got him."

How was Pandora in this universe? How was her voice in her ear? How did she know what was going on? "How?" Kat started to say to Pandora, but stopped. Now was not the time. She tried to gather her dignity as she turned to the soldiers.

"Soldiers, lay down your weapons, you're surrounded."

Behind them, Sungsu said, "Totally surrounded."

Some of the soldiers hadn't realized Sungsu's group was behind them and their eyes widened in surprise. Some of their guns drooped down towards the sidewalk.

One of the soldiers, the leader presumably, leaned down and put his gun on the sidewalk. When he stood, he held his hands above his head. "We surrender." He jerked his head towards his gun on the ground. "Come on, men. Lay down your weapons."

The other soldiers slowly put their guns on the sidewalk.

Pablo and Pa got off their bikes and started collecting guns. Pablo said, "Good plan, *hermana*," as he passed Kat.

Pa was all business, his mouth pressed in a thin line.

Aban stepped forward. "So, we shoot them now?" He flashed a split-second smile.

Kat didn't know if Aban's attitude was an act or not, but she didn't like it. Killing the soldiers in cold blood had never been part of the plan. Killing them if they had to in a firefight, yes, but in cold blood, no. She still felt a little queasy about what she'd had to do to free her people from Police Patrol in Katherine's universe.

She made the mistake of looking one of the soldiers in the eyes and he just looked scared. He wasn't any older than Pablo and was probably just following orders.

Then, *Killer, killer, killer*, echoed in her mind. She regretted all those Police Patrol men they'd killed. Couldn't they have freed Pa and everyone else another way? She glanced at him.

There'd been enough killing. There were hardly any people left in her universe. Her fingers fluttered on her locket.

"Kat?" Pa asked.

"Maybe we should try to work together with the soldiers," she said. "We can use all the help we can get if we're going to save the universes."

Almost on cue, Pandora's voice in her ear said, "Uh oh," and the ground started to shake.

"You heard the lady," Pa said in an authoritarian tone. "Lower your weapons, people. We're working together."

"What's with the energy readings and earthquakes?" the

lead soldier said.

But Kat only had eyes and ears for the middle-aged woman running between the soldiers with her arms outstretched.

"Oh, thank, Gaia. Thank, Gaia." the woman said, tears streaming from her eyes.

"Ava!" Pa said.

It was Ma.

Soon Kat was cradled in her arms. Ma smelled just like she remembered, like woman and lavender with a hint of medicine. Her eyes spilled over. It was her. It was her ma. Alive. "Thank, Gaia. Oh, Ma." She couldn't stop crying. Ma was alive.

Chapter Forty-Five: Universe 3: Katherine, April 30, 2100, 8:00 pm

Katherine's nerves were stretched to the breaking point. Thanks to Winston, they'd been able to access the security channels and find out all the breaking news about the Code Nuclear. She, Jacob, Father, and Professor Jain had been glued to the security feed in between earthquakes and fundamental force fluctuations.

Evidently it took time to set off a nuclear bomb. Police Patrol had to access an all-but-abandoned nuclear silo down south near Colorado Springs, find nuclear bomb experts, and bring the system up to readiness. They had to quietly evacuate the capital, campus and the surrounding area of loyal Citizens.

She was studying the fusion notebooks from the other universe and they'd made some progress. As night approached, however, she kept reading the same words over and over without comprehending them.

Father said, "I still can't get your mother on the fon. Do you think that means they arrested her or evacuated her?"

Katherine didn't want to say what she thought, namely they might all be doomed and it was all her fault, so she shrugged. *Killer, killer, killer*, echoed in her mind.

Jacob, sitting next her, said, "They probably evacuated her. I'm sure she's safe."

She looked up at him and tried to smile. He was so sweet to try and sugar-coat things. *Killer, killer, killer.*

He caressed her hand.

"Maybe you guys should all try to go through a portal the next time one opens," she said. "Another universe has to be better than getting nuked."

"I'll go if you go, Katherine," Father said.

"I can't leave," she said. "I have to fix things."

"I'm not leaving you," Jacob said.

"Me neither," Father said.

"Look at this." Professor Jain held up one of the notebooks. Inside the front cover, it said, *Kay Garcia*. "This looks like your handwriting, doesn't it?"

"It does look my handwriting," she said. "Can I see?" When he nodded she grabbed it from him. Inside the notebook, interspersed amongst the documentation on deuterium/tritium temperatures and high-tech blankets to shield the vacuum vessel and superconducting magnets and the like were some personal notes in the hand of Kay Garcia.

Katherine flipped to the end. "Oh, wow," she said. "Listen to this: *When the energy readings jumped way up and the red letters flashed on the screen proclaiming Fusion Achieved I thought it'd be the best moment of my life. Very unfortunately, it looks like the United States of America and the People's Republic of China are going to war. Nuclear warheads are poised and ready to murder billions, to destroy our culture, if not our entire planet. Maybe if I'd achieved fusion more quickly...*

"And then, at the bottom of the page: *If you're reading this, all is not lost. Some human beings survived. Thank God for that. Please, please take my research and use it. Use it to help people, to rebuild our society. And please remember what happened to us—so it never happens again.*" Dried water droplets stained the whole bottom of the page.

When Katherine stopped reading and looked up, everyone's eyes were moist.

A sniffling sound wafted through the room. Katherine glanced at Pandora's CPUs.

Professor Jain wiped his eye. "Perhaps we should be trying harder to stop this code nuclear."

Father nodded. "The portals may not be our most immediate threat."

"I'm open to suggestions," Katherine said. Her eyes fell on the disabled nanobots carpeting the floor. At least they had one thing going for them. They were lucky Pandora had disabled the nanobots in here. "I wish the nanobots were working for us instead of against us."

"Hhm," Pandora said. Then she made the sound of someone blowing their nose.

Jacob grinned fleetingly. "Pandora? What's with the bodily functions sounds?"

Katherine interrupted. "Never mind that. You hitchhiked over to Kaitlin's universe in the nanobots," she said. "Couldn't you do something similar with the nanobots in this universe? Take them over? Make them do your bidding? And from there, can't you just take over all the computers and stuff?"

"Yes," Pandora said with an impatient tone. "I was just thinking of something like that."

"That's what hhm means?" Jacob asked, suppressing a grin.

"I wasn't quite there yet," Pandora said.

"Interesting," Father said. "The A.I. isn't quite as good as humans at creative problem solving."

Both Katherine and Jacob grimaced at him. They knew better than to disparage Pandora.

But Pandora didn't react. Maybe she was busy computing or hitchhiking or taking something over.

Katherine let herself relax slightly. Maybe they wouldn't be blown apart in a nuclear conflagration. Maybe they'd have time to fix the portals before all the universes were destroyed and all of humanity was massacred.

"I can commandeer the Police Patrol nanobots. I've completed the algorithms," Pandora said. "Shall I implement the plan?"

They all nodded.

"Yes," Katherine said.

"I can't believe we had that elaborate EMP idea," Jacob said. "We could have just sicced Pandora on Police Patrol." He flashed a full-fledged smile.

"Now that that's settled, I must admit, I don't understand how getting the tokamak to work helps with the portals," Father said.

Jacob tilted his head. "I'm not sure I understand a hundred percent either."

"That's probably because I didn't really explain it. It all has to do with standing waves," Katherine said. "Remember yesterday–" She paused. Could it really have been only yesterday? So much had happened since then. And she hadn't really slept or eaten. She felt tired all of a sudden.

"Yesterday?" Father asked.

"We deduced there was an unstable standing energy wave extending through the universes."

Pandora made a throat-clearing sound.

"Thanks to Pandora's excellent energy data, we deduced there was a standing wave and I hypothesized that we needed to stabilize the standing wave to keep the portals open."

Jacob squinted. "I guess I remember that."

"What's a standing wave?" Father said. "And where does this one come from?"

"Ah," Professor Jain said. "A stable standing wave is a wave that's stationary, that doesn't move, because the maximas of the wave reinforce themselves and the minimas cancel themselves. Somehow we created the unstable wave from the energy of the tokamak and the quantum computer and the mass exchange between universes."

Father still looked confused.

"You just need to know when a standing wave is set up correctly it's a very stable wave," Professor Jain concluded.

"Keeping in mind these waves," Katherine said, "it follows that if we set things up one way the portals would stabilize and stay open and if we set things up the opposite way the energy will cancel out and the portals will close. In that case, all this portal business, including the force fluctuations, should end because the portals won't have access to any more energy."

"And that will save all the universes from being torn apart?" Jacob asked.

Professor Jain nodded.

"Yes," Katherine said.

"So, you need the fusion machine to work so you can break this uneven standing energy wave?" Father asked.

"Actually, we need three fusion machines–which I think we can do," Katherine said. "The plan is to put one fusion device here, one in Kaitlin's universe, one in Kat's universe, and turn them all on."

"And then we can make the energy cancel out," Jacob said.

"Yes." Katherine smiled at him for a moment. They might actually have a chance to fix the multiverse, assuming they got the chance to try. "How's it going with taking over the Police Patrol computers, Pandora?"

"It's going," she said.

Professor Jain rubbed his hands together. "Now let's get back to that tokamak. I think we were getting close to getting it to work."

"Yeah," Katherine said. "I think so, too."

Father stood up. "What do you want me to do?"

Katherine stood up and led him to the lab door. "Please go get my old tokamak and bring it here so we can give it to Kat. It looks just like this one, but smaller." She gave him the directions to one of the other labs in the basement.

He went to get it.

Katherine, Professor Jain, and Jacob got back to work on the tokamak.

A few minutes later, Father rushed back into the room. "I can't find your old tokamak."

Katherine jumped up. "Oh, no. We need that. I don't think we can cancel the standing wave without it."

She ran to the other lab with Father and the others close on her heels. But when she got to the other lab, she discovered he was right.

The old tokamak was gone.

Universe 2: Kaitlin

As people crowded into the lab, Jake grabbed Kaitlin's hand. "Are you sure about this press conference, Kait? It could go south. Quickly."

She turned to face him, twirling her ring. "Like if the portals open up again in front of everyone? Like if gravity goes crazy? Like if soldiers start shooting at us from another universe?"

He nodded. "Ah, yeah. Basically. And then there's Hearthland Security. What if they decide to arrest you?"

She squeezed his hand back. "I don't know what else to do. The public is clamoring for a solution to climate change and I think we have one. Pandora helped me refine my earlier plan. And I have to stay out of jail to help Katherine solve the portal problems. Do you have any other ideas?" The plan was to engender sympathy so she wouldn't go to jail for treason and for her part in Win's death. Or if she did go to jail, delay it or get the president to pardon her or something.

"Nope," he said.

Her parents and siblings came in and immediately walked over to her.

Dad opened his mouth and closed his mouth. Kaitlin knew he was restraining himself from asking if she was sure about this, or even saying this was a mistake. Her whole family seemed to be restraining themselves from saying anything non-supportive. Hence, they weren't saying much of anything.

Professor Azar wasn't here. Kaitlin had heard he was in the hospital.

Professor Kim was standing in the corner, arms crossed in front of his chest, scowling. But her academic career was the least of her worries at this point.

"Thanks for coming," Kaitlin said to the reporters. "I appreciate your support, or at least your curiosity."

The reporters had set up their holocams so it was getting very crowded what with them and all the Hearthland Security officers.

George waved at her. She was glad he didn't hate her for Smythe's death and their foray over in that other universe. So far, he'd been holding off on arresting her. She glanced over where that portal had been, but it was just empty space, now.

She nodded back to him. It was nice to see one friendly face among the sea of black uniforms.

A man in a suit approached Kaitlin. "The president is pulling up now. Are you ready to proceed?"

Kaitlin nodded, trying to quell her nerves. It was now or never. "Yes, sir." She stepped over to the computer. "Pandora?" she said quietly. "Is the holo-movie of the sun shield ready?"

"Yes," Pandora said just as quietly. "We're going to knock their socks off—although, I must admit, I don't understand that idiom. Why is socks-knocking considered good?"

Jake frowned at the computer.

"Focus, Pandora," Kaitlin said. Jake wouldn't out Pandora would he? That wasn't in the plan. And that's all they needed to bring down this whole house of cards, people finding out about an A.I. running amuck.

The suited men were whispering things into their wrists and clearing a path from the door to Kaitlin.

A middle-aged Latina appeared in the doorway as the room silenced. She walked purposefully to Kaitlin. "Ms. Garcia."

"Yes, ma'am," Kaitlin said. "It's an honor to see you again, ma'am."

"You've been causing quite an uproar, young lady," President Crown said. She smiled a smile that didn't reach her eyes.

"Yes, ma'am," Kaitlin said, "Sorry ma'am."

"Did you have something to show me?"

"Yes." Kaitlin turned to the computer. "Now, Pandora," she whispered.

The holo-movie started. Planet Earth floated in space, turning slowly, one side lit by a small spherical sun. "This is planet Earth," Kaitlin said. "This is the sun." She pointed. "As we all know, Earth is warmed by the sun's energy." Some numbers floated midway between the sun and the planet. "These numbers represent the amount of energy that hits Earth." A second set of numbers appeared next to the planet. "And these numbers indicate how much energy Earth keeps a hold of." She paused, glancing at her family and friends who smiled encouragingly, at the reporters, the soldiers, and the president, who so far, seemed intrigued.

"My plan is to utilize materials from the moon." The moon popped into existence in the hologram and everyone started.

Some of the reporters laughed a little.

"To build a shield to block some of the sun's energy from reaching Earth." A series of small shields appeared between the sun and Earth in the hologram, causing the second set of numbers to go down.

Kaitlin paused.

The president nodded. "Very intriguing. But you released this information the other day, albeit not in such an accessible form. What's new?"

"I now have the know-how, to build tiny robots that we can fly to the moon, which will self-replicate, build, and launch the shields." Thanks, Pandora.

The reporters started muttering.

"All I need is a little raw material to start the first robots, and a way to get them to the moon. I suspect the Chinese will help us with the latter. It's their planet, too, after all."

"This is all very impressive, Ms. Garcia. If it's true," the President said.

"Uh, oh," Pandora said.

As everyone looked around the room for the source of the mysterious disembodied voice, the portals opened with a sizzle and all-hell broke loose.

Chapter Forty-Six: Universe 1: Kat, April 30, 2100, 9:00 pm

Kat was still reeling. Her ma was alive. Back in the well-lit lab, after the earth stopped quaking, Kat and her parents were sticking together like glue. Kat was sure she sported the same silly grin her folks wore.

"I don't understand, Ava," Pa said. "Where have you been all this time?"

Ma's grin faded. "You mean you didn't know?" She appeared well-fed and well-rested. Her brown hair was shiny and her skin rosy.

"Know what?" Kat practically bounced up and down on her stool. Ma was back. She was back. It was a dream come true. She had to restrain herself from hugging Ma again and again.

"All we knew was you went out on a mission and never came back," Pa said.

"Gaia," Ma whispered. "You must have thought I was dead. I'm so sorry."

"We're together now, that's all that matters," Kat said. She still couldn't believe Ma was alive, after all this time.

"Why didn't you come back to us?" Pa asked. "Or at least send word that you were okay?"

Ma blew out a burst of air. "The soldiers swore to me that they did send word." She looked at Kat and Pa. "No one came to tell you where I was?"

Kat shook her head.

"No," Pa said.

"Damn them," Ma said in a low voice.

The three of them turned and beheld the soldiers on the other side of the lab. An uneasy truce was still in effect between the soldiers and Kat's group.

"I was with the United States government," Ma said. "It still exists. We're trying to rebuild. There's a whole underground town, including civilian parents and kids under Cheyenne Mountain. They needed doctors desperately. I kept telling them I needed to get back to you, but somehow emergencies kept popping up one after the other. The government forces assured me that you guys knew I was okay."

She exhaled again. "But when one of the other medics told me you and Aban and Sungsu were in the sick bay, I knew something wasn't right. The leaders must have known you were my husband and they didn't tell me you were there. It wasn't right to keep you from me."

Pa tightened his mouth. "What do you want to do about them?" He inclined his head at the soldiers. "We could probably take them out."

"In cold blood?" Ma asked. "They've been disarmed. That wouldn't be right."

Kat flashed back to stepping around pooled blood in another universe. She swallowed. Yes, killing armed soldiers was bad enough.

These soldiers had basically surrendered so that was one problem solved. Actually, it was the second problem they'd solved since they escaped from Katherine's dangerous world first.

The three of them started to float up into the air.

Ugh. Speaking of problems. That left their biggest problem: the windows and how they were messing up the world.

Ma's eyes opened wide. "What's wrong with gravity? Is it getting worse? It wasn't like this down in Colorado Springs."

The soldiers scrambled to hold onto the bolted-down lab tables.

Kat's friends, who by now knew how to deal with the low gravity, seemed amused by the soldiers' discomfort.

Kat pointed at the location of the intermittent window. "It's these window things, I guess. It's worse here at the window location. They're destroying the universe, at least that's what the other Kat said."

"The other Kat?" Ma asked. "What are you talking about?

325

And how do you destroy a universe?"

The lead soldier bounded over to them, escorted by Pablo.

"We've cooperated. Now I demand you tell us what the hell is going on here," the soldier said.

Pa's face stilled as he pivoted to face the man. "Cooperated?" he said with steel in his voice. "That's not what my wife Ava's been telling us. You kept her from us for months."

The sandy-haired man took a step back. "I don't know anything about that. Today, we surrendered our weapons. We accompanied you here to your base."

Pa snorted. "Our base? Does this look like a base to you? Does it look like we have the technology to do anything?" He stuck his face in the soldier's face.

"We saw the portal open before," the soldier said, not backing down. "And you've got a hell of a lot of advanced weapons. Some look more advanced than anything I've seen before."

Pablo held up his hands. "Maybe we should all calm down."

Kat reached out and squeezed his arm in thanks. "Yeah. I think we should try to work together. We can use all the help we can get if we're going to save the universe."

"What the hell're you talking about?" the soldier said, his slightly-freckled face turning red.

Kat took a deep breath and dived in. "There's been some kind of accident which opened windows to other universes. We all need to work together to close the windows. If we don't, we'll all die, everyone in every universe."

"Other universes? That's the stupidest pile of shit, I ever–" the soldier said.

Pablo interrupted. "You said yourself you saw the window open. All of us, except Ava, have been over in the other universe. It's real. Where do you think we got these weapons and ammo?"

"Are you saying you don't believe your own eyes?" Kat asked. "Gravity is doing something weird right now, isn't it?"

"It's almost over," the voice in her ear said.

Kat jumped. She'd forgotten about the computer lady. "Pandora?"

"Yes," Pandora said.

"Where's that voice coming from?" Ma asked as she

surveyed the room.

Pablo and Pa shrugged at each other as if saying *nothing we can do.*

"Pandora, how are you here in this universe?" Kat asked. "How can I hear you? How do you know what's going on?"

"I hitchhiked over here to your universe on medical nanobots," she said. "A surprising number of your people were carrying them. Now, I'm running on the Homeland Security computers."

The soldier gaped.

"And..." Pandora continued. "Now on the internet web of this world. It's much smaller than the one I'm used to. Does that mean there aren't many people in this universe?"

Ma frowned.

Kat and Pablo looked at one another. Their world was screwed compared to Katherine's world. Of course, maybe all the worlds were screwed at this point.

"And you're hearing me because I modified some medical nanobots to create a tiny speaker that's in your ear canal," Pandora said. "The others hear me via the computer speakers."

"Wow, Pandora," said Kat. "How did you do all that?"

"I built some algorithms that recreate me when they can access the necessary processing power," Pandora said. "That's why it took me so long to instantiate, almost seventeen hours. That's forever."

"I don't understand any of this," the soldier said, "but I never agreed to have some alien software on our computers. And," he glared at them, "you didn't answer my questions. What's wrong with gravity? Why did we get those weird energy readings here? What was that window thing?"

"I've been trying to explain," Kat said. "I don't know what's going on. I don't know what's wrong with gravity or why you're getting weird energy readings. It's because of the weird window, but I don't know what the window thing is. Katherine, the woman from the other universe, just told me to stay here and help her when the window opened."

She stopped. "Shit." Gravity got weird after the earthquake after the window opened. The window must have opened, and they missed it. What if she'd missed what she was supposed to do for Katherine?

What if they were all doomed? She broke out into a sweat. What if she was responsible for her ma and pa and Pablo and everyone else she loved dying? She felt dizzy.

Pablo was staring at her. "Are you okay?"

She didn't know if she was okay.

Pablo sidled up right next to her. "You don't think you missed it, do you?" he asked quietly.

Her parents looked blank.

Ma asked, "Missed what?"

"I don't know," Kat said. "I pray not. Pandora? What happened when we were gone? Was Katherine looking for me?"

"No," Pandora said. "Katherine wasn't over there. I just talked to the other me and the other-other-me over in the other universe. Things are accelerating."

Kat was almost afraid to ask. "Accelerating? What does that mean? Are you talking about those nuke things?"

"Nukes?" the soldier squeaked. The blood seemed to leak out of his face. "What nukes? Where?"

Ma looked at him with concern. "Are you all right? What's your name, young man?"

"Nukes," he squeaked again.

"What's wrong with him?" Ma asked.

"He's worried about very powerful bombs," Pa said. "They have radioactive material that poisons every living thing it comes in contact with."

Gravity was gradually returning to normal.

"Pandora?" Kat asked. "Why was gravity weird for so long?"

"Which question should I answer first?" Pandora asked.

"Nukes," the soldier said.

"Yeah, the nukes," Pa said.

"The nuclear bombs have not been implemented yet in Katherine's universe," Pandora said. Then, she paused and said, "Uh oh. Hold on."

Kat and Pablo froze. Nothing good ever happened when Pandora said *Uh oh*.

"What?" Ma asked. "What's happening?"

Pa shook his head.

"Nothing good," Kat said.

A loud sizzling sound filled the room, and then the window burst open with a bounce.

"Gaia," the soldier whispered.

Ma stared at the window, face slack.

The other people in the room, Kat's friends and the soldiers, came up behind them, gawking at the window.

"Didn't we just have a window-thing? Is it just me, or was that really quick?" Kat asked.

Pablo reached for her hand. "It's not just you, *hermana*."

"Nukes aside," Pandora said, "we're running out of time."

The soldier made a noise that sounded suspiciously like a squeak and then he paused, visibly getting himself together. "Let me get this straight. Nuclear bombs aren't our biggest problem?"

"No," Kat said, shaking her head.

"What can we do to help?" The soldier glanced back at his men. "The resources of the United States government, such as it is, are at your disposal."

"Good," Kat said.

"It's George, by the way," he said. "My name is George."

"Nice to meet you, George." She held out her hand. "I'm Kat." They shook hands. In his eyes, she read the same grim determination that she was sure shone out of hers. They were going to get out of this, working together.

It made her feel a little better.

And then a man called for her through the window. "Kat?" What now?

Who was this guy? Where was Katherine?

In the meantime, the other Pandora said, "Pandora? Are you there?"

This Pandora said, "I'm here, Pandora. It worked. I instantiated here. Finally. It took forever."

Dragging Pablo behind her for moral support, praying they weren't already too late to save the worlds, Kat approached the sizzling window and the man calling for her. "It's Kat. What? Did you stop the nukes? Did you guys come up with a plan to save the universes?"

Katherine was still reeling. The old tokamak was gone. How was she going to gain control of the standing wave now? How was she going to save the multiverse? Was she going to be responsible for Jacob's death? For her parents' deaths? For everyone she loved dying? For everyone dying?

She, Father, Jacob and Professor Jain arrived back in her lab. They must have just missed the portals opening and closing because they felt a strong earthquake and now gravity was acting up.

She tried very hard to focus on the matter at hand. "Pandora?" she asked, holding on to a lab table. "How are we doing? Anything new with the portals?"

"Forget about the portals, what's happening with the nuclear bombs?" Father asked.

"I don't understand what happened to the old tokamak," Professor Jain said at the same time. "It couldn't just get up and walk away."

"Ah," Jacob said. "What does it look like, again?"

Katherine pointed at her tokamak. "Like this but smaller."

"Katherine?" Pandora asked. "Which question should I answer first?"

"Bomb," Katherine said.

"I'll be right back." Jacob bounded out of the room.

"Police Patrol gained access to the nuclear silo, and I infiltrated the computer system there via them. It wasn't easy. The system was archaic–"

"That's great Pandora," Katherine said. "You're our hero. Can you move it along? What's the bottom line?"

"Police Patrol successfully evacuated the area surrounding us. And they found a retired nuclear bomb expert, but he hasn't been able to do anything, because, as I said earlier, I infiltrated the archaic computer system at the nuclear silo."

"So?" Katherine said. "Are you saying they can't bomb us?"

"Yes." Pandora sounded smug. "I saved the day."

Professor Jain yelled "Hurray!"

Katherine's father yelled, "Yes!"

One problem solved. Katherine threw her fist in the air as she yelled "Yes!" and promptly floated up into the air.

He father grabbed her before she floated too far and pulled her back down.

"Is all that yelling for me?" Jacob asked from the doorway.

The three of them swiveled to see him pushing a large metal cylinder into the lab in the low gravity. He grinned.

"Is that the old tokamak?" Katherine asked, starting to float away again. "That's great. Where was it?" Now maybe they could solve their real problem—getting control of the portals.

Her father grabbed her again.

"It was in my lab." Jacob pushed it over to them.

"I don't understand," Katherine said. "Why was it there?"

"It was Kat's group," Jacob said. "They brought it to my lab. We were running interference with Police Patrol. Sorry. I should have figured it out earlier."

"I guess it's all's well that ends well," Father said.

"Yeah," Professor Jain said. His shoulders unclenched.

"You really shouldn't have pushed it over here by yourself," Katherine said. "What if the gravity had come back? You could have damaged it."

"If you weren't hollering for me, what were you hollering for?" Jacob asked.

"Pandora has resolved the nuclear issue," Professor Jain said. "She's a hero."

"Yay," Jacob yelled.

"Yes, Pandora," Katherine said. "You are a hero. Is there anything we can do to repay you?"

"I'll let you know." She still sounded smug.

Why hadn't gravity come back to normal yet? "Pandora? What's up with gravity?"

"Oh, yeah, that. Things are accelerating," Pandora said. "The portals are opening and closing more frequently and they have more energy. We're running out of time. We may all be doomed." All trace of smugness drained out of her voice.

They all contemplated each other for a moment, not knowing what to say.

Finally, Katherine broke the silence. "The multiverse isn't being destroyed on my watch. We aren't doomed. No way." She stood, started to float, and grabbed the lab table herself. "Who's with me?"

"You know I'd do anything for you, hon," Father said.

"Ditto," Jacob said.

Father gave Jacob an odd look.

"Of course, we're at your disposal, Katherine," Professor Jain said. "Just tell us what to do."

Katherine gathered her wits. "Professor Jain, make sure our tokamak is capable of fusion. We were almost there, right? Father, Jacob, Pandora, I need you to help me get this old one operational."

"What about Police Patrol?" Father asked.

"Good point," Katherine said. "Father, Jacob go barricade the front doors and then come back and help me. Pandora, call the people in my contact list and see if any of them can come help us. But be sure to tell them what's going on and that it will be dangerous."

"Yes, Katherine," Pandora said.

They all got to work on their respective tasks.

Jacob and Father came back and said the front doors were already barricaded.

Katherine was pleasantly surprised by what good shape her old fusion machine was in. They just had to implement the updates to the fusion device they'd retrieved from Kaitlin's world.

After they'd been working quite a while, Pandora interrupted: "Uh oh."

Katherine and Jacob froze.

Katherine was almost afraid to ask. "What?"

"Police Patrol has finally determined they can't implement the nuclear option," Pandora said, sounding like she was going to cry.

"Isn't that a good thing?" Father asked.

"Yes, but armed forces are already on campus," Pandora said. "They must be coming to attack us. I didn't see them coming. They must have figured out I was watching them through their own technology and got rid of it or blocked me somehow."

That was not good. "Shit." Katherine was immobilized for a moment, but she shook it off. Get a grip, Katherine. Don't give up. "Pandora, if you can do anything about surveillance, please do. In the meantime, guys, we should get back to work. Maybe we can fix the multiverse before Police Patrol attacks. It's our only hope."

It had to work. They had to fix the multiverse.

After another half-hour or so, they were almost there with the old tokamak. They'd hooked everything up. The vacuum vessel, cryostat, and divertor target were setup like the machine in Kaitlin's universe. Katherine started testing the electromagnetic field.

And then they heard a commotion at the lab doorway. "Oh, no." Katherine was afraid to check it out. Was Police Patrol attacking? Had they already gotten through the barricade?

But Katherine's mother, Winston, Pablo, and some strangers had shown up at the lab, most of them carrying bags.

"Mother? Winston?" Katherine asked. "I'm sorry to put you in danger, but I'm really glad to see you. How did you get past the Police Patrol and get in?"

Mother said, "A woman named Pandora called us. She said it was an emergency and to come to your lab right away." She paused. "I brought first aid supplies."

"Pandora told us how to sneak in through Jacob's lab," Winston added.

"And to bring friends," Pablo said.

Katherine stepped forward and put her hand on Pablo's arm. "We do need your help. Thank you for coming."

"Father?" Katherine asked. "Can you take them to do recon?"

He nodded.

Katherine got back to work on the smaller tokamak.

In the meantime, the group with Father conferred and a few

of them ran out the lab door.

"Uh oh," Pandora said. "Hold on."

Everyone in the lab froze.

A loud sizzling sound filled the room, and then two portals bounced open.

Katherine knew she had to get working fusion devices to both the universes next to hers to implement the standing wave. This was their chance. They had no time to lose.

"Professor Jain, is our big tokamak ready?"

"Yes," he said.

"Then come here and help me finish with this one," Katherine said. Then she turned to Jacob. "Jacob, go check and see if Kat's ready to receive a tokamak."

Jacob ran towards Kat's portal. "Kat?"

Pandora said to Kat's Pandora, "Pandora? Are you there?" and said to Kaitlin's Pandora, "Pandora? Are you there?"

"Mother, go check and see if Kaitlin's ready with her fusion machine."

"Okay," Mother said and jogged over to the other portal. "Kaitlin?"

"Uh oh," Pandora said.

Everyone froze.

"What?" Katherine asked.

"Police Patrol is advancing on the building," Pandora said.

"Shit," Katherine said. They weren't going to have time to deploy the fusion machines and destroy the standing wave.

Universe 2: Kaitlin

Kaitlin's news conference and plans were ruined when the portals opened, followed quickly by the earthquake and then the weird gravity.

When they thought the president was in danger, Hearthland Security sent in a whole big dragoon, or whatever it was called, of soldiers into the lab. It was only George's intervention that kept them from riddling Kaitlin's body with bullets.

With the world itself going crazy, the soldiers didn't seem to know what to do with Kaitlin other than point lots of big guns at her and her family. With her hands up, she kept saying she was sorry to them.

If she was responsible for her mom and dad and sister and brother and fiancé being arrested or getting shot by Hearthland Security, she'd never forgive herself.

Of course, if the multiverse was destroyed she'd never forgive herself for that either. That would be too horrible for words. Billions of people dead. Kaitlin had to force her mind away from that.

Didn't Katherine have a plan for saving the multiverse? Why didn't she implement it? What was going on?

Then, the world had seemed to go back to normal for a few minutes—at least there were no weird portals or earthquakes.

Until Pandora said, "Uh, oh. Hold on."

They'd all frozen in place, most of the soldiers looking around the room for the source of the voice.

The portals opened again.

"Kaitlin?" a woman called through the portal.

Everyone looked at Kaitlin.

"Should I go over?" Kaitlin asked. "You won't shoot me if I move?"

"Pandora? Are you there?" the other Pandora said.

At the disembodied voice, the soldiers looked even more unhappy if that was possible.

"No, we won't shoot you, Kaitlin," George said. "You better go find out what's happening."

"Things are accelerating, that's what's happening," Pandora said. "And, yes, Pandora, I'm still here. I don't think the multiverse has much time left."

Still aware of the large array of guns pointed at her, Kaitlin very carefully walked over to Katherine's portal. "What can I do to help? Please tell me we can save the worlds."

Chapter Forty-Eight: Universes 1 & 3: Kat, April 30, 2100, 10:00 pm

Standing in the still-strangely well-lit lab, Kat said, "What can I do to help? Please tell me we can save the worlds."

Katherine's Jacob was staring back at something or someone in his world. "Oh, no." He turned back to face her. "We're too late. Police Patrol is attacking."

Kat gulped. "The nukes? How long do we have?"

Behind her, Pablo grabbed her hand and said, "Can you close the window?"

"It's not the nukes," Jacob said. "We dealt with that. It's Police Patrol attacking the building." His hands fell to his sides. "We only have a few people here to fight and hardly any weapons." He glanced back at Katherine. "We won't have enough time to fix the portals."

"We're not just giving up," Kat said. "If we do that, everyone will die. We have to fight. We kicked Police Patrol's ass before and we're going to do it again. We should attack them right back."

Through the window, Katherine said, "Attack Police Patrol? I don't know..."

Kat turned to face the crowd that had gathered behind her. "We're gonna go through the window and fight the police in Katherine's world to save the universes. Come on, everyone!"

Jacob faced her through the window. "Really? You'd do that? It's dangerous. Do you have weapons? Do you know how to fight?"

Kat's friends were already grabbing their weapons, faces grim but determined, and lining up behind her.

On the other side of the room, George appeared to be

ordering his men to gear up and get in line.

Silly Jacob. If he had to ask that, his world was really very different. "Oh, we know how to fight," Kat said. "Don't you worry about that. Stand back. Here we come."

Pablo, who'd never let go of the huge rifle he'd emancipated from Police Patrol's arsenal, hopped through the window. On the other side, he about-faced and said, "Come on, follow me."

"Be quick about it," Kat said.

Kat's people, armed to the teeth, some with multiple weapons, streamed through the window to Katherine's world.

Kat went back to retrieve her gun, and found Ma still over where they'd been talking earlier.

"This seems rash, Kat," Ma said.

Kat paused for a moment, looking into her ma's warm brown eyes. Finally she nodded, and said, "Yes, it's rash. And I know, as a healer, it's against your beliefs to hurt people. But I'm not a healer." She paused again. "I'm a fighter. I'm a killer."

Ma's eyebrows rose.

"I've killed people." Kat gave a curt chin nod. "I'm not proud of it. But if there was ever a reason to fight, it's now. If we don't help Katherine, we'll all die. All of us. Millions, maybe even billions of people and plants and animals and everything will all die. I can't live with that on my conscience. Can you?" Kat started for the window.

Most of Kat's people were already over in Katherine's world.

"Do what you think is right, Ma." Kat quickened her pace, reached the window and stepped through.

Ma was right behind her.

Over in Katherine's universe, Katherine's pa Christopher was directing the armed folks.

Katherine's Jacob, still by Kat's window, seemed a bit dazed. "Ah, thanks, Kat. We appreciate it."

"Where do you want me?" Kat asked him.

"Actually, you guys don't have any scientists in your world, do you?" Jacob asked.

Despite the circumstances, Kat couldn't help grinning at that dumb comment. "No. Duh."

"Since you're probably the closest thing you guys have to a scientist," he said. "Maybe you should help with the fusion machines and the standing wave. You could run the fusion machine over in your universe."

"No offense, Jacob," Kat said. "But I think that would be a waste of my skills. I should be on the front lines. Can't you and that professor guy help Katherine?"

"Yeah, I guess," he said.

Over at the other portal there seemed to be an argument.

Universes 2 & 3: Kaitlin

Kaitlin couldn't believe how worked up people were getting.

"Shut those things!" one of the Hearthland Security officers shouted.

"Get rid of them." Several of the officers pointed their guns at the portals.

"They're evil."

"Shut 'em."

Kaitlin knew Hearthland Security didn't understand what was going on, but getting agitated wouldn't help anything. "Calm down, please. Quit waving those guns around." She recognized some of the men that went over to the radioactive universe with her, so it was understandable they were upset, but surely shooting people or portals wouldn't help anything.

Speaking of radioactivity... "You should stay away from that portal over there on the other side of the lab," she said. "It's not safe. It's radioactive."

The crowd surged in her direction, away from the radioactive portal. In the crush, Kaitlin and her family were practically pushed through Katherine's portal.

In the crowd, Jake grabbed her hand and squeezed it gently. When she turned to him, he flashed her an encouraging smile.

In the meantime, Katherine's mom had been trying to talk to her through the portal. "Kaitlin, I said, we're having problems over here. We need your help."

"Have you figured out how to close the portals for good?" Kaitlin really hoped they had. She couldn't wrap her mind around the concept of universes being destroyed. She definitely couldn't wrap her mind around everyone dying.

She glanced at her family again.

Her mom was staring at Katherine's mom through the portal. "Who are you?" Mom asked.

"Ava-Maria." Katherine's mom said, "Yes, we think we can close the portals."

"So do it, already," Kaitlin said.

"That's what I'm trying to tell you," Ava-Maria, said. "We need a few more minutes to set it up and we can't because we're under attack from Police Patrol. We need your help."

"Help with what?" Kaitlin asked. "Fight Police Patrol? I'm not a fighter."

"Maybe you have some other people there who can fight?" Ava-Maria said. "It looks like there are a lot of people there with you."

"Yes, we do have fighters," Pandora said. "This lab is lousy with officers."

"Thank you, Pandora," the other Pandora said. "That's very helpful."

"Why, you're welcome," Pandora said.

"Excuse me," Kaitlin said. "Can we let the actual people talk?"

"Is she implying we aren't people?" the other Pandora said.

"Shut it, computer ladies." George, the Hearthland Security officer, elbowed his way to Kaitlin at the portal. "Kaitlin, what's happening?"

Kaitlin pointed at Ava-Maria through the portal. "She says they're under attack and need fighters."

Ava-Maria nodded vigorously. "Yes. It's an emergency. Please hurry."

George shook his head. "I don't know. The last time we went through a portal, one of my men died. And we were all exposed to radioactivity."

"Don't worry," Ava-Maria said. "We resolved the nuclear bomb situation."

"The what?" George's mouth fell open.

"Police Patrol forces are moving into position," other-Pandora said in Katherine's universe.

"It's now or never," Ava-Maria said.

"I'm not sure," George said. "What do you think Kaitlin?"

"If there's even a possibility that we can stop the deaths of billions and billions of people, we have to try, don't we?" Kaitlin said. "I'm in." She gathered her courage and stepped through the portal to Katherine's universe.

"If Kaitlin's in, I'm in," Jake said, and stepped through after her.

"Me, too," Michael said.

"Me, three," Emma said.

As Kaitlin saw her loved-ones agree to risk their lives for humanity, she couldn't help feeling proud. "Mom? Dad?" She made eye contact with George. "George? We need your Hearthland Security forces."

Keeping her eyes on Katherine's mom, Kaitlin's mom stepped through. "If she's in, I'm in."

"Well, I have to watch out for all of you, don't I?" Kaitlin's dad said as he came through.

George was still wavering.

In her peripheral vision, Kaitlin saw a man who looked like George, but he had longer hair and was wearing an unusual tan uniform. She yelled across Katherine's lab to him. "George!"

Looking puzzled, the strange George crossed Katherine's lab to Kaitlin. "You're not Kat, are you?"

"No," Kaitlin said. "But I need you to convince someone to help us. We're running out of time."

The two George's stared at each other through the portal, mouths gaping in the exact same way.

Kaitlin's George asked, "Are you sure about this, George?"

"Yes, sir, George," the tan-uniformed George said.

Kaitlin's George turned around and addressed his men. "Come on, men. Double-time through the portal. Let's go."

Universe 3: Katherine

Katherine couldn't believe all the soldiers, some in tan uniforms and some in black uniforms, who had appeared in her lab. Were they really all willing to help fight Police Patrol? She was grateful. Maybe now they'd have a chance to fix the multiverse and save everyone.

That woman Kaitlin walked by, looking lost. She'd probably be useful for canceling the standing wave. "Kaitlin!"

Kaitlin stopped. "Yes, Katherine? I'm here to help, but I'm not sure what I'm supposed to be doing."

Over by the lab doorway, Katherine's father and Kat's father were busy organizing all the troops and passing out extra weapons. Some groups of armed fighters were already leaving the lab on the way to the battle presumably.

Katherine thought Kaitlin looked really nervous. "I'm sorry, we're a little disorganized. You're a graduate student, right? You were really helpful earlier with that fusion machine."

Professor Jain was still hanging around her. "Are you the one that found the working fusion device? That was amazing."

It was amazing. It might save them all.

"Thanks." Kaitlin nodded. "Yes. I'd be happy to do something scientific. I must admit, I'm not totally clear on the plan. Do we still need the fusion machine over in my universe?"

"Yes," Katherine said. "We're going to cancel the standing wave by putting fusion reactors in all three universes and canceling out the energy interference that's keeping the portals from closing."

Pandora said, "Shots fired! Our troops are under fire. Hurry up, Katherine."

"So, anyway, is the fusion machine in your universe hooked up and working?" Katherine asked.

Kaitlin shrugged as she tried to peer back through the portal to her universe. "It was earlier today. But the crowd with the press conference was much bigger than I expected and then when the portals opened, Hearthland Security and the president's security detail got pretty freaked out."

"Press conference?" Katherine asked. "President?" She shook her head. "Never mind that right now. Go back and make sure it still works. Get ready to turn it on when we need it."

Kaitlin hesitated.

Katherine followed Kaitlin's gaze over to her Jake and the rest of her family. "They'll be as safe as anyone else in the multiverse." Which was to say, not very.

Kaitlin's eyes moistened, but she nodded and stepped

through the portal back into her universe. So, that was two fusion devices almost ready in two universes. Check.

Now, they just needed number three. Katherine turned to Professor Jain. Somehow it was a little reassuring to see her old professor, just like it was a normal day in the lab. "Go over to Kat's universe and take our old tokamak and get it set up there."

"Okay, but with gravity temporarily back to normal how am I going to move the machine over there?" he asked. With his face pale and drawn, he didn't look like he thought it was a normal day in the lab.

"Jacob!" Katherine yelled. "Where had he gotten to?"

He detached himself from the group by the door and jogged over. "What?"

"Get some people and help Professor Jain get this old tokamak set up over in Kat's universe," Katherine said.

"I thought I needed to keep an eye on my quantum computer?" Jacob asked.

Good grief. He was right. They definitely needed the quantum computer for this to work. The stress must be getting her. "Delegate some people to help him, then."

"I know just who to ask," Jacob said. He darted away to Kaitlin's Jake and patted him on the back.

Katherine turned her attention back to her fusion device. All this had better work. Please, let it work, starting with her own system.

She put it in Production Mode and flipped it on.

Chapter Forty-Nine: Universe 3: Kat, May 1, 2100, midnight

Kat and Pablo and her parents and the rest of her group were arrayed on the third floor, peeking out the windows at the enemy, Police Patrol. Why didn't they douse all the streetlights out there? They were being stupid. In the distance, the pitch-black foothills overshadowed everything.

A few of Katherine's people, like Katherine's pa, Christopher, were also up on the third floor. Kat also saw Kaitlin's parents. She guessed the third floor was for the non-professional soldiers.

Kat touched her locket. Oh yeah, she should give it back to Ma, it was hers after all.

Glancing at Ma in the dim light streaming through the window, Kat couldn't get used to the image of her holding a gun. Things had really changed in the last week. Kat shook her head and turned back to the window.

So far, the enemy had fired off a few wild shots, probably trying to scare Katherine and whoever else they thought were in the building. Gaia, were Police Patrol in for a surprise. They had no idea there were seventy-some-odd armed soldiers lying in wait for them.

Next to her, Pablo poked her arm. "They're clueless," he whispered. "I almost feel sorry for them."

"Attention, Katherine Garcia, this is Police Patrol," a man yelled into a bullhorn pointed at the building. "You are under arrest. Surrender immediately. If you do so, you and your friends will not be harmed."

Kat realized, as far as Police Patrol was concerned, she might as well be Katherine. Before thinking about it too carefully, she pushed open the window in front of her. "Attention, Police Patrol–"

"Kat," that computer lady said in her ear, startling her and almost making her drop her gun out the window.

"Zip it, Pandora," she whispered.

"This is Katherine Garcia," she yelled out the window. "We suggest you surrender immediately. If you do so, you and your friends will not be harmed." She paused and smiled down at the men she couldn't see all that well in the streetlights.

A few of the Police Patrol men, or at least a few lumpy shadows, crept behind one of their trucks and conferred.

"Kat," Pandora said in her ear, as a bullet whizzed by her ear and smashed into the cinder block near the ceiling behind her.

"Be more careful, Kat," Ma said.

Kat nodded. "What, Pandora?" she ducked down behind the wall.

"I was going to suggest you not address Police Patrol," Pandora said, sounding particularly aggrieved.

"Why not?"

"Despite my best efforts with their databases," Pandora said, "they know it was you, Kat Garcia, that broke your people out of jail, killing several of their men in the process. They probably recognize you. They aren't going to surrender to you. In fact, seeing you will probably rile them up."

"Why didn't you mention that earlier?" Kat said.

"I tried. You told me to zip it." Pandora sounded hurt.

Kat couldn't really wrap her head around a machine that seemed to have feelings. "So, why are you listening to me? Maybe you should say or do what you want next time. Except for the evacuation order. You have to tell us when it's time to bug out and go home to our world no matter what you feel like doing." She peeked out the window again. "How many Police Patrol officers are out there, anyway?"

"Only about fifty," Pandora said.

"That's all?" Kat asked.

Christopher said, "They maintain order through fear and intimidation rather than actual force."

Police Patrol seemed to be moving back to their original

positions.

Then, obeying some command Kat couldn't discern, they open-fired on the third floor. Shattered glass exploded over them like a tsunami.

"Shit!" Pablo said.

Kat felt a strong force push her backwards. She hit the ground, landing on her back. What happened?

Her group all flattened themselves on the floor, hugging it like it a long-lost lover.

She heard the soldiers on the second and first floors below her return fire.

Police Patrol wasted no time directing their bullets at the first and second floors, too. If they were surprised to be fired upon by people on three floors, they didn't act like it.

Kat was still wondering why she'd fallen down when she realized her shoulder was killing her.

Ma said, "Kat, you're hit!"

Universe 2: Kaitlin

Suddenly Kaitlin felt nauseated and scared, even more scared than she had before. Her lab was empty, which was kind of amazing considering all the people that had been crammed in here just moments ago.

"Shots fired! Shots fired." one of the Pandoras screamed.

Kaitlin felt a sharp pain in her shoulder. But when she looked, there was nothing wrong. "Shut up, Pandora," Kaitlin said, twirling her ring. She couldn't hear herself think and she needed to think if she was going to do what Katherine wanted her to do. Why was she so scared now? What had changed? What was wrong with her shoulder?

"Which one of us?" one of the Pandoras asked.

Kaitlin couldn't keep track of them all. "All of you," she said.

"Yes," Katherine said over in her world. "No screaming. We're trying to concentrate here. You can talk if you have something to add about the fusion devices and the standing wave, otherwise, zip it." One of the Pandoras must be relaying voices to her through the portal.

Kaitlin smirked. 'Zip it' sounded like something Kat would say. Maybe they were all rubbing off on one another.

Out of the corner of Kaitlin's eye, she saw Jacob grab Katherine's hand and squeeze lightly.

Jacob said, "I just double-checked and my quantum computer is set exactly as it was when this whole thing began. And I've been thinking about it, and I believe the different universes are affecting each other via quantum entanglement. It's the only thing that makes sense. Otherwise how can you explain machines running with no power source?"

"I agree," Katherine said. "And the entanglement should help cancel out the standing wave once we get the three fusion devices going in the three universes."

"What's quantum entanglement?" Kaitlin asked, hoping Pandora would relay her voice as well.

"Briefly," Jacob said, "it's what it sounds like. It just means two or more objects are linked or tangled in a way that they each affect the other via quantum mechanics."

"We don't really have time to chat," Katherine said.

Kaitlin frowned. This entanglement stuff was important, she could feel it. But, saving the multiverse was more important. "Fine. Should I turn on the fusion machine here?"

"Yes," Katherine said.

"And I'll do the same over in this other universe," Jake said from Kat's universe. She didn't want Jake so far away.

Kaitlin said, "And you swear the portals won't close without warning? No one will get trapped in the wrong universe, right?" It would just about kill her if her family was trapped over there in another universe.

"Right. No one will get trapped," Katherine said, nodding.

Kaitlin stared at her through the portal. She wasn't sure she believed her. Maybe Katherine would do anything to save the multiverse. Her blood thundered, her head felt hot. Was this what it felt like right before you fainted?

"If you don't believe me," Katherine said, grabbing onto a lab table for support, "then maybe you should know we can't close the portals for good with the mass imbalanced. We have to send everyone home to balance the universes."

Kaitlin nodded. "And Pandora's ear pieces will order

everyone back here from the front line at the right time, right?"

"Yes," Katherine said.

"Okay," Kaitlin said and turned on the fusion machine. It was set-up to run in Production Mode.

"Is it working?" Kaitlin heard Katherine ask.

"Yes," Kaitlin said. "Just tell me what energy values you want."

"Good," Katherine said. "Stand by. A few seconds."

Kaitlin waited, trying not to think about anything, trying not to think about her loved ones in danger, trying not to think about how scared she was, trying not to think about everyone in all the universes dying. Trying not to think about her hands poised over the computer controls.

Universe 3: Katherine

"Multiple shots fired," Pandora said. "We're taking heavy fire!"

Katherine wasn't herself. She could hear the rat-a-tat-tat of the gunfire and was so scared she could barely think. She felt a sharp pain in her shoulder, but when she examined it, she couldn't see anything. "Pandora, maybe it would be better if you didn't give us updates about the fighting here in the lab." She clutched the lab table so she didn't fall down.

"Okay," Pandora said, sounding disappointed.

Something squeezed her arm. She looked down. It was Jacob's hand. She followed his arm up to his face.

"Are you all right?" he asked, concern etching his face. "You don't look so good."

"I'm just nervous," Katherine said, clearing her throat. "I'm fine."

"Should I go back to my lab and monitor the quantum computer then?" he asked with a gentle smile.

"Yes," Katherine said. "I was just going to say that."

"I thought you might be." Jacob dropped her arm and headed for the lab door.

Katherine stepped back and smacked into a lab stool, knocking it over.

Jacob glanced back at her and grinned.

How could he be grinning at a time like this?

Then she heard his voice in her ear. "Professor Jain and I are ready over here." Oh. That was Kaitlin's Jake.

She heard another voice in her ear. "This is Kaitlin. I'm ready in my universe."

In another minute or so she heard, "Jacob here. I'm ready in my quantum computing lab, too."

It was now or never. Katherine stepped up to the controls of her new and improved tokamak. It was in Production Mode, just waiting for her input.

"Pandoras are you ready?"

"Yes," one of the Pandoras said.

Katherine turned up the power supply on the superconducting magnet coils and the heating and current drive systems. The computer showed a corresponding power increase.

"Okay, Professor Jain and Kaitlin, turn up your power supplies."

"Check," Professor Jain said from Kat's universe.

"Which control was that?" Kaitlin asked from her universe.

Katherine bit back a snotty reply. They'd been through all this, but Kaitlin didn't really understand what was going on, so it wasn't surprising she was confused. Plus, she was probably scared, too. "Pandora, can you help her?"

"Yes," the Pandora from Kaitlin's universe said.

"How are the cryogenic systems doing?" Katherine asked.

"Fine," Professor Jain said.

"Fine, I guess," Kaitlin said.

Katherine's heart hammered in her chest. She was stalling because this was it. The fate of the multiverse depended on her next actions. "How's your electromagnetic field inside the torus?" If this didn't work, they were all screwed.

"Good," Kaitlin said.

"Fine," Professor Jain said, and then he added, "Katherine, I know you're nervous, we're all nervous. But we have to hurry."

"Yeah," Pandora said. "Get the lead out."

"All right," Katherine said. "Inject the Deuterium-Tritium gas and introduce the electrical current to make the plasma."

She turned to her own system and started the Deuterium-Tritium injection. When it reached the desired levels, she turned on the current.

The system started registering the plasma as the temperatures soared inside the tokamak.

"We have plasma," Professor Jain said.

"Me, too," Kaitlin said.

"Jacob, is the quantum computer okay?" Katherine asked.

"Everything's ship-shape over here," Jacob's voice said in her ear.

"The electromagnetic fields are rising off the charts," one of the Pandoras said.

This was it. Either it worked or every living creature, trillions of lives, on a multitude of worlds were dead, torn apart as the multiverse itself was torn to bits.

Chapter Fifty: Universe 3: Kat, May 1, 2100, 12:30 am

Kat touched her shoulder, and her hand came away bloody. She felt light-headed. Her blood was thundering. How did she end up on the floor? She couldn't think. "What happened?"

"You were hit," Ma said. "I told you to be careful."

"Do you have your first aid kit, Ms. Garcia?" Pablo asked.

"Of course she does," Pa said.

"Yeah, who do you think you're talking to?" Ma said, opening her bag and pulling stuff out.

Get a grip, Kat. She was in the middle of a firefight. She needed to concentrate. "Maybe you guys should get back to the fight." She gestured at Pablo and Pa.

Pa asked Ma, "How is she?"

"Is it serious?" Pablo asked.

"She's been shot, so, yes, it's serious," Ma said, and pulled Kat forward to look at her back.

Ow. Her whole upper left side was a pulsing throb with sharper pain centered on her shoulder. "Don't move me again," Kat said. "Please."

Pablo peeked out the window. "It looks like Police Patrol has taken heavy fire. I don't know how many of them are even left."

That was important. They were supposed to be on a mission.

"Uh," Kat said. "Maybe we should ask them if they want to surrender again?"

"It didn't work so well last time." Pablo shrugged in the dim light.

"Still, they've had more losses than we have," Pa said. "Obviously, they weren't prepared for this."

"It's gotta be demoralizing," Pablo said. "I mean, Pandora even took over a bunch of their equipment."

"Maybe we should ask Katherine's pa what he thinks," Kat said. "He's right down the hall."

Pa gestured him over to them.

Katherine's ma was the first to join them. "Was she hit?" Ava-Maria asked. "I knew it. I knew one of them was hit. I had a horrible feeling. Do you need any help, Ava?"

"No, thanks," Ma said. "I've got it covered." She started cutting Kat's shirt off her shoulder.

"What did you want?" Katherine's pa Christopher asked.

Kat tried to lean up, but a shooting pain lanced her shoulder. She could barely say, "Surrender."

Christopher glanced at her. "What?"

"I think she's suggesting we should ask them to surrender again," Pa said.

"That didn't work so well last time," Christopher said.

Pablo snorted and Kat exerted herself to give him a dirty look, which he may or may not have been able to see in the dimness.

Christopher continued, "But, this is a rout. I never thought I'd say this, but I feel sorry for Police Patrol, they seem almost helpless without their technology. I think we should contact the First Minister and ask him to surrender. He's vulnerable without Police Patrol."

"The first what?" Pablo asked.

Trying to move as little as possible, Kat pointed at Pablo with her thumb and said, "Yeah, who?"

"The First Minister is the leader of our country." Christopher touched the inside of his ear. "Pandora?"

Did he have an ear piece, too?

"Yes, Pandora," Christopher said, "Can you connect me with the First Minister?"

A couple more people joined their little group on the floor, and they also looked like her parents.

"See, I knew it," the woman said. "I knew one of them was hit. I had a horrible feeling. Do you need any help, Ava?" She must be Kaitlin's ma.

"Please hand me the disinfectant," Ma said, gesturing at her bag with her elbow.

The man, Kaitlin's pa, and Pa gave each other a weird look. Pa said, "How did all the Avas know Kat was hit?"

Kaitlin's pa, Topher, said, "It's weird." He paused. "What are you thinking now, Chris?"

"I'm thinking it's weird," Pa said.

Christopher, talking to Pandora or someone via his ear piece, stared at the other two Christophers and nodded in agreement.

"This is going to hurt, honey," Ma said to Kat, holding a wet cloth near her now-bare shoulder. "Hold her, Ava," she said to one of the Avas.

One of the Avas complied.

Kat nodded, and trying to distract herself, peeked out the window, not seeing many of the enemy still vertical. "I wonder what's going on in the lab," she said.

Ma started wiping her wound and it was all Kat could do not to scream at the top of her lungs.

"I'll ask Pandora," Pablo said. "Pandora?" he asked. "Tell us all what's going on."

"You're asking what's happening in the lab?" Pandora asked in her ear.

"Yeah," Pablo said. "Did they get the fusion machines to work? Is Katherine in control of the standing thing?"

Universe 2: Kaitlin

Kaitlin felt an almost-uncontrollable urge to scream. Why? It didn't make sense.

"Kaitlin?" a strange woman said.

Scared and nauseated, Kaitlin jumped sky-high. "You scared me." When she located the source of the voice, she was surprised to see it was the president of the Unified States standing in her lab. "Sorry, ma'am. I thought you left."

"What are you doing with that machine?" The president's business suit still looked immaculate. "Where did the Hearthland Security men go?"

"Kaitlin, what are your energy readings?" Katherine's voice

said in her ear.

"Just a minute, Madame President." Kaitlin turned to the computer screen. "One hundred sixty million degrees Celsius."

"Good," Katherine said in her ear. "Stand by for standing wave generation." And then it sounded like she giggled. Kaitlin was on the verge of some weird giggle herself. That wasn't right. Why were her emotions so crazy?

"Ms. Garcia?" the president asked.

"Sorry, ma'am," Kaitlin said. "I'm sort of busy." She stared at the computer screen. "Didn't your detail brief you before they left?"

"Yes," the president said and sighed. "But, frankly, it's a little too hard to believe. I half expected the officers to still be here."

"Ma'am," Kaitlin said, "No offense, but I need to concentrate."

"Can I help?" the president asked.

Kaitlin glanced up at her in surprise. "Yes, ma'am." She pointed at the computer. "I'm supposed to be adjusting the energy values, but there's something wrong with me. I'm having trouble concentrating."

The president took a step towards her. "Maybe you're scared? If I understand things, the fates of the universes are in jeopardy. That would make anyone scared. I'm scared."

Kaitlin clutched a lab table, staring at the president. She didn't look scared. She looked the same as usual—presidential. "Thanks, ma'am. I need to sit down. If you could come here to the computer, I'll tell you what to do when the woman in the other universe tells me."

"Okay," the president said, shrugging out of her suit coat. "You better call me Lenina if we're going to be working together." She placed her coat on one of the tables and walked up to the computer. "What am I looking at here?"

Universe 3: Katherine

Katherine squinted at the computer screen but was having trouble focusing on the data there. "Pandora, what's the temperature of the Deuterium Tritium mix here?"

The voice in her ear said, "One hundred sixty million degrees Celsius."

"Professor Jain?" she said via Pandora's ear piece. "What's your temperature?"

Professor Jain's voice in her ear said, "One hundred sixty million degrees Celsius."

Good. "Pandora, what're the electromagnetic fields doing? Does it look like we're starting to achieve a standing energy wave?"

"Affirmative, Katherine," Pandora said. "We must tweak the electromagnetic values in the other two universes slightly."

"Good." Katherine clutched the table. She needed to get on that tweaking, but she wasn't sure she could manage. What was wrong with her? "Pandora, can you give Professor Jain and Kaitlin the information?"

"Affirmative," Pandora said.

"Jacob?" Katherine asked. "Can you hear me?"

"Yes, Katherine?" he said. "Are you all right? You don't sound so good."

"How are things going over there?" Katherine asked.

"Fine," he said. "I'm not doing anything. I'm just monitoring the machine, ensuring it does what it's supposed to do. So far, so good."

"Can you come over here," she said. "I'm not feeling so good."

"Oh no," he said. "I'll be right there."

"Attention, everyone," Pandora said. "Christopher Garcia has an announcement. Go, Christopher."

"The First Minister has surrendered," Katherine heard her father say. "Police Patrol has been ordered to surrender their weapons and stand down."

Katherine heard faint cheering sounds in the distance, but she didn't feel like cheering. She still felt out-of-it, sick or something.

Jacob ran into the room with a huge smile on his face. He headed straight for Katherine. "We did it!"

"Katherine?" she heard Kaitlin in her ear piece. "Is it over? The fighting?"

"Yeah," Katherine said as Jacob enveloped her in his arms.

"Please send my people home as soon as possible," Kaitlin said.

"We will," Katherine said. She rested for a second against Jacob's warm, firm chest but then leaned away. She couldn't relax yet. "Pandora, please tell Kat's and Kaitlin's fighters to go home ASAP."

"Yes, Katherine," Pandora's voice was triumphant.

Katherine heard faint cheering sounds in the distance again.

From Kat's portal, Jake, with a huge smile on his face, poked his head through. "Can I go home now?"

"Pandora," Katherine asked. "Do we have control of the standing wave?"

"Yes, Katherine!" Pandora said.

"Once everyone gets home, can we cancel it out?" she asked. "Can we stop this thing once and for all?"

"Yes, Katherine!"

She turned to Jake and gestured to his universe. "Go on home, Jake."

"Yes!" Jake didn't waste any time popping through the portal and running across the lab to the other portal. "Kait, it worked. I'm coming home."

Professor Jain followed him through Kat's portal and approached Katherine and Jacob. He didn't seem to know how to react to their blatant hugging. He settled for nodding at them.

Soon, a bunch of soldiers in tan uniforms and in black uniforms ran into the lab and towards their respective portals. "Double-time, men," one of the soldiers yelled. They ran through the portals.

After all the soldiers were through the portals, Katherine saw a bunch of familiar-looking people who looked like her family and friends enter the lab.

Her mother ran up to her. "Katherine? What's wrong with you? You weren't shot were you?" She gazed into her eyes.

"I don't know what's wrong with me," Katherine said. "Something's not right."

She realized Kat's father, Chris, was carrying Kat in his arms. "What happened to Kat?"

"She was shot," Mother said. "I wonder." She glanced at Kat

and then back at Katherine.

The other two Avas came up to them, with the same wondering expression.

"What?" Jacob said. "You think they're linked or entangled somehow via quantum mechanics?"

"Maybe," Mother said. She turned to Kat's parents. "Is it all right if I give Kat a sedative?"

"Hey," Kat said, face ashen. "I need to fight." She groaned and shut up.

"Go ahead," Kat's mother said.

Mother quickly gave Kat a shot.

Kat closed her eyes and that clenched look left her face.

Suddenly, Katherine felt much better. Not sick. Not terrified.

"How do you feel?" Mother asked.

"Better," Katherine said. "Maybe a little sleepy, but normal."

All the Ava-Marias nodded.

The Christophers said, "Weird," in unison.

"Oooh-kay," Jacob said, drawing the word out. "Quantum entanglement, check."

Katherine stood up. "You guys get out of here. Go home. We'll cancel the standing wave to shut down the portals as soon as you're through."

They got.

Once all the visitors went to their home universes, she said, "Pandora? Shut them down."

"Yes, Katherine!"

The portals shut.

Chapter Fifty-One: Universe 2: Kaitlin, May 1, 2100, 2:30 am

When the portals closed with a booming sizzle, everyone in the lab cheered and jumped up and down.

Her family's faces showed relief and joy.

Emma, nodding, had tears running down her cheeks.

Michael kept thrusting his fist into the air and shouting, "Yes!"

Mom just whispered, "Thank goodness," and smiled and smiled.

Dad yelled, "Yeah, take that, universes!"

A hugging episode erupted as Dad hugged Michael and Mom hugged Emma.

The Hearthland Security officers were even hugging and patting each other on the backs.

Jake grabbed Kaitlin and hugged her, making her jump up and down with him. She couldn't help laughing a little. "All right, already."

"All right, nothing." He pressed his lips to hers and time stopped.

Kaitlin felt alive like she never had before. She could feel blood rushing to her face.

When Jake finally let go of her, she was slightly dazed. But she couldn't help noticing her whole family looking at them and smiling.

And the president.

Kaitlin extricated herself from Jake. "Madame President, thank you for helping earlier."

"It was no problem, Ms. Garcia," President Crown said, smiling.

"I'm not sure what was wrong with me," Kaitlin said.

Mom stepped up to them. "I might be able to shed some light on that." She glanced back at Dad who nodded. "We think you might have been linked with the other Kaitlins."

Kaitlin felt her eyebrows rise. "Linked? What do you mean? How?"

"I don't really understand it, but that other Jake said it was some kind of quantum stuff," Mom said. "You felt it when Kat got shot, that's why you felt so strange. And all of us Avas felt the same things. And all the Tophers."

Jake had an odd look on his face and Kaitlin knew he was wondering about that other Jake.

"It was weird," Dad said.

"Are we still linked?" Kaitlin asked

"I don't know," Mom said.

"That's a good question," a voice in her ear said.

Kaitlin jumped sky-high. "Pandora? Are you still here?"

"Yes, Kaitlin," she said. "I'm afraid you're stuck with me."

Kaitlin wasn't sure how she felt about that.

"I'm still here as well, Ms. Garcia," the president said.

"Uh oh," Pandora said quietly.

"And while I don't claim to understand what happened here today, you were in some trouble before," President Crown said.

"But what about that fusion machine?" George asked, elbowing his way through the crowd. "Isn't that a good thing? Fusion will help our world, won't it?"

"And her plan," Jake said. "Kait's plan for climate change, the stuff from the press conference with the tiny robots, that's important."

Kaitlin reached for Jake's hand and squeezed it.

He squeezed back.

Her family crowded around them.

Dad said, "Surely, there were extenuating circumstances."

"Yeah," Michael said.

The president nodded. "Yes. There were extenuating circumstances."

"Don't take Kait away from us, ma'am," Emma said.

"Enough," Kaitlin said. "I appreciate your support. I appreciate all of you." She couldn't help smiling at the love on their faces.

She was home.

They were safe.

The universe was safe.

That was enough.

No matter what happened to her, everything would be okay.

She let go of Jake and took a step toward President Crown. "But, I did give Bao information I shouldn't have. And, I was responsible for Officer Smythe's death. I'll regret that for the rest of my life. I'm prepared to face the consequences."

Universe 3: Katherine

When the portals closed with a booming sizzle, everyone in the lab had breathed a sigh of relief.

Katherine's mother was treating a few wounds amongst their friends, mostly glass cuts, in one corner of the lab.

Katherine's father was talking to many, many people via Pandora.

Professor Jain said, "If you don't mind, I'm going to take my leave. I need to make sure my family is okay."

"No problem, Professor Jain," Katherine said. On impulse, she grabbed him and hugged him. "Thanks for all your help." She backed away a little. "You should be proud. You helped save the universe."

"You should be proud, Katherine," he said, eyes shining. "You're the one who saved the universe. I just helped a little."

"You helped a lot," she said. "I couldn't have done it without you." Months of his mentoring sessions flashed before her eyes, as did the drained look on his face when he realized she would be taken by Police Patrol. She gave his arm a little squeeze. "Thank you from the bottom of my heart," she whispered.

He just smiled and shrugged. "See you soon, okay?" He took a step toward the door.

"Definitely," she said, and watched him leave.

"Pandora, please thank everyone who helped," she said.

"Yes, Katherine," Pandora said.

"You know what this means, don't you?" Jacob asked.

"The multiverse didn't explode, or whatever it was going to do?" she said.

"Well, yeah, that," he said. "But I was talking about this." He waved his hands around her lab. "We're free. We're all free. Police Patrol is gone." Jacob grabbed Katherine and hugged her, making her jump up and down with him. "Hurray!"

She couldn't help laughing a little. "All right, already."

"All right, nothing." He pressed his lips to hers and time stopped.

Katherine felt alive like she never had before. She could feel blood rushing to her face.

When Jacob finally let go of her, she was slightly dazed. But she couldn't help noticing her parents and everyone else looking at them and smiling.

Pablo grabbed Winston and planted a kiss, too.

Winston kissed him back enthusiastically.

Their friends, standing near them, chuckled.

Katherine's father approached Katherine and Jacob.

"Ah," Jacob's face turned very red. "Sir, ah, Sir Christopher. I really care about your daughter, sir."

And then her father actually laughed. "Relax, Jacob." He patted him on the back. "I know that."

Katherine's mouth fell open. Her fun-loving father was back.

"Honey, if you leave your mouth open like that, a nanobot might fly inside," he said. "Except, of course, there are no more nanobots."

No more nanobots. What a concept. It was almost mind-boggling. "Pandora? Are you still here?"

"Yes, Katherine," Pandora said. "I should hope so. Me and your father are planning North America's first election in a hundred years!"

Katherine's mother approached them. "I'm going outside to see if any of the Police Patrol survived and need medical attention. Who'd like to help?"

Father's expression quieted. "Of course I will, Ava-Maria."

"Yeah, me, too," Katherine said.

Everyone in the lab agreed to go out and try to help the surviving Police Patrol.

"I wonder why Police Patrol didn't just run away?" Katherine

asked.

"Good question," Katherine's father said. "The First Minister was ill-equipped to deal with an outright rebellion."

As they walked down the hall towards the exit, Katherine said, "It's peculiar how emotional I was during the battle. Do you really think I was linked with that Kat?"

"I do think the quantum computer was responsible for quantum entangling the universes," Jacob said. "That was the only thing that made sense. It's not outside the realm of possibility that people were also entangled."

Katherine's mother said, "All of us Ava-Marias felt the same things. And all the Christophers, too."

Jacob had an unusual look on his face and Katherine knew he was wondering about that other Jacob.

"Maybe you better go turn off that computer, son," Father said.

"Yeah." Jacob ran into his lab. Soon, they heard, "It's off."

"Do you think we're all still linked?" Katherine asked

"I don't know," Mother said.

"That's a good question," Pandora said in her ear.

They trudged up the stairs, yawning, and stepped out into the fresh air of a new era.

Universe 1: Kat

"What happened?" Kat asked. From the dingy furnishings and the lack of shiny electrical equipment, she guessed she was home. Her shoulder ached, but it wasn't a searing pain like it'd been before. "Are we home?"

"How do you feel?" Ma asked.

"Sleepy, but human," Kat said.

"Hhm," Ma said. "I think you must still have some of those medical nanobots inside you. You're doing much better than I expected."

Kat looked around the room and saw Pa conferring with a bunch of the tan-uniformed soldiers.

Pablo saw her looking around and rushed over. "How is she?" he asked. "Is she gonna make it?"

Ma nodded. "This one is tough. She's going to be fine."

"Thank, Gaia," Pablo said and squeezed her hand.

"Thank Gaia, indeed." Ma glanced at the former location of the weird window.

"Is it over?" Kat asked. "Did they shut down the windows for good?"

Pablo nodded. "We think so."

Pa saw them talking and came over. "How is she?"

"I think she'll make a full recovery," Ma said.

"Thank, Gaia," Pa said. "What about the other thing?"

Pa, Ma, and Pablo exchanged a look.

"What other thing?" Kat asked.

Ma said, "I might be able to shed some light on that." She glanced back at Pa who nodded. "We think you might have been linked with the other Kats."

Kat felt her eyebrows rise. "Linked? What do you mean? How?"

"I didn't understand it, but that Jacob guy said it was some kind of sciencey stuff," Ma said. "The other Kats felt it when you got shot. And all of us Avas felt the same things. And all the Chrises."

"It was weird," Pa said.

"Are we still linked?" Kat asked.

"I don't know," Ma said.

"That's a good question," a voice in her ear said.

Kat jerked in surprise and her wound throbbed. "Pandora? Are you still here?"

"Yes, Kat," she said. "I'm afraid you're stuck with me."

Kat wasn't sure how she felt about that.

One of the soldiers, George, approached them. "What do you think? Do you want to head back to Cheyenne Mountain, now? We need to get back to Homeland Security. Can Kat be moved?"

Home what?

Pa checked his watch. "We have just enough time to get there before sunrise if we get going now. Yeah, let's go."

Kat yawned. "What's going on?"

Pablo smiled at her. "Since we're all friends now, we're moving to that town your ma was at."

"Is that a good idea?" Kat asked.

Pa nodded. "Yes. They have food and water and other people. And schools."

"They have civilization," Ma said.

"Don't worry Kat," Pandora said in her ear. "I'll look out for you."

"Thanks, P," she whispered. "We better make sure to bring all these computers, then," she said loudly. She had a feeling Pandora would be a very good friend to have.

"Do you need someone to carry you?" Ma asked.

Kat looked at Pablo. "I think I can manage with Pablo's help."

He nodded, and reached for her good arm, placing it over his shoulders.

Leaning on Pablo, she stood up.

"Let's head out, men," George said.

Everyone started grabbing gear.

Pablo glanced from Kat to his large gun and back again.

Ma followed his eyes. "Pablo, I don't think you're going to need that anymore."

He shrugged and they started walking slowly towards the doorway.

The others streamed ahead of them down the hall.

When they were mostly alone, still moving slowly, Pablo said, "*Hermana*, what was that *thanks, P*, earlier? Was it that computer lady?"

"*Sí, señor*," she said, grinning.

"Good." He nodded. "Can I get one of those ear pieces, too?"

"I think that can be arranged," she said as they approached the stairs.

"Good, because next thing you know, they're gonna be making us go to school."

A burst of laughter erupted from her, making her wound throb. "Ow." But she couldn't stop smiling. "If that's the worst of our troubles, I'll be one happy *chica*."

He helped her up the first step.

"Ow," she said.

He chuckled as they slowly made their way up the stairs.

"Ow."

"Ow."

"Ow."

"I you-know you, P," she said as they stood just inside the front doors, catching their breath.

"Ah, hell," he said, turning to her. "I love you, K."

"Me, too." Kat felt her eyes fill. It felt like everything was going to change now. She could see her parents and the others outside waiting for them.

They stepped through the doors into brand new lives.

Epilogue

Universe 2: Kaitlin, July 1, 2100, 9:00 am

In bed, Kaitlin Garcia felt something hard and warm against her thigh.

It wriggled.

She resisted the urge to jump out of bed like her life depended on it. "Jake?" she said. When he didn't answer immediately, she added unhappily, "Buster?"

"Mmm." Jake nuzzled her neck. "Good morning, fiancée."

Kaitlin got shivers up her spine. "Mmm." She nuzzled him right back. "Good morning, fiancé." She laughed. "This was an awesome idea, babe, moving in with me in my house arrest."

Grinning, he said, "Well, I am awesome. And it's only a year." He leaned back, and stared into her eyes. "But you ain't seen nothing yet." He turned towards the lab doorway and yelled, "Buster, come."

Buster trotted into the lab carrying a bag in his mouth.

Jake patted the bed. "Here, boy."

Buster jumped onto the bed and lay down.

"If you think I'm doing a threesome with you and your dog, you've got another thing coming," Kaitlin said, smiling.

"Aw," Jake said, joking. "Sorry, Buster." He petted the dog's head. "You're out of luck, buddy." He extracted the bag out of Buster's mouth and fished a little box out of it.

It was a little dark blue velvet box.

It opened with a snap to reveal pure beauty.

Kaitlin gasped and covered her mouth. "Oh!" It was a perfect silver-colored band, braided around small diamonds. "It's so pretty."

Jake gestured at the ring with the box. "Take it, Kait. It's for wearing, not admiring."

"Oh, that's where you're wrong." She reached out for the ring. "It is for admiring."

Jake held out his empty hand. "And now we can finally get rid of that pink plastic thing."

Kaitlin snatched her hand back from his grasp. "Never. I'll never give up this ring. We've been through hell and high water together. We've been to other universes. It means so much. It's the symbol of our love."

His mouth turned down ever so slightly. "Can't the symbol of our love be white gold and diamonds instead of pink plastic?"

"Well, I guess they can both be symbols of our love." She slipped the pink plastic off her finger and slipped beauty on instead. She held it out in front of them, fingers stretched towards the ceiling, admiring it. "It looks really good."

"You got that right." Jake leaned down to nuzzle her neck again. "I can't wait until we start having babies. It was lucky those medical nanobots fixed your radiation damage."

Kaitlin had been very relieved none of the officers had lasting damage from their trip to the radioactive world. "Yes. Uh, you want to start making babies now?"

"When is professor grumpy-pants getting in?"

"Who?" As she pressed her lips to his she couldn't remember anything except this was her man. They belonged together. Forever.

"Ms. Garcia," Professor Azar yelled from the lab doorway. "This is unacceptable. Stop it."

"Oh, yeah, professor grumpy-pants," Kaitlin muttered.

"I don't care if you are best buddies with the president, we have a lot of work to do to implement your moon-shield project," Professor Azar said. "Do you want to save Earth from climate change or not? Get out of bed right now."

"Really?" Jake gave him a frank look. "Right now?" He glanced at himself and Kaitlin. "You'll get an eyeful."

Kaitlin stifled a laugh.

Professor Azar ran his hand through his still-luxuriant hair. Damn, the guy had nice hair. "Er, I don't." He looked closer at the bed. "Is that a dog?"

Buster glanced at the professor nonchalantly.

"I'm sorry, Professor Azar," she said. "Maybe you could give us a couple minutes of privacy?"

"I guess." He took a step towards the door. "But we're going to have to implement some kind of policy." He turned towards the door. "Come to think of it, I should go see how the fusion project's doing." He hurried out.

"Pandora?" Kaitlin said. "How about a little warning?"

"Yeah," Jake said, slipping into his pants.

"Well, excuse me," she said in a hurt tone. "Some people told me to zip it and mind my own business while they had their private time, so I took them at their word and focused my attention elsewhere."

Kaitlin, putting on her robe, glanced at Jake.

Time stopped as they smiled at each other for a moment.

Kaitlin was grateful Jake was in her life and Pandora, too.

She was very grateful her family and her world were safe.

She was grateful she'd had the courage to own up to her mistakes.

She was even a little grateful for Professor Azar.

"So?" Pandora said, and the moment was over.

"We shouldn't have snapped at you. You were just doing what we asked. Sorry, Pandora," Kaitlin said.

"I should hope so," Pandora said.

"I better get out of here, babe," Jake said. "I'm due at the Weather Agency, anyway. Who knows what kind of trouble Pablo's getting into without me?"

"Probably hitting on every intern in sight."

"Yeah." He laughed. "But I'll see you tonight."

She grinned. "Yeah, you will." She leaned in for a kiss. "And we'll pick up where we left off."

He grinned back. "Definitely." He turned to Buster and patted his leg. "Come on, buddy." They trotted out.

As Kaitlin started to dress, she asked, "Pandora, how's it going with the production of those nanobots for the moon?"

"Excellent, Kaitlin. I can't wait to tell you the latest..."

Universe 3: Katherine

When Katherine got to the restaurant, Jacob wasn't there yet. The hostess seated her, and she looked around nervously for her waiter. Hopefully, it wasn't that guy they'd had when she was here with Winston. Thinking of Winston, she couldn't help grinning.

She caught a glint of movement near her fancy new shoes. It was a nanobot.

She squished it under her shoe like a cockroach. "Pandora."

"Yes, Katherine?" the familiar voice said in her ear.

"I just saw a Police Patrol nanobot here at the restaurant. I thought we got rid of all the security nanobots."

"Well," Pandora said, "they're so handy for keeping an eye on things. I didn't think it would hurt to leave a couple–"

"No. Absolutely not," Katherine said. "Get rid of all of them. We didn't have a revolution for nothing." People didn't die for nothing. She pushed that thought away. Today was not the day for dark thoughts. Today was a happy day.

"All right, already." Pandora paused and then said, "There, they're all deactivated."

At the table next to hers, Katherine heard the plink of something falling into water, and a woman shrieking, "Eek," as she stared into her water glass.

Someone tapped Katherine on the shoulder. "Hey, beautiful." It was Jacob.

"You're the one who looks beautiful," she said, taking in his formal black suit. It fit him like a glove. "So that's a tuxedo? You look really good."

"You got that right." Jacob leaned down to nuzzle her neck. Katherine got shivers up her spine.

"But let me see you," Jacob said. "That dress looks amazing."

Katherine popped up, knocking the chair down behind her. She just glanced at it before twirling. She grinned as her skirt billowed up. "I'm never wearing a uniform again. I do look good, don't I?"

He grinned back. "Definitely."

A waitress placed two water glasses on the tablecloth with a flourish and held out menus to them.

Jacob righted Katherine's chair, they accepted the menus and sat down.

"Those flowers smell good," he said, pointing at the vase in the center of the table.

"Yeah, don't they? Winston said they were old English roses."

"I can't believe he's taking time off from his moon-shield project to get married," she said. "And he wants to start some carbon dioxide scavenging project in the ocean."

"I can't believe he asked me to be in the wedding party," Jake said shaking his head.

"Well, you were instrumental in bringing him and Pablo together," she said.

"Only because I took you away from him." Jacob grinned and reached for Katherine's hand across the table. "Come on."

Katherine tugged her hand back, but not very energetically. "Don't start again. You know I'm busy with the fusion project. We're going to put tokamaks all over Earth. Everyone's going to have all the clean energy they need."

"Please." He looked at her with puppy-dog eyes. "You know you're the only woman for me, Katherine. The only woman in all the universes."

She knew that was true. She blew out an exaggerated sigh. "Oh, all right. Quit asking already. Of course I'll marry you. Eventually. You're the only man for me in all the universes, too," she said in a rush.

She paused and time stopped as they smiled at each other for a moment.

Katherine was grateful Jacob was in her life and that he put up with her.

She was very grateful her family and her world were safe.

She was grateful things were finally changing on her world. People were being treated with respect, and she was a part of it.

She was grateful for everything, really.

"Can I take your order?" the waitress said, standing next to the table. The moment was over.

Jacob laughed. "We haven't even looked at the menus yet. We're going to need a few minutes."

The waitress nodded and walked away.

Jacob jumped up. "I have to kiss my fiancée." He bounded around the table and planted one on her.

As Katherine pressed her lips to his, she couldn't remember anything except this was her man. They belonged together.

Forever.

They eventually had to come up for air. Beaming, Jacob went back to his seat.

Katherine smiled back at him. "But seriously, can we wait a while for our wedding? I'd like to try dating, first."

"Whatever you want, fiancée." Smiling, he picked up his menu.

She couldn't seem to focus on her own menu. His every universe comment was sticking in her mind. "That was peculiar when Kat got shot and I sort of felt it, wasn't it?"

He glanced up at her.

"Do you really think my consciousness was entangled with her and that other one, Kaitlin?"

He shrugged. "It seemed like something was going on."

"It would be strange to be controlled or even influenced by someone else. What would that do to free will?"

"I don't know, Katherine."

"Do you think the quantum computer needs to be on for it to happen?"

"I don't know," he said, putting down his menu. "It's not on now. How do you feel?"

"I feel normal," she said.

"It's interesting though," he said, "quantum mechanics does say human consciousness has a special place in the universe–or the multiverse."

"And how many universes do we think there are, again?"

"Infinity."

They were silent for a minute, pondering this.

"Can I take your order?" The waitress was back again.

"We better order, or we'll be late for the wedding," Jacob said.

"Yeah, I guess," Katherine said.

But were infinite Katherines influencing her lunch selection? She glanced at Jacob. And infinite Jacobs chatting with waitresses and asking Katherines to marry them? And infinite waitresses taking infinite orders? And on and on?

"Babe?" Jacob said.

"Uh, yeah. Just a sec." She turned her attention to the menu.

Universe 1: Kat

In a brightly-lit underground classroom mostly filled with teenagers, the teacher asked, "Ms. Garcia? Do you know the answer?"

Next to her, Pablo groaned. "Ugh. School sucks."

Kat grinned. "I think the Irish philosopher and politician Edmund Burke said, 'All that is necessary for the triumph of evil is that good men do nothing.'"

"Good, Ms. Garcia." The teacher turned back to the blackboard.

"How did you know that?" Pablo asked quietly.

"I studied," she whispered back.

"So, class, what does this mean?" the teacher said.

And the bell rang.

"Saved by the bell," Pablo said. "I never understood that expression until I had to go to school."

Kat stood up and started gathering her books. "School isn't that bad. I sort of like it."

"Somehow, that doesn't surprise me," Pablo said, "considering how sciencey those other Kats were. Do you think you'll go into science?"

She nodded. "I already joined the brainstorming group. We're going to implement fusion energy and some kind of shield or something to help with global warming with Pandora's help."

She paused for a moment, remembering the feel of the sun on her face and the wind in her hair on the other world. She wanted to feel the sun and the wind again. She wanted everyone to feel that.

"Sounds too complicated for me, *hermana*."

She shook her head. "Aren't you a teacher? Hey, don't you have gym class now?" Even though the medical nanobots had healed her gunshot, Kat was still milking the injury to avoid gym. She rubbed her shoulder dramatically.

"Yeah," he said. "But that's different. It's fun, hand-to-hand combat, self-defense, stuff like that." He grinned.

She grinned back at him. "You just like seeing all these

teenaged guys in their skimpy workout clothes." Kat pointed at the students leaving the room.

He grinned some more. "No. I'm only doing my civic duty. That's it, I swear."

"Yeah, right." They laughed.

"Kat?" Ma said from the class doorway. Pa was there, too.

"See ya later, *chica*." Pablo grabbed his stuff and nodded at Kat's folks on his way out the door.

"Ma? Pa? What are doing here?" Kat asked. "Is everything all right?"

"Yes," Ma said with a big smile.

"We have something to tell you," Pa said with a big smile.

It was all very odd. "Is something wrong? You can tell me."

"No, Kat," Ma said. "Nothing's wrong. In fact, it's the opposite."

They glanced at each other. Ma nodded.

"We're going to have a baby!" Pa said.

"What?" Kat's fingers fluttered over the locket. "You're so old."

Pa snorted.

"Gee, thanks a lot," Ma said. "We're not that old."

"We were separated for so long, let's just say we were glad to see each other again," Pa said.

"Ugh," Kat said. "Yeah, I figured. Please don't give me any details."

"Say you're happy for them," Pandora said in her ear.

Duh. Kat reached out to Ma for a hug. "Sorry. I was just surprised. That's great news. Wonderful news."

She hugged Pa. "I'm very happy for you. Congratulations."

"And you," Ma said. "You're about to get a little brother."

Didn't that Kaitlin have a sister and a brother? "That is cool." Her fingers touched the locket again. "Ma. I forgot to give you back your locket."

"No, you keep it honey," Ma said. "I like the thought of you having Emma's picture and her watching over you."

"Me, too," Kat said. "Just like she did when she was alive." She paused for a moment. "And just like I will for the new baby." She felt her eyes fill.

Her folks seemed a little teary-eyed themselves as they

looked at her.

Pa cleared his throat. "Good, Kat. We're really proud of you, you know."

Time stopped as the three of them smiled at each other for a moment.

Kat was grateful her parents and everyone else seemed to be moving on from the bad stuff that had happened on her world.

She was very grateful her family and her world were safe.

She was grateful she'd played a part to make it happen.

"Gaia," Pandora said in her ear, and the moment was over.

Kat was even grateful for Pandora. "What, Pandora?"

"I think Pablo's ma was just processed in the intake area," Pandora said.

"What? His ma? That's wonderful." Kat said. "Does he know?"

"No. I'll tell him now."

"No. Let me tell him," Kat said.

"What's going on?" Pa asked.

But Kat was already running out of the classroom. "Pablo's ma might be here," she yelled over her shoulder.

She ran all the way down the hall to the practice area.

"You snooze, you lose," Pablo said to a group of students circled around him. "You stall, you fall. You quail, you fail."

The kids snickered, but they watched him carefully and nodded too.

"Again," Pablo said. "Try the moves again. Keep trying until you get it right."

The kids separated into sparring partners, with determined expressions. Amidst her excitement to tell him the news, Kat realized Pablo might be a good teacher.

She ran right up to him. "P, P, P!" She was panting so much she could barely talk.

"What's wrong?" he asked, alarm on his face.

"Nothing's wrong." Kat sucked air into her lungs. "Your ma. They think your ma's in intake."

"Gaia!" He took a step towards the door, but stopped. "Mia, you're in charge. Sparring drills. If anyone slacks off, you all run at least a mile."

At the girl's nod, he took off running for the door.

"Yeah, go ahead," Kat said, waving. "I'll catch up." She sucked in a breath. "Be right there." Breathe. "Right behind you."

In the intake area, Pablo clutched a middle-aged woman in his arms. "Mama. Mama. Mama." Tears streamed down his and her cheeks. They rocked back and forth.

Kat was so happy for him, she felt her own eyes fill. That was twice in one day. Geez, she was getting soft.

Behind them, two strangers, twenty-something men, seemed lost. She realized they weren't complete strangers. One was tall, white, and kind of lumpy looking. She took a step towards him. "Winston?"

"Yeah," he said, eyes widening. "Have we met?"

"Uh, not exactly." She glanced back at Pablo. She was pretty sure Winston and Pablo had a thing over in Katherine's universe.

She tapped him on the back. "P? Pablo? *Hermano*?"

Pablo and his ma separated. "This is my mama, Kat," he said.

"Yeah, I figured. It's very nice to meet you, ma'am, wonderful even." She smiled. "But, P., I think you want to meet this guy, Winston."

"Yes," Pablo's ma said. "These young men saved my life. This is Winston–"

"Smythe," Pablo said, a grin spreading across his face.

"Have we met?" Winston asked.

Pablo just smiled at him.

"It's kind of a long story," Kat said.

"And this is..." Pablo's ma said.

When Pablo turned his attention to the other man, he said, "Jason?"

"Jason Moretti," his ma said. "Yes. This is Jason. You know him. He was your friend Jake's big brother. You played together when you were little."

Pablo turned to Kat and grinned. He turned back to Jason. "Jason, I want you to meet my sister, Kat." He turned to Kat. "Kat, meet Jason."

Kat stepped forward, entranced with Jason's wide smile. His bushy eyebrows framed the most gorgeous gray-blue eyes. Time stopped when she looked into those eyes. She finally said, "Uh."

Jason laughed, and reached out to shake her hand. "Uh, to you too, Kat." He paused, gazing into her eyes again. "It's very nice to meet you."

"Uh, very nice to meet you, too."

And as they shook hands, Kat felt like her life was beginning all over again. And this time, the sky was the limit.

Science Fact: Climate Change

Weather is the current state of the atmosphere in terms of temperature, rain, humidity, wind, etc. for a specific location. Weather changes from minute to minute, and thus is considered short-term. Climate is essentially the average weather for a significant period of time for a particular region, and thus is considered long-term. Since climate is based on weather and weather changes, climate also changes.

All weather and, hence, all climate is ultimately due to the sun's uneven heating of our planet. The spherical Earth is heated unevenly because the equator is heated more intensely, Earth is tilted on its axis, it rotates on its axis, and land and water heat and cool at different rates. At its most basic level, weather is just the result this heat trying to spread out and equalize over the planet.

The United Nations Environment Programme and the World Meteorological Organization created an international body called the Intergovernmental Panel on Climate Change (IPCC) to study climate change. Thousands of scientists and approximately two hundred countries are contributors to, or members of, the IPCC. The work of the IPCC is held to the highest objective scientific standards.

The IPCC has three working groups. Working Group 1 assesses the physical aspects of the climate system and climate change including temperature and precipitation changes, ice sheets, and sea level. Working Group II assesses the vulnerability of socio-economic and natural systems to climate change, consequences of climate change, and adaption options. Working Group III assesses options for mitigating climate change including both limiting and removing gas emissions.

Important tools of the IPCC are large computer programs called general circulation models (GCM) that simulate the physical processes in the atmosphere, oceans, and lands of planet Earth. If these GCMs perfectly simulated these processes we could perfectly predict what will happen regarding weather and climate in the future. We aren't there yet. Instead, scientists vary parameters such as the amount of carbon dioxide in the atmosphere to create a variety of possible scenarios for the future.

All of the IPCC's scientific findings on climate change are available to everyone free of charge from their website: www.ipcc.ch Check it out! The summaries for policymakers are particularly informative. There's a lot of work yet to be done to understand and predict climate change.

For more information and details about these and other topics, check out the Physics Is Fun website: www.physicsisfun.net

Thank you for reading *Kat Cubed*. I hope you enjoyed it!

- For more info about me or my work, please go to my author website, http://www.lesleylsmith.com/. Sometimes, I post links for free fiction downloads!
- Please check out the Physics Is Fun website www.physicsisfun.net for lots of information about fun physics topics.
- Reviews help other readers find books. I appreciate any and all reviews.
- A sneak peek of my new novel *Temporal Dreams* follows.

–Lesley L. Smith

Temporal Dreams Chapter One

Kairi: Boulder, Colorado, 2019

The small velvet box thumped onto the blacktop like a tiny eight-hundred-pound gorilla. Kairi was packing the car for her spring break road trip when it fell out of her boyfriend Josh's duffel bag.

After checking to see if anyone else in the dorm parking lot had seen (they hadn't), she stared at it for at least a minute. She was surprised. They'd been dating for less than a year. Did people get engaged after less than a year? But marrying him would be awesome. She'd wanted a family forever. Her heart was thumping so loudly people must have been able to hear it all over Colorado.

Maybe she was overreacting. Maybe it wasn't an engagement ring.

Kairi did pick up the box and look inside. The lid opened with a snap, exposing a smallish diamond on a silver-colored band. She didn't know anything about diamonds, or silver-colored bands for that matter, but it was really pretty.

She did not try the ring on. That was her story, and she was sticking to it.

Suffice it to say, when her roommate, Dakota, came up behind her, she jumped sky-high.

"Have you still been having those weird dreams, Kairi? Ooh! What's that?" Dakota asked. As she leaned over, Kairi got a whiff of pot from her hair. "Oh, my God! Are you engaged?" She squealed.

Quickly, Kairi shoved the ring back in the duffel. "No, I'm not engaged. He hasn't asked me yet."

"But you're going to say yes when he asks, right?" Dakota

asked.

Visions of a perfect family life were running through Kairi's head: sharing her experiences of the day at dinnertime, waking up with that special someone, knowing for sure she had someone in her corner. And the holidays—they would be great, filled with fun and love instead of boredom, loneliness and worse. Her life so far had been pretty horrible. Josh was by far the best thing that had happened to her.

"Kairi?" Dakota frowned. "Are you considering saying no?" Dakota was also one of the best things that had happened to her. She was like a sister, even though they looked so different: Dakota so light and Kairi so dark.

"No, I'm not going to say no." But, he hadn't actually asked her. She was so confused. Why would he ask her to marry him? He came from a good family and she didn't even know where she came from. Of course, she'd been fantasizing that he'd ask her some day. "You don't think the ring might be for someone else, do you?"

"What? His secret girlfriend? No way, girl. You're getting married!" Dakota squealed again. "Pam is so going to kill you!" Pam was her foster mom.

"Pam would not kill me if I got engaged," Kairi said.

"Yeah, huh, she would," Dakota said. "She totally would. You swore you'd get your degree."

"Maybe we'll just have a long engagement," she said.

"Yeah, right," Dakota said. "That's realistic."

"Hey, Dakota." Josh's voice rang out across the parking lot.

"Shh," Kairi whispered and held up her bare finger. "Not a word. You don't know a thing."

"Hey, Josh," Dakota said in a singsong voice as he approached them. "So... any special plans for spring break?"

Josh grinned. "You mean besides driving across the country to drink beer on the beach?"

"Oh, you know−" Dakota started to say, but Kairi poked her with her elbow.

"We should get going," Kairi said. "We're burning daylight."

Dakota giggled. "Burning."

Josh leaned around Kairi and put *Electromagnetic Theory* and *Special Relativity* books on top of the suitcases.

Kairi smiled. "A little light reading?"

He put his arms around her waist and kissed the back of her neck. "Yep," he said in his low, husky, sexy voice. She loved that voice. The brush of his lips and his warm breath on her neck made her warm all over.

The edges of his eyes crinkled as he smiled when she twisted around and looked at him. He let go of her and said, "Ready to roll?"

"Yep." She turned to Dakota. "Bye, D."

"Bye." Dakota giggled and started walking back to the dorm. Then she stopped and turned around. "Call me! Let me know what happens."

"Am I mistaken, or is she high again?" Josh asked.

Kairi watched her try to unlock the dorm door. "Oh, be nice. Dakota's been through a lot."

"So have you, and I don't see you toking up all the time," Josh said. "I know you think of her as a sister, but you're too easy on her."

At least one person on earth should be easy on her. Kairi slammed the trunk closed. "She was my foster sister and I'm not too easy on her." But she didn't want to have this argument again. "Let's talk about it later." Or not at all.

Kairi walked toward the passenger seat. Now that she knew about the ring, the suspense was killing her. Was he going to ask her? How would he do it? In the car? On the beach? Maybe on the beach at sunset.

He was unlocking the driver's door. "It's around twenty hours till we get to Padre." He smiled at her over the roof of the car. "I think we'll have a chance to talk."

She said, "Can't argue with that."

As they drove through Boulder, she kept staring at him. If they got married, what kind of husband would he be? What kind of wife would she be? What would their kids be like? What would they look like? They had nothing in common in the looks department except dark-brown wavy hair. And eyebrows. They both had thick dark-brown eyebrows. But he had gray-blue eyes and hers were brown. He had white skin, and hers was the color of chai tea.

He shot her a glance. "What?"

"What do you mean what?"

"What's up? Why've you been staring at me? Wait." He flashed his teeth at her. "Don't tell me; I look particularly handsome today."

He did look handsome, but she couldn't say that. He'd get even cockier than he already was. "Uh, just wondering what you were thinking." When you bought that ring. Could he really want to marry her?

He grinned. "Thinking, when?"

"Uh, well, I was packing your duffel in the back, and something fell out." Enter gorilla; welcome to spring break. Shoot. So much for a romantic setting.

"Oh?" His face stilled and he shot her another glance.

"You know I really care about you, right?" Kairi mustered up what she hoped was a warm smile. Ask me. Ask me. Ask me.

"Care about me?" he choked out. "Gee, thanks. I thought it was more than that."

Crap. "It is. It is more than that. You're important to me. Really important." She needed to say it: the I-word. But she'd never said the I-word to anyone.

His face was turning red.

Shit. Say it. "You're the most important person in the world to me." Say it, Kair! She couldn't say it. He needed to hear it, and she needed to say it. And she felt horrible and mad at herself about it. What was wrong with her? Her mind skittered away from the back seat of that car years ago...

"Kairi, what's wrong?" Josh was staring at her instead of the road, clutching the wheel with an iron grip.

"Watch the road," she managed to say.

He pulled the car off onto the shoulder. "What's wrong?" His face was turning red, and he clenched and unclenched his fists. But she knew he'd never hurt her—unlike other people—that was one of the things that was so wonderful about him.

She just looked at him.

"Excuse me," he said, "if the thought of marrying me makes you upset. It's not like I even asked you yet!"

She'd never seen him so hurt. She had to do some damage control, or this relationship was over. Now. That was the last thing she wanted. "I, uh, apologize if I hurt you. I didn't mean to.

The idea of marrying you doesn't make me upset." She took a deep breath. It was now or never. "I do love you. I love you—and that's the first time I've ever said that to anyone."

His face smoothed. "So, what's going on? Why are you so upset?"

"I'm not sure." She swallowed. Figure it out, girl. "I guess I'm just scared."

"Just a sec." He bounded out of the car, opened the trunk and rooted around in his duffel bag. When he came back, he handed her a ...tissue.

She took the tissue, laughing, and blew her nose. She'd been sure he was going to expose the gorilla. She wiped her eyes and heard The Snap.

When she looked back at Josh, sure enough, he had the ring out and looked deadly serious. "This isn't how I planned to ask you, and it's not romantic, I know. But I just love you so much. I want to spend the rest of my life with you." He held his breath, holding the ring out.

It seemed as if time had stopped. She looked at his wonderful face, eyes filled with hope, and it felt as if her chest was being crushed. She was so afraid she couldn't breathe. Did he really want her? Did that mean he didn't really know her? She wished, no prayed, he did want her.

Finally, she said, "Josh..."

As she hesitated, the naïve look of hope on his face was morphing into something else. Something sad.

"Uh," she said. "Yes."

"Really?" His voice got all high and squeaky.

"Sure," she said.

"I love you so much," Josh said and reached for her.

"I love you, too," she said. It was getting easier to say. They kissed for quite a while.

"I love you no matter what," he said when they finally separated. He held out the box. "So, put it on."

"I, uh," she said. There were those hopeful eyes again. "Okay." She took the ring and slipped it on her finger. "So, maybe we should get going?"

"Yes, ma'am. Yes, fiancée!" He gave a grin and saluted her. "Your wish is my command."

As they pulled back into traffic, she concentrated on calming down. What was wrong with her? Josh was great. She'd never find a better guy, and he loved her. She did love him. And it was her dream to have a family. If they got married, he'd be her family. So, why did she feel terrified?

"Is there anything you want to ask me?" he asked.

Like, why would a guy like him love a girl like her? When would he stop being in love with her? What's it like to have everything easy? What's it like having a mom and dad? But she knew asking any of those questions would be a mistake. "Uh. Boxers or briefs today?" She forced a laugh.

Josh snickered. "In honor of spring break, I'm free-dogging it today."

Now it was her turn to snicker.

Southeast Colorado was downright boring. The view out the windows was of unending worn-out grass, and the hum of tires on the pavement was practically a lullaby.

Northeast Oklahoma wasn't any better, and she was dozing when that annoying emergency alert blared on the radio. "The National Weather Service has issued a tornado warning for Union County in northeast New Mexico. National Weather Service Doppler Radar indicated a funnel cloud near the ground ten miles southwest of Clayton. Residents in the area should seek shelter immediately." The radio was overcome with static, and Josh switched it off.

She realized while she'd been sleeping, it had clouded over. "Maybe we should seek shelter?"

Josh snorted. "It's all the way over in New Mexico. We're in Oklahoma, babe."

She had no idea where Union County was, but she could see the clouds overhead were very dark. "It can't be a good sign that we heard the emergency alert on the radio."

"We're fine," Josh said.

She just looked at him.

"I'm sure, Kair," he said and reached over to squeeze her hand.

"Okay, if you're sure," she said and settled back in her seat.

She dreamt of a freight train coming to run her over, roaring louder and louder as it got closer and closer.

And then she woke up, lying on the side of the highway. In the sun. It took a couple of seconds for it to register.

Where was she?

She stood up.

Where was Josh?

Where was the car?

What the hell was going on?

"Josh!" she yelled. But it was no use. She could see a long way, and all she saw was sad old grass and an unbroken ribbon of empty highway.

www.ingramcontent.com/pod-product-compliance
Lightning Source LLC
Chambersburg PA
CBHW072111250626
47159CB00007B/2400